S0-AFN-919

CRITICS RAVE ABOUT SIMON CLARK!

"I'm going to seek out and read everything Clark writes. He's a true talent."

—Bentley Little, *Hellnotes*

"Not since I discovered Clive Barker have I enjoyed horror so much."

—*Nightfall*

"A master of eerie thrills."

—Richard Laymon, author of *Flesh*

"Clark has the ability to keep the reader looking over his shoulder to make sure that sudden noise is just the summer night breeze rattling the window."

—CNN.com

"Simon Clark is one of the most exciting British horror writers around."

—*SFX*

"Watch this man climb to Horror Heaven!"

—*Deathrealm*

"Clark writes with compelling characterization and indelible imagery."

—*DarkEcho*

THE FACE IN THE DARKNESS

When Pel peered through the bars at the mosaic set into the floor the shock winded her. "My God," she breathed. "*It's him.*"

Icy shivers tickled down her spine. She leaned closer to see the face looking up at her from the floor. The artist had cunningly created a portrait from tiny fragments of glass and pottery embedded in mortar. Even more cunningly, the artist had contrived a picture of a man's face that appeared to gaze up as if from a dark void in the ground. A prisoner gazing from a pit. There was no background detail other than what appeared to be shadow. That in turn, forced the observer's eye to meet the eyes of the man in the portrait. To challenge them. That stare hit you head-on. She could feel herself drawn into a battle of wills with that man.

Pel found herself not just looking AT the eyes but gazing into them. At that moment, it seemed as if she'd fall into those wells of darkness if she let go. . . .

Other *Leisure* books by Simon Clark:

THIS RAGE OF ECHOES
DEATH'S DOMINION
THE TOWER
IN THIS SKIN
STRANGER
VAMPYRRHIC
DARKER
DARKNESS DEMANDS
BLOOD CRAZY
NAILED BY THE HEART

GHOST
MONSTER

SIMON
CLARK

LEISURE BOOKS NEW YORK CITY

For Janet

A LEISURE BOOK®

December 2009

Published by

Dorchester Publishing Co., Inc.
200 Madison Avenue
New York, NY 10016

Copyright © 2009 by Simon Clark

All rights reserved. No part of this book may be reproduced or transmitted in any form or by any electronic or mechanical means, including photocopying, recording or by any information storage and retrieval system, without the written permission of the publisher, except where permitted by law.

ISBN 10: 0-8439-6179-1
ISBN 13: 978-0-8439-6179-9
E-ISBN: 978-1-4285-0777-7

The name "Leisure Books" and the stylized "L" with design are trademarks of Dorchester Publishing Co., Inc.

Printed in the United States of America.

10 9 8 7 6 5 4 3 2

If you purchased this book without a cover you should be aware that this book is stolen property. It was reported as "unsold and destroyed" to the publisher and neither the author nor the publisher has received any payment for this "stripped book."

Visit us online at www.dorchesterpub.com.

GHOST MONSTER

THIRTY YEARS LEFT

Rebecca watched the man. Love and rage clashed inside of her. Conflicting emotions tried to batter each other into submission. Yet one couldn't triumph over the other. As she crept up on him through the long cemetery grass she saw herself snatching up a piece of shattered gravestone then hurling it in his face. However, a second later she imagined his mouth on hers, as he pushed her back into a bed of wildflowers. And there, between the tombs, she'd breathlessly beg him to take pleasure in her body.

Cold October winds blew from the ocean. They sang through the abandoned mansion on the cliff top—a sad song of lost hope; a ballad for abandoned lovers. That breeze brought with it the musky smell of the derelict's shuttered rooms; it streamed through Rebecca's long red hair. In that strange mood of hers it felt as if the ghosts of Murrain Hall roughly ran their fingers across her scalp, tugging curls sharply enough to elicit a surprised gasp.

For a while, she stood beside a graveyard angel; one corroded by storms into an ugly, hunched thing. *What now? Do I go back to my car and forget what happened last night? Or do I get hold of Jacob? Then keep my hands on him until he tells me what I want to hear? Damn him . . . I wish I'd never set eyes on his face.*

Despite the urge to drive out of here, Rebecca found that her feet carried her through the cemetery to the mausoleum. This brick-built building was no bigger than a prison cell.

The side nearest to her presented an opening that extended the full length of the structure. Normally, it would be sealed by a gate made of iron bars so thick you'd think the barrier had been placed there to keep a thousand desperate prisoners locked inside. Now, the gate had been swung open on its big oily hinges.

The subject of her rage—and her passion—worked diligently within. Dear Lord, he could have been a surgeon the way he carefully attended to that vile thing. Talk about being scrupulous! This smacked of obsession . . . a morbid obsession that sent a trickle of goose bumps up her thighs.

Rebecca Lowe didn't even want to *think* his name. Yet it spurted from her mouth with so much heat it made her lips tingle, as if she'd been suddenly kissed: *"Jacob Murrain!"*

Her shout didn't even make him pause. He continued polishing the mosaic set in the mausoleum floor. An oil lamp hanging from its ceiling washed him in a rich amber glow.

Rebecca forged through the long grass. Over the swelling mounds that marked burial plots. Deep beneath her feet there'd be cavities of utter darkness that housed skeletons by the hundred, softly decaying burial shrouds and a deathly, eternal silence.

"Jacob Murrain!" Rebecca burst into the little building.

The man remained on his knees. With a slow rhythm he wiped the mosaic.

She hissed, "Why must you do that? I couldn't even bring myself to touch it."

Without looking up, he said, "You shouldn't have followed me here."

"I needed to see you again."

"Why?"

"You know why."

Shaking his head, he used the cloth to rub the ugly image there on the floor.

Speechless with pent-up emotion, Rebecca glared at the man. Jacob Murrain was lean from working in the forest.

Midforties, yet not a gray hair flecked his black hair. His broad face always appeared tanned, even in winter, which accentuated his pale gray eyes.

She asked herself: *Why am I obsessed with that face?* And even as she persuaded herself to aim a kick at him, as he crouched there, she found herself panting, "Make love to me." Her eyes bore into his head. "Like you did last night." He didn't respond. "Jacob! Prove to me that you don't regret spending the night in my bed."

"We're not kids, Rebecca. I'm forty-five. You're . . ." He didn't finish the sentence. Instead he paid close attention to the mosaic eye with its fiery red pupil.

"I know we're not children," she said with some heat. "I've been married. Had two sons. Not that that stopped you being excited by my body. Listen, Jacob—last night, I let you do things that no man has ever done to me before."

"I've got bad blood, Rebecca." At last he straightened his back. "I've got *his* blood." He nodded at the mosaic. "Just like him, I'm a Murrain." Taking a breath, he explained, "Murrain blood poisons us, and it poisons everyone we care about."

"You care about me?"

Jacob tipped fluid from an old brandy bottle. From the bubbles in it she figured it was a mixture of detergent and water. Outside, the wind blew hard. It rustled grass around the tombs. Then it caught the pinnacles on the church tower. It produced a sound that made her shiver. Voices whispering. That tone of whisper was reserved for the town gossips, when they sneeringly speculated how long her latest love affair would last before yet another disastrous and acrimonious breakup. *For the last twenty years I've been the talk of the town*, she thought sourly. "*Here comes Rebecca Lowe, the red-haired seducer of men.*" She sighed. *If only I could have a relationship that doesn't get complicated. Just once. Please God . . .*

Now here she was: obsessed and loving and hating in equal measure.

Why Jacob Murrain? He's as much a town pariah as I am. The family's always had a bad name. Devil Murrain, they call them. Shaking her head, she watched him lavish care on the hideous mosaic. If only he'd caress her bare skin, like he stroked the cloth across the face of his ancestor.

In an attempt to draw him into conversation (and so maybe elicit an answer to her question about him caring for her) she said, "Ghost Monster. That's what we called that picture when we were children. We used to come up here and say to each other, 'I dare you to put your arm through the bars and touch the Ghost Monster's face.'"

"That would be a stupid thing to do."

"Why? It's only a *stupid* picture."

He paused to survey the results of his cleaning. The eyes of the mosaic portrait appeared to burn in the lamplight. Lips were parted to reveal bright teeth. "This is my ancestor Justice Murrain."

"I know. He had the blood of a thousand men and women on his hands. Families down in the town still scare their children with the story. Then the kids come up here and dare each other to touch the Ghost Monster. And it still gives them nightmares."

"So it should. Then it gives me nightmares, too."

The physical intimacy of a few hours ago gave her permission (at least in her mind) to ask Jacob the question people longed to ask but never dared. "Why do you do this?"

"It's got to be preserved. I clean it every week. Then every two months I apply a coat of resin to make sure the mosaic fragments stay cemented in place."

"But it's more than that, isn't it? You're obsessed. You're up here in all weathers, moping over the damn thing—cleaning, polishing, gluing the bits back down, fixing the tiles on the mausoleum so the rain doesn't come in. You've even been seen at midnight, checking that the lamp hasn't gone out. It's crazy!"

"No, it's not. The lamp must stay burning."

"But you're not tidying this thing up. You're guarding it, aren't you? As if it's made out of gold."

"It's our family tradition."

"Why?"

"Because if I didn't you'd die. Everyone in the town would die."

The answer shocked her as much as a slap in the face. "Jacob? You really believe that?"

Calmly, he said, "This is a portrait of Justice Murrain. Never a more evil man lived round here. When he died he refused to lie where he was put. His spirit continued to haunt these cliffs. It was another ancestor of mine who created the mosaic. How it works, I don't know, but it holds Justice Murrain's spirit in the ground."

"That's insane."

"Ask the townspeople. If they've got the guts to agree with me they'll confirm it. This image children call the Ghost Monster is a prison for my ancestor's ghost."

He stood up to reach the lamp. Turning a little wheel, just beneath the glass chimney, caused the wick to grow longer. In turn, that made the lamp burn brighter. Amber became bright yellow. That intensity of light almost forced Rebecca to close her eyes. Once more her anger got the better of her.

"So if I smash this picture to pieces it will release the ghost of your ancestor?" She gave a harsh laugh. "I know why you're saying these things, Jacob. I've seen through you. You're thinking, 'Now I've had my fun with the woman I'll scare her away with a ghost story.' Well, I'm not so easily scared!"

Suddenly, he turned and gripped her elbow. The grip hurt, but it was sweet hurt, too. Despite herself, she wanted him to hold her in a crushing embrace. His pale gray eyes locked onto hers.

"Rebecca. You listen to me. I'm not joking. And I'll give you this warning: Life is going to get dangerous for us here. A new harbor is being built down the coast."

"What the hell are you talking about?"

"They've dredged out the channel for oil tankers. That's led to shifts in seabed levels to the point it's eroding the coast here. You've seen how the cliff has been collapsing onto the beach. Part of the old hall has already fallen into the sea."

"What's that got to do with your stupid picture!" Rebecca stamped her foot onto the portrait of the grim-faced man. He appeared to be gazing up out of a pool of black liquid—just a pale moon of a face, with burning eyes and parted lips that revealed teeth that would have been more suited to a feral dog. She stomped on it again. "Did your ancestor hear that? Will he grab me by the foot?" That laugh became wild-sounding.

"Don't do that, Rebecca."

"Scared?"

"Yes, I'm scared. As you should be." His grip tightened on her arm. It made her heart beat faster. "The cliff is eroding. Soon the sea will have taken what's left of Murrain Hall across there. In a few years it will eat its way through the ground, devouring the church and the cemetery. The ocean will rip this mausoleum apart. Then it will annihilate the mosaic." His eyes blazed into hers with a passion that made her tremble. "Then my ancestor will be free. Do you understand? He'll want his revenge on the town. That will include you and everyone you care about."

"You're not mad," she spat. "You're a sadist. Trying to scare me half to death, so I won't bother you again." She gave it one last try. "Make love to me here, Jacob. I can make you feel like you're in paradise."

"Why can't I make you understand? It's started to go wrong already. People have seen a figure in the ruins of the house. He's starting to come back into this world. My ancestor Justice Murrain is on his way. As the cliff crumbles it weakens the hold of the mosaic. At the moment he's just an image . . . he can't hurt you. But it won't be long before he will wreak havoc."

"Bastard." Anger convulsed her. "How dare you cast me

aside like I'm a dirty old rag? Last night I gave you so much of my body, Jacob . . . Now you won't even talk to me. At least not properly. Instead, you spout ghost stories about your ancestor. Why don't you just tell me to go to hell? I'd know where I was with that. I've heard it enough in the past."

"Rebecca—"

Her push caught him off guard. He tried to brace himself with his right foot, but the shoe found no grip on the smooth stone floor, and he slipped heavily onto his hands and knees.

Show him how you feel. Break something!

If only she could shatter the mosaic. The leering face of Jacob's ancestor that he so closely guarded. It would be satisfying to gouge the fiery eyes. Then she noticed the lamp. Keeping the thing burning obsessed the man to the extent he'd come out here at night to tend it. Before he could climb to his feet she grabbed the lamp from its hook.

Then she fled with it, laughing. She laughed even louder when she heard his protests. *Dear God, the man sounds like a child whose favorite toy's been stolen.*

Rebecca, holding the lamp high, ran through the graveyard. She hadn't given much thought where she'd take the light. This felt good . . . hell, it felt so damn fine to have stolen it from Jacob—that's all that mattered. Just to torment the man. Maybe she could even use the lamp as a bargaining chip?

Rebecca's path took her toward Murrain Hall. Part of it had already fallen into the sea due to the cliff being eroded. The dark structure that remained was a forbidding pile to be sure. Its little windows were more like those in a prison. The blocks of stone were somehow lumpy-looking. The black slate roof resembled the scales of a cobra. The whole place resonated with loneliness, despair, and lives blighted with suffering.

Still gleeful, still intent on mischief, she raced through the stone archway that led into the courtyard. It was darker there. The evening light seemed to prefer to avoid this area.

The bleak edifice of the house loomed over Rebecca—a cliff of bleak stone in its own right.

Still holding the burning lamp high, she saw the figure standing there, framed by the doorway of the house.

Laughing, she said, "Oh, Jacob? You caught up with me quicker than I thought you would." She ran her hand down her hip. "Then maybe I provided you with an incentive?"

At that moment, in the yellow flare of the lamp, she looked fully into a familiar face, with those darkly handsome Murrain features. But then Rebecca realized this man wasn't *Jacob* Murrain.

It felt as if her heart had been wrenched from her breast. With a piercing scream she started back. Her heel caught against a fallen branch. When she fell onto the ground the lamp broke against her chest. Inflammable oil drenched her clothes. Then the burning wick was on her.

After that she didn't much care about the man who watched her. Or the fact that he wore the same face as the one in the mosaic. The one that as a lively, impish little girl she'd called: "Ghost Monster."

FOUR DAYS LEFT

CHAPTER ONE

"Here comes trouble."

Pel Minton looked in the direction that Nat pointed. Hurrying along the cliff-top path, like lives depended on it, came a man with a mass of black hair that streamed out in the cold wind from the sea. The long coat he wore billowed raven black. Walking wasn't easy for him; he needed the wooden cane he wielded to take the pressure off his right leg. If he was in pain, however, he didn't yield to it. All that mattered was reaching the site of the archaeological dig here in the cemetery.

Pel zipped her fleece against the invading cold. "So what have you done to upset him, Nat? Stolen his girlfriend?" She smiled. "Just hope he hasn't brought his gun."

"This is England." Nat grinned back. "When Brits get riled they don't start shooting, they just get aloof and very, very polite."

"Well, that guy looks as if he's here to rip our heads off."

Nat shoveled soil from the hole he was standing in. "That's Jacob Murrain. Whenever we start digging in this cemetery he hobbles up and tries talking us to death." He tapped his forehead with muddy fingers. "Senilityville."

"Senile? He can't be a day over forty?" Pel watched the approaching man. He was tall, lean and there was a youthful energy that, despite the limp, powered his stride.

"The gods must have let him keep his looks in exchange for his sanity. According to the police he's over eighty."

"The police?"

"Yeah, we had to call the cops a couple of times. He doesn't like us excavating here. When we refuse to quit he sits in a trench, or climbs onto the bulldozer."

By this time, the man was around a hundred yards from them. Pel saw the determined expression on his face. "So why is he hell-bent on stopping the excavation?"

"Just wait until old Jacob gets here—you'll hear it from his own lips. It's truly amazing." Chuckling, he returned to scooping out more of the soil.

Pel Minton sieved graveyard dirt through a mesh filter onto a plastic sheet. Tiny splinters of human bone, mainly fragments of skull that resembled gray cornflakes, were retained by the mesh. Despite being the mortal remains of the local inhabitants since ancient times, these went into a hopper disparagingly marked DROSS. These shards of bone had no archaeological merit as they came from disturbed soil. What Pel had been instructed to search for was quickly datable material, such as pot fragments, coins, shoe buckles, clothing pins—these were the true archaeologists' treasures. Artifacts that could whisper the secret of their age to the expert who had an "ear" for such things.

Pel Minton had left Providence the day after her twenty-first birthday to travel the world. Pel wasn't the kind of person to dwell on self-image. She didn't mournfully gaze into the mirror for hour upon hour. *Life is to be enjoyed* was her pet mantra. Her best features, she decided: almond-shaped eyes, good jawline, long-tapering fingers. Worst feature: hair. And what mad hair! Her unruly, crazy splash of hair bugged her. It never looked right. If only hats were fashionable again, she could hide her frizz under a beret, or even bury it out of sight beneath a gargantuan Mexican sombrero.

As for character: likable enough to have loads of friends. However, people often confessed to her that she could be a handful. An electric storm in the shape of a single American female. For some reason, whenever she got into a new relationship Pel Minton disrupted lives—like a twister in a chicken shed. She couldn't figure out how or why, but she turned her new friends' world topsy-turvy. Now every time she met a potential new pal, or new boyfriend, she'd find herself thinking, *Watch out! You don't know what you're letting yourself in for. I'm dynamite!*

Six months ago, Pel Minton had joined an archaeological excavation in England. Despite there being little in the way of wages, the work suited her. Accommodation came free (rudimentary, to be sure: either a house-share with other diggers, or a tent), but it was a great way to see Britain, and she loved the mystery of peeling back layers of earth to reveal Roman villas, or Saxon forts, or whatever lay hidden. A couple of months ago, the opening of a battlefield grave revealed skeletons with arrowheads embedded in the bones. A sight as thrilling as it was grisly.

This dig, however, would be different. Today was catastrophe day. She eyed the approach of the old man, who appeared so uncannily young. Only the walking cane hinted at infirmity.

The head of the dig, Kerry Herne, employed a bullhorn to toss out quips and encouragement to a dozen or so colleagues, who toiled in trenches, or sieved dirt for finds. Aged forty, outrageously glamorous, with long, windblown hair, she raised the mic to perfect lips. "Give it your best shot, people. We're waiting for word on the church ruin from the authorities. Meanwhile, we've got to finish these test trenches tonight. It is really—and literally—a case of time and tide conspiring against us. Where you're digging now will be ocean in a matter of days. Fish will be doing whatever fish do where you're standing—d' your hear, Nat Stross?"

Nat saluted her with a shovel; a mass of soil mixed with bone fragments cascaded down his neck, which earned him laughter from his colleagues.

Kerry grinned as she thumbed the mic button. "Archaeologists interpret the dirt, Nat, we don't use it as a fashion accessory." All the time she shot glances in the direction of old Jacob Murrain. Clearly, she knew what lay in store for her when he reached the dig.

"Keep sieving, Pel." Nat shook dirt out of his jacket. "We've another ton to lift before bedtime."

"Slave driver."

"Aw, go on, you love it. Then you have to love this work with a passion, because we don't do it for the money. Am I right?"

Pel gently tapped him on the head with the plastic mesh. "Next you'll be telling me we get our reward in heaven. Whoa."

"What you got there?"

She gently wiped the dirt of centuries from a metal disk the size of her thumbnail. "Coin . . . no, it's a silver button."

Nat whistled. "That's high society. Make sure it gets put with the A-class finds on Kerry's table."

Technically, Nat was her boss, but despite being built like a heavyweight boxer, he was gentle as a kitten. And he never gruffly ordered her about, unlike some of the other archaeologists, who endlessly chivied their lowly "dirt monkeys," as they termed their assistants. When Nat asked her to do something he always made it sound like caring advice from a friend.

Taking the silver button (Regency, she surmised) to the trestle table, where the particularly valuable finds were set out for Kerry's perusal, allowed her to catch her breath. It had been a busy five hours, and this was her first day at this particular site. Because coastal erosion had been munching away the coastal cliffs at such a ferocious rate, the archaeologists were on a rescue mission, which turned out to be little more than a "rip and grab" job. They were compelled to yank potentially valuable artifacts out of the ground fast before the sea took them.

As Pel threaded her way through the headstones, with her

precious find in hand, she had the opportunity to appreciate how hard her colleagues worked. There were a dozen slit trenches in the graveyard. Another one had been started alongside a freestanding mausoleum in redbrick. Little bigger than a garden shed, it contained one of the most chilling pieces of "primitive art" ever seen. At least, that's what Nat claimed. *Tempting to take a quick peek*, she thought, *but we can't waste a minute. The ocean's going to take all this in a few days. Time's running out.*

As she walked through the long grass she sucked cool sea air into her lungs. Clouds scudded through a blue October sky. On the cliff top stood the remains of a church. The square tower still remained intact but the other end of the church, containing the altar area, had tumbled down onto the beach as the ground had crumbled away beneath the foundations. Now roof timbers stuck out into the cold breeze; the bones of the church laid bare by its gradual destruction. She scanned the terrain behind the doomed church. Largely undulating grassland, it suggested loneliness. The nearest house lay in the direction of town, perhaps a mile away. While the only road, serving this unpopulated section of coast, seemed to only venture here grudgingly. Little more than a dirt track, it had nearly broken the suspension of the vans as they'd driven up here. Strangely, as the road was seldom used, a pair of trucks, with matching crimson cabs, were thundering up the incline toward the church. *Maybe they're salvage merchants coming to collect masonry from the church*, she mused. *They better be quick, there's a chance it will have flopped down onto the beach in a few hours.*

Breathing deeply, Pel savored the tingling scent of ozone on the air, blending with the subtler aroma of freshly turned soil. Her parents would be surprised at her choice of work; after all, she never was one to get her hands dirty; now, however, Mother Nature's own good earth decorated her fingers.

Kerry smiled from where she sat at her finds table. "Ah-ha, more treasures?"

"A silver button."

"Excellent. You know, you've a good eye, Pel. Most people would have thought this to be just a grubby pebble. It takes some doing to see an underlying design through the dirt."

"It's practice, I guess."

Kerry gave her an appraising glance as she slipped the button into a plastic envelope. "We don't want to lose you. You're a valuable member of the team now."

"Thanks, but I still plan to leave for Berlin at the end of the month."

"I wish you could be persuaded to stay. The pay's awful, as you know, but this is valuable work. And you're just so bloody good at it. You're intuitive. You can read subtle clues in the landscape. We wouldn't have picked up the medieval jar last week if you hadn't checked the walls for cavities." Her line of sight wandered across to the church ruin. "Oh no, he'll kill himself . . . the place is falling apart." Kerry picked up the bullhorn and shouted, "*Sir! You, sir. Keep out of the ruin. It's unstable . . . sir!*" She frowned. "That's odd."

Pel looked in the direction of the church. One of its exposed roof beams swung in the breeze as if inviting them to get closer. "What's wrong?"

"I thought I saw someone against the base of the tower. Like they were"—she shrugged, baffled—"trying to push it over the cliff." Kerry rubbed her forehead. "It's these sixteen-hour days. I'm going nuts." She smiled. "You don't see anyone do you, Pel? Dressed in black?" The smile remained, yet her expression suggested someone who needed reassurance.

Pel tried to lighten the mood. "You are going nuts. There's no one there. It's probably just a shadow cast by the clouds."

"Yes, you're absolutely right. Anyway, I shall be having a very large gin and tonic in the pub tonight. I'm sure I'm even cataloging finds in my sleep now. Oh no, here he comes." She nodded in the direction of the cemetery gate. "Mr. Murrain."

"Why's he trying to stop the dig?"

"He's obsessed with the mosaic in the little building over

there." Kerry adopted a deep voice to imitate that of a man's: "'Keep the light burning; you've got to let me keep the light burning.'"

"The light? What light?"

"Oh, the man's convinced himself there's . . . damn, he can't do that!" Kerry spoke into the bullhorn, "*Mr. Murrain. Please stop what you're doing. This is work of international importance, Mr. Murrain. We can't allow you to disrupt it.*"

Kerry dashed toward the intruder who'd climbed into a trench. Pel watched with that mixture of shock and fascination that comes when a situation appears as if it will erupt into violence. Nat went along to back up Kerry. They weaved through the headstones toward the man. What then? Would they restrain him? Nat wouldn't normally resort to force, but if the old man got so riled up he decided to attack? She had a sick feeling in her stomach—the one that told her a situation was about to turn ugly. It was, but not in the way she anticipated.

The other diggers had stopped work now. They stood in their trenches to watch the outcome. Already they could make out Mr. Murrain's cries on the shiver-making breeze: "You mustn't destroy it . . . you can't even touch the mosaic . . ."

Kerry approached the man slowly now. "Coastal erosion will destroy the mosaic anyway. We're not going to damage it. It's going to be lifted out in one piece and taken to a museum."

"It must stay here," roared the man. "It mustn't be touched. And I've got to keep the light burning. If I don't we'll all be in danger."

With the mosaic lying at the focus of this argument, Pel decided to snatch a look through the iron railings, which formed one side of the mausoleum. It had to be something pretty special to get the old gent so worked up. And Nat did say that the mosaic's picture was the strangest he'd ever seen.

Even as she cut through the grass to the building, she

could still hear Mr. Murrain pleading with Kerry and Nat. "Listen to me," he shouted. "Instead of moving the mosaic you should be urging the authorities to build a seawall here. It's still not too late to save the land. We'd be safe then."

"I'm sorry, Mr. Murrain. That's beyond our remit. We can't persuade anyone to build a seawall to stop the erosion. It's too late—"

"Yes, it will be too late!" railed the man. "You know what the town's children call the mosaic? They say it's the Ghost Monster. And they've named it Ghost Monster for good reason! If you insist on removing it, then I'm warning you that—"

A roar of engines drowned Mr. Murrain's prediction, or threat, or whatever it was he was trying to tell Kerry and Nat.

Those guys are eager beavers, Pel thought. The two trucks swayed as they powered along the road that would take them along the edge of the cemetery to the ruined church. In each cab a man sat at the wheel, their eyes hidden by sunglasses. Dear heaven, the guys were in an insane hurry. That little track wasn't built for those kind of speeds.

Pel shot a glance back at Kerry, now in earnest conversation with the old man waist-deep in the trench. The others were returning to their work as the threat of violence seemed to be receding. Little did they know . . .

Pel quickly approached the mausoleum. *Just one little peek, then I'll get back to my sieving*, she promised herself. *Well, there's the light that he was so worried about.*

An old-style lantern hung from the ceiling inside the building. It shone its amber light down onto . . .

She never got a chance to see what the lamp did shine its light down onto. With a massive crash the first truck powered through the fence. In an explosion of splintered timber rails the vehicle shot through the cemetery. The second truck followed. Both machines smacked into headstones. Stone crosses, carved angels, plaster cherubs—they burst into fragments as the trucks battered them into the earth.

Pandemonium. Archaeologists scattered for cover. Pel froze. The drivers must be deranged. Why on earth would any sane human being want to race trucks in a cemetery? One truck skidded sideways, its wheels hurled up sod, along with dark geysers of earth; its rear end fishtailed into a finds table, sending it cartwheeling into a hole. Then the big machine spun out of control; its rear wheels pitched down into the main excavation works. There its driver revved the engine uselessly as tires spun against soft muck.

Distracted by the crash of the truck, she forgot to check where the other one was. When the thunder of a motor battered her ears she glanced in the direction of the sound.

The second truck swept through the grass toward her. A marble angel rose above a grave between her and the cab's grill. A second later the steel beast annihilated the angel.

Pel knew she was next. There was no time to run. The front of the cab filled her vision. The engine howled. All she could do was close her eyes. Then wait. Five, four, three . . .

The concussion came sooner than she anticipated. Breath jolted from her lungs. She descended into darkness.

CHAPTER TWO

They say if you are attacked by a lion you feel a detached calm. The teeth gripping your throat don't hurt you. You are strangely at peace as the animal savages your body. You are tranquil. It's like going to sleep in softly engulfing darkness. These thoughts went through Pel Minton's mind as she was hurled sideways. Logic dictated the truck's fender had smashed her ribs . . . and probably the entire front of her skull.

But as she fell into a place that was cool and dark there was no pain.

It only hurt when an object snagged her earring.

"Ouch. That stings!" Even more surprising than the lack of pain from what must have been a dozen broken bones, was the way her lips effortlessly ejected the words.

"Sorry." An Englishman's voice. "But whatever you do keep your head down."

A powerful hand pressed against the side of her head. Strangely, it felt like someone held her head against their chest. But who on earth . . .

Then a monstrous roar. Her eyes snapped back into focus.

Above her, a black tire sailed just inches from her face. This, followed by the underside of a truck. All too clearly she saw the spinning drive prop, along with dirt-encrusted steel struts; a moment later: a greasy rear axle and yet another tire. Then, above her, deep blue sky.

At that moment she understood. Someone had thrown

her bodily into the narrow test trench near the mausoleum. Just two feet wide and eighteen inches deep it resembled a shallow grave. One that had just saved her life. Or at least the one employed by a stranger to save her life.

When she sat up there was sudden silence. The truck had come to rest, nose first, against the mausoleum. Steam rose from the cab. The engine, thankfully, had died.

When she turned to thank her savior she experienced a giddy sense of disorientation. For there sat Mr. Murrain. Only he didn't look quite like the Mr. Murrain who had limped into the cemetery to berate the archaeologists. Although this Mr. Murrain had the same shock of black hair framing a broad face—one set with a pair of large gray eyes that had such an uncannily pale gleam. No. This version of the man was definitely far younger. Twenty-five at most, she guessed.

With an expression approaching amusement, he noticed her bewilderment; also, the fact she glanced between the man who still sat alongside her in the trench and the one standing with Kerry fifty yards away.

"That's my grandfather. Then you'll know all about old Jacob Murrain." He gave a dry smile.

She shook her head.

"Oh?" The smile broadened. "You soon will. A little thing like this"—he nodded at the truck that had crashed into the mausoleum containing the mosaic—"won't distract him for long." Swiftly, he climbed to his feet, before brushing the soil from his jeans and white T-shirt. He offered his hand to help Pel stand. "I'm Jack Murrain. Are you sure you haven't heard of the Murrain clan?"

Once more, she could only give a little shake of her head. The shock of being almost crushed into eternity by the truck started to work its way into her nerves.

"I'm surprised," he said brightly. "According to the locals we're a family of demons." He studied her with those unnerv-ingly pale eyes. "You're not hurt, are you?"

"I'm fine." Even so, a tremble ran through her. Only it

wasn't fear. She'd spotted the driver of the truck that almost killed her. "You damn idiot," she yelled. "You nearly hit me!"

The burly man advanced on her, eyes blazing. "Then you should have got out of the bloody way!"

"Why were you trying to run me down?" She met him head-on, fists clenched.

"I wasn't after you, you stupid bitch. I was trying to flatten that bastard." He jabbed a finger at the mausoleum. "I'd have done so, too, if I hadn't had to brake 'cos you got in the way!"

"Calm down, Ross," Jack told him. "You owe the lady an apology."

"I'll do no such ruddy thing. Out of my way."

The trucker went to shove Pel aside. Instead, Jack Murrain grabbed the big man, then flung him onto the mound of soil heaped beside the trench. In the same moment, Jack pinned the man down with one knee between his shoulder blades; the other knee shoved the man's face deep into the soil. The trucker struggled. His muffled cries became guttural choking. Jack exerted more pressure against the back of the man's balding skull.

"Ross. I know you can hear me. When you calm down, I'll let you go."

By this time Kerry strode through the grass; her voice boomed through the bullhorn. *"Everyone stay calm. Don't tackle the drivers. Leave them to me!"* The woman was steaming angry. No wonder. The excavation site had been wrecked.

But running up through the cemetery before her came the second driver. He clearly resembled the first one whom Jack held facedown in that mixture of earth and disturbed human bones. They were about the same age, too, midforties. The man bristled with aggression. For the second time today Pel felt the sick sensation that foretold of impending violence.

"Let go of my brother," bellowed the man.

Jack retorted, "Scott. The pair of you must be out of your minds. What do you think you're going to gain by driving trucks through that thing?"

"Because it's all your grandfather thinks about. If we bust it we make the bastard suffer. Now, let go of my brother."

"Ross can get up when he stops behaving like a jerk."

"I'm warning you, Jack."

"And I'm promising you that if you so much as touch me, or anyone here, then I'll knock you into that hole and fill it in myself."

Jack noticed that the fight had gone out of the guy he held facedown in the dirt. Quickly, he got off then rolled him over. The half-choked man sat up. In between gasping for breath, he spat out chunks of graveyard soil; no doubt, with the odd flake of human skull, too.

Pel glanced round. Kerry and Nat had reached the little gathering by the trench. Elderly Mr. Murrain had joined them, too.

"Idiots," growled the man who resembled Jack so much. "What do you think you're playing at?"

Still uppity, Scott grunted, "You're going to pay for what you did to our mother. For starters, we're going to smash up the place, seeing as you love it so much."

"Love it!" The old man choked back his astonishment. "I despise it. But it's my curse to maintain the mosaic . . . and make sure idiots like you don't vandalize it. That's my grandson's curse, too. When I'm gone, he's got to guard the mosaic with his life!"

Ross had recovered enough to chip in, "The cops couldn't get charges to stick against you, Jacob. But we'll make sure you pay for what you did to our mother."

"That was thirty years ago," Jack protested. "Besides, my grandfather didn't do anything wrong."

"She got half her face burned away."

"The woman stole the lamp," Jacob said. "I tried to stop her."

Pel watched this with growing fascination. For all the world, it seemed an old vendetta had flared up right under her nose. Something connected with the mausoleum, and the mother of these two men. Old Mr. Murrain protested his innocence. He also insisted there'd been an accident, yet had she noticed a shift in his gaze that hinted at guilt? Previously, this venerable senior had been so rock-sure. He'd been on a quest to stop the team from digging. He'd positively radiated conviction that the archaeologists must desist. Now that the brothers spoke about their mother Mr. Murrain had become edgy, uncomfortable.

He's hiding something. Pel's insight made her heart beat faster. *This is a man with a secret.*

"Get those vehicles out of here," Kerry ordered. "Otherwise, I'll call the police." Then she turned to the old man. "Mr. Murrain, you must leave, too. That goes for your grandson."

"Jack saved my life," Pel blurted. "He hasn't done anything wrong."

"Everything will be much calmer if these four gentlemen leave the site. Then we can start repairing the damage and getting back to work."

Nat returned from checking on the mausoleum. "The iron screen's a bit busted but the building's okay."

"What about the mosaic?" Jacob Murrain showed the same anxiety as a father inquiring about his sick child.

"Not so much as a scratch."

"Thank heaven for that. But I'd like to see for myself."

"No way." Kerry spoke with feeling. "That's enough excitement for today. Now, everyone who isn't authorized to be here please leave the site. And take those filthy machines with you."

Scott felt compelled to fire a parting shot. And to Pel's ears it was a fantastically mystifying, and electrifying, parting shot: "Kids call that picture the Ghost Monster. You only have to see it to know why. And another thing"—his lip curled—"everyone here. Yes, every damn one of you. Take a look at the picture of the Ghost Monster. After that, study these two here—Jacob Murrain and Jack Murrain—then tell us that all three aren't one and the same. Like peas in a pod they are! They're the devil!" With that strange accusation the men went to retrieve their trucks.

"See they don't misbehave again, Nat." With a splash of dark humor Kerry added, "If you have to, knock their heads off with a shovel."

As her words died on the breeze a thudding reached them. The sound of giant footsteps stomping this way—or so it seemed. Then someone pointed at the church. All of them turned to see the wall nearest the cliff shed its building blocks, as if they were stone tears, into the ocean below.

CHAPTER THREE

They stood on the cliff top to watch the steady fall of the church into the surf.

Nat smiled at her. "So how was your first day on-site?"

Pel took a deep breath. "Well, we got hassled by a madman raving about the mosaic. The cemetery got trashed by psychos in trucks, and then I nearly got killed when one tried to ram the mausoleum . . ." She found herself grinning, despite the mayhem. "Is every day like this here?"

"No, absolutely not." He feigned shock. "This has been one of the quiet days. Usually far more exciting things happen."

One of the archaeology students clapped his hands. "Whoa. Watch out, there goes the arch!" A stone arch that had supported a section of roof began to sag as if it had become soft as rubber. "Victorian Gothic, wouldn't you say?"

A low sun turned the stonework bloodred. Dark lines suddenly ran through the masonry. The ornately carved arch bled dust into the evening air. A moment later it collapsed, taking roof timbers with it. Debris splashed into waves fifty feet below them. Archaeologists and humble diggers (the so-called dirt monkeys) fell silent. All saddened by the death of the old church that had seen thousands of baptisms, weddings, funerals, and services galore down through the years.

Pel shook her head. "This is insane. Couldn't anyone have saved it?"

"Budgets are too tight to move entire buildings. All we can do is snatch artifacts out of the ground before the sea eats up the coast."

"It seems like desecration to me. Such a lovely old building."

"They managed to remove some of the historically valuable features, such as the font, the bells, and the stained-glass windows." Nat pointed out ships to the south. "That's what's causing the problem. Those are dredging a channel out of the seabed for the new port. This area's suffered coastal erosion for centuries but they've just gone and made it a whole lot worse. Five years ago, the North Sea out there advanced a yard every year. Now it's more like a yard *per day*. If you look out to sea to that dark area—the one about two hundred yards offshore—that's a mass of rubble underwater. Twenty years ago it was dry land, complete with the remains of a big house. The sea claimed that, too." He smiled. "Murrain Hall. No prizes for guessing whose ancestral home that was."

"You mean the guy who saved my life?"

"Ah . . . I was referring to old Mr. Murrain, but it's obvious that his grandson made a big impression on you."

"If he hadn't pushed me into the trench I'd be sleeping in the morgue tonight."

"Nicely put. But as it is, you'll be sharing a house in Crowdale with the rest of us. Have you got your things in there yet?"

"No, they rushed me here from the water mill excavation. My bag's in the back of the van."

"You'll love it. They even have a shower that works this time." He gave her a shrewd look. "And it's right next to the Raven's Nest Tavern."

"Why should that interest me?"

Nat winked. "Because that, Pel, my dear, is where young Jack Murrain spends his evenings."

"Idiot. I don't find him attractive." The words came out

right, but the tone was wrong enough to make her blush. *Oh my God, I do find him attractive.* In her mind's eye she saw his face framed by that wild blaze of dark hair. Then there were those large gray eyes. *Windows to a melancholy soul.* She bit her lip. *Stop it. I do not fancy him. Period.*

CHAPTER FOUR

Brothers Scott and Ross returned from the failed wrecking spree at the cemetery to find their mother at the door.

I wish she'd cover up that mess, Scott thought, then immediately cringed inwardly with sheer guilt. That *mess* was his mother's face. While the right-hand side of her face was flawless, even beautiful for her sixty-five years of age, the left side resembled the face of a doll that had been held over a flame. Mottled with reds, browns, yellows, it had, all those years ago, melted. Her left eye had become a drooping slit. The eyebrow had never grown back. The flesh on the ruined side simply hung down as if in the process of sliding from her skull, dragging one corner of her mouth down with it.

They were big men, yet they flinched like little boys when she unleashed her tongue. "Jacob Murrain telephoned me. The first time he's spoken in thirty years. He says that you drove trucks through the graveyard. You tried to smash up that old mosaic of his ancestors." The good eye blazed. "Why didn't the pair of you flatten it into the ground? Why has it taken you all these years to get back at him for what he did to me? Go on, look at this." She pointed at her scarred face. "His doing, that."

"Ma, don't! We tried—"

"And failed. Do I have to tell you what he did to me?"

Ross trembled. "You've told us hundreds of times."

"Another telling won't do any harm, then, will it? I was at the mausoleum when he was cleaning that damned picture.

He chased me down into the ruin that used to stand on the cliff. Went wild with me he did, then smashed a burning lamp on my head. It burned me up like I was in a furnace. The police said it was an accident, but you know better, don't you boys?"

They nodded in that submissive way of theirs when faced with Mother's wrath.

She nodded. "Jacob Murrain thinks he can scorn me for thirty years, then talk to me like nothing happened. 'Rebecca,' he whines. 'Rebecca, curb your boys.' Hearing that monster say my name sickened me. Now then, the pair of you know the hospital can't do anything more for me. They say my heart's only good for a few more months."

The big men had tears in their eyes as they listened.

"I've demanded nothing from you either as boys or men, other than you do your best to live a good, honest life. But Jacob Murrain is as good as my murderer. My heart's damaged because of the misery of looking like this." She touched her ruined cheek. "If you can make that devil of a man suffer just a tenth of what I've gone through, then I'll leave this world a content woman." Her good eye fixed each one of them. To Scott it felt like a splinter of glass going through his chest. "Promise me you'll do that for me, lads. Make Jacob Murrain suffer."

"We'll break his neck, Ma."

"No, that's what you *won't* do. Listen to me . . ." She beckoned them to her, so she could put her arms round both at the same time. The scent of lavender filled their nostrils. Without liberal use of it, Ma exuded an odor of death. Softly, lovingly, she breathed, "I don't want you to lay a finger on Jacob Murrain. Instead, you're going to break his heart. This is how you'll do it. Destroy the things he cares about." She licked her lips. "Hurt the people he loves. And the people they love. Make his life hell on earth. Do you promise, lads?"

Ross and Scott sincerely promised they would. Scott's heart beat harder. *We've crossed the point of no return. What happens next? Who will we hurt? And how?*

Anger had left her now. Tired, she turned her left cheek to them. "Kiss Ma's poorly better."

She'd asked that of them since they were boys. *Kiss Ma's poorly better.* Then they'd kissed her scarred flesh. Scott still went to the bathroom to scrub his lips afterward. *Kiss Ma's poorly better.* His mouth brushed the corrugations in her cheek. She put her hand behind his head so she could push his face firmly against that cold, dead scar tissue.

CHAPTER FIVE

Pel had to stifle her *ooh-eee!* of sheer ecstasy in the shower, lest the other dirt monkeys suspect she was erotically tangling with a man. But after a long day of sieving graveyard dirt it was bliss to be able to blast herself free of that grit coating her body. When Jack Murrain had thrown her into the trench the dirt had worked itself into every secret corner of her anatomy. Add to that, she now sported bruises on her buttocks, thighs, and shoulders after the narrow escape from the lunatic trucker. The bruises, while not hurting, left her skin unusually tender. When she gently soaped those "war" wounds of the day there was a bittersweet sensation. The beautiful magic of the hot shower at least managed to transform hurt into a sensual tingle.

Only a bad thing happened—a very bad thing. She smiled. When she soaped her body the mental image of Jack Murrain returned to her so vividly her skin goose-fleshed. Damn it, she even recalled the pressure of his body on hers. That muscular weight as the truck surged on over the trench above them. What a way to meet a guy. Inches from death. And in a hole littered with skeletal remains. *Just imagine the best man's speech at the wedding banquet.*

"There you go again," she told herself. "Letting your imagination run away with you."

After turning off the shower she stepped out of the stall onto the mat. The bathroom of the house she shared with the other diggers wasn't all that bad. Though the fixtures were dated they were clean. A previous owner in a fit of narcissistic delight had covered one wall with mirror tiles, so she had a full-length and steamily naked companion in the form of her reflection. Her body had become tighter and slimmer after all these months of digging England's soil to expose the past. Her efforts to uncover mysterious Roman temples, medieval pot kilns, Elizabethan armories, and a host of other sites had rewarded her with the fit, athletic body she'd always aspired to. If only the girls from her old school could see her now. Her Providence friends wouldn't recognize the new Pel. However, sadly, regrettably, *annoyingly*, she was also single. This state of affairs had bugged her for the last three months. After the relationship with a guitarist had petered out she'd become cursed with . . . *what's the phrase that best described being single? A singleton? Singlehood? A lone maiden? A bird without its song? Bread bereft of butter? A slipper without a foot? No, too Freudian. A Pel Minton without a Jack Murrain?*

"Quit it." She vigorously toweled herself. "No more crazy romances. Find a regular guy." Her mouth still managed to retain that tang from the dig site. Proximity to the sea made the soil taste salty. "Ugh, toothbrush where are you?"

A moment of rooting through her bag delivered a distasteful truth. She'd forgotten to bring her toothbrush, along with a bunch of toiletries, from the other house that she'd been occupying with her colleagues. Well, it couldn't be rescued now. It was an hour's drive back to her old quarters.

"Okay, there's a simple fix. Buy new." The downside: it was ten o'clock. She didn't know the town at all, let alone if there'd be any stores open. Nevertheless, she dressed in a sweater and jeans, pulled on her shoes, then collected her jacket on the way out. At this time of night an English coastal town in the fall would be chilly, or "bloody parky" as the Brits were inclined to say.

This house was a big old thing on four floors with lopsided staircases, doors that shut themselves, or opened themselves, apparently on their own mischievous whim. Most of the furniture looked fit for the museum. A smell of fried food permeated it from cellar to attic. Of course, fried sausages, bacon, eggs, and hash browns became the breakfast of choice for archaeologists, facing a day's labor out in a blustery field.

Pel's plan had been to ask one of her housemates where she'd find the nearest drugstore (and maybe beg for a merciful peppermint to take this salty taste off of her tongue); only she discovered that everyone had slipped out in search of beery delights in local taverns. At least that's what the note said on the kitchen table.

Pel, you'll find us in the Raven's Nest—wink, wink. Nat. She knew full well he'd play matchmaker with her and Jack Murrain.

"Not on your nelly, buster." Wrapping a white scarf around her neck, she opened the door then stepped out into the nighttime street. The cold drove her back on her heels it was so intense. For the good the clothes had done her she might as well have left the house naked. A regular hubble-bubble of voices came from the Raven's Nest Tavern next door. With its windows steamed up she could at least safely pass without Nat seeing her. Because Nat would relish persuading her to go into the bar where she could "accidentally" find herself reunited with her heroic rescuer.

She'd used the phrase "heroic rescuer" flippantly, but wasn't Jack the genuine hero of the day? He'd risked his own neck to save hers. "Maybe I should go in and offer to buy him a drink."

No! She was slipping into the mind-set of flirting with the stranger. "Saving your life doesn't confirm nuptial rights, you know." Setting her expression to stern self-denial, she hurried down the sidewalk in the vague hope it headed toward the town's shopping center. She saw no one in the lonely thoroughfare. The silent, narrow streets engulfed Pel as completely as if she'd been swallowed into the dark belly of some primeval beast.

CHAPTER SIX

Pel Minton moved through the deserted streets. They were lined with three-story houses in a brick the color of raw beef. These houses had no front gardens—front doors opened directly onto the sidewalk; each house was connected to the next so there was no break in the tenement. At that lonesome time of night it seemed to Pel that she walked in a deep canyon. Streetlamps bled orange that was reflected by the windows; they could have been watchful amber eyes as she passed by.

Doesn't anyone live in these houses? The question made her shiver. *The town looks deserted. Or perhaps everyone goes to bed at ten?* In the distance, she could hear the dull roar of surf. Ocean scents reached her on the cold air that seemed intent on invading her clothes. On telegraph poles were homemade signs: WE NEED SEAWALLS, NOT TANKERS! STOP COASTAL EROSION! SAVE OUR HOMES! When she did pass a house, with a light burning in the front room, she heard a TV carrying a debate on the state of the coast. The sound ghosted after her. *"A spokesman for the construction company responsible for the new port insisted that coastal erosion had always been present in the region. While he agreed that seabed dredging had resulted in a rapid increase in the rate of the loss of once-dry land, he stated that the cliffs would stabilize again soon. Campaigners against the new oil terminal claim that without adequate sea defenses hundreds of homes will fall into the ocean. While vast tracts of agricultural land are . . ."* When the voice of the newsreader faded away it became uncomfortably silent.

Pel shivered. *What on earth am I doing? I'm wandering round in a strange town at night. I haven't a clue where the stores are. How do I know there aren't muggers waiting for me round the next corner? Come to that, do I know my way back to the house?* Unsettling thoughts. A sense of vulnerability infiltrated her sense of security. All the roads looked alike—canyons of houses; lots of shadowy areas that might harbor killers for all she knew. *You're risking being attacked for a new toothbrush,* she scolded. At last, a break in one of the rows of houses that formed such forbidding ramparts of brick.

The narrow alleyway led to an elevated area of ground. She decided to check it out in case that somewhat higher point afforded her a glimpse of the shopping area. At least then she'd have her bearings. *Although don't go too far. It's dark over there.* She let her mind-chatter continue to distract her from being frightened. Of course, imagination fed the mind-chatter. Turning it bad. *Are those voices? Can you hear approaching footsteps? Isn't this the kind of place a Jack the Ripper would lurk? Just waiting for a fool of a girl to enter alone? What does the point of a knife feel like? That stab-stab-stab! What would it be like to watch the steel blade slice your belly?*

"Get out of the alley," she told herself. "Get out fast."

She turned. Then froze. Blood thudded in her ears. Her lungs locked up tight. She couldn't breathe. Because there, blocking the exit of the alleyway into the street—and relative safety—was the silhouette of a figure. A tall man, in a darkly billowing coat. Though she couldn't see his face she *knew* he stared at her. What's more, the head tilted to one side. He examined her. Assessed her. Rated her. She felt naked beneath his probing stare.

Don't show fear . . . Don't show fear.

"Hello." She took a step forward. "Are you lost? Can I help you?" Okay, those were totally random questions, but they were all she could pluck out of her panicked mind. What did he intend to do to her? Because, hell and damnation, that's what his posture suggested. *I've got plans for this woman,* his body language hollered loud and clear. *I've plans for her. She will do nicely.*

Determined not to show fear Pel advanced on the figure. In that light he was just a shape cut from shadow. She couldn't tell what clothes he wore, or even glimpse so much as a glint of an eye, but all of a sudden she knew one important fact. *He's a Murrain. That hair; the posture; the lean physique. Definitely Murrain!*

"I'm not frightened of you. What do you want?" Now she rushed toward the motionless figure. *Is it the grandfather, Jacob Murrain? Or the man who saved my life today? He's followed you, Pel. He wants to put his hands on your body again. He lusts after you.*

The figure changed. That shadow silhouette had become so much *more* than a man. The shadows seemed to boil as if a blacker essence flowed out from its chest. Waves of brutal cold struck her. She gasped. Her legs faltered. All of a sudden the strength went from her knees. At that moment it seemed as if some external power had invaded her body. She'd never felt so weak, or so helpless. She couldn't even shout.

Her toe stubbed an uneven flagstone. A second later she bumped down onto one knee. *Now it happens. This is where he attacks . . .*

She closed her eyes. Her heart pummeled her ribs. In her mind's eye she saw his hands—Murrain hands!—reaching toward her. *Fight him. Scream! Kick!*

Pel opened her mouth to yell her defiance.

She blinked. The ocean sounds grew louder. When she lifted her head she saw the figure had gone.

CHAPTER SEVEN

As luck would have it, Pel Minton found a mini-mart at the end of the street. The brightly lit store couldn't have filled her with more joy than that lovely hot shower earlier in the evening. It felt so warm and so safe to push through the glass door into a place stocked with everyday things. It smelled enticingly of pastrami. There were racks of candy, shelves of canned beans, carrots, peas, stew, meatballs. She even smiled at the sight of England's infamous black pudding in the chill cabinet. Nat, with great relish, had introduced her to this delicacy. "Try some black pudding," he'd told her. "You'll love it."

Black pudding comes in a cylinder of reddish brown paste, speckled with white (uncharitably, it could be described as moistly soft "matter"). It tastes metallic; a little peppery.

"It's okay," she'd said hesitantly on tasting it. "A kind of salami?"

"It's made from congealed blood," Nat had explained with relish.

Too late to spit, as she'd already swallowed, she'd grimaced, flapping her hands in the air. "Gimme a drink! Quick!"

He'd chuckled with sadistic glee. "Here's a nice English beer—warm—just how they like it. Ha!"

Now she found herself staring at the infamous black pudding in the chill cabinet. Meanwhile, the mini-mart customers stood in line, with their late-night purchases, as a middle-aged woman served them. On a TV an old episode of

The Simpsons played. For the millionth time Bart tormented Homer to distraction. That episode she'd seen so many times it had grown as familiar to her as her own fingernails. Yet this is the strange thing. When TV programs are imported into Britain from the States they seem to undergo a distinct change. As if whatever entered this old country passed through a field of transformation. Pel knew the technical reason why *Simpsons* episodes on British television screens assumed a different appearance. It was because that America used the NTSC TV system of 525 lines, while the UK employed PAL, generating 625 lines. Here in Britain, TV images were electronically carved with remorseless precision; colors were much colder. Even when she curled up to enjoy a bar of chocolate, she discovered that her familiar US brand had been manufactured in England. With slightly different ingredients, the chocolate had a restrained taste, as if holding back its normally rich bounty. A ghostly version of chocolate, she'd decided. Phantom fare.

England! They drive on the wrong side of road. In butchers' stores pig trotters are proudly displayed. There's peppery blood pudding—some delicacy (for vampires, yes). Police wear helmets shaped like the female boob. They don't carry guns. Bacon here is soft not crispy. Chairs can be uncomfortably small. Often the locals speak an incomprehensible version of English. An American fanny is in a different part of the body to an English fanny. Something that caused red faces when she complained to a rail conductor that gum left on her seat was stuck to her fanny. And yet . . . and yet . . . her mind was becoming attuned to the English way of life. Okay, she wasn't a blood pudding muncher yet. But she'd learned the notorious "warm beer" referred to a British beer known as "bitter." Made with different ingredients to regular beer it was, like red wine, supposed to be served at near room temperature.

It had taken time, but now she'd grown to like this little island. And one thing she did savor were the layers of history beneath her feet. She loved her job. It excited her to scrape away the soil to reveal all those hidden layers. It was like reading a book of secrets. To tease the meaning out of an old Roman coin, or piece of Viking pot, had become strangely addictive.

The Simpsons' theme bounced from the TV. She realized she'd been browsing here without even picking up what she needed. Quickly grabbing a basket, she added a toothbrush, toothpaste, a bag of peppermint humbugs, body spray, and a hairbrush.

Being in the store had a calming effect. It eased the memory of that disturbing encounter with the figure in the alleyway. *So it might have been one of the Murrain men looking at me. That doesn't mean he wanted to rip off my clothes, does it? Get a grip, Pel.* The company of other customers did make her feel better. Even so, a shiver ran down her spine when she recalled that silhouette. It seemed to emanate such a strange aura; as if its emotion formed a field around it that touched all that came near.

When she'd paid for her goods she walked briskly along the main road. Now she had her bearings she'd be back at the house in ten minutes. Thankfully. She longed to get out of her clothes now, then slip into the warm embrace of the bed. But the day hadn't done with her yet. Even with the time heading toward midnight it had one more curveball to throw at her.

As she crossed the road she noticed a man sitting on a wooden kitchen chair on the sidewalk. There was an empty chair beside his. He appeared a giant of a man, with huge pale hands that gleamed in the streetlight. The oddness of the scene was amplified by the fact he had bare feet. In this cold night air that must have been numbing, to say the least.

The man watched Pel approach. *Oh no, he's going to invite me to sit next to him. This is all I need.* His eyes glistened. He'd been weeping.

Then the giant spoke in a boy's voice: "Just look at him."

He put his arm around the back of the chair next to him, as if cuddling a little friend. "Look what's gone and happened to him."

Later, she'd chide herself for responding, but his voice had been meltingly plaintive. So she found herself sympathizing (or, more accurately, humoring the man's fantasy that he had an invisible friend sitting alongside him).

The man continued. "I'm worried about Bobby."

"Is Bobby poorly?"

"He's very, very frightened," the giant said in that little-boy-lost voice, but then added in angrily mature tones, "And it's all your fault." He snapped to his feet.

Dear God, he was almost seven feet tall. His eyes burned at her. Anger made his entire body quiver.

He took a step forward then bellowed, "It's all your fault. You and your bloody diggers. You're breaking up the picture—the Ghost Monster. I touched it when I was little. Little as him." He pointed to the empty seat. "Touched the Ghost Monster! It made me what I am today! I know things aren't right here!" He punched the side of his head. The force of the blow made such a loud crack it sickened her. "I'm not . . ." *Smack!* He thumped his own head again. ". . . right in . . ." *Smack!* "HERE!" He took another step toward her; a huge volcano of anger ready to erupt into violence. "The little chap's frightened. He saw Justice Murrain tonight. After all this time . . . he's come back to walk round these streets . . . Justice Murrain's looking. He's watching us all. Because soon he'll be back properly . . . and then he'll do what he wants with us. You'll see him. He's a crow man; all in black. He's been let out of the picture. And it's all your doing . . . you and them bloody diggers!"

Behind him, a door opened. As light spilled into the street a white-haired woman hurried out, crying, "Horace . . . Horace." Although Pel couldn't make out individual words, other than "Horace," the woman appeared to be soothing the big man. In seconds, she'd gently guided him back into the house.

Pel anticipated words of apology from the woman, or some explanation why a troubled man, who wasn't usually allowed out by himself, surely, came to be sitting on the sidewalk, waiting to accost passersby. The door shut without the woman even glancing in Pel's direction.

"Don't give me a thought. I'm fine. After the day I've had nothing surprises me anymore. I'm going to walk round the corner there, and no doubt the devil will be waiting with a couple of martinis. Sleep well! Don't let the bedbugs bite!"

The street was deserted once more. A church clock struck the quarter hour. Nearly midnight.

Pel sighed. With her carrier bag of toiletries she trudged, tired and emotionally bruised, in the direction of the house.

My first day in Crowdale. I sieved human bones (among other things) from graveyard soil for five hours straight. Then a madman interrupted the dig. After that, the lunatic truckers smashed up the place. I nearly get killed. A stranger I can't get out of my mind saved me. Tonight I saw him, or a relative of his, stalking me in an alley. Just a little while later another lunatic (the town must have them in abundance) accuses me of terrifying his imaginary friend, Bobby. I've scared him because we've unleashed some kind of vengeful spook on the town. Nodding, she murmured to herself. "Yes, that's what I call an eventful day. Wow-wee, I can't wait to see what tomorrow brings."

Just five feet from the front door a hand fell on her shoulder. *This is it, the death blow. It can't be anything else.*

She turned to see Nat's grinning face . . . and beer-flushed cheeks.

"Come for an ale."

"No thanks."

"We want to celebrate your first day on the Murrain site dig."

"I didn't think you liked English beer?"

He giggled. Someone might dismiss the man as a happy-go-lucky drunk. Yet she'd seen him ever so tenderly lift a child's bones from the dust of years. "Human sacrifice," he'd murmured. "It wasn't at all rare for stonemasons to bury a child in a wall's foundations. They believed a child's ghost made the building stronger." Now, here on the pavement, he beamed like a jolly uncle. "English beer. Bitter." He used the local name, "bitter," for the brew. "Blessed, life-enhancing bitter. It's weird—once that flavor buries itself in your taste buds you find yourself craving that first pint of the night. I love English beer. *I just love it!*" Clearly, he'd been indulging in his new love affair with the brew all night.

"I'm going to call it a day, Nat."

"Aw, c'mon. We can sleep when we're dead."

"Elegantly put, Nat. But it's just been one of those days, you know?" She unlocked the door.

"Jack Murrain's in the bar."

She paused.

Nat burbled on. "He's been there all night. Ha, looks to me as if he's waiting for someone."

"Sweet dreams, Nat." Pel closed the door behind her. Then she mounted the stairs to her bedroom, hoping that her dreams, even if they weren't sweet, wouldn't turn into nightmares.

CHAPTER EIGHT

Bulmann parked the truck as close to the church as he dare. Even the vibrations of the motor made the walls, which now overhung the cliff's edge, flutter as if they were made out of paper. Not long now before the whole blasted lot ended up in the drink.

When he opened the door he noticed the dashboard clock recorded a time of just eight minutes to midnight. The nearest town lay miles away. Nobody would be near enough to give a damn about a flashlight moving in the church. Who'd care anyway? Soon fish would be swimming in its rubble.

Bulmann knew, however, that it contained one last treasure. He'd climbed its fifty-foot-high square tower that morning before the archaeologists had fetched up to start digging holes in the graveyard. Entering the church didn't present a problem. The local museum had removed its oak doors, which were supposedly built from the coffin lids of medieval monks. Not that he gave a flying crap about that.

In a few paces, Bulmann had reached the narrow entrance to the church tower steps that spiraled up to the roof. A bulky figure came shuffling down, grunting with bearlike aggression.

"What's wrong, Miller? Too bloody heavy for you?"

"Carrying this doesn't bother me. It's Steve. He's yakking like a daft old woman up there."

"Damn it. Get the lead out to the truck."

Miller hefted the stolen roll of roof lead toward the door.

"Make Steve get a move on. There's cracks appearing in the walls."

"Don't worry yourself. It won't come down with you in it. This end of the church is still on solid ground."

"Yeah, if God doesn't smite us."

Cursing to himself, Miller lumbered outdoors with a hundred pounds of metal in his arms. Then again the church's interior was steadily becoming the outdoors in its own right. The altar end of the church had fallen into the sea. Now a quarter of the building had gone; it left one end yawningly open to the night sky, with views of moonlight on the ocean.

Pity we couldn't have got the roof timber, mused Bulmann. That would have paid for a new swimming pool in his Spanish villa. Well, the lead from the tower roof would keep him in creature delights for a week or two. There's a girl in Skipton whom he'd promised to take somewhere special. In return for something even more special.

Grinning, he climbed the spiral staircase. Soon he emerged from the hatchway onto the roof. Here, the sheets of lead had already been rolled by Miller and Steve into hundred-pound bundles.

"Steve. Stop jerking around up here; get that lead shifted down to the truck."

Instead of obeying his boss, Steve nodded in the direction of the graveyard as a cold wind whipped around their ears. "See that?"

Cops? Alert to being caught, he scanned the dark area of ground. "What do you see?"

"It's the Ghost Monster."

"What?"

"Ghost Monster. That's what we called it as kids."

"Steve. Pull yourself together or I'll chuck you off this damn tower."

But Steve's face shone. Bulmann couldn't tell whether it was excitement or terror.

Steve said, "You're not local so you won't know the story."

"I don't want to know any frigging stories. I want that lead in my truck."

"We used to ride our bikes up here as kids. It was a bravery test to reach through the iron fence and touch the Ghost Monster's face. Look, you can see the lamp burning there. Old Jacob Murrain keeps it lit."

Bulmann used a meaty paw to cuff Steve's ear. "Pick up that lead."

Steve appeared hypnotized. The blow didn't faze him. "The Ghost Monster, the kids' name for the picture. But really it's a mosaic of Justice Murrain. They said he was the devil."

"You're fired. Go home." Bulmann picked up the heavy roll of lead. "Get away from here before I break your face."

Bulmann climbed down through the trapdoor with his cumbersome load.

Above him, Steve shouted, "Don't you see? They've been messing around with the Ghost Monster. That's something you never should do."

"Go to hell, Steve."

"I know they've damaged it somehow. I've seen him."

Bulmann ignored the man.

"I've seen Justice Murrain. Down there on the path. He's back!" His voice rose into a screech. "Bulmann, he's back!"

Bulmann didn't care. He paid more notice to the cracks in the walls. Miller was right. They were worse now than first thing this morning. The entire cliff face must be rotten. It offered as much support to the ancient church as if it were no more rugged than a soggy cardboard box. *Still, we're going to get this lead—all of it.*

He continued down the spiral of steps. The dead weight of metal in his arms wanted to drag him down faster. On this downward spiral he could see only a yard in front of him at any one time.

So, when he turned the spiral to find that a man had climbed halfway up the tower to meet him, they weren't any more than eighteen inches apart.

Bulmann froze. The man seemed nothing but shadows and a pair of eyes. They burned into him.

"Get out of my way!" Bulmann thundered. Yet fear flowed through him like a river. He'd never experienced terror like it. The thunder continued. However, it wasn't the echo of his voice in the confines of the tower. He knew only too well what produced that sound.

Cracks in the walls writhed like snakes. Then suddenly they were fissures through which he could see the night sky. He'd never heard a sound so loud. Slowly at first, then with lethal speed, the entire church tower toppled over the edge of the cliff. Bulmann didn't live long enough to feel the wetness of the ocean. But before he died he experienced the agony of tons of masonry grinding him to a mulch of blood and shattered bones.

THREE DAYS LEFT

CHAPTER ONE

He returned with the same ocean waves that devoured those butter-soft cliffs of boulder clay. Fishing boats lay in the sluggish waters of the harbor. The first light of day caressed a sign that stated CROWDALE BOAT BUILDING & REPAIR. Once he entered the town it was much darker there. Houses at either side of the narrow roads formed shadowed canyons that even streetlights couldn't dispel.

It seemed to him that he'd recently woken from a deep sleep. Thought hadn't entirely connected with memory yet. There was vagueness about his identity. Yet he sensed that would be short-lived. When he passed through all those dozens of houses to glimpse people still asleep in their beds he sensed a momentous change in the air. He was approaching a huge event. Soon there would be a profound transformation.

Just what he wasn't sure. But he could sense its approach. Extraordinary events. Miracles. A transfiguration. That sense of wonder at a secret about to be revealed made him excited.

So much so, he didn't question how he could breeze through those redbrick walls as if they were nothing more than mist. Or how he could rise up through floors as if he were a bubble rising in a glass of ale. When he ascended through a man and woman coupling on the bed his mind filled with the man's lust. The woman lay beneath the man as he jiggled his hips. Dutifully, she murmured, sighed, then glanced at the clock on the bedside table.

The one who'd drifted into the bedroom poured itself into the man's head. Now HE was stabbing himself into the woman. She took notice of this. A gasp of surprise. Her brown eyes opened wide. "What's got into you . . . you've turned into a tiger."

Lust blazed. He pounded his groin against female beauty. It helped him remember. This had happened before a long time ago. He'd taken pleasure in female flesh like this. Now! To burst like a dam inside of her! That's what he longed for . . . this ecstasy . . . it had been so long ago since he'd experienced it.

He knew he'd taken possession of the woman's husband. So he made the husband's hands titillate the woman's dark nipples until they were hard. Then he was kissing her neck . . . her ears . . . kisses turned into bites. The woman moved to his rhythm. She was loving it . . . she was begging for more. She'd abandoned herself to this storm of sexual gratification that raged inside her flesh.

No . . . he was leaving too soon. He looked down on the man and woman fucking on the bed. His senses had disengaged from the husband's. Not finishing the coupling as nature intended angered him. But he was slipping away through the walls again.

Once more he was outside, floating through the dawn as lightly as a feather on a breeze. Brickwork engulfed him; then he was in a brightly lit bakery where men kneaded soft white mounds of dough. They chatted to each other. Never once did they look in his direction. He realized he was invisible to them.

What drove his spirit didn't allow him to linger. Once more he moved through walls. Wires formed patterns in the plaster. He saw copper pipes beneath floorboards as he passed through. Beneath the floor of one house, in a little back room, the bones of a baby occupied a dusty pillowcase. Against a delicate skull, a tiny pink teddy bear.

He moved faster. A sense of urgency burned in his nerves.

This voyage excited him, yet frustrated him. What was he supposed to do? What was his purpose? He appeared to be searching for something. Yet what was it? What must he find?

Into a police station. Through the bars of a cell two policeman argued with a man tattooed with swastikas. The lunatic threw punches at a wall; blood gushed from the broken skin of his knuckles.

"Cool it, Standish," called one of the constables. "We'll put you in the jacket again if you don't lie down and shut up."

The drifting one entered the lunatic's head. He saw dreams of killing the policemen . . . then setting fire to the building and dancing in the flames. Rage mangled the lunatic's mind. Hate was his reason for living. So he raved and swore as he punched the wall. For a moment, the drifting one calmed the lunatic. He was learning how to control minds.

The swastika-covered man turned to the two policeman, placed his palms together as if praying. "I do beg your pardon, gentlemen. My intemperate outburst must have been disturbing for you to apprehend. As Caesar might have declaimed in ancient Rome: *fiat justitia, rust coelum.* Ergo: let justice be done, though heavens fall. However, *dum spiro, spero. Et hoc genus omne.*"

The policemen were dumbstruck. One approached the bars to stare in at their prisoner. "Standish, what on earth is that gibberish?"

"Gibberish, gentlemen? Gibberish? That, my dear sirs, is the language of better men than we. It is Latin. The divine tongue that graces heaven."

The drifter was gone. The lunatic spat, "What you looking at, cop?" Then he returned to punching the cell wall. Bared knuckle bones shattered. His curses became screams.

Telephone wires, a gull perched atop the pole, a mail van in the street, a boy on a bike delivering newspapers. The drifter saw them all as he searched the town for something that was so important it put his senses on edge. Though the drifter had no flesh that sense of urgency burned him until he longed to howl. But what did he search for? What was his goal? He didn't know. But instinct would tell him when he found it. He was certain.

A moment later his presence ghosted through a three-story house. In a bedroom a big man crouched beside an empty chair.

"I'll protect you. I'll keep you safe." He spoke to the chair like it was a person. "I know you're frightened, Bobby. He won't hurt you; I won't let him."

The big man suddenly glanced up. For a second he seemed to see a phantom shape floating there. Yelling, he covered his face with his hands then tried to scramble under the bed as if he were a little boy.

Then the wall appeared to touch the drifter's face. More rooms came and went. Men, women, children: either asleep in their beds, or early risers shedding nightclothes.

Where was this *thing* he searched for? It maddened him like an itch he couldn't reach. If he didn't find it soon his mind would dissolve back into the mist that had held it captive for centuries. *Where is it? Where is she?*

The instant the formless cluster of shadows that was *he* entered the room he understood. Lights flashed inside his mind with the force of lightning strikes. Yes, he searched for a woman. Not just any woman.

This one lay on the bed. Aged around twenty she slept deeply. His presence loomed over her. He fixed his gaze on a calm face framed by tight curls. Her body appeared to glow with the promise of something special. The emotion that filled him had such power that he felt changes take place within himself. Whereas he'd been nothing but shadows, now he noticed that pale hands hung down from his sides. He flexed the fingers. A new strength flowed into him. In the mirror he saw patches of darkness in the air assume the shape of a figure. A pair of eyes burned.

This shape wouldn't last long, he knew that, but this was

the start of something extraordinary. A power grew within him. Soon it would allow him to unleash vengeance—utter vengeance on the town. The sleeping woman drew his attention once more. He leaned over her, staring down at her closed eyes, above which arched a pair of dark eyebrows. The lips were perfectly shaped. He longed to kiss them. To look at her was akin to inhaling an intense perfume. It went beyond beauty; her closeness intoxicated him. Could he reach into her as he'd done with the husband ravishing the woman? Or the lunatic in the police cell?

Light falling through the window grew stronger. As it intensified he realized his mind was melting away. The figure in the mirror dwindled to nothing more than a stray shadow.

Yet before he dissolved entirely into a mist of unthinking nothingness three facts presented themselves. Firstly: he knew that he'd return. Secondly: soon he'd be free . . . properly free. Thirdly: the woman's name. He deciphered it on what appeared to be an oblong broach, which also contained a miniature portrait of the woman: *Pel Minton*.

CHAPTER TWO

Pel Minton pinned the name badge that displayed her photo ID to her sweatshirt. After checking her reflection in the mirror she left her bedroom, determined to grab a decent breakfast before the ride up to the dig site.

Most of the team were already sat around the big kitchen table. They were upbeat. Excavation of the Murrain site (as they now dubbed it, considering the family's ties to that locale) was a race against time. It got their adrenaline running. They loved the challenge of rescuing archaeological finds before the entire caboodle dropped into the sea. Fried bacon aromas enriched the air to the point it made her stomach rumble.

Nat nibbled at a piece of dry toast.

Pel ruffled his wiry hair. "Are you still in love with English beer, Nat?"

He groaned. "Never again. If you see me with a glass of bitter smash it out of my hand. Please." Everyone laughed. He put his hands over his ears. "Not so loud. There's a poor archaeologist suffering here."

A guy frying bacon responded with, "Ten hours shoveling grave dirt will make you as good as new." He sliced black pudding into the bacon pan. "Hey, Nat. I'm cooking you breakfast. Bacon, black pudding, sausages."

"Sadist," Nat grunted. "I'll wait outside for . . ." He gagged at the sight of fat bubbling in the pan. "That's just evil." He fled for the front door.

As Pel sat down to a bowl of cereal another of the dirt monkeys, a petite redhead of thirty, read a text on her cell. "Kerry's got reports back on those pieces of pottery from the north end of the site. They're confirmed as first-century Roman so we've got to put in another trench there this morning."

The dozen people in the kitchen wolfed down their food. Despite their appearance—sometimes they resembled wandering vagabonds—they loved their work and were truly dedicated. Pel found herself growing so fond of them she'd begun to dread the idea of moving on. But she'd committed herself to traveling through Europe. If she formed any more attachments to the country, or to these lovably quirky characters she'd never escape again.

The vans arrived, driven by the senior archaeologists. The more humble dirt monkeys clambered into the back to drape themselves among the shovels, sieves, metal detectors, trestle tables, and assorted tools of the excavator's trade. Nat sat in the front with his head through the open window in the hope a cold blast of air would dislodge the hangover.

"If I feel like this tonight," he declared, "just bury me in the graveyard."

Twenty minutes later, when they arrived at the dig, a startling sight made him forget his headache. "Ye gods!" he shouted, startling everyone in the van. "The church!"

The van came to a rest by the graveyard gate. Instantly, everyone tumbled out before racing down to the cliff. A great chunk of earth had dislodged during the night. As it fell into the sea it had taken what remained of the church with it. Pel had set off to follow the group, who were clearly fascinated by the demise of the old building. However, she realized this might be her only opportunity, on what promised to be a furiously busy day, to catch a glimpse of the mosaic that had caused so much controversy yesterday. She pushed through the gate then walked up the path that led to the mausoleum—a ten-by-ten structure in brick with a black slate roof.

The cemetery bore its wounds, of course. Yesterday, the trucks had smashed many an ancient tombstone. An angel's stone head lay on the path. Twin furrows in the grass revealed where tires had ripped through during the rampage. The trenches were just how they'd left them last night, fortunately. It would be simple enough to continue the digging-and-sieving operation this morning.

And on this chilly morning the graveyard sat peacefully amid the green pastures of England. Doves cooed in a tree. One of the last butterflies of summer, with papery white wings, flitted over a patch of lavender. The substantial difference today was the disappearance of the church ruin. Not that it should have come as a surprise. Coastal erosion encroached by three feet a day. The church on the cliff's edge could have hung on for only a few more hours at best. As she walked along the path she glanced back at her friends on the cliff's edge. They pointed down to what must have been a scattering of debris on the beach. October sunlight glinted on the sea. In the distance, dredging vessels that were the cause of this destruction still glided back and forth as they ripped up ton after ton of seabed. A boost to the local economy that the supertankers would bring would outweigh the loss of a few square miles of grassland; at least, that's what the politicians argued.

Pel reached the building at the top of the graveyard. The truck had buckled the iron bars that formed a protective screen across the mausoleum's entrance. Also, there were fresh-looking cracks in the brickwork. However, the structure appeared reasonably intact.

When she peered through the bars at the mosaic set into the floor the shock winded her. "My God," she breathed. "It's him."

Icy shivers tickled down her spine. She leaned closer to see the face looking up at her from the floor. The artist had cunningly created a portrait from tiny fragments of glass and pottery embedded in mortar. Even more cunningly, the artist had contrived a picture of a man's face that appeared to gaze up as if from a dark void in the ground. A prisoner gazing from a pit. There was no background detail other than what appeared to be shadow. That, in turn, forced the observer's eye to meet the eyes of the man in the portrait. To challenge them. That stare hit you head-on. She could feel herself drawn into a battle of wills with that man.

And what a man? *He's the image of Jack Murrain,* she told herself. *That face—and those eyes—had looked down at me like that after we fell into the trench.* She shivered again. *The resemblance is uncanny.*

Pel found herself not just looking AT the eyes but gazing into them. The burning pupils in the center of the large gray irises pulled a nerve inside of her. Her hands found the iron bars. She needed to hold on as vertigo tugged hard. At that moment, it seemed as if she'd fall into those wells of darkness if she let go.

"He's looking into me," she murmured to herself. "He's reading my mind." The insane notion frightened her. Yet why did she feel excited, too? There was intoxicating power in that portrait's stare. She could feel it stealing through her mind . . .

"So what do you think of my picture?"

The shock of hearing the voice so close made her flinch back.

"Sorry, miss. I didn't mean to scare you."

"You didn't," she said quickly, not wanting to be taken for a dizzy kid.

"I come up here every morning to check on that devil." Jacob Murrain nodded at the mosaic. "I've got to keep the light burning. Usually, I'm up here at daybreak but it's harder to get out of bed these days. Old age is catching up with me. And my leg's playing up again." He gave the bars a tug to test that they were still fixed securely to the brickwork. "The truck hit this thing hard yesterday. I'm surprised it's still standing." He turned those gray eyes, which so closely resembled those of the face in the mosaic, toward her. "My grandson encountered you yesterday, didn't he?" The man smiled. "In my day, a young fellow swept a pretty girl off her feet in an entirely different way." He checked the cracks in the brickwork with a "Tut-tut," then: "You weren't hurt?"

"I'm fine. Your grandson saved my life. I should thank him in person."

"I'm sure he'll like that." He met her eye. "You don't find it disquieting? The family resemblance? Jack looks so much like me. And I look so much like him." He indicated the mosaic again. "That's Justice Murrain. Born, regrettably, 1700. Died, thank the Lord, 1751. He lived in Murrain Hall—the remains of that cursed house lie out there under the ocean. Along with the church, I see. Parts of the church dated back a thousand years. Justice Murrain worshipped there—though what he worshipped won't be found in the Bible." He produced a key from a pocket in his black coat, then opened the padlock before pulling open the iron gate. Hinges shrieked. "I keep the lamp burning. Can you smell roses? That's because I use scented oil. If I don't, a bad odor starts to linger. It comes from Justice Murrain there. Even though the devil lies ten feet down in a sealed iron coffin, right beneath the mosaic, he exhales the stench from his lungs."

Pel had expected Jacob to rave again. But this morning he appeared so calm and so sane. The only odd comment was about his entombed ancestor breathing bad air out through the mosaic.

"Yesterday I got myself into an upset," he confessed. "I thought you were going to start digging out the mosaic."

"It's got to be removed," she said. "If we don't the sea will keep tearing away at the cliffs until it reaches here. Then, like the church, it falls into the water."

"So it's of historical importance then?"

"Absolutely."

"But it's far more important than that. It's vital. This likeness of my ancestor keeps his evil soul trapped in the earth. If it's destroyed or moved"—the man shrugged as he lowered the lamp to the floor—"then everyone in the town will suffer at his hands, just as it suffered in the past when he was flesh and blood."

Pel's curiosity got the better of her. "Why, what did he do?"

"Justice Murrain brought the torments of hell to the town. Do you really want me to reveal the things he did? And what he did to torture his own wife?"

Just then, Jacob Murrain could have been opening a door for her to step through. Okay, a metaphorical door. But Pel sensed that she was about to pass across the threshold to another world—one that was dangerous and strange and alive with the promise of new experiences. Some of which would be frightening. There would be wonders, too. A trickle of excitement ran through her body as her mind played a trick on her. She pictured herself standing there, a slim figure in blue jeans next to Jacob Murrain. For one dizzying instant she couldn't tell whether the figure was the octogenarian, Jacob Murrain, or twenty-five-year-old Jack Murrain . . . or was it someone much older? The black coat now resembled a billowing cloak: one as dark as the heart of a tomb.

Those vast gray eyes filled her vision. The world had grown dreamlike.

"Do you really want to hear the life history of Justice Murrain?" he whispered. "Local people say that to even know about how Justice Murrain satisfied his appetites is to give the man a toehold onto your soul."

Do I accept? If I say yes I will be making a deal with the man. I'll have bought into the Murrain legend. There'll be no going back . . .

"You must tell me you want this." Jacob's gaze became a deep pit. "You have to say the word 'yes.' After that, open your heart to the words you'll hear." Then came the clincher, which surprised, yet excited her, too. "You won't hear the story of Justice Murrain from me. It will come from the lips of my grandson, Jack Murrain—the man who, yesterday, risked his life to save yours."

Her heart thudded. "Yes. I accept."

No! Why did I agree to such a thing? What's going to happen to me now? Thoughts of meeting Jack Murrain had provoked such sensual excitement. Those thoughts had been nothing less than an erotic caress. But now a sense of danger roared through her. Pel couldn't set the emotion in words, yet she knew she'd exposed herself to a risk that would come prowling from the unknown.

A voice snapped, "Mr. Murrain. You're not going to interfere with my team today, are you?"

Pel blinked, as if waking from a trance. The diggers were already back in their trenches.

The head archaeologist fixed the man with a fierce glare. "We don't want a repeat of what happened yesterday. Pel, here, was very nearly killed by that lunatic in the truck."

"Those men were nothing to do with me, Ms. Herne." Jacob Murrain's expression was as grave as it was wise. "My goal in life is to preserve the mosaic of my ancestor. While I've breath in my body I will keep that light burning."

"It's our intention to save the mosaic for posterity, too, Mr. Murrain."

"Then persuade the authorities that we need a seawall building here. The mosaic of Justice Murrain must remain not only intact, but stay here above his grave. It keeps his spirit fixed in the ground."

"We've been through all this before, Mr. Murrain. Now if you'll excuse me . . ."

"A seawall. Beg them for it."

"The politicians won't fund the building of a seawall, as well you know." Then Kerry turned to Pel with a reassuring smile. "Pel. Help me mark out these readings on the ground, please."

"Pel." Jacob Murrain's face glowed. "*Pel.*"

She shuddered. *Oh my God, now he knows my name.* Inexplicably, she was gripped with a fear that somehow he could use her own name against her. Right at that moment she didn't believe she was in the presence of an elderly man, but some kind of warlock. *Then every English village had its witch. And its own monster, too.*

"Good day, Mr. Murrain." Kerry took Pel's elbow so she could guide her away from the mausoleum. When they were out of earshot she asked, "Pel, are you all right?"

Pel nodded, feeling anything but.

Kerry eyed her with concern. "What did he say to you?"

"Oh . . . nothing much. Just stuff about the mosaic."

Pel hadn't told Kerry the full story. That was because if she suppressed the ominous sense of danger, which now gushed through her, it might simply vanish. But it didn't do that at all. Instead, she recalled images of her father hooking fish in the ocean. Now, like one of those doomed fish, she felt a great barbed hook of sorts implanted in her soul. Trouble was coming. Nothing she could do would allow her to wriggle free.

CHAPTER THREE

The brothers Lowe paid their money. They got what they expected. The woman they took it in turn to screw was no
stranger to the needle. She was a gaunt, used-up scrap of a
thing. In years gone by, Ross and Scott would argue about
who went first, then usually settled the dispute with a cut of
the cards. Now Scott Lowe wasn't that bothered who rode
the prostitute's weary bones first.

The time was coming up to eleven in the morning when
Scott stepped out into the yard to check the trucks over.
Meanwhile, brother Ross ushered the brown-haired woman
into a timber cabin that served as the office to their haulage
business. When he was younger Scott had peeped through
the blind to see how his brother treated the women they paid
for sex. Okay, Ross was eager enough. With a lot of lusty
grunting, he'd pull up skirts, tug off knickers, then push the
woman down on her hands and knees to pump her good and
hard. All the times Scott had watched his older brother slamming his hips into her butt he never saw the man look the
woman in the eye.

The October day turned out to be a kind one. With light
winds and sunshine it didn't seem so much like the start of
winter. So Scott whistled to himself as he checked the trucks
for damage. Yesterday, when they smashed up the cemetery
(not to mention sending those archaeologists running for
their lives), had been the most exciting thing he'd done in
years. The idea of getting revenge on Jacob and Jack Mur-

rain, the damned ghouls, excited him, too. Neither Scott nor Ross had any family other than their mother. So their lives consisted either of driving trucks, or spending evenings in the pub. Sometimes the occasional hour with a tart for hire. There were days he'd ask his reflection in the shaving mirror, "Isn't there anything more to life than this?"

He tugged long grass from the wheel arch of the truck's cab. Dear God, he'd nearly run down a woman yesterday. What had gotten into him?

Scott paused by the cabin to check if Ross had finished yet. He heard his brother's grunts. "Bitch . . . you dirty bitch . . . bitch, you . . . uh . . . take this. You have it, dirty little cow."

Yup, he was still on the job, and talking dirty, too. It didn't take much to imagine the chubby belly of his brother smacking into the scrawny ass of the addict. He'd probably be yanking the hair on her head, too. To pull her back onto his hot rod.

Scott wondered if he'd have time to check the tire pressures before it was his turn to ride the woman. This afternoon they had to haul a bunch of scaffolding to the new oil refinery down the coast. He fished a pressure gauge from his jacket pocket. Before he'd reached the first truck he saw a figure approach through the bushes.

Damn, she never comes down here. Something must have happened. He intercepted the woman. In the sunlight the burned side of his mother's face seemed to glow with the most lurid orange and yellow blotches.

"What's wrong, Ma?"

"I've got to see you and your brother together. Now."

"Ross is busy, Ma. He's talking to the harbormaster about a new contract."

"It can't wait. I need to speak with Ross immediately ."

But right now Ross entertained a woman in the cabin. Ma headed purposefully toward the door. If she walked in, Scott knew full well the sight that would slam her right in the eye.

Her eldest son would be ramming himself into a prostitute, who'd be perched on the sofa on her hands and knees. That would be a spectacle. A big, balding man, all reddened up with excitement, poking lustily into a skinny little figure that's as pale as milk and water. It would be like watching an ape-man humping a ghost.

Let Ma walk in on them. Just you see how she'll react to that little sex scene! He had to bite the inside of his cheek to stop laughing out loud. God, it would be a crazy thing to let her surprise the pair, going at it doggo. But then, recently, he was in the mood for doing crazy things. Maybe it's knowing the coast is being munched away by the ocean? Even solid ground isn't solid anymore. In the town there was an expectation that extreme and unpredictable events would soon be taking place.

"Ma. Ross has got his hands full in there." Inwardly, he chuckled over his choice of words. *Go on, push it further!* "He won't want to break off at this stage. If he's interrupted now it'll only mean a mess for him to clear up later." *No, you've gone too far. She's staring at the door.* "The harbormaster's contract is an important one, Ma. If Ross can clinch the deal, we'll have a steady income shipping fish for the next twelve months. No, Ma, wait until he's got the terms nailed."

"The harbormaster, you say?" The melted side of her face glinted, as if it turned clammy in the October sunshine. "He's in there, negotiating right now?"

Scott nodded.

"I'm your mother. Don't you think I know what you get up to in there every Tuesday morning? He's got a tart in there, hasn't he? One of them drug girls from the probation hostel?"

Scott was astounded. She knew all along?

"What you do with company profits doesn't interest me. But when it comes to some harlot coming between you and making Jacob Murrain pay for what he did"—she touched her ruined face—"that's as bad as humping a whore in church." Her chest heaved. "I'm not long for this world, Scott.

When you've got even with Jacob, and I'm in the dirt, that's when you can have as many tarts as you want. You can cover yourself with their mess for all I care."

"Ma—"

"When I'm dead fill the house with them. Take them in my bed!"

For years Scott had been emotionally blocked. Now, the dam burst. "I never wanted to pay for sex, but you twisted our minds! I couldn't talk to girls because you'd poisoned Ross and me. Nobody else in Crowdale would have anything to do with you, so you spent years brainwashing us that the town hated Ross and me, too."

"And so they did. They've always despised our family."

"Was that a reason to convince your sons that they were outsiders? Lepers? Two men who would be scorned by everyone for miles." His voice rose. "Ma. You fucked us up."

"You'll be the ones to get fucked up . . . with parasites . . . a dirty little rash." The intact side of her face assumed an expression of gloating. She loved purring those words. "Go with prostitutes and you'll wind up in trouble so deep you'll never claw yourself out."

Scott didn't want to deliver the knockout blow of truth. But at that moment he was so enraged he couldn't stop himself. So he stood in the yard full of trucks that fronted a busy street and he bawled, "You say we'll end up in trouble over prostitutes? Of course, you're the one who knows, aren't you? I've heard the truth, Ma. Thirty years ago, you were Crowdale's famous whore!" When he looked into her good eye he saw the same expression as those fawns he rode over in his truck. An absolute expression of horror. They knew the wheels would crush them flat. And now he couldn't stop his juggernaut of bitter words slamming into the woman who gave him birth. "You earned money from the men between your legs. When I was at school the kids told me that there was nothing you wouldn't do for cash. You met cargo ships in port then fucked the entire crew!"

Softly, his mother began to weep. She walked back up the path toward the house. He'd gone too far . . . way too far. There'd be a price to pay for revealing she'd been the town's most notorious whore.

With a groan of resignation he knew that when she asked him to act against Jacob Murrain he'd agree. Because guilt at his accusation would become unbearable; already his heart felt heavier than iron in his chest. Perhaps if he offered to kill Murrain's grandson that would be enough to win his mother's forgiveness? Anything . . . he'd do absolutely anything . . .

CHAPTER FOUR

In the graveyard, Kerry and Pel used aerosols to spray vivid orange marks on the grass. After fifty minutes of this activity, parallel lines radiated out from the mausoleum, like the spokes of a wheel. The redbrick building that contained the dour mosaic of Justice Murrain formed an oblong hub at the center.

"Are you sure you're okay?" Kerry asked. "You seem preoccupied."

Pel put on a brave face. "I'm fine. I just wasn't expecting Mr. Murrain to come popping out like that."

"He's been buttonholing members of our team ever since we arrived. It's always with some dire warning that terrible doom will befall everyone if we remove the mosaic." She gave Pel a genuinely sympathetic look. "He didn't say anything else to worry you?"

"No. Truth be known, I'm more concerned about those bozos coming back for another wrecking spree in their trucks."

"I'm not sure I did the right thing letting them leave. Perhaps I should have called the police." Kerry gave a pained shrug. "But if I had, the police would have wanted to interview the team; we'd have lost time we can't make up. Every minute counts now. And now this." She unfolded a plan of the graveyard. "I didn't expect Geo-Phys to find a whole system of earthworks buried under the topsoil." The Geo-Phys team used electronic equipment to sense variations of the magnetic field in the ground. A computer translated that data into a map of what lay beneath the surface. In effect, the equipment allowed them to see what lay buried under the sod.

"Have we marked it all yet?"

"Just about. Their readings indicate that the main arm . . . or spoke of the earthwork runs down that way to the cliff. Centuries ago, it might have connected this area with a henge or tumulus; of course, that lays out there in the briny now." Kerry indicated the sea. "Which means our impossible workload to investigate this site is now doubly impossible."

"We could bring in lights and continue the dig after dark?"

"At a pinch we might have to do that. The scanners detected what might be an Iron Age burial at the end of the main spoke. As that's right on the cliff's edge we'll have to give that priority." Kerry mused, finger against lip. "If we devote all our manpower to it we might be able to open up the tomb vault in no more than an hour. Of course, it's unorthodox . . . painfully unorthodox for we sensitive archaeologists." She grinned. "But it's either that or watch the whole lot go plop into the drink."

"I don't mind skipping lunch, if it helps."

Kerry appeared touched by the gesture. "No, Pel, I insist on diggers taking meals. You lovely dirt monkeys have got to keep your strength up. But thanks, anyway. But we'll mark the tomb's location before we break for lunch. I want to bend Nat's ear about all this, too."

Nat did some ear-bending of his own. Although the radiating spokelike arrangement of earthworks was invisible to the naked eye he'd been eagerly walking the lines marked by Kerry and Pel in orange paint.

"My God, it's fantastic!" he enthused. "Kerry, this has got to be the find of the year. You know what we've got here?" Nat's eyes twinkled. "Prehistoric earthworks."

"And they're overlaid by a later Christian site."

"Which is in keeping with most English churches. Pagans converting to Christianity still revered their old temples." He crouched, so he could look along two parallel orange lines painted on the grass. They led from the cliff's edge directly to the mausoleum. "This has probably been holy ground for the last eight thousand years."

Pel had to remind the excited man of one painful fact. "And in a couple of weeks, at most, it will be underwater."

"I know. To lose a site like this is tantamount to sacrilege. And it gets worse. Geo-Phys have been running a new computer program to refine their results." He produced a sheet of paper covered with what appeared to be blotches, but to Nat's trained eye it formed a window to a subterranean world. "Look, you've got the mausoleum in the center forming the hub. This suggests that two-hundred-year-old building has been erected over a far more ancient structure. I'd bet my wages that you'll find a Roman temple under there . . . then under that will be a prehistoric Celtic site. From that specific point these spokes radiate. They might be sacred groves, possibly linear mounds. The enhanced results reveal that the outer end of the spokes have been linked by what might be a ditch. So, in effect, the ditch forms something like the rim of a wheel enclosing the entire site."

Kerry checked the images. "So—a distinct boundary to separate holy ground from the ordinary secular landscape beyond."

Nat smiled at Pel. "I'm elated because we've found something unique. I'm also distraught because this beautiful feature, where Britons have worshipped from eight thousand years ago as pagans—until a few months ago as Christians—is going to be ripped apart by the ocean." He looked at Kerry. "If we hammer on parliament's door, will they bring in the army to shore up the cliff? That will buy us time, not just to continue the excavation, but lobby the government to build a proper sea defense here. Something to keep that beast"—he jerked his head at the ocean—"at bay."

Kerry wrestled with the dilemma. "They've not inter-
vened anywhere else. We've had to sacrifice some wonderful
historical sites."

The big man had tears in his eyes. "This place is so . . . *so*
important. We're talking world heritage class."

"I'd need to get the backing of everyone from the local
mayor right up to the prime minister." Kerry's voice quivered
with excitement. "It will cost millions."

"And already it might be too late." Nat pointed at the
readout. "They'll have to start work within hours to have any
chance of stopping the erosion."

Pel scanned the rough grass of the graveyard with those
orange paint marks forming the outline of a vast wheel. "So
how did this place work? What was it for?"

Kerry hugged herself. "Think prehistoric Vatican. A place
where ancient people traveled to from all over Europe. They
came here to worship and to perhaps seek a magic cure for
illness."

"See those radiating lines?" Nat asked. "How they con-
verge on the most intensely sacred center of the temple area?
Those will be spirit roads along which not just mortals would
walk. Those are the highways of the gods . . . and for the
ghosts of the dead. They'd approach the holy epicenter along
those from all points of the compass. The area within the rim
of the wheel shape would be a meeting place of heaven and
earth. Once inside here, the ancients believed you could talk
to your gods. The living might bring presents for dead ancestors and meet them face-to-face."

Kerry added, "Think of it also as an occult savings bank.
The spirits of the dead could be summoned, then—through
sacred ritual—be joined with the ground here. That is, the
ghost would be embedded into the earth."

Pel's flesh tingled. "You mean the place where the mausoleum sits is a kind of anchor? It anchors ghosts to this world?"

Nat grinned. "Yup, to stop them flying off. It would make
this place supernaturally strong. Where the sick would be

miraculously healed. It might also have been used to imprison evil spirits."

Pel's voice rose. "But that's what Mr. Murrain has been saying. He told me this morning that the ghost of his ancestor Justice Murrain is embedded in the mosaic. It holds him captive."

Nat sighed. "Something which he clearly believes. And if we believed in such things as malicious spooks, and troublesome phantoms, this is the time to get really, really worried."

"Why?"

Nat showed her the printout that revealed a shadowy line that encircled the site . . . or nearly encircled the site. "The ancients created a mechanism here, or so they believed. It was a machine built from mounds, ditches, standing stones, and timber posts. Just like a computer processes information, so this temple processed beings from the spirit world."

Pel began to see a pattern in the plan's blotches. "But a quarter of it has already fallen into the sea."

"Exactly," Kerry affirmed. "A whole section of rim has gone, along with parts of the spokes—the spirit roads."

"So the machine is literally falling apart," Nat told her. "The ancient people who worshipped here would be frightened if they'd known this was going to happen. They'd realize it wouldn't function properly." As a cold wind sighed from the sea Nat gave an expressive shrug. "If Murrain shares the same belief, he'll be convinced that his ancestor's ghost is already starting to break free."

Clouds looming over them suddenly made the world a gloomier place. Chill fingers of air touched Pel's face. When she looked up the slope she saw a darkly clad figure standing against a line of bushes. At that moment, she didn't know whether she was looking at Mr. Jacob Murrain. Or someone else who resembled him. When she looked again the man had gone.

CHAPTER FIVE

"Joe, I dare you."

"I'm not scared."

"You are." The older boy made chicken sounds. "Scared—pant-filler scared."

"I'm not. It's just stupid. I mean, what's the point?"

"Everyone says you're a coward, Joe. Prove that you're not."

The girl said, "Don't listen to him, Joe. We came up here for a bike ride, not to mess about on the edge of the cliff."

The older boy made chicken sounds again. There was no humor in it; he was being mean.

"Stop it, Neil. And leave Joe alone, or we're going back into town."

"So you're taking orders from a girl now, Joe? Jelly belly."

A teacher assessment day meant they'd got a day off school. Everyone had heard about the church falling into the sea, so crowds had come up to see it for themselves. Of course, with the church, or rather the rubble from it, lying in the surf, there was nothing interesting to see now that the *actual* collapsing part was over. The three—Neil and Bethany, aged fourteen, and Joe, thirteen—had cycled round the lanes hunting for excitement. They'd briefly paused to watch the archaeologists. There were holes in the grounds. A couple of people sieved earth through a mesh. A guy with a metal detector had been scanning the ground. A pair of women had been painting orange marks on the grass.

"Boring," Neil had declared.

Joe wouldn't have minded staying a little longer. He'd planned to ask if he could see the finds table. He'd done that before and been rewarded with the chance to hold a medieval spearhead. There'd also been a dozen Roman coins. It had given him a buzz to touch money that had been used to buy stuff like wine, cloaks, and swords centuries ago. The archaeologists had been happy to chat with Joe, once they realized he had a genuine interest in the excavation. One had held up the smallest coin: it bore the picture of Poseidon, god of the ocean. The man had smiled. "Two thousand years ago this would have bought you a cooked mouse. The people round here used to jab a stick through the head of the mouse, roast it over a fire, then eat it like a lollipop."

A second archaeologist had added dryly, "The mouse would have been flavored with honey. Which is infinitely better food than they give us here on-site."

Unlike Joe, Neil wouldn't stick around to watch the excavation. He longed for the kick danger would give him. Then Neil got a juicy thrill from smashing windows. Sometimes he let down car tires, then laughed when their owners stood scratching their heads, no doubt wondering if they'd got a puncture. So, Neil being the eternal risk-taker, suggested they cycle down to the cliff.

"Toby Lomax told me about this," he said, as he laid down his bike on the grass. "Now watch me. 'Cos you're both going to do it."

Neil approached the edge of the cliff.

Joe's stomach muscles clutched tight. "Careful. There's a fifty-foot drop here."

"I'm not scared."

"Don't come running to us if you break your legs," Bethany quipped.

"It'll be more than broken legs," Joe warned. "You'll bust like an egg."

"Shut up, jelly belly." Neil knelt at the edge of the cliff, so he could see the yellow sand fifty feet below.

Yeah, Neil, you're not brave, Joe told himself. *What you've got is a lack of imagination. You can't picture yourself dropping over the edge like a lump of dirt. Then hitting the beach so hard you break every bone in your body.* Joe closed his eyes for a second. In perfectly sharp detail he could picture annoying Neil Chambers toppling over. He'd scream for his "mammy" as his legs kicked the air on the way down. Splat!

Joe was imaginative. He could imagine the ancient Roman invaders living in their villas up here. He was intelligent, too. This week the kids had been getting excitable at school. Suddenly, there'd been lots more fights. There'd been trouble in class. Kids had been fidgety. Joe had noticed birds had started to migrate. The season had changed. The first frost of winter had appeared a couple of nights ago. *Thousands of years ago humans used to migrate, like the birds still do. The urge to migrate is still in our genetic memories. Children have the instinct to move on to some other place. But because we have civilization we've stopped migrating, but the urge is still in our blood. When the seasons change that urge possesses us; it makes us restless. We're no longer ourselves. History doesn't just lie underground. It lies inside our minds, too. One day we will have* psychological *archaeology.*

Now, at the top of the cliff, which had all these cracks running back through the soil from where it was giving way, Neil planned some crude archaeology of his own. Here they were screened by bushes from the archaeologists in their trenches, but it was still within the precincts of the graveyard.

"You're mad, Neil Chambers," Bethany told him. "Don't you know that right at the edge of cliffs you get an overhang where roots hold the soil together. If that gives way . . ."

"Shut your spit flaps, Bethany. Now watch me." The youth lay flat on his stomach, then wormed toward the edge of the cliff until his head jutted over the edge. That done, he reached downward.

"You'll kill yourself," Joe warned.

"I'll kill you, jelly belly, if you don't be quiet. Uh . . . I can feel 'em!"

"What've you found?" Bethany was interested now.

"Ah, wouldn't you like to know?"

Joe realized what it must be. "It's the graves underground. The cliff's dropped away."

"Bingo, jelly belly." Grinning, Neil brandished a pale object in his hand. "When you look down you can see bones jutting out from the cliff. It's like cutting a cake in two and seeing the fruit inside."

He flung the fragment of skeleton at Joe, striking him on the chest. When it fell onto the grass Joe recognized it as a piece of skull.

"Those are human remains, Neil. It's disrespectful to chuck 'em."

"Frightened, jelly belly? Scared the ghost will come along and twist your nuts."

"I'm going home." Bethany picked up her bike. "You've gone too far."

Laughing, Neil pushed himself to his feet, then flung something resembling a stick. A child's thighbone struck her cheek with enough force to make her cry out.

"Hey!" Joe shouted. "Stop that."

"Crybaby."

"You're a bully," he said. "Whenever you get bored you start hurting people."

"Oooh, write it all down. I'll read it the next time I'm on a long, boring bus ride."

Joe picked up his bike, too.

"Cowards," Neil jeered. "Show us you've got some guts, Joe. Get down here at the edge of the cliff and pull out some bones."

"Give it a rest." Bethany sighed. "We're not interested."

The wind blew harder. Dark fists of cloud punched the horizon. Surf hissed over the sands as the tide turned.

Neil snarled. "I'm sick of you sticking your nose in, Bethany. How's about this, then? I'll hold on to your legs as you reach over the cliff for the bones."

"No."

"Tough. I'm going to make you anyway. I hope you've got a head for heights." He grabbed the girl's arm before she could pedal away.

"Neil, stop it!" Joe shouted.

"Like you're going to make me? Remember who made your mouth bleed last Christmas." He dragged Bethany, together with the bike, to the cliff's edge.

"Neil, let go!" Fear snapped through the girl. By this time, they were ten feet from the sheer drop.

"Stop it." Joe climbed off his bike.

"Not a chance. She's bone picking, like I did."

"Leave her alone." He ran to the youth.

But Neil shoved the smaller boy aside as if he were nothing more than a doll.

"Stop it, Neil," Bethany pleaded. "You'll let me fall."

He chuckled. "Your family will leave flowers here if you're killed. Then I'll come up here and kick them over the edge, too."

Joe saw he could do nothing to physically stop Neil forcing Bethany toward the edge of the cliff. Instead words erupted from his lips. "Neil. I dare you to do something."

"What's the point? You daren't take risks."

"Yes, I will. Come with me?"

"Where?" The bully eyed Joe with suspicion.

"The Ghost Monster. Watch me touch its face!"

"You daren't touch a teddy bear's face, jelly belly."

"I dare you to touch it, too."

"That Ghost Monster dare's for little kids."

"So you're not coming with me?"

"Nah."

Joe made chicken clucks.

That incensed Neil. "Okay." He let Bethany go. "I'm going to make sure you touch the Ghost Monster. If you don't I'm going to beat you to crap."

They were at the mausoleum in two minutes. The archaeologists were using picks to attack a small area of ground near the cliff. They swarmed over it like ants, as if lives depended on digging the pit.

The three leaned their bikes against the brick structure then snuck round to where the iron grill protected the mosaic. The bars were easily wide enough to reach through. For a while, all three stared at the face, as it peered up out of the shadows. Joe found his gaze drawn to the gray eyes centered with pupils that possessed a wet, shiny slickness. *Like real eyes,* he told himself.

"Hello, Mr. Murrain," Bethany said.

Both boys saw how she'd turned away from the iron bars to look down the slope.

"Idiot," Neil grunted. "Who are you talking to?"

"I thought I saw Mr. Murrain standing there by the graves." The girl appeared troubled. "I'm sure I did."

Neil shrugged. "Bloody time of month."

"Touch the picture," Joe ordered.

"You touch it."

"Remember the story?" Bethany had turned back to the mosaic. "If you touched it, then the devil would get you."

"Kid stuff," Neil uttered.

"I dare, if you won't." Slap! Joe's palm smacked down into the center of the Ghost Monster portrait. Its gray eyes peered out from either side of his fingers.

Neil pretended to be bored. "Okay, jelly belly, I'll touch it now, if it makes itty-bitty boy happy."

Joe didn't move. He remained in a crouching position, arm extended through the bars, hand flat against the picture of Justice Murrain.

"Shift out of the way, doofus." Neil tugged Joe's hair.

The boy still did not move. Nor did he seem to feel the yank of his hair.

"Can't you hear me? Move your lard butt."

No reply.

"Shift." Neil jabbed his toe into Joe's back. "Next time, I'll give you a proper kick, then you'll know about it."

Joe crouched at the bars, staring at the face inside the mausoleum.

With sadistic pleasure Neil gave Joe a sharp kick. Joe didn't even appear to register the blow, though it must have hurt.

"Hey, stop that, Neil," Bethany protested.

The breeze carried a body of cold air from the sea. The grass flattened as if invisible feet marched through it.

Neil gave a menacing snarl. "If you don't move, I'll knock your teeth down your damn throat."

Without turning, Joe murmured, "So, been watching your stepmother through the keyhole again? She makes merry with the sailor men."

Neil recoiled in astonishment.

Joe continued smoothly. "That performance excites you, doesn't it? A regular hornpipe of pleasure, uhm?"

"Shut up."

"You love to peep through that keyhole."

"Joe. I'm warning you."

"Told your father, eh, boy?"

Joe still remained in the same position, crouching at the bars, his hand on the mosaic. The image's gray eyes peered up out of the ground.

Bethany took a step back. Joe's voice had altered. It had become much, much deeper. That, and the phrasing. As if someone uttered words that were unfamiliar.

"I know what you crave, boy." Joe spoke with rich pleasure. "You long to use your father's di-gi-tal camera. You promise yourself to cast images of your stepmother's frolics onto a web . . . no, onto THE Web . . . for all the world to see."

With a roar Neil lunged at Joe. Clearly, he intended pounding the boy. However, Joe leaped to his feet. His expression had undergone a profound transformation. He leered at the bigger youth.

When Neil swung his fist, Joe easily swept the punch

aside. Then he grabbed Neil by the hair and slammed his face against the iron bars. Bethany stared in horror.

Neil must have figured his skull colliding with the gate had been a pure accident. He flung a savage punch at Joe's face. Once more the smaller boy smashed Neil's head against the ironwork. This time the teen's face turned bone white as a river of red gushed down from his fringe.

Joe blinked. "Neil, what happened to you? How did you cut your head?"

Bethany stared in total shock.

He took a clean tissue from his pocket then held it out for Neil, so he could press it to the bloody cut. However, Neil backed off. The youth was terrified of Joe. Awash with blood, Neil grabbed his bike then cycled away down the lane in sheer, blind panic.

Joe turned to Bethany. "What happened?"

At last, she broke eye contact with him then cycled away as fast as she could. Before she fled, however, she'd uttered these mystifying words as she pointed at the mosaic. "*You were him!*"

CHAPTER SIX

"Hurry it up," Pel warned. "It's starting to give way."

Nat and Kerry tied the rope to the towing pin on the van. The other end of the rope had been secured to the slab of stone that covered the ancient tomb.

"Nearly there," called Kerry. After checking the knot, she ran to the van to jump into the driver's seat.

Nat wore a bitter expression. "This isn't archaeology, it's criminality."

"The crack's widening," Pel warned. "I can even see the beach through it."

"Just two more minutes, then we'll lift the stone." Nat signaled Kerry to start the motor. "Take up the slack, but don't pull yet." Then he motioned to the diggers who still sweated in the deep hole they'd dug on the cliff top. "Everyone out. Stay right back. If the rope snaps, it'll take your face off."

The team didn't need telling twice. They backed off a good fifty feet or so.

Pel remained close, however. She had to be near enough to judge whether the section of cliff top that contained the Iron Age tomb would fall into the sea. To distract herself she imagined describing her situation to friends back home in Providence. *Okay, picture this. I'm standing just three feet from the edge of the cliff. The beach is fifty feet below. In just two hours we've dug a hole ten feet deep to expose a tomb that's more than 2,000 years old. At any moment the entire thing could collapse. Fissures run from the cliff to the excavation pit. They're opening*

*wider by the minute. I can even hear the grass roots ripping as
more cracks appear. This is a race against time. So, as a last-ditch
attempt to break open the grave, we've tied a rope to the stone
that seals the tomb, the other end's tied to a van. My boss is just
about to tow it clear. The archaeologists have to dive in. Scoop
out the contents. Then vamoose. Or it's certain death.*

Pel's heart pounded her ribs. A furious hammering.
Adrenaline made all the colors so vivid—she'd never seen
grass as green. The tombstone slab had the luster of onyx.
The soil appeared to shine as if sprayed with gold. While the
rope that connected the van to the stone blazed a brilliant,
dazzling orange.

Now, the rope grew taut. When Kerry eased the van forward the line quivered. A sense of pent-up energy animated
it. If it snapped now. Dear God . . .

Nat shouted, "Pel, you're too close. Keep clear of the rope.
And, for the love of God, don't get too close to the cliff."

Vibration from the van's motor shook the ground. A crack
opened that was so wide her boot slipped through until she
was ankle-deep. She moved away from the fissure—that
move took her closer to both the quivering rope and the
cliff.

Nat yelled, "Pel, get away from there. I'm ordering you!"

She held up a finger. *Give me one more minute.*

"No," he bellowed. "You'll be killed! Run!"

Suddenly, the van moved forward, hauling the stone slab
upward. Instantly, she saw the dark void it had revealed.
Gleaming there: bones.

She thought: *A grave like this has to be high status. A chief.
A priestess. Who knows? Even a god in human form.* Prehistoric religion was shadowy, mysterious. *Every single find like
this is precious.*

Nat shouted, "I'm calling this investigation dead. We're
quitting it. I'm not paying for it in human lives!" Then louder:
"Pel, get away from there!"

The wall of the pit sagged at the cliffward side. From here, she could see that barely a foot-thick wall of soft earth separated the tomb from empty air beyond the cliff's face. Nat would have approached her, but the taut cable between van and tomb slab prevented him rushing to drag her away.

Pel made a fateful decision. "Rob!" she called to one of the diggers. "Throw me a finds box. The big red one!" Rob hesitated. "Quick! Before we lose it."

He tossed her a red plastic box that could have comfortably accommodated a microwave oven.

"No! Don't you dare!" Nat screamed. "You'll be killed!"

Pel sat down on the edge of the pit; then as if it were a kids' slide she skidded on her rear to the bottom. At the far side of the pit the earth wall fell outward. Now Pel had a clear view of the ocean, along with the beach a lethal fifty feet below.

Quickly, she positioned the box alongside the grave. Then as gently, but as swiftly as she could, she lifted the bones out of the tomb vault—a void that was little larger than a child's bed. Into the box went the top of a skull that ended just below the nasal cavity; after that, ribs, femur, collarbones, pelvis, half a dozen vertebrae. In the soft black mulch at the bottom of the grave lay implements for the afterlife—an ax head, flint arrowheads, a corroded iron knife blade, then a black pot the size of a melon. She reached deeper to extract jet beads, bone clothespins, and a stone head that was no bigger than her fist. Then she realized that it was harder to reach the bottom of the vault.

"Dear God," she hissed. "It's sinking away from me." All around her, the sides of the pit spilled a golden rain of dirt. People shouted that she must get out. A rumble grew louder. Suddenly, it felt as if she stood in an elevator that had begun its descent.

With a desperate surge of energy she reached into the tomb one last time. She seized a man's heavy jawbone still set with creamy white teeth. Then she clawed her way back up the side of the pit with one hand while she dragged the plastic box behind her.

"She's not going to make it," Nat shouted. "The whole lot's falling from under her."

Kerry flung herself chest-down at the edge of the pit, then reached out her hands. "Forget the box! Leave it! Give me your hand!"

Instead, Pel thrust the box up at her boss. Her hair and mouth were full of dirt that gushed down from the rim of the pit. Rob dashed forward to grab the box. Then Nat and Kerry seized a hand each and yanked Pel from the pit—just as the ancient grave fell down onto the beach with a sound like thunder.

CHAPTER SEVEN

When Pel's colleagues had dragged her to safety Nat yelled in her face: "IDIOT!" For a moment she thought he'd push her roughly away. Instead, he hugged her with such relief that she couldn't breathe. Then he went to sit with his back to a tombstone where he wept like a little boy. After that, it went a bit of a blur. The next time she felt clear-headed enough to check her watch forty minutes had elapsed from the time she'd scrambled out of the collapsing grave pit. A half-drunk mug of coffee rested on the trestle table in front of her. A cool wind blew her hair. Her hands were streaked with yellow earth. In assorted trenches, dirt monkeys were hard at work again, digging, sieving, sorting finds. She drained the cup. Whoever had made it ensured it was caffeine-rich enough to kick-start her senses. No sooner had she set down the mug then Kerry and Nat marched purposefully toward her along a graveyard path.

"Oh no," she groaned to herself. "This is where I get fired."

Kerry appraised her no doubt tousled hair. "I've a good mind, Pel Minton, to put you over my knee and give you a good, hard spank."

Nat rolled his eyes. "Kerry? Do you have to? The last thing I need right now is erotic imagery of you disciplining young women. My heart's still pounding like crazy." Despite being shaken, he managed a smile. "I've experienced every emotion

imaginable today. Elation at the finds. Guilt at rushing exca-
vations. Sheer freaking terror of you jumping into the grave
pit. Now Kerry gets me steamy with images of her spanking
your butt. I ask you."

"You're going to fire me, aren't you?" Pel asked.

"Fire you?" Kerry's frosty expression warmed into a grin.
"We're here to thank you."

"Praise you. Adore you," he added with a flourish.

Kerry continued. "Come across to the finds table. If you're
up to it?"

"I'm fine. Never better."

She followed Kerry back to a table where the objects she'd
rescued from the tomb now lay in plastic trays.

"Right." Businesslike, Kerry pointed at the trays. "It's
too early to be certain yet; however, these artifacts appear
to originate from overseas. The blue beads there are Egyptian. All this points to it being an extraordinary burial of
an extraordinary individual. The grave goods were brought
across half the world at a time when most people lived
in tents made out of animal hide and bones. So, tell her,
Nat."

He beamed. "It means that now we know this is a hugely
important site. Temple Central, as we have dubbed it, must
be preserved. Kerry is taking what you so bravely, coura-
geously, magnificently *rescued* back to the university. Then
she's contacting the appropriate government officials."

"Cross all fingers, and pray to your god of choice." Kerry
took a deep breath. "We hope . . . just hope . . . that we'll be
granted a preservation order for this site. It's just too important to surrender to the sea."

Nat's eyes shone. "If we get the order then they're going to
have to build sea defenses. Even if it means mobilizing the
army."

Pel absorbed the spectacle of what seemed just moments
ago a humble grab bag of artifacts from the tomb. A few
bones, flint tools, a crudely fashioned stone head.

"It gets better." Nat laughed. "Are you going to tell her, or shall I?"

Kerry twinkled. "You spotted it, so go ahead."

"See the skull?" He indicated the upper part of the skull. The dome of the cranium, orbits, and nasal passages were intact, but the upper jaw was missing. "Look closer."

"What am I seeing?"

The man clearly relished the moment of revelation. "Examine the forehead."

The smooth cream-colored bone with its customary hairline markings, where the skull plates had fused, appeared normal. "What's wrong with it?"

"Nothing. But it could turn out to be an amazing find in its own right."

"How?"

Kerry's smile broadened. "Doesn't it appear familiar? The broad forehead. The prominent brow bones. The unusually large eye sockets."

"You are joking?"

Kerry shook her head. "Nat has an instinct for spotting similarities. And he's invariably right."

"It's a Murrain?" She stared in astonishment. "Surely there's no way of knowing that this is the skeleton of Mr. Murrain's ancestor."

"Ah," breathed Nat. "I agree. This is when archaeology becomes guessology." He lightly stroked the ancient skull. "But familial likeness can continue down the bloodline for millennia. If we can link the remains of this old gentleman here with one of the Murrain gentlemen from Crowdale, we will have established the oldest link between specific skeletal remains and a living human being."

"But you can never be certain, can you? It'll always be just a guess."

"This is where I ask you to point out the most important find on the table. Go on, Pel. Pick an object."

She pointed at the stone carving.

"I'll put you out of your misery. It's the jawbone!"

"The jawbone? Surely, that's not . . . ah." A thought struck her. "DNA."

Kerry pursed her lips in approval. "Absolutely. If we're in luck, we can cut open the tooth and extract the DNA belonging to the occupant of the grave. Then to prove our hypothesis all we need do is obtain a DNA sample from one of the Murrains."

Nat grimaced. "However, they're not exactly happy to see us here. Especially when we have to rip up the mosaic of the more recent ancestor Justice Murrain."

"I'll do it," Pel said with conviction. "I'll get a sample from Jack Murrain."

"Really? You don't have to do—"

"I'll bring you one back. Trust me."

Both exchanged glances. This meant a lot to them.

Pel continued, "Because if we can prove that Jack Murrain is the ancestor of Mr. Iron Age Murrain here that will clinch the protection order, won't it?"

"Indeed it will," breathed Nat, still in awe of the discovery. "So far, here in Britain, archaeologists have matched DNA from skeletons in Avebury to living people in its neighborhood. It's been proved that the same families have lived in the vicinity of that town from before the birth of Christ to modern times."

"With this skeleton," Kerry added, "we might be able to prove the Murrain family have lived on this coast for the last five thousand years. Who knows, it may go further back than that. Murrains might have hunted wooly mammoth here."

"Just in case you did offer to approach Jack Murrain, we asked the local police for a DNA kit." He produced a polythene bag from his pocket. "After all, it's vital to prove the link as quickly as possible."

"How do I . . ." She nodded at the bag containing latex gloves, Q-tips, test tube, and labels.

"You need to obtain a specimen of Jack's body fluid. You'll appreciate that's where we can easily extract DNA."

"Body fluid. Right."

"In this case, saliva is fine. Just have him rub a Q-tip along his upper gum."

Pel took the bag. "I'll have Jack's sample in my hands tonight. One way or another."

CHAPTER EIGHT

"I'll kill him, Ma. Just say when."

"Listen to me, boys. Revenge can't be rushed." The woman with the burned face set mouthwatering steaks in front of her middle-aged sons. This wasn't just their favorite meal, this was leverage. They became malleable when she filled their bellies. "There were harsh words earlier." Her good eye bored into Scott. His cheeks flared red with shame. "But we're all friends again now, aren't we? I love you both very much. Now eat up, don't let it get cold." They attacked the fried beef. "Remember what I told you before. We're going to make Jacob Murrain suffer. But don't strike him. Damage the things he likes. Hurt the ones he loves. I've been suffering this disfigurement for thirty years." She touched her scarred face. "Now you're going to ensure that Jacob suffers, too. I want him to crack. To fall apart. Then come begging forgiveness. I want to see him on his knees in front of me." Ma spooned mayonnaise onto their plates. "You're going to start tonight. You're going to wipe that arrogant look off his face."

CHAPTER NINE

Pel Minton let the hot water caress her thighs. This shower was heaven-sent.

Okay, she thought. *You're going to turn up at Jack Murrain's door and brightly say, "Give me a little of your body fluids. Because I need your DNA." That's a doozy of a first date.*

She soaped her stomach. "It's not a date," she murmured. "I'm going to his house for the sake of science."

But then why am I so excited? And what will his reaction be when I appear out of the blue?

CHAPTER TEN

Horace sat on his chair outside on the pavement. An empty chair stood beside his. People were walking home from work along the street.

Whenever a man or woman caught his eye he cried out, "Look at Bobby. The little chap's frightened." He indicated the empty chair.

"Lunatic," hissed a woman as she quickened her step to get away.

"I saw the man last night in my room," Horace insisted. "All in black he was. Big black crow! The little chap here got really, really frightened." The woman didn't even glance back at the giant as he sat in the chair next to his invisible friend. "I saw him walk—whoosh—right through the wall." A group of teenagers mooched by. "And another thing. I can see shadows flying all around the houses. Lots of them. There's more and more of them with every hour that goes by."

The youths shouted taunts.

"Watch out," Horace called. "They're coming to get you. When they do, you'll be sorry."

A teen kicked over the empty chair, and then the group ran away, laughing.

"Hey! You knocked Bobby off his chair. You've made the little chap cry. You'll pay for that. Them shadows are over your heads. They're following you!" He picked up the chair, then patted the seat for his invisible friend to climb back up. "I know only we can see him, Bobby. And only we can see them shadows in the air. But all those nasty people will suffer one day. Them shadows are going to do something rotten to Crowdale."

The man's put-upon mother came out of the house. "Horace, you can't sit out here, shouting. You'll have the police here again. Now come inside where I can keep an eye on you."

"Can you see the shadows, Mammy? They're all flying through the sky. I see them as clear as I can see your face."

"'Course you can, Son." With that, she ushered him inside.

CHAPTER ELEVEN

Anger. Knowing he'd been wronged. No sense of taste. No sight. No smell. No hearing. Neither hot nor cold. Since the night of Murrain Hall being set ablaze he had been adrift in a mist of rage. That had been the predominant emotion. Anger coupled with a lust for revenge. Apart from that, there'd been few other thoughts inside his mind.

But now he knew that his world was set for change. He'd begun to remember incidents from his life again. His marriage to the witch-whore. The birth of his son, whom he despised the moment he'd set eyes on the blood-smeared brat, still oiled from his mother's womb. Lately, he found himself in Crowdale again. The town's buildings had changed. Yet its inhabitants still enraged him.

At last, however, excitement illuminated his spirit.

He was starting to break free of a prison cell that had held him captive. His servants were being released, too. Soon he would be in control of his destiny once more. Though he had no lips to smile—yet—an electrical impulse registered the sensation that would have led to a tightening of his mouth. That sensation intensified when he, at long last, recalled his name. Justice Murrain. *Yes, my friends, not long now . . .*

CHAPTER TWELVE

Pel Minton found the address that Kerry had given her. The Murrain home was the last house out of town, situated on a lane that led to the churchyard and its controversial mausoleum. The twin-storied property sheltered under a tile roof, which glowed deep red in the sunset. Tellingly, it stood apart from neighboring dwellings. As if it shunned the rest of Crowdale. Or did Crowdale shun it? Rather than boasting a garden, it stood in a rough pasture of ankle-deep grass. All in all, a lonely-looking house. I am solitary, it seemed to say, but I don't care. Because you and I have nothing in common.

And here I am arriving out of the blue, she thought. *A surprise visit from an American stranger. A girl with a dangerous reputation for turning lives upside down.*

Pel slipped her hand into her jacket pocket where the DNA kit nestled. Suddenly, the idea of standing there on the threshold of the Murrain household and cheerfully announcing, "Hi, I've come to collect a smear of your body fluid," seemed peculiar to say the least.

A cool breeze ghosted from the sea to send a shiver up her spine. This house really did seem as solitary as the mausoleum, which contained that chilling and gloomy mosaic. "What is it with you, Murrains?" she murmured. "Do you all live in houses that look like tombs?" She stepped through the gate, with all the trepidation of entering that clinical room in a morgue, where they did the cutting.

The first thing she noticed, as she walked up the gravel drive to the house, was the pickup in the garage. The second, that two men were busy jabbing screwdriver blades into its tires.

"Hey, what the hell do you think you're doing? Stop that!"

Both men looked up at her. In their forties, they were thickset with blotched faces. The eldest grunted, "You've not seen anything. Go home." He drove the point of the screwdriver into the rubber. With a fierce hiss the tire deflated. The pickup sank down until the cab sloped sharply.

"You!" she shouted. "I know the pair of you. Both of you were at the graveyard yesterday, driving those trucks like madmen!"

"Oh, one of the diggers, are you? Well, this is none of your business. Clear off."

"It is my business. *You* clear off."

One of the men advanced menacingly with the screwdriver. In her mind's eye, she saw him plunging its sharp point into her throat. Already she could envisage blood gushing down her chest.

"You two cowards don't frighten me." Even so, her legs turned gel-like. "Get away from here!"

He took another step closer.

The other barked, "Leave her, Ross. We've no argument with her!"

"Interfering little bitch," Ross grunted. "That devil boning you, huh? Is he going to put a bastard in your belly?"

"Ross." The other man sounded edgy now. "We've done here."

"Not yet, we haven't. Remember what Ma said?"

Pel decided to establish an air of authority. In a clear, forceful tone she said, "Leave now. Or I'll call the police!"

"Do as the young lady says."

The voice from behind Pel startled her. She glanced back to see Jacob Murrain emerge from the house. For an elderly man his hair was thick and perfectly black. He went to stand beside Pel.

In a strong voice he said, "Scott Lowe, your brother, Ross, has always been a thug. I expected better of you."

"Thirty years ago you as good as killed our mother."

Ross advanced, with a pit bull growl, "Burned half her face off, you did. Even if the law did nothing, we're going to make sure you suffer for that."

"You are trespassing. It's time to leave."

"They punctured the tires," Pel said. "You should call the police."

Ross gestured with the screwdriver. "The cops will do nothing to help a Murrain. They'll be glad to be rid of you all."

Pel put herself between Jacob and the thug. "The pair of you, just piss off!"

"Get out of the way!" Ross lurched forward.

"Before you touch him, you're going to have to get by me first."

Scott grabbed Ross's arm. "We've done enough. Remember what Ma said!"

With an expression of reluctance, Ross allowed his brother to tug him back down the driveway. Even so, he couldn't resist shouting, "Murrain. Next time you won't have that scrap of a woman to save your neck!" Then both stomped back to a car parked on the lane. After it had roared away it seemed almost unbearably silent.

Jacob took a deep breath. "Well . . . it's over for now." He turned those large gray eyes to regard her. "Won't you come inside for a drink? I daresay we both could use a piping hot coffee."

"Aren't you going to ask why I'm here, Mr. Murrain?"

"Pel Minton, isn't it?" He smiled. "Jack's been talking about you."

Now the confrontation had passed she felt weak enough to be blown away by the sea breeze.

"You're cold," he told her. "Come inside. Jack'll be home in five minutes. He's just gone to make sure the lamp's burning over my damned ancestor."

Standing there, like some lost waif, would have been pointless. Besides, she was on a mission. She nodded her thanks then entered the Murrain house.

CHAPTER THIRTEEN

"Thanks for keeping those apes off my grandfather," Jack Murrain told her as they stepped out of the house. "I don't even want to imagine what would have happened if you hadn't been here."

By now, night had fallen. A frostiness in the air gave it teeth to nip her nose.

"You risked your neck to save me yesterday," she replied. "It was the least I could do. I'm sorry I couldn't stop them puncturing the tires."

"No worries. I can patch them so they're good as new. Let's say we're even, then." His smile broadened. "Regarding the lifesaving, that is."

"You know, you should report those two to the police."

"We Murrains have a strange relationship with the town. They seem to have an instinctive need for us to be here; only they don't really like us. When there's been trouble before the police make sympathetic comments, but nothing concrete gets done."

"That's discrimination."

"I agree. But it's a fact of life. We deal with it."

In the light of the driveway lamp she regarded the man. Although he was in his midtwenties he had the same wise, if slightly melancholy expression as his grandfather. They both had a head of thick black curls. Their eyes were large, a pale gray, and had an uncanny way of gazing deeply at objects, and people. After she'd been invited into the house by Jacob

Murrain she'd spent twenty minutes drinking coffee and chatting to him. Pel's colleagues had insisted he was crazy. A madman with an obsession about the Justice Murrain picture in the mausoleum. He seemed compelled to care for it, and he had that mantra about the lamp: "Keep the light burning." Yet Pel found Jacob Murrain to be perfectly pleasant, inordinately levelheaded, and utterly sane. A gentleman with a heartwarmingly gentle manner. Tonight he never mentioned the mosaic (although Pel found herself wanting to comment how much both Mr. Murrain and his grandson Jack resembled the portrait of their ancestor Justice Murrain. Also, what was Justice Murrain's story? She found herself consumed with curiosity). However, Jacob chatted about how sad he was to see coastal erosion eating away the landscape. How he'd witnessed many a home fall into the sea. He'd also pointed out photographs on the wall of himself in his youth (a dead ringer for Jack), his wife, and his son (another one who shared the same Murrain features). He'd asked her about her own life as a digger for the archaeologists. Pel confessed she adored her work, and although her own parents and sisters lived in the States, and that she missed them, she found herself enjoying herself so much in England it would be a wrench to move on.

Then Jack had arrived. Over another coffee he'd listened intently as his grandfather explained what had happened. Including how Pel had defended him from the thugs. Jack had been angry about the threats made by the Lowe brothers. Something in his eye told Pel he dearly wanted to visit the brothers, then pound some sense into their thick skulls. However, his grandfather calmly smoothed the incident over. That it was just an isolated outburst. Everything would settle down again soon.

Now Pel walked side by side with Jack along the driveway to his car. It was a white Mercedes that must have been old as Jack himself.

He ran his finger along its elegant wing. "My grandfather's

pride and joy. By sheer chance, I'd taken it up to the grave-yard instead of my pickup. Something tells me those thugs would have made a mess of the paintwork. They know he spent years restoring the Mercedes. He found it in a barn up the coast. A farmer had stowed chicken feed in it to stop rats gnawing the sacks." His gray eyes alighted on hers. "So why did you come up here?"

She felt the plastic bag in her pocket. "What would you think of me if I told you I came here for your body fluids?"

His eyes widened.

Laughter escaped her lips. "I'm sorry, I couldn't resist see-ing your expression. More specifically, I require, if you con-sent . . ."

"Go on." That gaze sank into hers.

"A sample of your DNA."

"You know . . . and this might surprise you, Pel . . . but I've never had a girl ask for my DNA before."

"Yeah, does sound kind of funny, doesn't it? Then what do girls usually ask you for?"

"They ask: 'Will you please stop peeping in through my bedroom window at me.'" He was amused by her shocked re-action. "That time I couldn't resist seeing *your* expression."

"So, the Murrains have a sense of humor. I like that." Pel tugged out the plastic bag. "Right. We could do it here."

"Oh . . . the DNA thing. Shouldn't I be lying down when you extract the . . . uhm, whatever it is you need."

"Nothing so intrusive. I just need to swab your mouth with a Q-tip."

He feigned disappointment. "Is that all?"

"Yup."

"It seems coldly functional."

"I'm not always a coldly functional girl, you know." She zipped up her jacket against the chill night air. "Sometimes I dance, have fun with friends, generally let my hair down. That sort of thing."

"You could perform the procedure here. But it wouldn't be right to let you walk home in the dark."

"Are you planning to let me extract your DNA in the car after you've driven me back?"

"Still sounds coldly functional, doesn't it?" He scratched his eyebrow. "Why don't we go out for a meal? After all, you still haven't explained why you want my DNA."

"It's part of a secret cloning experiment. We want to fill the world with Murrains."

"See, you've got a sense of humor, too." Jack smiled. "Good. We can swap jokes. So . . . what do you say to dinner?"

CHAPTER FOURTEEN

After letting his grandfather know his plans, Jack drove Pel into town. The classic Mercedes was as comfortable as a lounge sofa. Pel found herself in good spirits. She and Jack chatted like they'd known each other for months.

"There's a Greek restaurant," he told her as he parked in a side street. "The Athenaeum, it's one of my favorites. You do like Greek food, don't you?"

"After a day's digging you could spit-roast an entire goat and I'd call it a snack."

He grinned. "I like a girl with a healthy appetite."

They strolled through the town. A few people hurried to the pubs, otherwise the center seemed fairly deserted tonight. Jack led her toward a street that had been glassed over to create a quirky shopping mall. All the stores were closed, but a couple of bars flashed neon signs to alert people they were serving drinks.

"The power supply is playing up tonight," Jack observed as they approached automatic doors that opened and shut without being triggered by anyone. Lights suddenly dimmed, too, until streetlights bathed them in a bloodred glow. "It must be the cold snap. Everyone's turning their heating up."

"Just hope the power station hasn't fallen into the sea. Everything else seems to be tumbling in."

"Tell me about it, Pel. My grandfather can't sleep for worrying about that damn mosaic."

"Do you believe that if it's destroyed it will bring doom and carnage?"

Jack's face hardened. "It's important to my grandfather. I didn't think you'd be one of those that mocked."

"No . . . I didn't mean . . ." *Hell, time for damage control.* "I'm not mocking your grandfather, Jack. I know it's important to him. The archaeologists do, too. They're as keen as him to save it. Because in days from now the sea will have taken that, just as it's gobbled up the church."

His expression softened. "I know you're trying to do the right thing. Only my grandfather is adamant it shouldn't be moved." He shook his head. "Adamant? That seems too tame a word. To be honest, Pel, I sometimes think the sheer trauma of trying to protect the mosaic will be the death of him."

They walked beneath the glass roof to an escalator that softly purred as its steel steps ascended to an upper walkway. Lights still grew dim before reluctantly brightening again. On the screen of an ATM Pel noticed that dark patches skimmed through the bank's animated logo. Clearly, that wasn't intentional. The shadows resembled death's-heads. As they rode the escalator it suddenly juddered to a stop, leaving them at a standstill between floors. The few people mooching about the place exchanged glances, then shrugged. Power outages were nothing new. However, there was something odd about this. The way the electricity flow appeared to be restricted as if some force was slowly strangling the very cables that carried it.

When the escalator didn't restart the pair climbed to the top.

Jack crossed the walkway to the taverna door. Above it, Greek-style lettering spelled ATHENAEUM.

"After you." He held open the door.

Pel smiled her thanks and entered. Scents of roasting meat and spices greeted her. A sigh of pleasure escaped her lips. Now she really did feel hungry. At that moment, her near-death experience in the tomb earlier in the day seemed impossibly remote. The slightly disquieting pleasure of being here with Jack Murrain stimulated a train of thought: *Why am I attracted to him? This isn't what I planned when I arrived*

*here in Crowdale, is it? No more ties . . . stay a free spirit. At
least for the time being, anyway.*

A senior waiter greeted them with a pleasingly Greek-accented, "Good evening. I'm delighted you joined us tonight. We have wonderful specials on the menu. Lamb with mint and yogurt. Or, if you prefer, swordfish steaks baked over charcoal. Very nice." He settled them into a cozy booth, then left them to chat.

"So, Pel, are you going to reveal why you crave my DNA?"

"Only if you reveal what's so special about Justice Murrain and his mosaic."

Jack smiled. "Ladies first. The DNA?"

A young waiter appeared with slicked-down hair. He held out three menus.

Jack nodded a greeting. "Evening, George. But there's only two of us."

The waiter frowned. "I was sure I saw three of you come through the door together."

"Just the pair of us, George."

"I could have sworn your grandfather was with you." The frown deepened. "At least a gentleman that resembled your grandfather. In a long black coat."

Pel noticed how uneasy the man had become. "The lights have been playing tricks tonight."

"Maybe so." Repeatedly, the waiter glanced in the direction of the door, as if trying to solve the problem. "Can I bring you a drink while you make your choices?"

"Pel, I can recommend the retsina wine," Jack said.

"Retsina it is, thanks."

As he was driving, Jack ordered himself a large Coke with ice and lime.

"Okay," he began. "Body fluids. Why mine?"

Pel explained about the finds in the Iron Age tomb. For the time being, she avoided mention of the dramatic way she'd rescued the artifacts from the grave, just before it plunged down the cliff face. When Jack heard that Nat suggested the skull in the grave resembled those of the Murrain family to such an extent he suspected a blood link the man was genuinely impressed.

"I can't wait until I tell my grandfather. He always insisted Murrains have lived in this neck of the woods ever since there was a Britain." He smiled. "So he may well be right after all."

"If the pathologist can extract DNA from the tooth I found in the tomb, then it can be compared with DNA from your sample." She poured them both glasses of water from a carafe. "If a link can be proved, the archaeological site will be awarded a special protected status. With that, there's a chance the government will rush in temporary coastal defenses, so a full assessment can be completed."

"Would that mean the mosaic can remain where it is?"

"I'd be lying if I said yes, Jack. That's a decision for government officials to make."

"But there is hope?"

"Yes, there's hope."

"So my DNA sample is vital?"

She nodded. "As far as I know, there's only yourself and your grandfather, who are local bloodline Murrains."

"We are the only Murrains *period*—as you Americans say. We're the last of the line. The only two full-blood Murrains in the world. And from what you suspect, after your discovery today, the end of a very, very long line." The waiter brought the drinks. Jack raised his glass to Pel. "Here's to body fluids and to all the treasures they contain. And to you, of course, for protecting my grandfather."

Pel began conversationally, "The last of the line? Your grandfather showed me a photograph of his son, who looked just like . . ." She grimaced. "Oh, I'm sorry. He didn't say, but your father must be—"

"Dead. Yes, unfortunately. No, don't apologize; you weren't to know. My father went away to work on the rigs. He died when I was three years old. Murrains don't fare well away from Crowdale. Once we leave these few acres of dirt behind we have a tendency to . . . well, wither away and die."

"That's what your grandfather told you? It sounds as if he's finding reasons for you to stay."

Jack nodded. "It would break his heart if I left. He's told me ever since I was tiny that it would be my duty to safeguard the mosaic." He studied the menu. "The stuffed vine leaves are good."

"Jack." Her fingers encircled his wrist. "You promised me that you'd tell me about your ancestor's mosaic. You can't keep me in suspense any longer. I want to know."

"It's a rather gruesome tale. I was going to leave it until after dinner. Disturbing things happened. It could ruin your appetite."

"No, tell me. I'm pushy. Mysteries make me squirm. I want answers."

"First, we'll order the food, and then I'll reveal all." Once the waiter had written down their choices on his pad Jack took a swallow of Coke. "Okay, as you know, I'm the last of the Murrains. You'll also be familiar with the fact that surnames often reveal the occupations of our ancestors—there's the obvious ones like Carpenter, Taylor, Bowman, Farmer, and so on. Then you get Cooper, which means barrel maker, or Tanner, who cures animal hides. Some surnames reveal an ancestor with a disability, such as Shillito, meaning 'silly toe.' Probably that disability recurred so often in a family that the description of the condition stuck as a surname. Murrain comes from an archaic French word for 'carcass.' In times gone by, if you said an animal had gone 'Murrain' you would be saying it suffered from a disease." He regarded her with those gray eyes, which were infused with such wisdom and an underlying sadness. "Hardly a pretty name to attach to such a long dynasty. Uh?"

"Go on."

"Are you sure you want to know more about our erstwhile clan?"

"Yes, like I said: I'm pushy and inquisitive. I'll squeeze the truth out of you if I have to." She deliberately kept her tone light. Although she did crave to hear the facts behind the mosaic that had, indirectly, nearly cost Pel her life.

The first course arrived, a light seafood salad. For a moment or two they chatted about the food as they squeezed lemon juice onto a delicious-looking assortment of fish. Then Jack began talking in a matter-of-fact way. "These are the bare facts. Justice Murrain was born in 1700. He inherited the hall that his father had built, and the thousand acres of farmland that went with it. We still own what's left—twenty acres of forest that we manage for timber and firewood. The Murrain family were highly respected; they treated their employees well. Until Justice Murrain came along, that is. There were rumors that in his teens he shot the local blacksmith because he didn't care for the expression on the man's face. Justice Murrain was evil. He was evil to animals, to servants, to his own family. There were rumors he suffocated his own father because he wanted to inherit the family property before he was thirty. Nothing could be proved. Criminal investigations were rudimentary back then. And if you could bribe the local magistrate, well"—Jack cut a bloodred tomato—"you could literally get away with murder." He continued briskly, "Justice Murrain craved wealth, so he turned the house into a 'Bedlam'—an infirmary for the criminally insane. The authorities paid him well to make sure all the psychotics and violent crazies were taken out of society and put into his care. Then my ancestor really got down to work. He turned his mental patients into a private army. They guarded Murrain Hall. Nobody dare go within miles of the place. He sent squads of lunatics out to rob and murder travelers on the main highways. Not only did he keep their possessions he took possession of the corpses, then forced relatives to pay exorbitant burial fees. And because he'd corrupted the local magistrate he could spin some yarn to the authorities that the killings were the work of outlaws, and nothing to do with him. During the 1730s my ancestor was responsible for highway robbery, extortion, blackmail, kidnap, plus a huge protection racket that involved Justice Murrain's gang of deranged men and women—they marched into town every market day and forced families to hand over their cash. Anyone that complained would be beaten. If they tried to notify the authorities outside the area, the thugs would return to hang one of the family from the gallows in the market square. Justice Murrain created a blanket of terror over Crowdale. Nobody dare speak out. He demanded more and more money from them, to the point the townspeople's children began to suffer from starvation." He paused to regard a pink flake of salmon on his fork as he, no doubt, saw the reign of terror in his mind's eye. "They say Justice Murrain became as mad as his army of psychotics. Progressively, he became more delusional. When his wife gave birth to their first son he thought she'd brought a rival into the world to destroy him—no doubt he recalled that he'd killed his own father. In a fit of rage he threw his wife to his henchmen. What the lunatics did to her you can imagine. Anyway, she died of her injuries. Justice Murrain hated his baby son. Loathed him so much, he cut off the thumb and forefinger of each hand; that way, he reasoned, the boy could never use a pistol to shoot his own father." He gave a grim smile. "I told you it was a hell of a story."

Pel shivered. "It's terrible enough about what he did to Crowdale—no wonder they have issues with the Murrains— but the way he treated his own son? Even most tyrants protect their own children."

"Justice Murrain broke even that rule. To maim your own child is as evil as you can get. It breaks the laws of nature. Even animals will die to protect their own young. His treatment of his baby son is beyond my understanding anyway."

"Yet your family protect Justice Murrain's portrait in the mausoleum."

"That's covered by the final part of the story. In 1751 Justice Murrain presided over a private army, which he now called his 'Battle Men.' By this time, he kept his son in a kennel with the dogs. I daresay, the dogs treated the boy a damn sight better than his own father. Then, at long last, the priest in Crowdale managed to smuggle a letter out to his bishop. The letter detailed Murrain's crimes. Within hours a contingent of soldiers arrived at the hall to arrest my ancestor. Justice Murrain ordered his men to fire on the soldiers; when some of the king's men were killed by musket-shot all hell broke loose. The soldiers were determined to avenge their comrades, so they set fire to the house, then bayoneted all of Murrain's henchmen. As for the man, himself, they say he rode out of the courtyard on a huge stallion, saber in hand, and wearing a long black cloak that flapped out like the wings of a raven. He could have escaped, because the soldiers were on foot; however, he chose to ride three times around the church—'widdershins' they call it, if you circle a church in a counterclockwise fashion. Something the superstitious never do, because it invokes the devil. Then he rode the horse back into the courtyard of the burning house, where the debris collapsed on him." He held out his hands. "And that was the end of Justice Murrain. Legend has it, his bones lie under the mosaic."

"The son? The boy with his forefingers and thumbs amputated?"

"He survived to continue the bloodline. It was he, James Murrain, who eventually rebuilt the hall. At the same time, locals complained that they were being harassed by the ghosts of Justice Murrain and his thug army. So James Murrain had the mausoleum built. And using his own mutilated hands, just three fingers on each, he created the mosaic portrait of his own father. The fragments of tile, glass, and pottery that make up the mosaic, like a jigsaw, came from the ruins of the original house that burned down."

"So this portrait trapped the ghost of Justice Murrain and all the ghosts of the thugs that served him?"

"That's what James Murrain and the townspeople believed."

"And what your grandfather *still* believes."

"Each to his own." He pushed the plate aside.

"But what do you believe, Jack?"

The man merely shrugged.

"Jack, your grandfather is determined that you stay here to guard the mosaic, and to keep that lamp lit."

"That's going to be immaterial, isn't it? Either the sea will take the portrait, or your archaeologist friends are going to uproot it for a museum."

She held his gaze. "You still haven't told me what *you* believe will happen when the mosaic is moved. Will your ancestor break free?"

At that precise moment the lights went out. The darkness absolute.

CHAPTER FIFTEEN

Kerry Herne, chief archaeologist on the Murrain site dig, found it nigh impossible to stay away. So, alone, she patrolled the cliff top, flashlight in hand, sweeping the beam back and forth to check for any more telltale cracks in the earth—those cracks that would alert her to another section of cliff marked for destruction.

A frost added daubs of white to the grass. Orange lines on the ground showed where Temple Central (as they had dubbed it) lay buried in the graveyard area.

"I must be mad coming up here alone," she murmured as she neared the cliff's edge. Surf roared across the beach fifty feet below. Her face tingled with cold. There were times she stood up here and willed the sea not to rob her of the excavation site. When she did so, she felt as obsessive as old Mr. Murrain. Both guarded the area as if it meant more to them than life. She glared at crumbling sections of cliff thinking, *Please don't fall. We need to dig into you tomorrow. There are wonderful artifacts here of huge historical importance.* Other matters preyed on her mind, too. Had Pel got hold of Jack Murrain's DNA sample yet? Would government officials be sympathetic to her plea that the cliffs be protected from the surf?

Kerry found herself following the line of the "spirit roads" that she and Pel had marked out on the grass. In the gloom, she glimpsed centuries-old headstones. Some of which carried the name "Murrain." The family's roots here were deep. Very deep. Up ahead stood the mausoleum. Its oil lamp burned inside, casting a glow onto the frost-covered grass. At this time of night the archaeologists' trenches resembled open graves—but what elongated graves they were. The graves of giants.

Wayward thoughts, but then this place has that effect on you. Kerry followed the line of the spirit road back through the graves to the cliff's edge. Almost immediately a deep groaning sound began somewhere under her feet. "Oh, no, not again. Please no."

The cliff top formed a slab of dark earth in front of her. Beyond that, the twinkle of starlight on the sea. The ground shuddered. The pained groan rose in volume. Kerry directed the flashlight at parallel orange lines that ran right to the end of the cliff. They were moving. Slowly at first. Then faster . . . faster. With a lurch in her chest, she knew what happened to those thirty square yards of once-solid ground. Accompanied by a roar, many tons of soil and rock—and a section of spirit road, containing who knows how many precious ancient artifacts—tumbled into the surf below. She recalled Nat's speculation about this complex of prehistoric earthworks. About it being a mechanism that controlled supernatural powers. At least that's what the ancients had believed. Now another part of that mechanism had been destroyed.

Such a forlorn sense of loss rang through her. The coast was dying. Her precious archaeological site was dying with it. She imagined how distraught the ancient men and women would be to see the destruction of their holy ground, those people who worshipped here thousands of years ago. They'd know that the temple that contained their gods, and the spirits of their ancestors, was being broken by the ocean. Such annihilation would be releasing entities that should never, ever be released. Those prehistoric people would wail at the impending chaos. The world of humans, and the world of ghosts, would be on a collision course. The results would be catastrophic.

CHAPTER SIXTEEN

Horace sat on his straight-backed chair in the street again. Cold didn't bother him. Nor did it worry Bobby, his imaginary friend, on the seat beside him. Both stared into the darkness.

Seven-foot Horace hadn't developed as other children do. He had a talent for seeing things that other people couldn't. Like his loyal friend, for instance. Lately Bobby had become badly frightened, and he'd uttered this ominous sentence: *Shadows are doing what shadows shouldn't.* Horace liked to repeat the little fellow's observation. Those twisty S words tickled his tongue. *Shadows are doing what shadows shouldn't.* They were, indeed. Shadows flitted along the line of houses. They floated through walls. They shot through roofs. He'd even seen them ghosting up through the rugs in his bedroom.

Then everyone who knew Horace knew that he saw lots of stuff that nobody else ever did. Like the time he ran to the harbor, yelling he could see pirate ships sailing toward the town. He witnessed foxes that walked on their hind legs in the supermarket. There were bats the size of cows living in the town-hall roof, according to Horace. His neighbor Mr. Brodrick had been found dead under the Christmas tree ten years ago. Yet many a night Mr. Brodrick would appear at his door to say to Horace, "Come into my house. Bring the little fellow. You can watch me stir my Christmas pudding. Then we can play hide-and-seek . . . in the dark . . . you'll love that."

Those things Horace saw all the time. Tonight, as the town-hall clock struck ten, he would be treated to an entirely different spectacle.

"They're coming," Horace told his imaginary friend. "They're almost here." Horace's heart pounded. He'd never felt as tense as this before. He could hardly breathe. *"Bobby! They're here!"*

A profound sense of change crept into the world. The canyon formed by the row of houses at each side was deserted. Drapes were all drawn shut. Frost glinted on the blacktop. Then something strange happened. The darkness at the end of his street underwent a transformation. There was darkness still . . . but it pulsed blackly. As if the shadow of a heart throbbed there. A pulsating essence of blackness.

For a moment he was entirely alone (apart from his virtual friend). *Then he was not alone.* Because walking majestically along the center of the road came a figure. A tall figure in black made entirely of shadows. A figure with a mass of raven hair. A garment billowed around him until it resembled wings. And the man had such a cruel face. He walked proudly . . . pleased with himself . . . immensely pleased. And he moved with such dignity that it seemed he led a parade.

Horace's heart pounded. He couldn't breathe.

He watched the man in black approach. It was the crow man that he'd glimpsed before. But this time he was no longer alone. Smoothly, like they were fish swimming through the sea, came more figures. Ghost men and women. Dozens of men and women. They possessed strange faces . . . with yawning mouths, and smiling mouths, and leering mouths, and mouths that were not human. They didn't walk—they glided with fluid grace, either at street level, or along the rooftops of houses, or they dipped below the surface of the road only to reemerge again. Horace recalled how dolphins swam. How they vanished below the sea before bursting forth once more. These shadow people weaved through road tar, as if it were no more solid than water. Some darted in and out through the walls of the houses. Lights flickered on and off.

The crow man approached. A smile played on his lips. His gray eyes locked onto Horace's face.

The man pointed a long shadow finger at Horace's chest. "*I take him.*"

Horace understood the brutality of being alone in the face of such danger. All those things he'd seen in the past—the cow-size bats, the pirate ships, the shopping foxes—no longer seemed real. But the man in black did. So did his phantom army. All too real. All too frightening.

Horace tried to flee back home to his mother. But a movement from above caught his eye. The crow man had risen into the night sky. Then that shadow figure plunged downward right into the center of Horace's face.

When Horace opened the door to his home his expression had changed. The voice that came from his lips had altered, too. His diction had an unfamiliar precision. The tone: a gloating quality. "Mother. It's me. It's your loving boy. Mother, I've brought you a surprise." He closed the door behind him.

Later, neighbors told police about the screams they heard through the walls. Terrible, terrible screams.

TWO DAYS LEFT

CHAPTER ONE

The chimes of midnight from the town-hall clock mourned the death of the old day. A new one had begun as Jack walked her back to the house. After the power outage they'd dined by candlelight for a while in the Greek restaurant. While they'd been there, Jack had popped into the bathroom to collect the DNA sample. This was simply achieved by scraping a Q-tip against his upper gum, then placing it into a test tube, which he sealed, and handed back to Pel.

Within twenty minutes or so of capturing that potentially valuable drop of body fluid, the power had been restored. Yet as they strolled along a chilly canyon, formed by the rows of houses, the lamps still kept dimming to a dull orange. Jack had confessed his ambition to travel. Yet she sensed that deeply woven into Jack's thoughts was his grandfather's longing that he continue the Murrain family tradition of protecting that mosaic in its mausoleum. And to keep the lamp burning there. They formed a trinity—lamp, mausoleum, and mosaic. Their purpose to hold evil Justice Murrain's ghost locked up tight in the ground. Or so Jacob believed.

A hundred yards away, police cars had gathered. Blue lights whirled. An ambulance moved off slowly from the parked vehicles. The ambulance driver didn't appear to be in a hurry, suggesting either there was no real crisis, or more grimly, their patient was beyond a high-speed dash to the hospital.

The midnight drama had brought people out of their

houses. One woman, clad in a toweling robe, stood on her doorstep as Jack and Pel walked by.

Without even bothering to check whether she knew them, the woman called out in an excited voice, "That lunatic down there . . . the one who always sits outdoors on the chair . . . has done his own mother . . . bashed out her brains on the kitchen floor. It's time they put a rope round his neck . . . of course, hanging's too good for him. They should put him in a room with . . ." Her voice trailed off. From that expression of excitement, all stirred up with moral outrage, her face morphed into a leer of utter delight. Beaming at them, she stepped back into the house.

"Are your townsfolk always like this?" Pel asked. "Does murder make them cheerful?"

The street lamps dimmed again. Even the whirl of blue lights on the parked police cars became a gloomy purple.

Jack's eyes gleamed. He suddenly appeared preoccupied.

She touched his arm. "Are you all right, Jack?" There was an oddness about her surroundings now that she couldn't quite put her finger on. Shivers ran across her skin. Every few seconds she seemed to catch a glimpse of something out of the corner of her eye. As if a shadow had skated past on a house wall. However, when she checked there'd be nothing there.

"Jack? What's wrong?"

He licked his lips as if the taste of his own skin was new to him. Then he studied his hands in the police cars' pulsating blue lights. An expression of bafflement broke into a smile of wonderment. The man had seen something amazing. But what?

She didn't like this now. A voice in her head begged her to run. Not to look back. Hell . . . to run until she was free of Crazy Town. Because that's what it was becoming.

A man dashed by them after a screeching cat. He'd armed himself with a walker that he slashed through the air.

Seconds later, a heavily built man blundered out of the dark. He recognized Jack.

"Oh, Murrain . . . you shouldn't even show your face round here, y' bastard. Nobody wants you in town. Get outta m' way." The man intended to shove Jack aside as he stumbled drunkenly home.

Jack smoothly grabbed hold of the man then shoved his bloated face to the wall.

"Lemme go," barked the drunk. "You want to mix it with me, eh!"

With an expression that seemed so alien to Pel, Jack seized the drunk by his hair, then scraped his face along the rough brickwork. The wall worked as well as a grater. It scraped a layer of skin off the man's nose and chin. He went from threats to blabbing for mercy.

Chuckling, Jack shoved the man on his way. His adversary clearly had all the fight ground out of him. He clamped a heavy paw to his grazed face as, whimpering, he blundered away into the darkness.

"Jack." Her blood pounded. "My God, was there any need to do that to him?"

That's when he pounced. Dragging Pel into the shadows, he seized hold of her; his arms were steel bands; she couldn't move.

Then he pressed his mouth on hers. She'd never felt such remorseless pressure before on her lips.

CHAPTER TWO

Throughout Crowdale perhaps as many as a hundred people started to act out of character. In an apartment overlooking the harbor a husband woke to find his wife admiring her naked body in the mirror.

"Nice," she murmured.

"Tilly, it's gone midnight," he grunted. "Come back to bed."

"That's what I intended." Tilly leaped onto her husband. Straddling him, she worked herself into ecstasy, just by rubbing her groin against his stomach. His surprise yielded to erotic excitement. In moments she'd impaled herself on his penis, then bounced up and down hard, her knees on either side of his torso. As he lay on his back he marveled. She'd never ridden him with such gusto. Lately, their sex life had been nonexistent. Now she was a women possessed.

In the gloom this robust woman moved her hips, like a lap dancer, grinding away for all she was worth. Soon, she quickened her pace, flung her head, so her long hair swished; then she let out a roar of curses as the orgasm shook her. In the white heat of ecstasy she dug her thumbs into his eyes. His scream shook the perfume bottles on the shelf.

In the kitchen of the Italian restaurant the chef laughed hysterically. He forced the face of a waiter into a bowl of chopped tomatoes as he ran the sharp wheel of a pizza cutter across the young man's bare back. Why, in no time at all the possessed chef had etched a bloodred pattern like so—XXXX—all the way from the base of his waiter's neck to the buttocks. Meanwhile, the waiter's shouts were muffled by juicy slices of tomato.

With a flourish, to finish his XXXX design on the man's bare back, Chef ran the pizza wheel down the cleavage of his backside. More blood squirted. The waiter's scream soared to a high-pitched screech. It made the torturer laugh so much he had to pause to wipe tears of merriment from his eyes. Chef had just cut the guy a new corn chute, and it brought Chef such joy, such boundless, inexpressible joy.

One o'clock in the morning. Two men had been in the process of stealing fuel from vans in a yard. So: *not* the most awesome crime of the year, but the two friends, who'd been sharing heroin needles for years, had woken from a narcotic stupor to find they needed another fix. Therefore, a big, spectacular heist wasn't required. A few gallons of fuel in a drum could be sold, no questions asked, to a neighbor. The cash would buy enough magic powder to tide them over nicely until morning. Then they could engage in some profitable shoplifting in order to purchase yet another round of exciting needle time.

They'd pried off a fuel cap without much trouble. Now, liquid spurted down the siphon tube into a plastic drum.

One of the junkies rubbed a bloodshot eye as he crouched beside the container. "It's half full. Make sure the other end of the pipe stays down far enough into the fuel tank. Careful! Air's coming through. Push your end in deeper."

His friend suddenly stiffened. He grasped the back of his own neck.

The first one, who crouched, said, "What the hell's wrong with you?"

The second one kicked the drum so fuel cascaded over his pal.

"You idiot," hissed the first, "wha' ya do that for?"

In suddenly peculiar accents the second posed a question: "Does this nectar from the iron honeypot burn?"

"Stop acting nuts; otherwise you'll have to find your own dope money."

The second produced a lighter. For a split second he seemed to be figuring out how to operate it. As if the device was unfamiliar.

The first addict's eyes stung too much from the splashed fuel to notice what his amigo fiddled with. A tingle of heat against his cheek, however, told him he was in danger.

"Get that thing away from—"

Fumes from the fuel reached the flame of the lighter. Both men were engulfed in the fireball. One died screaming. The possessed man danced in the incandescent heart of the billowing flame, laughing.

On the cliff top Kerry Herne felt it enter her head. To her, it seemed as if a cold, solid object had penetrated the front of her skull. Following that, a sense of her "self" being displaced from its customary seat of consciousness. Before she could even ask herself what had happened to her she whooped with excitement. There in the darkness the flashlight fell from her fingers. Then those fingers explored the contours of her body.

When they found her breasts they eagerly ripped open her jacket, then tore at the shirt until flesh had been bared. With a sensuous delight her possessor squeezed her full breasts. A moan of pleasure escaped her lips.

That expression of delight turned to one of cold fury when her eyes picked out the lantern's glow in the mausoleum. With an animal snarl she raced through the cemetery toward it. On the way she wrenched the head off the statue of a weeping child that adorned a tomb. The head, complete with soulful eyes, and stone tears, was about the size of a volleyball in her hands, yet she handled it effortlessly. She sprinted past gravestones. Being alone in the dark didn't bother her, for it was her possessor who called the shots now.

In seconds Kerry had reached the iron gate of the mausoleum. Madly, the possessed woman used the carved head to pound at the ironwork. Its nose shattered. An iron lug gouged the eye. Her knuckle caught a bar. Blood gushed from her hand. As she hammered at the gate, crimson speckled her naked breasts. All that mattered to her possessor was to break down the gate. Once inside, she could wreck the mosaic. Then the Justice would be free forever. With him would emerge the men and women who obeyed his every command, no matter how grievous, or foul, or sadistic.

Her vision blurred as she struck the iron bars. Pieces of stone flew from the stone head. One raked a scratch on her long, pale neck. But pain didn't matter. Exhaustion didn't matter. All that did matter was to enter that hateful building: to destroy the portrait whose spell had bound Justice Murrain and his servants into the earth for more than two centuries. True, its grip on them already weakened. From time to time, they could briefly escape, but to smash the portrait would break its power for good.

A figure slammed into her. A pair of strong arms forced her against the gate. A hand managed to wrench the statue's head from her fingers, then fling it aside.

"Let go, let go!" The voice that *wasn't* Kerry's thundered from her throat.

"No. I won't let you destroy it."

She managed to turn her head a little. The face, framed with dark hair, just inches from her own, possessed a nerve-tingling familiarity, yet a strangeness, too.

"You're not him." The words gushed with rabid ferocity from the possessed woman's lips. "You're not the Justice! Let me go!"

"I'm Jacob Murrain. Justice Murrain's ancestor. And I will lock his spirit into the earth. And back into that earth will be banished all those evil souls that have sworn allegiance to him."

She struggled. But the man held firm. She tried to squirm round, so her naked breasts would be pushed against him, with the intention of distracting him, but no, he could have been hewn from solid oak. There was no shifting him. Not one inch.

When Kerry Herne's possessor realized it would be futile to remain embedded in this lovely piece of woman flesh, however much it yearned to stay, it released itself from her brain with an enraged howl.

Kerry flinched at the cold iron bars pressed against her skin. Dazed, she murmured, "What have you done to me?"

Jacob Murrain spoke gently. "I'm sorry if I hurt you. But I couldn't allow you to break into the mausoleum."

"Break into the mausoleum?" Kerry echoed. "Why on earth would I want to do that?" She noticed her bloody finger in the light of the lamp. At the same time she saw her exposed breasts. Shivering, from both cold and naked fear, she closed her jacket, then held it shut by folding her arms. She blinked. Random memories flickered across her mind's eye. Images of her desperately attacking the gate. Shards of stone bursting from the stone head, as she pounded the bars. "I did attack the mausoleum." A sound taut with hysteria. "But why? I devote myself to protecting it . . . but at that moment I wanted to see it smashed. It would have been lovely to break the mosaic into a million pieces . . ." She gulped. "Oh my God, what's happened to me?"

"You're well again now. Don't be afraid." The man rested his hand on her forearm. A tender gesture of reassurance. "You should go home and rest."

"But what happened to me, Mr. Murrain? Have I gone mad?"

"Allow me to escort you back to the car. If you wish, I can explain then."

Kerry managed a weak smile. "Such chivalrous manners, Mr. Murrain. You should have been a knight in armor."

"You could be closer to the truth than you imagine. Before this is over we may have to slay a singular demon."

Though they walked through darkness, beneath a sky of

glittering stars, his sense of direction was faultless. Then she knew he'd been attending to the mausoleum and its grim portrait for more than half a century. Although she felt bruised, and even though her senses felt as if they'd been fed into the psychological equivalent of a food blender, a sense of resolve took hold within her. She wanted answers to what had befallen her. And if she had to question Jacob Murrain all night she'd get to the bottom of this.

Meanwhile, Jack Murrain all of a sudden stepped back from Pel. A second before he broke off the kiss she felt a tremor run through his body with such violence that he'd jerked his head forward, breaking the skin of her upper lip.

Gasping, she leaned back against the house wall. The blue lights of the police cars still whirled down the street. From one of the bedroom windows came hysterical laughter. From another, sounds of sex—but sex undertaken with such gusto one of the partners bleated, *"Oh-oh-oh-oh!"*

The thought hammered through her skull. *This is Crazy Town. Get out while you can!*

Jack ran his fingers through his black mane. "Pel? What happened, just then? What did I do to you?"

"Let go . . . I'll shout the police . . . they'll hear me!"

"I'm sorry. I don't know what came over me. Oh, no. Your lip's bleeding. Did I hit you?"

Pel stared at him in shock. His face reflected the glow of the streetlight. "You mean you really don't know?"

"I remember we were talking. A woman told us there'd been a murder, then . . ." His expression became one of horror. "Then a sense of pressure against my head. After that . . ." He shrugged, baffled.

Pel broke free of his grip. "Don't play that game with me."

"What game?"

"Pretending you've lost your memory. Listen, Jack, you know full well you roughed up that drunk. Then you"—she backed away—"made a meal of me."

"Made a meal of you? What do you mean by that? And how did you cut your lip?"

By this time, he directed those questions at her back. Pel Minton raced along the road. She stopped running when she reached the house she shared with her colleagues. And only when stout door timbers held Crazy Town at bay did she sigh with relief then climb the staircase to bed.

CHAPTER THREE

At the ungodly hour of two in the morning Kerry Herne stood naked from the waist up in the cold night air. She'd ditched her torn shirt and jacket into the backseat of the car. A sea breeze, as cold as ice cream, poured across her bare skin. She drew a fleece from the rear parcel shelf of the car, then grateful for its warmth—and protection of her modesty—quickly donned it, before zipping it up to her chin.

The car stood on the dirt track that led to the graveyard. By starlight she could make out the oceanlike dark expanse of pasture. At that moment, it seemed as if she'd been conjured into a landscape of elves and giants. The trees in the gloomy landscape were towering structures. The gravestones could have been humpy, goblin-size men. Normally, she wouldn't have found such objects troubling, but after what she'd endured tonight, when she seemed to lose her wits, and then attacking the mausoleum, even vines climbing up the cemetery fence had all the ominous intent of tentacles bursting forth from the ground to strangle the unwary.

Taking a deep breath, she adjusted the collar of the fleece. That done, she sat in the driver's seat beside Mr. Murrain.

"Tell me what happened," she demanded.

"You're cold," he told her. "This can wait until the morning."

"No way, sir. Tell me now."

In the darkness of the car he resembled the mosaic portrait of his dead ancestor to an unnerving degree. "Your body was invaded. One of the spirits freed itself from the mausoleum long enough to take control of you."

"You mean *possession?*"

"Without a doubt."

"How can you know?" To her surprise she found herself not pouring scorn on the allegation that she'd been possessed—if anything, she wanted evidence to corroborate the statement. Because if some malign force had not taken possession of her, then the only other conclusion was that she'd lost her sanity.

In low, gentle tones the man explained, "This has happened before. You can find similar accounts to what occurred tonight in newspaper files of the *Crowdale Gazette*, and in the court records. Uncannily similar accounts at that. In 1863 one of my ancestors responsible for caring for the mausoleum became more interested in playing cards than his ancestral duty. The structure began to decay. Townspeople reported that certain neighbors would suddenly behave strangely at night—often this behavior would be violent or of a sexual nature. There were murders, assaults, arson attacks. Most of the damage was directed at the mausoleum. By morning the person who'd behaved violently would be their old self again. They'd be astonished by the accusations against them. It wasn't long before a local priest identified the evil that affected them was possession." He sighed. "Possession by evil spirits from the mausoleum. Many of those that were possessed would make it their mission to destroy the mosaic of Justice Murrain. If it is destroyed the monster's ghost will be free to go on the rampage forever."

"How did they stop it happening again?"

"You know the story of Justice Murrain? How he housed the criminally insane in Murrain Hall, which once stood on the cliff here? And that he turned the lunatics into his own private army?"

Kerry nodded. "I researched the local history before we started the dig."

"Local children for generations have called the mosaic the Ghost Monster—more accurately, however, it is a ghost prison. It contains the evil spirits of my ancestor and his Battle Men. It is now the Murrain family's role to safeguard the mosaic. To maintain the building, and keep the light burning. So you might ask me how they stopped that plague of possession back in 1863? It is simple. My family made sure that the building was restored. Soon those cases of possession stopped. Life went back to normal. Ms. Herne, I believe there is some mechanism that holds the evil in check beneath the mosaic, but, as importantly, if the building is properly repaired after any damage occurs, that mechanism heals itself. The power is restored automatically. Forces are at work that share the attributes of Mother Nature. That is, they are self-regulating, and just as animals and plants spontaneously heal themselves after injury, so the forces that operate beneath the mausoleum do likewise. Tonight the integrity of the mechanism was damaged in some way. It allowed the spirits a temporary release. One took possession of you. It willed you to try and break through the gate, so you could smash the mosaic, and so release Justice Murrain and his henchmen for good. But the power reasserted itself in a way that can only be described as miraculous. Then, as if it still held the evil spirits on a long leash, it could draw them back. And you became yourself again. Your mind took back control of your body." His voice acquired a more defensive tone. "Go on, Ms. Herne. This is where you ridicule what I've told you. Possession by an evil spirit? Survival of my ancestor beyond the grave? Voodoo? Witchcraft? Black magic? Why don't you scorn me all the way to hell and back?"

"Mr. Murrain. If you'd told me that even two hours ago I'd have laughed in your face." Kerry shuddered. "But after what I experienced out there in the graveyard tonight? It felt as if an ice-cold fist had been forced through my forehead into my brain. There was no stealth involved. It was violence! My mind—that thing I call *myself*—was beaten back until some entity took its place. A *something* that abused me, violated me, then moved my arms and legs as if I were nothing more than a plastic doll." She breathed deeply. "And believe me, I have the bruises to prove it."

"At last, at long last." He was pleased. "We are beginning to understand each other."

"And respect each other."

"Naturally."

As a measure of that newfound trust she found herself telling Jacob Murrain about the discoveries over the last couple of days. How a prehistoric ritualistic site, which they'd dubbed "Temple Central," formed a complex of radiating lines that the worshippers believed were "spirit roads." What's more, an earthwork ringed the plot of land: a special area that would have been holy ground to the ancients. Kerry added, "The mausoleum site lies at the heart of Temple Central. I know the son of Justice Murrain built the mausoleum, and he didn't put it there by chance. He knew *exactly* what he was doing. I suspect legends, handed down from parent to child, within your own family, would have singled out those few square yards as being an incredibly potent location. It may well have been where the temple altar was placed. The holy of holies. A zone of powerful magic. The man who decided to contain the spirits of Justice Murrain and his Battle Men here understood the workings of this occult mechanism. He appreciated how it can bind spirits to the earth, as it were, and keep them jailed."

"But you say that the earthwork is being destroyed by the sea?"

"A large chunk of it went tonight. I watched it fall onto the beach."

The man shook his head sadly. "I believed if I could safeguard the mausoleum building everything would be well.

But you've told me it is only the central component of a larger mechanism. Now I know that parts of the mechanism, namely the earthwork and the spirit roads, have been damaged it explains everything." He took a deep breath. "Because part of it has been lost that means my ancestor, the despised and hateful Justice Murrain, is starting to break free."

"If what you say is correct then we're in trouble." Kerry knew this was the time to make that leap of faith *and to believe.* "The power that traps the spirits of Justice Murrain and his gang must be at its weakest during the hours of darkness. When part of Temple Central collapses into the ocean it allows them to escape for a while. But, so far, it's only temporary." She spoke with utter certainty now. "The mechanism has been able to heal itself. When it does, it draws those entities back into the earth. Once they're back evil is contained. They can do nothing to harm the outside world."

"How long the mechanism continues to self-repair is the important consideration now. There may be a tipping point; a point of no return. If any more of the site is lost, then my ancestor might escape the mosaic, even though it's still intact. Should that happen, he will exact his vengeance on the surviving Murrains. He reviles his own bloodline. And he will inflict brutal suffering on the town. He will bathe in its blood. Who will be able to stop him? *How will they stop him?*"

"Mr. Murrain, we are allies now," she said firmly. "We must stop the coastal erosion once and for all."

"How?"

"My team uncovered a skeleton yesterday, possibly between four and six thousand years old. We suspect it might be one of your ancestors. If we can prove the skeleton's link with living descendants today, namely, yourself and your grandson, then we should be able to persuade the government to protect the site."

"You do realize you might already be too late?"

"We've got to try, Mr. Murrain. For all our sakes—even if it's the last thing we do."

A sea breeze hissed through the gravestones. It could have been the sound of an entire army of ghosts whispering momentous news: that the eve of a great battle was drawing near.

CHAPTER FOUR

Pel Minton arrived at the dig site later than everyone else that morning. She'd been instructed to remain at the house to wait for a courier to collect the DNA sample she'd taken from Jack Murrain. A leather-clad woman had arrived on a Harley at nine thirty. Pel quickly signed forms on the courier's clipboard; then she'd watched the woman stow the container that held the precious swab into a foam-lined pannier. A moment later, the Harley had roared away, bound for a university lab where the DNA would be extracted.

When Pel did reach the site the sense of urgency she found there was palpable. Straightaway, she could tell coastal erosion had taken another bite out of the cliff. Nat stood up to his neck in a pit where he extracted pieces of a cremation urn together with burned bones.

"Roman! Third century!" he shouted with a distinct note of desperation. The cliff's edge was only ten feet from the pit he stood in. Elsewhere, diggers attacked the earth with feverish intensity. Yet more people sieved for finds. Archaeologists clustered round tables set out amid gravestones; they were recording the latest artifacts, either photographing, labeling, note-taking; all had worried expressions.

The ocean's getting closer, she told herself. *Soon the Murrain site will be under the ocean.* All would be lost here, unless the government designated the historical site with a special protection notice. Of course, then would come the hard labor of contractors installing a barrier at the base of the cliffs to save them from the surf's pounding.

Kerry Herne fought to apply clamps to the edge of her finds table to prevent the sterile sheets from being carried away by the wind. When Kerry saw Pel she beckoned her frantically.

"Pel? The DNA sample?"

"As of thirty minutes ago on its way to the lab."

"Thank heaven for that," said the chief archaeologist with feeling.

"I'll say."

Then both women eyed each other. Pel noticed the scratches on Kerry's throat. Two of her fingers were bandaged as well. Meanwhile, Kerry must have seen Pel's swollen upper lip.

Both women exclaimed in unison, "What happened to you?"

Kerry gave a grim smile as she fastened a G clamp to the table. "You first."

"I met Jack Murrain last night. He took me out to dinner."

"Oh."

"Then he went nuts. He all but shoved some guy's face through a wall; then he got passionate."

Kerry turned a laptop, so the screen faced Pel. A wireless link piped in a local TV channel. "I've been watching the local news feed. Last night a good portion of the town went nuts. There've been outbreaks of violence, vandalism, assaults—often committed by people who are usually perfectly law-abiding. See for yourself."

Pel watched an anchorman reading the news on a split screen. The other screen showed footage of a familiar row of homes. Police cars stood outside a house where a pair of empty chairs sat side by side. *"Many townspeople will be familiar with Horace Neville, known as the Gentle Giant by neighbors. Last night, Horace's mother, Lucy Neville, sixty-three, was brutally killed in her own home. Screams alerted neighbors who called the police. All the police spokesman will say, at the mo-*

ment, is that a man, who resides at the Neville address, is in custody."

"I was on that road last night," Pel exclaimed. "I saw the police cars." Then she added with some force, "And that's where Jack attacked me."

"Jack Murrain might not have been himself."

"In all honesty he scared the hell out of me." Pel frowned. "What do you mean *not himself?*"

"I mean *literally* not himself. I spoke to his grandfather last night. We're agreed there's a problem here."

"A problem that's bigger than the site falling into the sea? Something to do with what happened to Jack last night?"

"And other townspeople acting out of character." As she spoke, Kerry set out fragments of pottery—new finds from the excavation. "It's too dangerous to remain in Crowdale at night. I'm arranging accommodations for our team in Calder-Brigg."

"But that's an hour's commute away. We'll lose valuable time working on site."

"Can't be helped, I'm afraid. Our team's safety is paramount. Will you photograph the fragments of the funerary bowl? I need to collect the rest from Nat."

"Kerry, you've got to tell me what's happening. This involves me, too."

"There isn't time now. Sorry."

"Kerry?"

Kerry, however, hurried through the graveyard to where Nat worked in the pit. The brief conversation with Kerry left Pel with a burning curiosity. How could coastal erosion be connected with Jack Murrain's bizarre behavioral switch last night?

Just why would it be dangerous to stay in Crowdale overnight?

The Murrains are at the center of this. Pel Minton decided there and then she'd get to the bottom of the mystery.

CHAPTER FIVE

They'd taken his clothes away. For examination, they said. A policeman had given him a white paper coverall with a dinky elastic hood. Then he'd been locked in the police cell. Horace Neville didn't know why he was there. Something to do with his mother? That's what he'd been able to infer from conversations that he'd overheard between police officers and the ambulance driver. But events of the last few hours confused him.

Yes, he remembered sitting on his chair in the street, alongside the little fellow. The one everyone else insisted they could not see. Some were even cruel enough to say Bobby didn't exist. That upset Horace. Worse, it made the little fellow very sad. Then Horace remembered that just before midnight a procession marched up the street. Shadowy men and women. They weren't confined to walking at ground level. Some scurried across the rooftops, weaving round chimney pots, or hopping over TV aerials. Others appeared to swim under the blacktop of the road before popping out again. That would have amused Horace, as a rule, only last night it had scared him. Even scarier was the man in black who led the procession. He was tall, very thin, had lots of black hair. And he looked a lot like Jacob Murrain. Only it wasn't he. Horace was certain of it. The gray eyes were terrible to look at. They made Horace's heart clamor painfully in his chest.

Then it all went dark. When he knew where he was again

he sat in the back of a police car. He had blood on his clothes, though he hadn't hurt himself. So if it wasn't his blood, where had it come from?

Mystery, mystery, mystery. Horace didn't like it.

He turned to his imaginary friend, who sat on the cell bunk beside him. "What happened to us? Why have the police put us in here?"

Too frightened to reply, Bobby remained silent.

"Will they let us go soon, Bobby? They won't hurt us, will they? 'Cos I won't let 'em hurt you. You're my friend. I'll keep you safe."

Bobby smiled.

Horace continued in that same reassuring tone. "'Cos if they try and hurt us we'll run away. I'm good at running. I run right fast. I'll pick you up and—whoosh!—dash to a place they'll never find us."

The giant of a man went to the cell window. Chimes from the town-hall clock told him it was four o'clock. Already the sun hung just above the rooftops. Dark soon. Horace Neville felt a shiver of excitement. He didn't know why. Only he sensed something special would happen with the arrival of night.

CHAPTER SIX

On the dot of four the diggers started to pack their tools and the day's archaeological finds into the vans. Most were unhappy about the hour's drive to Calder-Brigg. Plenty asked the same question: *What's wrong with the house in Crowdale?*

Pel noticed that Kerry simply evaded the question by saying that she was too busy to discuss it, but it was all down to budget overspend (a semiplausible catchall explanation, Pel reasoned).

A determination to keep digging ensured that Nat remained in the pit near the cliff's edge. He'd uncovered more Roman cremation urns. Come hell or high water, he was determined to remove them before the day's work was finished; he doubted if that plot of land would still be here in the morning. All day they'd heard the thump of rocks falling from the cliff.

Pel had been carrying one of the trestle tables to a van when a voice startled her.

"Here, let me help you with that."

"Jack?" She held the four-by-four-foot tabletop in front of her, as if it were a shield.

"Pel, I'm not here to cause trouble."

"Damn straight you aren't. Go away."

"I attacked you last night, didn't I?" His large gray eyes locked onto hers. "If I hit you I didn't mean it. You've got to believe me, Pel."

The breeze ran icy fingers through her hair. "Are you honestly saying that you can't remember how you attacked me?"

"I must know what I did. It's eating me up. All last night I was wondering if I'd . . ." He gave a painful shrug. "If it was bad . . . you know, criminal . . . tell me, and I'll turn myself in."

"Surely, you remembered what happened?" Her arms ached from carrying the table, so she set it down. "We went out to eat at the Greek restaurant."

"I remember that. But later everything became sort of . . . it's hard to describe. Indistinct. Blurred, as if I stopped seeing clearly."

"You don't remember roughing up the guy who threatened you?"

He shook his head.

Pel continued, "Or grabbing hold of me after that?"

He winced at the accusation. Such a forlorn expression impressed itself on his face that her heart went out to him.

"It's all a blank. Tell me how I hurt you."

"You idiot. You kissed me!"

"How?"

"How do you think? Do you want me to sketch a picture?"

"My grandfather said you were intelligent, Pel. He told me you've got brains."

"As compliments go it's secondhand. I hope you'd have the balls, Jack, to judge some of my qualities for yourself." She clicked her tongue. "Now that you're here you can carry this table to the van."

Jack appeared confused and relieved by turns. "I kissed you. That's all?"

"No other parts of your anatomy were involved. Though you managed to kiss me so hard you made my lip bleed."

"I'm sorry. It's just that I don't remember kissing you. And all I'd had to drink was Coke. I can't even blame alcohol."

Pel regarded him. "Kerry said you weren't yourself last night."

"How can she know? I didn't . . . uhm . . . approach her, did I?"

"*Approach?* I'm taking that as your euphemism for passionately pouncing on females?"

"My grandfather said you were smart." He reached the stage now where his relief allowed him to smile. "I don't make a habit of 'pouncing' on a first date."

"I didn't know it was a date. All I wanted was a smear of your body fluid."

"The sample's safe, then?"

"It's already at the lab. Some white-coated scientist will be dissecting your DNA even as we speak." Her tone hardened. "Do you think the lab will find a DNA marker for pouncing on American girls?"

The comment made him uncomfortable. "My grandfather seemed to know what had happened to me, but he's not telling."

Pel opened the van door. "Same goes for my boss, Kerry Herne. She appears to know something, too. She was talking to your grandfather last night. So why are they shy about sharing their secrets?"

"Especially when it involves us."

She found herself eyeing Jack's face. His concern touched her. What's more, the events of the last twenty-four hours had forged a bond between them. "We should confront them. They should tell us what they know."

"Why don't we meet up again tonight? Then we can develop our strategy." He grinned. "Also, I can buy you a drink by way of apology for . . . *pouncing*."

"According to Kerry, your behavior had become abnormal. She seems to think that others from Crowdale have been acting out of character, too."

"I could pick you up from the house at seven?"

She shook her head.

"Okay, eight?"

"I'm sorry."

"Oh." He'd interpreted her refusal as a rebuff.

She reached out to touch his forearm. "Jack. I'd love to. It's just that we're being bused back to Calder-Brigg."

"Surely you've not finished work here, yet?"

"No . . . there's a problem. Kerry's concerned we might be at risk, somehow, if we stay in Crowdale."

"Risk of boredom, maybe. Listen, I'll talk to my grandfather tonight, then see you here tomorrow morning. I might have found something out by then. After all, I'm entitled to know why I went crazy last night."

On impulse, she tested him with a challenge. "Or you could drive over to Calder-Brigg tonight and buy me that drink? But if you're too busy . . ."

His grin was a boyish one. "I'd like nothing more. Give me the address."

"They haven't told me where we'll be staying yet. If you give me your number I'll text it to you later." She handed him paper and a pen. "Of course, if you find yourself daunted by a feisty American girl, you could always stay here in Crowdale—and wait and see if everyone goes nuts again." She grinned back at him. "It might be the safer option. Old boyfriends say that I'm a bit of a handful."

He jotted down the number, then handed it to Pel.

"I'll be there no later than eight," he told her.

"In the meantime, if *you* go nuts, be sure to call ahead and warn me." She touched her lip. "There's only so much bruising a girl can take, you know?"

Anxious, fretful, nerves jangling, Kerry Herne shepherded stragglers to the waiting vans. They'd cleared the site of equipment. Only Nat remained in his pit, determined to extract the last cremation urn from the earth. This was a rare find, he'd insisted. From inscriptions scratched on potsherds he'd gleaned that there'd been some kind of mutiny in the army here seventeen centuries ago. Many Roman soldiers had been killed in a night of orgiastic violence. If he teased as many artifacts from the tomb as he could, then he might be able to piece together the full story.

Kerry stood at the graveyard gate. Everyone else waited in the convoy of vans and cars. Nat's head appeared from time to time above the soil mound. Beyond him, the sea turned dull as iron as daylight faded.

"Nat. We've got to go."

He held up his hand.

Five more minutes? Damn, I want out before sunset. It's not safe here at night. Kerry shuddered; she recalled how some brutish intelligence had invaded her mind last night. Without a doubt, there'd be trouble if they stayed.

Taking a deep breath, she murmured, "Calm yourself. It won't be properly dark for almost an hour yet. We've plenty of time to get away. They can't touch us by day. As long as there's light we're safe." At that moment, she had a sudden urge to find an excuse never to return but, call it professional pride, call it hubris, she knew to the roots of her bones that she wouldn't stay away from the graveyard. Not only must they finish the archaeological investigation, they must also find a way to preserve the mosaic. "It's that or die trying," she murmured with such dark humor she shuddered, the coldness of eternity in her blood.

Nat gently pried a shard of bright orange Samian ware from the earth. On it were scratched words in Latin. Plenty of time to decipher those later. Even so, he itched with curiosity. Strange events occurred here in AD 300. Roman soldiers went berserk and then attacked their comrades. He needed to know the full story.

Carefully, he placed the piece of pot in a finds tray. At that moment he froze. A groan burst from his lips. For all the world, it felt as if a hunk of cold iron had been rammed through his forehead. A second later, he clawed at the side of the pit.

"Bury me alive, would ya! Bury me with blood in my veins? I'll kill ya. I'll rip ya sideways, so help me!"

The walls of the pit appeared to close on him. The stench of damp earth clogged his throat. Why did this seem so familiar? How could he know what it was like to be laid in a grave? Then to feel cold soil pour over his face.

Hands grabbed hold of him. Bellowing, Nat fought to be free. Faces . . . his enemy's faces loomed overhead. They were here to destroy him.

Howling, he lunged at the woman, hands at her throat.

"Nat! It's me, Kerry. Calm down!"

All of a sudden the strength bled from him and he dropped to his knees.

Gasping, he stammered, "W-What happened to me? I can't remember . . . everything went strange . . ."

"Don't worry, Nat. It's not your fault." Kerry's face was grim. "You weren't yourself for a while."

She told him not to worry, but Nat realized he'd never seen his boss look so worried before. It was still daylight, the evening sun had broken through, the sea shone blue. He heard her mutter, "Oh God, they're not restricted to the night. They're breaking out during the day." With those, to him, inexplicable, yet peculiarly unsettling comments, Kerry helped him to her car for the drive to Calder-Brigg.

CHAPTER SEVEN

From the cell Horace Neville watched the sun set. Darkness seeped over the town. In those shadows were yet deeper shadows. They moved with a predatory menace. The same eager stealth as hunting wolves. One moment he stood at the barred window, asking himself why he'd been locked in this little whitewashed room, with its single bunk, when a cold pressure started above his eyes.

It could have been the start of a crushing headache. Yet after a moment's resistance, as if his brow held some invasive force at bay, until it could repel it no more, there was a sense of yielding. Then his mind was thrust aside with all the contempt of a carjacker bundling a driver from their seat behind the wheel, then taking their place.

The possessed giant of a man stood patiently, a smile playing on his face, his eyes burning with a keen intelligence. Eventually, the steel flap in the cell door flicked down. A constable set down a plate of sandwiches on the flap, along with a paper cup containing milk.

"Eat up, Horace, lad," said the middle-aged man. "The police doctor will be along later to check that you're still healthy and in one piece."

The prisoner didn't answer.

With a regretful sigh the constable added, "I've known you for years, Horace. I've seen you many a time sitting on a chair outside your front door. If it helps, I don't believe you knew you were hurting your mother." He tapped the sandwich plate. "Now, eat up. When they transfer you it might be a while before you're fed again. Did you hear me, Horace?"

The big man in the paper coverall turned to fix the constable with a glaring, insightful eye. "I'm not this . . . Horace you speak of."

"Suit yourself, lad. I know you have your little fantasies."

The prisoner curled his lip. "Fantasies? There'll come a day when you wish to God that you're faced with mere fantasy and whimsy."

"Eat your sandwiches."

"What does this name mean to you: Justice Murrain?"

"Now, now, Horace. Enough of the silly talk."

"Justice Murrain. You know that name, don't you? In Crowdale it is not so much a soubriquet as a legend. So, sir? What do you think of my new flesh? Quite a giant, eh? A veritable tower of mutton." He laughed. "I'll keep it for now. It serves a purpose. Regard these fingers, sir. Aren't they formidable? They could belong to an ape."

"Don't start behaving the lunatic, Horace." The policeman had grown nervous. "Just tell them what you did, lad. The death of your mother was probably an accident."

"Her death an accident? Ha! Hardly. Neither will yours."

Rattled, the policeman stood back from the cell door.

The prisoner spoke swiftly. "I know there are still Murrains in the town. Bring one to me."

"You're not allowed visitors."

"Surely I am, sir. A mental defective locked away in your jail must have the right to advice and guidance from an independent party of sound mind. Isn't that so?"

"The court can authorize—"

"Courts be damned!" He loomed toward the cell door. "Bring a Murrain here to me. It's time I was reacquainted with men of my own blood."

The constable, now safely beyond arm's reach of the prisoner, did not budge.

The possessed man gave a secret smile. "If you don't agree

I can arrange a display for our amusement. What if, for example, I had the power to make your good lady wife stroll naked through the streets to this jail? Might that persuade you to obey me?" His smile grew wicked. "During that walk, she would offer the services of her ample womanhood to any passing gentleman."

The policeman's nerve broke. He hurried back along the corridor with the prisoner's laughter ringing in his ears.

CHAPTER EIGHT

Rebecca Lowe sat in front of the mirror. She was in an armchair; her sons stood at either side of her.

"See that face," she breathed as she stroked the disfigured half. "Jacob Murrain did that to me. He used the lamp from that shabby little building in the graveyard." Her finger stroked a line across skin that was by turns puckered, or smooth as plastic. "Jacob Murrain has been mocking me for thirty years. He destroyed my beauty . . . and I was beautiful, boys. Every man in Crowdale desired me."

In the reflection she saw her sons as well as her burned face. Scott appeared uncomfortable when she talked about how sexually desired she was by the males of this little coastal town. *Then I was. Even the mayor himself had moaned with pleasure when he finally got the chance to undress me that Christmas Eve . . . before Jacob Murrain killed my looks.*

"So," she said, "when are you going to make me proud of you?"

Scott replied, "We only have to wait another week or so, Ma. Every day the cliffs are being eaten away by the sea. By the end of the month, Murrain's building in the cemetery will be gone."

"Murrain must suffer, but not from what the sea is doing naturally. He should know that it's our family that has revenged itself on him. You must break his heart."

"But how, Ma?" burbled Ross in those thick tones of his. His bald scalp reddened as emotion gripped him. "We already punctured the tires on his grandson's pickup. What more can we do?"

"Isn't it time you confronted his grandson? Frighten him."

They shuffled uncomfortably.

"Jack isn't a weakling, Ma."

Ross agreed. "Last night he tried to shove Bill Tawny's face through a wall."

"That's right. Bill saw him with some woman from the dig. Jack pounced on Bill for nothing."

"Is this woman Jack's girlfriend?"

"We saw her at his house." Ross shrugged. "I guess so."

"Good." Rebecca pulled her hair forward to hide the scars. "If you can make her life a misery that will make the son unhappy, which in turn makes Jacob suffer. Do you follow me, boys?"

Ross would stolidly obey. Scott showed signs of unease.

"Remember what the doctors are saying?" said their mother. "My heart won't last till Christmas. You don't want me in my grave, knowing that Jacob Murrain is still sneering at me, do you now?"

Tears sprang from Ross's eyes. "Don't say that, Ma. You're not going anywhere. Them doctors know nothing."

Tellingly, Scott didn't make a comment. Then Scott always was the smarter of the two.

Rebecca nodded. "The girl is the key. Use her to make Jacob Murrain suffer."

CHAPTER NINE

A middle-aged policeman led Jacob Murrain to steps that descended to a row of cells. The gates of every single one were open, bar one at the end. When the policeman saw Jacob had noticed the vacant cells he explained that the other occupants had been moved out, either bailed, or transferred to another town. This was a small station in a little town. Law-enforcement resources were limited. Yet the killer in the only occupied cell required special attention.

As he descended the steps in front of Jacob, the policeman suddenly stopped. "I shouldn't be doing this, you know?"

"Then why do it, Constable?"

"Because I don't know what I've got down here."

"Horace Neville, isn't it? As far as I know, he's the poor guy with learning difficulties. I've seen him sitting out in the street, but I've never spoken to the man."

"That's him. For years he's told folk he's got an invisible friend." The constable laughed. It sounded more like a sob. "At least it's supposed to be Neville."

"Then why have you asked me here? I don't understand."

"Because he demanded that you come and talk to him."

"Demanded? How can he demand anything?"

"Because he can!" The constable spat the words, like they tasted foul in his mouth. "Look. He warned me if we didn't bring you here he'd make my wife walk to the police station naked."

"*What?*"

"Forty-five minutes ago I had a call from my neighbor. He said he'd seen Sheila heading up the lane toward town. As she walked, she was taking her clothes off. The neighbor and his wife brought her here wrapped in a blanket. Is that a compelling enough reason I agree to what the maniac wants?"

"Dear God in heaven." Jacob began to suspect what lay in wait for him at the end of that tiled corridor. "Did you speak to your wife?"

"She doesn't know me. Everyone she meets she begs to be fucked."

"Very well." Jacob steeled himself. "Take me to him."

"Keep back from the gate—well back! Horace Neville won't be as you remember him."

"I don't doubt it."

Together they walked along the corridor. In the cell, a shadow was waiting.

CHAPTER TEN

"Calder-Brigg could be a million miles from Crowdale." Jack Murrain regarded the flow of cars past the multiplex cinema. The faces of the town's people were somehow brighter. Back home everyone had dour expressions, as if some insurmountable problem worried them.

Pel Minton smoothed down the material of her dress as they waited in line for the ticket booth. "So, you're glad you came to see me? Or do you wish you were back at grandpa's house, polishing your collection of cricket balls?"

Jack laughed. "You are crazy, Pel Minton. I don't have a collection of balls, cricket or otherwise."

"I thought all Englishmen played cricket?"

"The other kids tended to shy away from us Murrains."

"Ah, the Murrain family curse."

"If anything, we have been cursed. The Murrain family have devoted their lives to protecting that damn mosaic of my equally damned ancestor." He wore a lost expression. "Only when I'm here in a big town like this all that seems unreal. I mean, why should I follow in my grandfather's footsteps and go marching up to the mausoleum to sweep it clean, then fiddle around with that stupid oil lamp?"

Imitating an old man, she croaked, "Keep the light burning, Jack. You must keep the light burning."

"Now I'm here all that seems dreamlike. The obsessive behavior—cleaning the mausoleum, tending the lamp, checking that nobody's vandalized the mosaic." He glanced round at crowds of happy people, heading to the bowling alley, or clutching burgers from the building with the big M. "But my grandfather is sincere, you know? He's made me promise to look after that pile of old stones when he's gone."

"I'm sorry, Jack. I shouldn't have joked about it. The mosaic means a lot to your family."

"And everyone else, it seems. Your archaeologist friends are busting their rumps to save it." He pulled banknotes out of his pocket, as they approached the booth. "My treat. I hurt you last night. The least I can do is pay for the film."

Pel told him not to bother with popcorn. After a day's hard work on the Murrain site all she wanted was to feel a softly cushioned seat beneath her then to settle down into the velvety, comforting darkness of the cinema. Already trailers were being screened, so they had to fumble in the gloom to find empty seats. A bunch of kids laughed at teaser clips from a new blockbuster comedy.

"I should warn you," Pel told him. "I laugh out loud when I see funny stuff on-screen."

"Good," he said with feeling. Then, marveling at being in such a cheerful place, he said, "When I get away from Crowdale I feel brand-new. It's like a weight lifted from me. For goodness' sake. I feel excited. I'm happy."

"You should leave Crowdale forever."

"There are days when I want nothing more. And now I'm here, just an hour's drive from home, it feels like a holiday. I want to shout stupid things. Tell jokes. Hear laughter. Dance. Sing. Do reckless things. Throw my shoes into a fountain."

"Kiss a girl?"

"Hell, yes."

"So what's stopping you?" Pel clamped a hand at each side of his face, then kissed him on the mouth. Her bruised lip had still hurt, but when her mouth touched his the hurt became a delicious tingle. Neither broke away. The kiss went on until the trailers ended and the credits rolled for the start of the film. Then, at last, they sat back in their chairs. His hand found hers in the gloom. She held it there on her lap. Tightly.

delicate muscle. Rachael bites into . . . The face crept toward the turkey spiked and the proffar pulled her the stop of the him. Then Yeslan, they catanak in their chains this time found here in the ghosst. She had it there on my legs Tydley.

CHAPTER ELEVEN

Jacob Murrain approached to within six feet of the cell, mindful to be beyond arm's reach of its inmate. The policeman, scared-looking, stood even farther back down the corridor.

Through the bars, Jacob could see the bulky figure of Horace Neville. Taunted "the village idiot" by local kids, the giant gazed out through the cell window, his back to Jacob. For a moment, they remained silent; nobody moved. Then Jacob took one silent step closer to the bars.

Horace spoke without turning. "I'm sure our constable, there, would advise you to desist from approaching the cell any farther."

"You wanted to see me, Mr. Neville?"

"Neville? Ah . . . that's the name of the flesh that clothes my wits."

Jacob surmised that the quick voice and precise diction he heard now didn't match Horace Neville's usual speech patterns. He began to suspect he knew the reason. "Why did you want to speak with me?"

The giant continued to gaze out at the town. "The surface of it all has changed . . . true, most of the buildings are different, the hard black surface on the roads is intriguing. Vehicles move without horses." His nostrils flared as he inhaled. "But Crowdale's underlying *stench* is the same. Do you know what that smell is, sir? It is fear. Ignorance. Stupidity. The men and women of Crowdale have always wallowed in it. Why do these townspeople have to be so weak? It makes me angry to see them cringing. Even the constable, there, cowers—just like a dog before a raised fist. Now if—"

Jacob interrupted, "Did you want me here to be your passive audience, so I could listen to your rather tedious observations? If you require nothing more than that, then you can bore those four walls. Good night."

As Jacob turned to leave the prisoner laughed. "Ah, I like that. You've fire in your heart. The Murrains aren't cold as cod yet."

"So, what do you want from me?"

The man in the cell turned to fix Jacob with his uncannily sharp eyes. "Do you know who I am?"

"I'm told your name is Horace Neville."

"But *you*, sir, know my real identity don't you?"

"Of course, I do."

"And what is my name, sir?"

"Justice Murrain."

"Ah, at last! I'm speaking to an equal. Someone with a mind."

The police officer spoke up. "What's going on here? Why is Neville using a different name?"

The prisoner laughed. "Don't waste your time telling him, Jacob Murrain. He wouldn't understand. Now . . . will you, my descendant, the vessel of my blood, shake me by the hand?" He thrust a huge fist through the bars.

"You belong in the ground! The son you mutilated, your descendants, all the way down the bloodline to me, have sworn to keep you there: dead and buried!" He met the man's stare. "If need be, I'll sacrifice my own life keeping you there. You are poison, Justice Murrain."

"Tut-tut, Jacob. I made mistakes in the past, for sure. But now I am free I will correct those mistakes. This time I will do the right thing." He seized the bars as he spat the words. "Last time I let Crowdale live. Not this time. I'll kill every one of them. I'll break the babies in their cradles. Then I'll burn the town back to bare earth!"

"I'm fetching the straitjacket," said the constable.

Jacob Murrain shook his head. "This is temporary. Justice Murrain isn't free yet. Not completely. Come daybreak, he'll be drawn back to the mausoleum."

The constable frowned. "I don't understand. Justice Murrain? He lived here hundreds of years ago. The man in the cell is Horace Neville. He can't even buy chocolate by himself. He's stupid. Congenitally stupid."

Jacob eyed the possessed figure. "For the time being, the man in there is no longer Neville. And he's far from stupid. Justice Murrain was extremely intelligent. Oh, a psychopath to be sure. But he had a formidable mind."

The prisoner hissed, "*Has* a formidable mind. Don't speak of me in the past tense, Jacob. And you are right. I'm learning fast. I've been able to move around the town for some time, ever since that prison on the cliff top started to fall into the sea. I know about the internal combustion engine. I've seen machines that fly. I've learned new words: telephone, computer, Internet, electricity, refrigeration, television, celebrity culture, pop music—do you want me to sing the latest hit song?" He grunted with pleasure. "See, I am intelligent. Ferociously intelligent. I've sifted through the trappings of modern society. Most of its technology isn't as advanced as I'd have hoped. People surround themselves with electrical novelties and pretend they're civilized." He leered through the bars. "It will be quite satisfying to rip society asunder."

At last, the policeman grasped what was happening. "I can deal with this. I'll go fetch my shotgun. When I give him both barrels that will shut him up forever."

"Tell him, Jacob. You can destroy this flesh, but?"

"He's right." Jacob sighed. "You won't stop Justice Murrain by killing this individual in the cell. His ghost will simply take possession of another body."

"Ah . . ." The prisoner held up a finger. "Now comes the moment when I reveal the reason why I summoned you here, my dear descendant. This body I'm occupying is only a makeshift conveyance. I've no intention of riding in this ungainly behemoth for long." The smile became a cunning one. "No, indeed, sir. My intention is to become a Murrain again. A living, breathing Murrain, with strong hands that will seize this world and shake it up once more. Now, Jacob . . . there's no need to step away from me, or wear such a worried frown. I won't take possession of you. No, sir, you're far too old." He spoke with chilling clarity. "Listen to me, Jacob. Earlier, the constable revealed that you have a grandson by the name of Jack. He is mine, Jacob. All mine. I will occupy his body. He will become Justice Murrain."

CHAPTER TWELVE

Kerry Herne was worried. In the Calder-Brigg motel, which the excavation team were using as a temporary base, she sent e-mails to her university colleagues, who were pressing the government to build sea defenses. That wasn't her immediate concern, however. Kerry recalled how last night she'd spoken to Jacob Murrain. The man had been convinced that by day everyone would be safe. That there'd be no more instances of possession. And that the spirits of Justice Murrain and his thug army, which rejoiced under the name "Battle Men," would remain trapped in the earth during day-lit hours. Night was the dangerous time, Jacob had insisted.

Only here at the motel, an hour's drive from Crowdale, did Kerry feel safe. That there'd be no repeat of the occurrence last night when some brutal force had invaded her mind, then forced to abuse herself. Outside, the lights of cars slid by. She was tempted to slip on her coat and simply walk through the crowds heading out to bars and restaurants. The sheer "ordinariness" of it all would be reassuring. Because what worried her was this: despite Jacob Murrain's assurance that they'd be safe by day she'd witnessed what had befallen Nat Stross that afternoon. The sun had been shining. The graveyard dig site had been bright. Yet Nat had shown every sign that some other personality had overwhelmed his normally cheerful demeanor. He'd gone from carefully extracting Roman pots to screaming in a very un-Nat-like voice that he didn't want to be buried alive. When Kerry had gone to him she'd noticed his expression was un-Nat-like, too. There were something feral about it. Like an animal caught in a trap—fear mixed with pure viciousness. What's more, he hadn't recognized her when she'd tried to help him.

So, okay, the episode had lasted mere minutes. But she'd seen how he'd become some *other* person. And the sun had shone down.

Kerry murmured to herself, "You're mistaken, Mr. Murrain, they don't just come out at night. Nobody is safe now. They can strike by day."

CHAPTER THIRTEEN

After the film Pel and Jack were strolling through the town center when Jack picked up a voice mail on his phone. He moved away from an Argentinean restaurant that was not only bustling with people, but played tango music loud enough to drown out most conversations.

Pel watched him stand there, phone pressed to his ear. With the large gray eyes and mane of black hair, his looks were timeless compared with the other men passing by, who were clearly working hard to be fashionable. *Don't watch him,* she told herself; however, lately she'd found it hard to take her eyes off him. And after that kiss in the cinema she realized this was the start of something. For some reason it seemed as dangerous as it was thrilling. She'd not felt quite like this with a man before. A voice in her head warned: *Back out now while you can. Go on that trip to Germany you've been promising yourself. Now's the time to escape . . .* Yet the sensation that tickled along her nerves was undoubtedly delicious. She yearned for Jack to touch her again. Hell, not just touch . . .

He came back to her through people streaming toward the bars. A puzzled smile played on his lips. "I've just listened to a voice mail from my grandfather."

"Is something wrong?"

"I'm not sure. At least, I don't think so. But he's asking me to stay away from Crowdale tonight. And not to go back until daylight."

"It's nothing to do with those two thugs again who threatened him?"

Again, he could only give a baffled shrug. "He insisted that I shouldn't worry . . . but he's also adamant that I stay here in Calder-Brigg tonight. He wouldn't have asked me to stay unless he had good reason." He scratched his head. "What I have to do now is find a bed for the night."

She slipped her arm round his waist. "Something tells me that will not be a problem." A moment later she found his mouth with hers. Excitement, like lightning, flashed down her spine.

CHAPTER FOURTEEN

The four men had been drinking since early that evening. When one of them got word that his ex-girlfriend had been seen driving her new flame up to the section of cliff known locally as Make-Out Mount, the men had hatched their plan. The clock on the dash recorded eighteen minutes before midnight when they stopped the van behind the car on the cliff top.

Mitch was pissed that Bex was seeing another guy. It had driven him into a blazing rage when she walked out on him three months ago. He'd smashed up the apartment, killed her dog, and beaten up her brother in the street. There were no limits to Mitch's rage. His drinking buddies spurred him on. They got all hot, sweaty, and excited when they saw him thrash a guy. Usually, a couple of meaty punches from his fists were enough to floor Mitch's adversary. Of course, that didn't get them off the hook. Mitch liked to stomp heads. Crack, crack, blood all over the place.

So Mitch's buddies were already squealing with excitement by the time they reached the remote spur of cliff, 150 feet above pounding surf. Now for another kind of pound time. Bex's new cuddly bunny was gonna get it.

When Mitch drove up to the car the action had started already. In the blaze of headlights they could see that Bex braced herself on all fours on the backseat while Billy-boy, the new boyfriend, did his impression of a mating dog as he slammed into her. Both were knotted so deep into the love-making that they didn't even notice the van arrive.

"Are those two blind?" shouted Drake. "Look at him! Billy's rodding her senseless! They've not seen us! How can anyone not see the fucking headlights."

Mitch went wild with jealousy. "I'll kill them. I'm going to stuff his balls down his throat."

Before the van had even stopped he leaped out. Through the glare of headlights he charged the fucking pair. Mitch punched Billy so hard it uncoupled his cock from Bex's flesh. With blood cascading from his mouth, Billy slumped back.

Bex, at last, realized things had gone to shit. Trying to tug up her pants, as she attempted to evade her ex, she started screaming. Mitch aimed a kick at her butt.

Then Mitch turned to Drake. "You still got that camera phone?"

Drake pulled it from his pocket.

Mitch snarled, "You film what I do to these two. Then I want you to send that film to everyone who knows these pair of fuckers. Got that?"

"Be my pleasure, Mitch."

The others whooped to encourage Mitch. The man was nothing more than a slab of hard muscle and no brain. If he wasn't boring out women he was busting guys' faces. Now he intended to do both. And knowing Mitch it could even be at the same time.

Fourteen minutes to midnight. He slapped Bex down with the palm of his hand. She slumped down beside her bleeding boyfriend. Her half-naked body gleamed in the headlights.

"You film this, Drake."

"Sure thing, boss." He pressed the phone's record button. A copycat image of what happened in real life appeared on the little two-inch screen.

Billy-boy tried to climb to his feet. Mitch felled him with a kick. Sweet Jesus, how that kid screamed. It sounded like a flock of seagulls had caught fire.

The drunken men laughed. Mitch turned his attention to the woman who had once shared his bed. A hellcat of a women who had once writhed and sucked and bit and screamed with pleasure.

Sure was screaming now. But pleasure had frig all to do with it. Mitch had decided to drag her round the car by her hair.

Thirteen minutes to midnight.

As he filmed the cliff-top fun, Drake felt a sudden pressure against his head. "Aneurysm." The word suggested bloated arteries giving way under pressure. A ruinous explosion in the brain. He froze, still filming. Now Mitch rode Bex—beautiful, naked Bex. Rode her like a donkey; she shuffled on all fours, he astride her back. Two of Mitch's buddies cheered. Billy-boy whimpered; he held his bloody face in his hands.

Twelve minutes to midnight. A sense of a hard, cold object being forced through his skull made Drake lock up tight. He became statuelike. Yet he still held the camera phone up to film Mitch rain punches down onto Billy-boy's face.

Eleven minutes to midnight. Drake's mind had been displaced by an intruder. One of Justice Murrain's henchmen was in the driver's seat, so to speak. The possessor enjoyed the spectacle of torture through Drake's eyes. Not only did he marvel at the little box in his hand that captured Mitch stomping on the naked gentleman's stomach, but he understood how it worked. It was so very easy to extract knowledge of this instrument—this phone—from the mind that he'd subdued. The possessed man smiled. Oh, this would be enjoyment indeed.

Yet, sadly, it would be a brief excursion from the grave tonight. The possessor knew that the pull of the mosaic and all its powers would be strong. He wouldn't be able to resist for long. Soon it would draw him back into the ground until the next time. For shame. 'Tis a pity. He smirked. Never mind. He'd extract maximum pleasure from this little nighttime passion play on the cliff.

By this time, the big muscular one, known as Mitch, had removed his heavy leather belt from his pantaloons . . . no, the correct modern term is *blue jeans*. With this formidable leather strap he whipped the naked buttocks of a buxom beauty. Each blow made her breasts dance as she shuffled on her knees. Oh, could England still be as merry as this? The possessor giggled. Relish these games. Applaud such invention.

He watched the man deliver five more swishes with the belt (goodness, how each swish ended with a mighty SLAP when leather struck buttock). The possessor felt a great force tug at him. Alas, not long now. Soon he would be drawn back into the earth to wait with his fellow Battle Men until the next release.

Eight minutes to midnight. Quickly, he returned to the van. There he found a large hammer tossed among a mess of other tools in the back. Once he had secured a comfortable grip on the wooden shaft he returned to the bloody panto-mime. Mitch directed mighty swings with the belt on the back of beauty's legs. Oh, those screams. Those woman sounds . . . they set alight his veins.

But time was running out.

Seven minutes to midnight. Holding the camera phone in one hand, the possessor filmed the back of the heads of the two men, who yelled encouragement at their brave friend. The slayer of the she-dragon; she who clutched her buttocks while yodeling, "Uh-uh-eeew!"

The possessor smashed the hammer into the back of one gent's skull. The other turned in surprise. Without missing a beat, he cracked the hammerhead into the center of the bul-bous nose. Blood erupted, filling the air with droplets. In the light from the cars it turned the night all misty red. A second blow knocked a goodly portion of brain from the skull.

Neither the woman nor the one known as Billy-boy noticed. They were soundly being made tender by Mitch's beating.

Five minutes to midnight. Quick. It's starting. The pos-sessor had begun to lose his grip on this young buck's flesh.

Now Mitch knelt on the women's naked breasts as his big hands gripped her throat. She looked up at him in surprise through a wash of soft hair. It seemed as if she'd been taken unaware by this turn of events. Man seed and lady blood made gloriously crimson her thighs. Now her life drained away as she lay there beneath strangling hands.

The possessor restrained his next blow. *Clunk*. The hammerhead tapped Mitch's temple. It merely stunned him. He flopped down onto the half-asphyxiated Bex.

Swiftly, the possessor rolled Mitch's two dead friends over the edge of the cliff. With those disposed of, he dragged the senseless Mitch to the car; once there, he hauled him into the passenger seat. Then, in a flash, the possessor ensconced himself in the driver's seat. It didn't take more than a moment to filch from the displaced mind the knowledge to start the car's motor, then set the machine in forward motion. Directly toward the lip of the cliff. Nothing but fresh sea air beyond. The possessor put his arm round Mitch's neck then pulled him close, until the sides of their heads touched.

The possessor still held the camera, so he could film them both. His thumb found the send button. He'd dispatch those images recorded tonight to everyone in this device's phone book. But not yet . . . just a few more seconds.

Mitch woke as the car neared the cliff's edge. He struggled to break free.

"What the hell're you doing, Drake? Let go!"

The car's nose bumped up over the lip of soil. Stars filled the windshield. After that, a perfect view of a nighttime sea. Then the car's nose dipped for a view of the surf 150 feet below. The machine dived downward.

Mitch was screaming. The possessor was filming—and enjoying every moment.

One minute to midnight.

Air howled by the car. Soon it traveled faster than it ever did before.

The possessor hit SEND. Mitch cried with terror. Footage

of the night's bloody events flashed from phone to transmitter, then to dozens of homes in the county. Phones on bedside tables began calling out to their owners that video clips were being received.

The car struck.

Midnight.

ONE DAY LEFT

CHAPTER ONE

At seven thirty Pel Minton, already dressed, opened the motel room blind. Bright October sunlight flooded in. A figure beneath the bedclothes groaned.

"Wakey, wakey," Pel sang out brightly. "Come on. Up and at 'em. The bus will be here at eight. You don't want to be late. Trenches to be dug. Ten tons of English soil to be shifted by supper time!"

In the motel room an assortment of beds and sofas yielded half a dozen females—a mixture of archaeologists and dirt monkeys. Kerry had managed to cram her team into every available space.

A red-haired student kicked back her sheet. "Why is Pel so nauseatingly cheerful?"

Another grinned. "Didn't you hear the news? Pel has a new man in her life."

"Come on, spill the beans." Redhead was enthralled.

"She was out with him last night. It's Jack Murrain. The grandson of nutso Jacob Murrain, who guards the mausoleum."

"No!"

Pel laughed. "We had a date, that's all."

Redhead answered a knock at the door. "Well, well, speak of the devil." She kept the door ajar by only an inch or so. "Morning, Mr. Murrain. I'm afraid not all of us are dressed yet. Yes, okay, I'll let Pel know."

One of the other girls giggled. "He's keen to see you again."

Redhead smirked. "Perhaps he's been out early to buy an engagement ring." The smirk became laugher. "He wants to see you right away . . . probably down on bended knee in the corridor." She deepened her voice to mimic Jack. "Pel Minton, dear heart, I am but a humble woodcutter. However, will you make me the happiest man in the world and say 'I do.'"

Another girl poked her head from under a blanket. "Pel? Do you think there's a chance a good-looking guy will save my neck today? I need a new boyfriend, too."

Pel grinned. The ribbing was good-natured; she knew it would continue for the rest of the day—at least. As she stepped through the motel room door, she wondered why Jack needed to see her so urgently. Last night he'd slept on a camp bed in one of the rooms occupied by the guys on the team. She and Jack had agreed to meet at eight, so he could drive her back to the cemetery dig site. The rest would travel in a convoy of cars and vans. An unpleasant thought struck her. Maybe he's going to backtrack on last night. *We had a great evening, but I'm not ready for commitment yet. It was just a bit of fun, right? See you, around, Pel.*

Pel found Jack in the reception area. He'd bought her coffee from the machine. A middle-aged guy sat behind the desk watching TV. Apart from that single member of staff, the pair were the only people in the room. Jack indicated a corner where chairs had been arranged around a low table.

"What's the matter, Jack?"

"Grab a seat. I need to show you something."

"Jack. Something's wrong, isn't it? I've never seen you look so serious."

He pulled a phone from his jacket. "Listen. A couple of nights ago it seemed as if Crowdale went crazy. Me included. Yesterday, my grandfather begged me not to go home."

"Your grandfather's okay?"

"I hope to God he is. I haven't been able to reach him yet." He thumbed buttons on his phone. "Anyway, that wasn't why I needed to speak to you."

"Oh?" Here it comes. *Pel, I don't think we should see one another again.*

Instead of uttering words of rejection, he showed her the phone's screen. "When I switched it on this morning I got this. A series of video clips." He grimaced. "They're not pleasant."

"So, why—"

He interrupted. "Because I'm sure it has a bearing on what happened the other night. Watch." Thumbing a control, he held the device so she could see the screen. "As I say, you're going to see some intense stuff."

Jack hadn't exaggerated. At first, it seemed typical phone footage captured when people had been hitting the liquor hard. The outdoors scene had been lit by car headlights. An area of rough grass. Laughter, shouts. Drunken horseplay. In seconds, though, Pel realized she witnessed a vicious attack. A guy with his pants round his ankles got a thrashing from a young thug built like a heavyweight boxer. Then came a flurry of other shots, revealing a half-naked woman being ridden like she were an ass, then beaten with a belt. Moments later, the attacker knelt on the woman, strangling her.

"Dear God, this is awful. Don't show me any more."

"No, you must." Arm quivering with tension, he held the phone closer.

Now, she saw two heads on the little screen. It could have been the kind of gooey shot lovers take; they sit side by side, their heads touching, as both look into the camera that one of them holds. Straightaway, Pel realized that these were two young men in a car. The car jolted over rough ground. One of the men, the thug who'd beaten up the courting couple, sagged down, clearly only half conscious. The other wore such a leering expression of delight on his face that it made Pel feel physically sick. Pure evil blazed from the guy's eyes. This was someone who drank cruelty like an alcoholic gulps vodka. This individual feasted on sadism. Inflicting suffering was his true love.

"I don't want to see what happens next. It's going to be awful."

"Keep watching," Jack insisted.

At that moment on-screen a remarkable transformation occurred in the car. The flesh of the guys' faces rippled. The thug recovered consciousness. His eyes went wide. The expression of horror managed to horrify Pel in its own right. Then something really strange happened. All this crud that accumulates in old cars—paper cups, gum wrappers, cigarette packets, lighters, coins, maps, pens, lengths of string, paperclips—all of that, which normally languishes in storage compartments under the dash and in doors, abruptly drifted upward. Coins, pens, silver foil, beer bottles, you name it, became weightless. This, and the way the men's faces rippled, reminded her of astronauts floating in zero gravity out in space. That's when she examined the screen closer. Through the car's rear window she could identify a cliff top in the taillights. It receded at a hell of a rate.

Screams came from the thug. The other guy wore a happy smile.

The screen crashed to black.

"Oh, my God," Pel breathed. "This was filmed as the car fell from the top of a cliff." She shuddered. "Jack, how did you get this?"

"A guy I know sent it to my phone just around midnight last night."

"He's sick."

"He's dead." Jack switched off the phone. "The happy-looking soul in the movie you've just watched is . . . was Drake Epworth. He filmed this; then he must have pressed send just before the car hit the beach. The other guy was Mitch Gill, a nasty piece of work, the town bully. He was the one attacking his ex and her boyfriend."

"Then this Drake Epworth must have been even worse. Who films their own suicide?"

"Yeah . . ." Jack said, doubtful. "Only he wasn't that kind of guy. He was sneaky. He liked to gossip behind people's backs, but this wasn't his style, if you could call filming your own death 'style.' He worked for us from time to time, when we needed an extra pair of hands with the logging, that's why he had my number. I've known him for years. Yet when I saw his face on that screen this morning it was like I didn't know him at all. As if something had got into him. Insanity? Drugs? Only it seemed to be more than . . ." His voice tailed away as his attention was caught by the TV. "There's your proof the film wasn't a hoax."

Pel turned to the TV. It showed footage of a mangled wreck lying in a pool of water. The clerk had the sound turned down to the point where she only heard snatches of the newsreader's commentary. ". . . remains of a car found on the beach this morning . . . police say it's too early to say . . . bodies of two local men . . . Mr. Gill, released from prison last month, where he'd served . . . next of kin have been informed . . ."

Jack Murrain was a man in a hurry. He found it hard to sit still.

Pel said, "I'm sorry about the loss of your friends."

"They were no friends of mine. Truth is, the town's better off without them. Especially Gill. He'd done plenty of prison time for nearly killing people because he'd taken a dislike to their faces." He stood up. "If you'll excuse me, I'll try calling my grandfather again. I'm worried about him."

He went out through the doors to stand outside. She appreciated his charming manner. He considered it bad form to make a call in her presence. Not that she minded. Come to that, there was a lot she didn't mind about Jack. Often, she found herself picturing his face when he wasn't there. And if there had been a vacant room in the motel last night, then those hours of intimate darkness might have turned out very differently. As it was, they'd found themselves bunking in separate rooms. Of course, there was always tonight. "If Crowdale hasn't gone totally nuts by the time we get there," she murmured to herself.

Jack returned. "Something is wrong," he told her brusquely.

"My grandfather has asked me . . . well, demanded, really . . . that I stay out of town."

"Why?"

"He won't say. Other than to trust him, and to find an old friend of his in Calder-Brigg, who'll be able to spare me a room."

"He didn't give you any clue about what's happening there?"

"None."

"So what are you going to do, Jack?"

He flashed her a rather wild smile. "Disobey him, of course. I'm going right back there to talk to him face-to-face."

"You'd disobey him?"

"He's been a father to me, Pel. If he's in danger I'm going to be at his side to meet it head-on." He pulled out his keys. "Grab your things. I'll meet you at the truck in thirty seconds."

CHAPTER TWO

The cops' change in shift brought new guards for Horace Neville—or at least the *individual* officers believed was Horace Neville. If anything, that morning, rumors circulated that the wife of one of the constables had been brought to the station in a manic state of mind, not to say undress. As the constable had hurried off duty to get his wife home he'd called out, "Watch Neville. He's changed. Don't trust him."

Three police officers were instructed to take their murder suspect, Horace Neville, by car to the county's police HQ in Calder-Brigg. There, the prisoner would be interrogated by detectives expert in handling psychiatric cases.

A sergeant approached the cell. He'd known Horace Neville for years. Ever since Horace had been the unusual child, who'd run down to the beach, where he'd rush into the surf, because he said he saw pirate ships sailing by and he wanted to join them. The sergeant, nor anyone else, saw any pirates. Neither did they notice the other marvels that Horace Neville claimed to behold: everything from foxes shopping in the supermarket to the invisible companion who sat with him outside his home.

The sergeant pushed his face toward the bars. Beyond them, Horace, a giant of a man, a hitherto gentle giant, stood gazing out as the sun rose over a blustery Crowdale. He wore a paper coverall; undoubtedly, his bloody clothes were now being scrutinized by forensics.

The big man murmured without turning, "*Veni, vidi, vici.*"

"What was that you said, Horace?"

The man spun round. "I said I want my mother. I'm frightened. I want her."

The sergeant sensed that Horace, who normally behaved like a little child, was secretly laughing at him. A fierce intelligence burned in his eye. Then Horace's voice quavered. "I want my mother now. Take me home."

"I'm sorry, son." The sergeant spoke gently. "We can't do that. You see, your mother's had a bit of an accident. So, for now, we're going to drive you over to Calder-Brigg, where someone needs to talk to you."

"Doctors?" Horace's voice had the timbre of a scared little boy. "I don't like doctors."

"No, another policeman. Don't worry, they won't be nasty to you."

"Can I have some clothes, please?" His huge fingers scraped at his chest. "This pajama thing is scratchy."

"Once you get to Calder-Brigg I'm sure they'll fix you up with some proper clothes, son. The constables are here now. We'll take you out to the car."

"Oh, now?" Was that a glint of eagerness in his manner?

"That's right, Horace. A nice drive to Calder-Brigg. Nothing to worry about."

He produced a set of handcuffs. "We'll have to fasten these to your wrists, Horace."

"No."

"It's the rule, son."

"I'll be good, mister."

The sergeant knew Horace's way of speaking from past meetings. Now, however, the inflection had changed. When he said smartly, *I'll be good, mister*, it came across just a bit too glib. The sergeant eyed the big man on the other side of the bars. Horace smiled.

"I really do promise to be good as gold, mister."

The sergeant handed the handcuffs to another constable. This officer had less patience.

"Come closer, then put both your hands through the opening in the gate."

Horace, smiling, consented. The constable snapped on the cuffs.

"Okay," the sergeant said. "Now, we're good to go. You can let him out, Johnson."

The constable produced a key then unlocked the cell.

"We've got the car parked just outside in the yard," explained the sergeant. "There'll be three of us with you in the car. You'll sit in the back with me."

Horace nodded. When he walked purposefully from the cell into the corridor, his wrists manacled, the sergeant held up his hand.

"Whoa, aren't you forgetting someone?"

The constables chuckled. The sergeant glared at them. Horace merely frowned; he didn't know what the man was talking about.

The sergeant nodded at the cell. "Who are you forgetting?"

"Who am I forgetting?" Horace stared at him.

"The little fellow. You know, your friend who sits next to you, when you're on the chairs outside the house. Bobby?"

Horace merely appeared annoyed; then the sergeant noticed his eyes slip out of focus, as he searched for a memory. At last, a dopey grin came back to Horace's face. "Yes, the little fellow. Come along, Bobby. We're going in a car. Can he sit on my lap?"

The constables smirked. One couldn't resist saying, "He can bloody well sit inside the engine for all we care."

The sergeant knew about Horace's imaginary friend. If he humored the big man it might make his journey to the outside world less fraught. Of course, at some point the man, whatever his mentally restricted state, must be made to understand that he'd beaten his own mother to death.

When they reached the car the sergeant felt a tug of unease. It lacked the toughened glass screen between the rear seats and those of the front. Until he'd spoken to Horace

Neville that morning, a lack of a security screen hadn't been an issue, but the sergeant's instincts made him suspicious of Horace. The man just didn't seem like his usual self. Normally, the giant would shamble along in an ungainly, clumsy manner. Today, he moved with precision; he carried himself as straight-backed as a soldier. Strange.

However, the glint of sunlight on the cuffs reassured the officer. The chains would safely contain the man.

"Okay, Horace, I'll help you get into the car. Sit down, then swing those big legs of yours behind the driver's seat. That's it."

Soon the car pulled away from the police station into the town's busy streets. However, within a few miles they joined a deserted country road that led toward Calder-Brigg. Horace didn't speak. He watched the passing scenery with interest, as if much of it was new to him. A train pulling out of a rural station was especially fascinating.

The only time he did speak was at a crossroads. Horace murmured, "Ah, yonder lane ran down to Murrain Hall."

The driver accelerated along the highway. There was little in the way of morning traffic out here. In that relaxed state that comes with being a passenger in a car the sergeant suddenly recalled what Horace had uttered in the cell that morning. *Veni, vidi, vici.* The sergeant's long-dead history teacher would have nodded with satisfaction as the cop recalled a fact from one of his lessons. *Veni, vidi, vici.* It was Latin. It meant: I came, I saw, I conquered.

The sergeant regarded the giant squashed into the backseat beside him, just as he lifted his manacled hands. Horace—or at least the figure they identified as Horace—gave a cold smile. At the same time he snapped the chain links on the cuffs.

Then there was screaming. Terrible screaming. Before he died the sergeant realized those screams vented from his own lips.

CHAPTER THREE

Pel Minton would have dearly liked to accompany Jack Murrain to check on his grandfather. This had all the makings of an intriguing mystery. She wanted to find out why certain people in the town were acting so strangely. There'd been unsettling news reports on the truck's radio as Jack had driven toward Crowdale. In addition to the two guys riding the car over the cliff's edge to their deaths, there had been random outbreaks of violence. Witnesses repeated the telling phrase that the perpetrators "weren't themselves."

Pel checked the time, as Jack maneuvered the truck along narrow country roads. If only she could grab a few moments to hear why Jacob Murrain was so desperate for his grandson to remain in Calder-Brigg. However, she knew she'd be missed at the dig site. Now, it was a case of all hands on deck. Time was short. Already the ocean would have claimed yet more dry land.

Jack braked the truck at the cemetery gates. Already, early arrivers from the team had started work. The mausoleum lamp still lit its interior in a rosy light. Meanwhile, away over the sea, a bank of thick black clouds advanced menacingly toward the mainland.

"Looks like stormy weather's on its way," Jack observed. "I'll give you a call and let you know how my grandfather is as soon as I can."

"Thanks." She opened the door. "Be sure to let me know if I can be of help. I'll see you later." For an instant, she paused.

After the kisses of last night she wondered if it would be repeated now. Though the anxious way he tapped his fingertips on the steering wheel signaled that he was preoccupied with hurrying home to check on his grandfather. "And Jack?"

He glanced at her.

Pel smiled. "Be safe."

Jack nodded. A moment later he gunned the truck back up the lane.

Pel zipped up her jacket against a biting wind. Figures on the dig site were hunched, muffled things. That cold really tore through you. Pel hoped someone had remembered to bring the flasks of hot coffee. They'd need it today.

She made her way amid the gravestones to the trench she'd occupied yesterday. One of the archaeology students brushed soil away from a pair of skeletons lying side by side.

"Twin burial," he said. "Probably a family tragedy. See burning to the finger bones? My guess is they both died in a house fire." He shook his head. "Rush mats on the floor, thatched roofs, open fires? A deathtrap. We don't have time to examine this one properly. I'll photograph the bones in situ. Once I'm done, would you cover them with soil for me?" He gave a sad smile. "Treat them gently, won't you, Pel? They died young."

Who says there's no room for sentiment in archaeology? She'd seen more than one seemingly brusque archaeologist, who loved nothing more to cuss, swear, and crack tasteless jokes, turn away with a tear in their eye when excavating the bones of children.

More vehicles arrived. Soon the team were near thirty strong. Most worked in the excavation trenches in the graveyard. Nat chose to dig a test pit perilously close to the cliff's edge. He desperately wanted to uncover a section of Temple Central earthworks before they fell into the sea. For once, Kerry was nowhere to be seen. Usually, the whirlwind of a woman would be zipping round, checking finds, offering words of encouragement, or helping manhandle stone slabs that would defeat many a muscleman.

Pel worked hard. Even so, curiosity about Jacob Murrain's plea to stay out of town became a maddening psychological itch. Thirty minutes after starting work, a car roared up to the archaeologists' parked vehicles. Kerry shot from the driving seat, climbed the graveyard fence, then ran through the long grass. She beckoned them as she approached.

"Gather round, people!" The wind seemed to want to shout her down. An icy blast of air gusted through the cemetery, hurling dirt into people's eyes. "Just two minutes of your time, please. I'll make this fast."

They formed a semicircle, all bulky in their layers of sweaters and fleeces. Dark clouds swamped the once blue sky. *Jack's right. A storm is coming. A ferocious one at that.* Pel had to put her arm round a tomb's stone angel to stop herself being toppled by the gale.

"Is that everybody? Nat, you hear this, too. Then I'll let you get back to the dig!"

Nat hauled himself out of the pit, then loped from the cliff to where a strange audience had gathered—one that seemed to consist of both human beings and stone tombstones that, for all the world, appeared to have gathered to hear Kerry's words.

She had to fight torrents of frigid air to make herself audible. "Listen. At the risk of being melodramatic . . . I bring good news—and a warning." The winds nearly toppled her. The woman steadied herself with a tombstone that bore a skull and crossbones. "Good news first. Preliminary test results are back on the prehistoric skeleton—the one found at the entrance to Temple Central—and with the saliva swab Pel Minton obtained from Jack Murrain." She grew with triumph. "They are a match! We have established the oldest blood link between skeletal remains and a living human being." Immediately, there was applause and shouts of YES! "That means the Murrain family have lived in this area for at least five thousand years. Temple Central is unique. Overnight, it has become one of the most valuable heritage sites in the world."

Nat didn't so much as shout as erupt. "Thank God, Thank God!"

"Thank Pel Minton, too; she got both samples. And nearly died in the process when the cliff gave way."

Nat bounded over the graves to hug Pel. "Kerry. Do we get special status?"

"Yes!"

"So we get that damn seawall?"

She grinned. "Absolutely. Work starts at daybreak tomorrow. Contractors will stack what are basically steel cages full of rocks at the base of the cliff. Ladies and gentlemen, we have saved the Murrain site."

"Joy, oh joy!" Nat dropped on his hands and knees to kiss the ground. "Temple Central will be preserved. I'm going to devote my life to excavating it. Ye gods, I'll write a book! Make TV documentaries! Then die happy! And be buried right here!" Clasping his hands together, he laughed until tears streamed down his face.

Kerry grinned. "I may be totally wrong, but something tells me that Nat is pleased."

Nat jumped to his feet to waltz circles with another dirt monkey. "Kerry, they've got to give us the contract for a premier investigation. No more dig and grab."

"First things first. We need to stabilize a mile of cliff, and all this ground."

Nat shook his fist at the ocean. "Don't you dare take any more of my precious site. I won't let you. My sheer willpower will stop you. Back, Neptune, back!"

"Nat, don't tempt fate. Haven't you heard of 'hubris'?"

Pel spoke up as gales moaned through the cemetery. "Jacob Murrain should be told. After all, it means the mausoleum and the mosaic will be saved, too."

"Absolutely." She tossed the car keys to Pel. "You know where he lives. Tell him the good news. Mr. Murrain is our ally now."

Nat remembered something. "You said you had a warning, too?"

"I have indeed." Hard particles of white bounced against the grass. Hail stones. Whoppers at that. "Please listen carefully to what I have to say. Other tests have revealed that there are spores in the soil. Fungus spores."

The team were baffled by the warning.

"Fungus?" Nat scratched his head. "What's so dangerous about that? We encounter fungal spores all the time."

"Not like these, you don't. They contain toxins that are related to the chemical found in LSD—that's tabs of acid to the streetwise here."

"There's a risk we might get high?"

"The spores affect the brain," Kerry told them. "You might hallucinate. Behave out of character. Even imagine that a spirit, or ghost, has taken control of you."

Many of the diggers laughed.

"No, I'm serious." And her expression was *deadly* serious. "Working conditions here, seeing as we're on top of a cliff, are hazardous. If anyone's reasoning, or self-control, is impaired by the spores, then we . . ." The hail fell faster. ". . . then we might be in danger. If you feel at all strange . . . disorientated . . . or simply don't seem yourself, then put up your hand and tell your supervisor. Likewise, if anyone notices a colleague behaving oddly tell me or a senior team member. Then we'll get the affected person away from here fast. Okay?"

Everyone appeared puzzled by the warning but they chorused their okays.

Kerry smiled. "The main thing, we have won a victory. We're going to save this archaeological site. Now, my dears, dig your little hearts out." She shielded her face against stinging particles of ice. "Or at least until the hailstorm stops us."

They returned to work. Kerry gave Pel a thumbs-up, then nodded at her car. Pel hurried toward the cemetery gate. She couldn't wait to see the Murrains' faces when she revealed that the mosaic would be preserved. The only oddity that niggled: Kerry's warning about narcotic spores in the soil. She'd heard of psychoactive spores forming naturally on rye infected with ergot (where it could become dangerously toxic) but never in the dirt beneath your feet. Kerry had used the phrase "not feeling yourself." The newsreaders had repeated the same phrase used by witnesses to violence in the town. Specifically, that the people responsible for the attacks "weren't themselves." Then a couple of nights ago Jack "wasn't himself" when he rammed the drunk's face into the wall, then kissed her so roughly he cut her lip. What's more, he couldn't remember doing either the day after. Curioser and curioser.

The force of the hailstorm didn't allow her to dwell on the mystery. Pieces of ice the size of grapes hurtled out of a black sky. When they struck exposed skin they stung like hornets. Pel dashed the rest of the way to the car, then all but flung herself behind the wheel. *Dear God. Whiteout.* Hail rattled furiously against steel. In the graveyard, the diggers scattered before the force of the storm. Some hunkered down into the trenches, their hoods pulled over their heads. Others sought refuge in tents used as temporary store places during the day.

Nobody will venture out in that, she told herself, for fear of being flayed. At least these savage hailstorms tended to be short-lived. Once visibility had improved she'd drive to the Murrain family home with the good news.

She hoped with all her heart that Jack would have good news about his grandfather when she arrived there. Because, right now, she suspected that something had gone seriously amiss in Crowdale.

CHAPTER FOUR

Kerry Herne sheltered beneath a canvas awning not far from the mausoleum. The glow from the lamp inside, so faithfully tended by Mr. Murrain, turned the falling hail golden.

On the one hand, Kerry wanted to celebrate that they'd saved this historical site from coastal erosion (or as good as: soon defenses against the surf would be in place). Yet on the other hand, fearsome worries plagued her.

For one, she knew the truth: evil forces were at work here. She'd been briefly possessed by one of the devil spirits. Yesterday, Nat had been invaded in the same way, too. The perfidious ghost had driven aside his mind, then taken control. Not only did she believe what Jacob Murrain had told her, that the mosaic was basically a prison cell for the ghosts of Justice Murrain and his henchmen, *but*, and this was really important, she knew something that the man didn't. The spirits weren't restricted to possessing people by night. They could also invade a person's mind by day. That's why she'd invented a story about the soil being contaminated by fungus spores that had the same hallucinogenic properties as LSD. Clearly, it would be an uphill task to convince her team that they were in danger of demonic possession. Until one experienced it for oneself, it was a difficult truth to swallow. So, the explanation based on psychoactive spores had been the most expedient. Despite her colleagues' puzzlement, Kerry was confident that they had believed it. Okay. It was a gamble to continue the dig here, yet she knew she couldn't halt it now.

After all, it would take time to install the barrier at the base of the cliffs. And how would she explain to her superiors why she'd stopped work on site? The threat of coastal erosion was a compelling argument to continue the excavation.

God willing, her team would be untouched today, and they wouldn't experience the brutal presence of an alien mind supplanting their own. If they did, however, at least she'd gone some way to prepare them. At the first sign of a problem the affected individual could be bundled away. With their limbs gaffer-taped together, if need be.

The wind blew harder. Kerry Herne shivered, as she crouched beside trays full of bones from human beings who worked, played, and made love here before the great pyramids of Egypt had even seen the light of the African sun.

CHAPTER FIVE

For an octogenarian, Jacob Murrain's eyesight was near perfect. After the blizzardlike hailstorm had abated, he witnessed a figure approach the house along the hilltop path. Even at a distance of a full quarter of a mile Jacob identified the man immediately. For a while, Jacob stood there on the front lawn, to watch Horace Neville's advance toward the house. Not that it was Horace Neville anymore. Though they were still hundreds of yards apart, Jacob knew that the man's eyes met his with a fierce glare. What's more, the approaching figure moved with a confident swagger. This could be a rich landlord visiting his poor tenant.

When Horace marched through a field gate a hundred yards away Jacob Murrain did the wise thing. Calmly, he withdrew to the house, then locked the stout door behind him. That done, he climbed the stairs to the landing where he opened a window that overlooked the driveway.

He could view his visitor plainly. The giant still wore the paper coverall issued by the police. His bold confidence appeared to increase with every step he took.

Jacob leaned out a little so he could check the road that led to the house. So far, it was deserted. As were the surrounding fields. The only other house was a good half mile away, so Jacob didn't expect any casual visitors to drop by. A good thing, too. Because if they did, Jacob didn't rate their chances of surviving more than a few moments.

The thing that wore Horace Neville's body stopped ten yards from the house. A smile spread across the giant's face when it saw Jacob looking out at him from the upstairs window.

A cold breeze tugged at Jacob's hair; however, it wasn't the chilling power of the weather that made him shiver; it was the gloating triumph in his visitor's eye.

Jacob's voice rang out with a clear strength, "I know who you are."

The man aped a child's voice. "It's so co-cold, Mr. Murrain. Aren't you going to let me and the little fellow inside to warm our ickle-lickle hands?"

"You don't fool me. Horace Neville's been pushed aside, hasn't he? The man I'm speaking to right now is my ancestor, isn't that right?"

The giant smiled. "How on earth could you prove that?"

"Proof be damned. You are Justice Murrain. You know it. I know it. So no more games!"

"In that case, show me your good manners. Invite me in, sir."

"Never."

"Do you prefer me to kick down your door?"

"You can try." Jacob remained calm. "But I've built this house like a fortress. Reinforced doors. Steel bars over the ground-floor windows."

"So you've been expecting me all along?"

"Don't flatter yourself, you devil. Because of what you did more than two hundred years ago the Murrain family have been treated like criminals. The town despises us. Trouble always comes looking for us, so I made sure our home would keep unwelcome visitors out."

The giant patted his chest. "Ignore the fact that I occupy the body of the idiot. To all intents and purposes I am Justice Murrain. Consider me to be that man. So I am your forefather. Accord me respect."

"Never. You are a monster. I've devoted my life to protecting the mosaic. That was the prison that kept you, and the scum who followed you, locked down tight into the ground."

"It's failing. Those occult chains that bound us there are breaking one by one. As you see for yourself, I'm out. So, dear kin of mine, aren't you going to ask me how I threw off the constable's shackles? Or how I learned where you live?"

"You think you're smart, but you're not. If it wasn't for the sea eroding the cliffs you'd still be trapped under the mosaic. It isn't your clever mind that got you out of the mausoleum, it's geology. The cliffs are boulder clay, not solid rock."

"Maybe God made me free. To punish all you sinners."

"God? You've been delivered here by Satan."

"Sticks and stones, my good sir. In truth, I came across a gentlemen walking in a field over yonder. It's surprising how easily I made him tell me your address. What struck me so forcibly is that how fragile men are these days. I'd swear his bones were no stronger than the stems of a flower." He shrugged. "The police officers were no more robust, either."

"You bastard."

"Jacob, I'm not here to defend myself to you. You're of no importance to me at all. I'm here for your grandson."

"Jack's not here. He won't be back for days."

"Is that so?" The body that Justice Murrain occupied turned to face the direction of Crowdale. "I saw Jack Murrain steering that vehicle of his into town. There's no road out in that direction, so it suggests to me he's on some errand and will be back shortly. Am I not correct?"

Jack Murrain had rushed back that morning to check that his grandfather wasn't in any trouble. Jacob had been able to assure him that everything was fine, and that he'd merely wanted his grandson to have a night out in a town where the lights burned brighter. Of course, he still needed to find a way to keep Jack out of Crowdale, until Justice Murrain, and his henchmen, were either contained or destroyed.

Jacob leaned out of the window again to check the road. No sign of Jack—yet. But he could drive round the corner any moment. Jacob cleared his throat. "Jack has work to do. He'll be gone for hours."

"Before my informant had the temerity to expire so quickly, I did glean that your only source of income is a forest that lies over the hill. 'Tis such a shame that our noble family have been reduced to the status of woodcutters." His glare intensified. "So you are a liar, old man. Jack doesn't go to a place of employment in the town. Then what errand is he running for you? A new handle for your broom? Oil for the lamp? Or . . ." He spat the words, "Rubber incontinence pants? New sheets? Because you befoul your bed at night? Batteries for your hearing aid? Ha! See, Jacob. You underestimated me. You think I arrived here wielding the mind of a man from the 1700s. But I can reach into the idiot brain of Horace Neville." He slammed his fist against his chest. "Then I rip out facts about this modern age. I'm fluent in its idiom. For example, do you like M&Ms? Which is your favorite color? Do you prefer *The Simpsons* TV cartoon to the shopping channels? Which microwave meal do you shovel betwixt your flapping gums?"

"I wish I had a gun right now, Justice Murrain. I'd shoot you dead, so help me."

"Fetch a knife from the kitchen. Even an electric knife." Justice Murrain gloated on Jacob's unease. "Then I'd gladly let you cut off my head. Because you know full well that though this body would die, I will not. Me! Justice Murrain! Your illustrious ancestor, will simply be freed from this flesh. Yes, I may be forced to return to the mausoleum for a spell, but then I will soon be free to find another host again."

"Host? You even talk like a parasite."

"You've been trying to distract me, Jacob. Quite simply, I am here for Jack. I want to be a Murrain again. A flesh-and-blood Murrain. You're too old, too used up. Jack Murrain is what I need right now. I shall transfer myself into his fresh young head." He wore a self-satisfied smile. "Jack's body will be my vehicle." The smile widened. "When Jack grows old I will then transfer to his children."

"He doesn't have any children."

"But I've seen him in the company of a young lady—and such a beautiful, desirable lady. Once I have taken possession of Jack Murrain I will make the lady my wife. See, Jacob? It is all so simple. I have it all planned out." He sighed with pleasure at his own foresight. "After I'm done with Jack in thirty years or so, I will transfer to his son. Then in another few decades I will skip lightly into the skull of his son. And so on. I will be immortal." He grinned. "And you will be nothing more than a stench in your grave."

"And I suppose your Battle Men will do the same? So you have your henchmen for always, moving from human being to human being, like the parasites you are."

"Ah, envy, sir. It runs thick in your voice."

"Envious? I'm nauseated." Then a revelation struck Jacob. "Wait. I'll take you up on your offer."

"Offer?"

Jacob's pulse quickened. "You invited me to cut off your head. I'll do exactly that."

Currents of air cried around the eaves of the house, then tapered into a sigh as they flew among the trees. Justice Murrain kept his eyes locked on Jacob's. The arrogant stance appeared to weaken.

Jacob sensed his advantage. "Surely, you've no problem with that, have you, benighted ancestor of mine? Because, as you told me, the moment that body dies you simply vacate it. And after a short spell back in the mosaic you will be able to find another body to possess."

For a split second Justice Murrain wore a hunted expression. The blip in his confidence confirmed to Jacob that he wasn't as sure of himself as he first appeared.

Jacob spoke with growing authority. "There's a problem, isn't there?"

"Oh, this body I've occupied has its annoying shortcomings. I readily confess that although strong it is clumsy. It's rather like riding a laming horse." He held up a finger. "No, I must use a modern example. To occupy this body is like driving a car with a malfunctioning—"

"Ah-ha! I know what's wrong. You are trapped in there. Go on, *confess* that! You thought it would be so easy to possess the body of an imbecile. But you're the imbecile! Horace Neville suffered brain damage when he was born. A brain like that, with all the neural pathways messed up? Easy to get into—hard to get out!"

"That's not true!"

"You're stuck in there. You've got yourself trapped in the body of Horace Neville. So what now, Justice Murrain? I've seen your Battle Men occupy men and women in the last few days, but it's only very briefly, isn't it? They soon lose their grip and get sucked back into the Ghost Monster. That's what local children call the mosaic. What a lovely name, heh? The Ghost Monster is a prison for the souls of the damned. But there's a real danger for you that the Ghost Monster is beyond your reach. If I cut your throat, will your spirit die with Neville's body? Will you be destroyed forever?"

"I'll kill you!" With a howl of fury Justice Murrain climbed the trellis beside the front door. When the giant tried to stretch up to the window, where Jacob stared down at him with such loathing, his fingertips fell inches short. As he endeavored to reach the window ledge Jacob caught hold of his wrist.

"Justice Murrain. A human body is holding you prisoner. That means you're human, now . . . and vulnerable."

Jacob pushed the man's wrist away from the window frame. With his balance gone, and occupying such a clumsy body, the giant toppled backward onto the path outside the front door. Over 200 pounds of meat and bone made a hell of thump. Instantly, Justice Murrain grimaced with pain. As he lumbered to his feet, he held his elbow. Animal-like growls issued from his throat.

"So." Jacob's satisfaction was immense. "You feel pain. I'm glad about that. The question remains: if that body is killed, do you finally die with it?"

"I don't care, you pathetic little man!" Justice Murrain gripped the injured elbow in his other hand. "Because look who is coming up the road. Here is your beloved grandson." He laughed. "Watch me leave this." He cuffed the side of his own head. "Then watch me invade the mind of Jack Murrain. See how I use him. Witness what I do." He spluttered with laughter. "Then you will watch him put his hands around your scrawny neck."

Jack's pickup rumbled along the road. In less than three minutes he would be turning into the driveway. What would he make of this chuckling giant, clad in a paper coverall?

"He will soon be here, Jacob. Watch what happens when I transfer." The voice became a gloating hiss. "Then I, Justice Murrain, will live forever and ever."

Jacob pulled a phone from his pocket, pressed the keys, then spoke these words: "Jack. Sorry to spring this on you, but I need you to go over to Calder-Brigg. Yes . . . if you will, son. It has to be right now." A quarter of a mile away the pickup pulled over. An expression of absolute fury distorted Justice Murrain's face. He realized he'd been thwarted. Smoothly, Jacob continued. "Go to Albert's workshop. You'll find him there, if you're quick. Ask to borrow his shotgun. There's a rat in our garden. A big, ugly thing it is. I want that rat dead before it causes any damage."

The pickup accelerated away, quickly dwindling into the distance.

Furious, Justice Murrain pointed at Jacob. "Hear this: I will take him. His body is mine. Then I'll break your skull!"

Justice Murrain loped away across the fields. In the white suit, the giant resembled a pulpy maggot that had been gifted a pair of sturdy legs. Within moments, Jacob had lost sight of the possessed man. What he hadn't lost sight of was this: sending Jack to Calder-Brigg had been a temporary stay of execution. Justice Murrain would be back. *That—just as everything born will eventually die—is a certainty.*

CHAPTER SIX

The moment the hail stopped clear visibility returned. In the car, Pel Minton started the motor. Even as those last bullets of ice struck the graveyard, the diggers returned to their trenches to winkle out fragments of Roman pottery, or search for flint implements in Temple Central.

Pel eased the car from the line of parked vehicles, which would take the team back to the motel at the end of the working day. However, her journey to Jack's house to tell him, and his grandfather, that the mosaic would be saved was short-lived. She'd barely covered a third of a mile when a dip in the lane landed her in a deep, crisp drift of hailstones. She'd been traveling slowly, so there wasn't much in the way of a jolt, and probably not even any damage to the fender. However, the tires lost all traction. After a few wheel-buzzing attempts she realized the car had become well and truly stuck. This section of lane only served the graveyard so there'd be no traffic, either to present a danger of collision, or any opportunity for assistance.

Pel debated her best course of action. Walk back to the graveyard (and face some ribbing; after all, she'd stranded a car in what was only a small drift of hail), or sit it out? Despite the cold, she noticed that the ground temperature must still be relatively high. Already, hailstones were turning to gray mush. What's more, the mound of ice that held her only just reached the bottom of the car. Surely, this would be short-lived. Once the ice had melted she'd be on her way.

Switching off the motor, she zipped up her jacket. *Wait it out,* she told herself, *you'll be able to drive away in a few minutes.* Pel opened the car door; a deluge of cold air flooded in. Happily, the beads of ice were liquefying. With a sense of relief she shut the door again. That done, she settled into the seat, arms folded, her chin buried deep into her collar.

She'd donned so many layers of sweaters and T-shirts beneath the jacket her own body heat toasted her flesh nicely. Through the windows, which had started to mist up, she could make out a line of trees. Beyond those were open fields. Meadows rippled as winds tore through them. At that moment, Pel enjoyed the coziness of being comfortably cocooned in the car. The trees swung back and forth with the gentle to-and-fro rhythm of a hypnotist's watch on a chain. Her eyes followed the side-to-side motion of those great elms. Soon Pel had begun to yawn. She snuggled deeper into the seat. Yawned again. *It wouldn't do any harm to close my eyes for a minute, would it?* An enticing notion. *Why not? Nothing's likely to hit the car, is it? After working in the cold outdoors this is pure luxury.*

Pel closed her eyes. A sensation of being ever so gradually dipped into warm honey stole over her as sleep made its stealthy advance. At one point she gazed at lazily waving trees; then she floated into the world of dreams.

In the dream, Pel Minton strolled back through time. She found herself in the sacred arrangement of circular ditches and mounds that formed Temple Central (long before the cemetery existed). White pathways radiated outward from the concentric earthworks. In the center, a figure. This man was unmistakably a Murrain. Or at least hailing from the ancestral line that would become the Murrain dynasty one day. The same mane of black hair adorned his head. The same large gray eyes gazed from a deeply tanned face. Dressed in a mixture of animal skins, purple-dyed fabrics, and even skillfully woven vines, the shaman's clothing combined the world of animals, plants, and materials spun by humankind.

Deep in the dream's embrace, Pel Minton glided through sunlight. As she did so, she noticed dark shapes flit along the straight pathways into the heart of Temple Central.

Pel didn't know how she understood this, but she knew they were the ghosts of the pagan dead. They were flowing along those tracks to join their ancestors in holy ground. Just as she knew that procession of swift shadows were spirits, so she realized that Jack Murrain's ancestor beckoned them into a loving embrace. The earth ring, formed by mounds and ditches, were symbolic arms that hugged the spirits. They were being welcomed to their new home, a pagan afterlife, where their souls would nourish green forests, and help breathe new life into the wombs of animals and humans alike.

I like this dream, Pel thought warmly. It's not often some conscious part of her was aware that she was asleep and dreaming. This was one of those rare occasions. She strolled toward the ocean. The sky darkened. Thunder growled. Behind her, the shaman raised his hands. He appeared to be beckoning her. Nevertheless, she continued walking. Ahead stood a mansion in dark block-work. Spindly chimneys rose in fingers of stone above the sharp line of the roof.

So I've advanced 5,000 years in just a few paces, she mused. A sign on the gateway bore stark black letters: **MURRAIN HALL**. Ah, the Murrain ancestral home. The dream's gift was that it enabled her sleeping self to picture the ancient house so vividly. Thunder grew louder. A darkness swept over the countryside until all she could see were lights shining through the windows. Now she found she couldn't stop herself from approaching the massive front door of the house. Her feet quickened. Yet dread filled her. She didn't want to go into that place. Something awful waited for her there; she was certain. Glancing back, she appeared to be looking along one of those "ghost roads" that radiated from the sacred site. At its center, the shaman ancestor of the Murrains; he waved at her. A gesture to return. Not to go forward into the house.

Only that fabulous figure in animal hides, vines, and purple raiment had become blurry, indistinct. A shadow of a shadow . . . a ghost of a ghost . . .

"I want to wake up now. I want to stop dreaming."

But an implacable force drew her toward the entrance of Murrain Hall: a forbidding building—one that could have been built from the bones of slaughtered innocents. Those bones were cemented by their blood. A symphony haunted its rooms; that music was wrought from the sighs of the dying.

Unseen powers rushed Pel Minton through the entrance into the vast interior of the mansion. Inside, it resembled an ancient church; one adorned with Gothic arches and bulbous pillars. Candles rendered from the flesh of murder victims illuminated it.

Though she desperately wanted to stop her feet from taking her farther, she found herself entering the huge Gothic hall. Now she noticed men and women sitting cross-legged on the stone floor. They were corpses, somehow pretending to ape life. At an altar heaped with human body parts stood a tall man with a mane of black hair; his gray eyes burned at her from the gloom.

His lips curled into a leering grin. "Welcome, my love." His voice washed over her in waves of utter darkness. "I am Justice Murrain." Then he addressed the congregation of the dead. "This, ladies and gentlemen, is my new bride." His lips were a raw, oozing slit in rotting skin. "And you are here to witness our wedding. You will watch us upon the matrimonial bed—when we become mated as one. You will hear her sighs of pleasure. You will bask in the scent of her body as she writhes naked. Be good, my friends, be faithful, and I will grant you a sip of her passion. For we all, in essence, will be wedded to this woman's flesh . . . one way or another."

At last, Pel retreated from the satanic altar, and the demonic figure. Even as she managed to flee he let out a peal of laughter that hurt the bones in her head. *"Battle Men! Bring me my bride!"*

That unholy congregation rushed her. Fingers stained with dried blood grasped her limbs. Men and women, alike, eagerly tore off her clothes. Then, howling with joy, they carried her, naked, to Justice Murrain, her bridegroom.

"No!" She punched out.

The sound of the car horn brought her instantly awake.

Perspiration rolled down her forehead. Her clenched fist still pressed against the horn in the center of the steering wheel. The bleating wail made her flesh crawl, for the dream overlapped reality. She could still smell the rot of the dead, carrying her along the aisle. Eager arms wrapped around her chest. Yet the grip of corpses was the only seat belt that she still wore. She released the catch with a sigh of relief.

Pel's lips were dry. Breathless, trembling, she unzipped her jacket. Her heart beat a wild rhythm against her ribs. The moment she moved her hand away from the horn the bleating wail mercifully stopped. The silence managed to be immediately oppressive. *Dear heaven, how long have I been asleep?* Dazed, she glanced about her. The car's windows had misted up. Vague shapes beyond the glass were discernible, and little else. The waving giants ahead must be trees, she told herself.

When she glanced back through the rear window a pale, billowing shape appeared. She stared at it with that dumb incomprehension, which comes after waking abruptly from a deep sleep. A white sheet blowing in the breeze? She frowned. The rear window had misted up so thoroughly she couldn't make out any detail, other than a nebulous white shape that expanded and contracted. It grew larger. The white pulpy object appeared to be topped with an oval blob.

A face! The moment Pel knew it was a figure she knew she had to get away from there. It didn't look right to her. The way it approached was unequivocally ominous. Because she knew, at last, that it ran toward her.

Pel hit the central locking switch. Then she clawed at the keys hanging from the one in the ignition. Her fingers were clumsy from being bunched up inside her sleeves as she slept.

When she pawed the keys she couldn't grip the fob of the vital ignition key.

"Come on, damn you!"

All around her, only opaque grayness of misted windows. She could have been sitting in the middle of a table-tennis ball for all she could see of the outside world.

Then . . .

Thank God!

The key turned; the motor spun into life. Then her heart lurched in her chest so violently she thought she'd vomit, for a huge pulpy figure slammed against the driver's door. It fumbled with the handle. Thank goodness she'd remembered to lock the doors.

She engaged drive. Wheels ripped at the rug of hailstones. For all the frantic shaking of the car, as she floored the gas pedal, it didn't move forward one inch. The tires couldn't bite against road. *You're going nowhere.* A bare fist struck the side window, just inches from her face. It did it again—a huge thump of a sound. A star crack appeared.

Ease off the gas, she told herself, *then apply it gently. Coax the car out of the ice slowly.*

Yet every atom of her body howled to dump gas into the motor by the gallon, so she could take off like a rocket. But that wouldn't work. She'd only find herself sitting here, wheels spinning fruitlessly, until the psycho, whoever it was, could break a window then haul her out. Then she could do nothing . . . as he broke her arms for fun, or dangled her over the edge of the cliff by the hair (oh yes, her imagination wasn't tardy: it supplied gruesome images of her tortuous murder).

A huge fist struck the side window again. This time it turned milky white as cracks ran through every inch of it.

Gas . . . apply gradually. Gentle acceleration. Don't rush this. Pel forced herself to operate the car with all the delicacy of a surgeon paring membranes. She didn't even consider wiping the fog from the glass. *No time. Just get the car moving.*

Then get the hell away from Mr. Psycho, trying to batter his way into the car!

Eureka! The car rolled forward. She pressed the pedal a wee bit harder. The speedometer's needle trembled as it began to climb. Then tires bit blacktop. A surge of power connected with wheels, wheels connected with firm road. Pel accelerated. The next time the fist crashed against the car it struck the back window. A hole appeared in tempered glass. An arm clad in white . . . in what appeared to be a protective suit . . . entered the car with all the loathsome intent of a pale snake worming its way into a baby's crib.

Floor it! The car rocketed forward. Glancing back, she glimpsed a face. *My God, isn't that the same guy I saw in Crowdale? The strange guy who sat on a chair outside his house and muttered about his friend being "poorly."*

Jolting, from running off hard road onto uneven earth, stopped her deliberating about her would-be attacker for the time being. Frantically, she scrubbed her hand over the windscreen to shift the condensation. Soon, she'd cleared an area the size of a soup plate that allowed her at least a half-decent view of the way ahead. It took mere seconds to drive off the grass at the side of the road and back onto blacktop again.

That done, she didn't even glance back to see if the madman vainly tried to follow her, as she raced along the country road to the Murrain house.

CHAPTER SEVEN

Ross Lowe didn't consult his brother, Scott, about his plan. Scott tended to be the one who wanted to discuss things like "implications" and he was quick to identify flaws in any plan that Ross would suggest. Even though, at forty-five he, Ross Lowe, was the older brother.

As he watched his mother brush her hair down over the burned half of the face he told her, "I'm going to do it today, as soon as it's dark."

"You're a good boy," she purred. "I know you're going to make me proud." She caught her breath; at the same moment she pressed the palm of her hand to her breastbone. Ross asked her in panic if she was all right. The woman smiled; instantly the smooth burn scar puckered into yellow ridges. "Don't you worry about me, Son. I'm going to keep this heart going, rotten though it is, until I have the satisfaction of seeing Jacob Murrain suffer."

"Tonight, Ma," Ross blabbered, eager to please. "I promise."

CHAPTER EIGHT

Pel Minton found herself pulling into the Murrain driveway in front of Jack, who was driving his pickup. By now, the windows of the car that Pel drove had thoroughly demisted, mainly due to the rear window having a whacking great hole in it.

When Pel climbed out of the vehicle the same time as Jack climbed out of his, she guessed both their expressions wore the same mixture of surprise and concern. She noticed he carried a rifle or shotgun in a soft case, while he'd seen the damage to her rear window.

"What the hell happened?" he asked.

"What the hell's with the gun?" she shot back by way of reply.

"I got a call from my grandfather, adamant that I drive over to his friend's in Calder-Brigg to pick up a shotgun . . . something about a rat in the garden." Clearly, he was more concerned with the damage to her car than any rodent infestation. "Someone lob a rock at you?"

Jacob Murrain appeared at the house door before she could answer. "Inside, the pair of you. Quickly!"

So, before she had a chance to elaborate on the damage, she consented to being hurried inside. Jack followed, wanting to know what troubled his grandfather. "If it's Ross and Scott again, I'm going to knock their idiot heads together."

"I wish it was Ross and Scott." Jacob's heartfelt statement made Pel and Jack exchange puzzled glances. "Come through to the living room. I'll lock the door."

With Jack in the room, holding the shotgun, and Jacob busily bolting the door, Pel felt she was adrift from reality. What's more, this shared the same occult quality as earlier, when she'd dreamed about a Murrain ancestor welcoming ghosts to the sacred site—and just before her nightmare encounter with Justice Murrain, who'd greeted her as his bride-to-be. Now that really did set icy shivers dancing on her backbone.

"Grandfather, Pel's had some trouble. Her car's been damaged."

"Well, my boss's car, actually. I hope she'll take the news well."

Jacob encouraged her to sit down in an armchair by a blazing log fire. He repeatedly glanced out through the window, a decidedly anxious expression on his face. "So, my dear, what happened?"

Pel explained that her boss had asked her to deliver good news. That works would begin in the morning to protect the base of the cliff from further erosion.

"The mosaic will be left where it is?" Sheer relief swept through Jacob; so much so, that he appeared unsteady on his feet. He sat down on the sofa. "Thank providence for that. But what happened to the car?"

"Well," she began, wondering how much detail to give. Falling asleep in the driver's seat seemed pretty dumb to admit, even though it was stationary at the time. "On the way here, the car got stuck in a drift of hail. As I waited for it to melt, so I could get moving again, the windows misted up. Then I noticed a figure, all in white, running toward the back of the car. I locked the doors. Just in time, too, because he started punching the window. Luckily, I managed to get the car moving forward. As I did so, he gave me one last parting shot. He thumped the rear window so hard he smashed it."

"Who the hell would do a crazy thing like that?" Jack was astonished.

"All dressed in white, you say?" Jacob nodded, grimly.

"The man who attacked your car was here earlier. It was Horace Neville. The white garment is a suit to protect forensic evidence. But to quote a phrase used a lot in the past few days, 'He wasn't himself.'"

"Horace Neville?" Jack set the gun down on a table. "No one would disagree that he's peculiar. Everyone in Crowdale's seen him sat outside the house, talking to his imaginary friend. But he wouldn't attack a car."

"Jack, believe me, he's a changed man." Jacob went to the window to scan the fields. "A couple of nights ago he murdered his own mother. This morning he killed three policemen as they were taking him to a specialist unit in Calder-Brigg."

"And he was here *after* killing the police officers! What on earth did he want?"

Jacob took a deep breath. "He wanted *you*, Jack. Earlier, when I saw you driving toward the house, I phoned and asked you to fetch the shotgun. The business about the rat was the first thing that came into my head."

"Well, you can't stay here. For all we know, Neville might come back. I'll drive you over to Calder-Brigg."

"Jack. Whoa . . . stop there. I'm not going to Calder-Brigg."

"Of course you are. It's not safe here. I'll make sure that Pel gets back to her people at the dig site. If they don't know already, they've got to be warned, too. And the police have to be notified."

"No, Jack. I've got to take care of the mausoleum."

"Mausoleum be damned!" Jack crashed his fist down on the table. "Grandfather. I'm sick and tired of your obsession with that bloody mosaic. Leave it alone. The archaeologists are going to take care of it."

"Jack, it's—"

"No, for once, you to listen to me! You don't know how much I hate that mosaic. Do you know the times the kids at school taunted me about that . . . the Ghost Monster! I had to endure their mockery, their jokes." Eyes blazing, Jack let the anger rip. "The times I defended your obsession with the thing. How I tried to justify it. But I felt like the only kid at school who believed in Santa Claus. They were laughing at me. I was treated like the school idiot—all because of that damned picture of our ancestor!"

"Son, I'm sorry. But—"

"But nothing! You haven't a clue what I endured . . . what crap I had to go through every day. Me! The Ghost Monster boy! The other kids called me names so I beat them. That got me into trouble with the schoolteachers. And I never told you what it was doing to me. Because for year after year I believed in you. You swept the mosaic, kept the lamp burning, guarded the mausoleum. I really and truly believed that you were protecting us all somehow. That because you safeguarded the mosaic you were safeguarding Crowdale. That made me so proud."

"That's exactly what I did. You will, too, someday."

Pel watched in silence as the younger Murrain unleashed all that pent-up rage.

"It's over! I'm not indulging in this sick devotion anymore, to a pile of stones in the graveyard. Listen, I was fifteen years old. I started to see a girl who was new to the school. 'Don't have anything with Ghost Monster boy' the other kids told her. 'He's a weirdo. He and his crazy grandfather will have you down on your hands and knees washing a freaky face every day.' Of course, she exited from my life like a shot. That's when I saw through your *quest:* to keep the mausoleum in one piece. Your obsession was destroying my life. As simple as that. My childhood was sacrificed—sacrificed on the altar of your love affair with that brick hut and its ridiculous picture."

After that, silence, apart from the crackle of burning logs on the fire. Both men appeared exhausted by the outpouring of Jack's rage.

At last Jacob murmured, "Son, don't you think I went

through the same when I was your age? It is the curse of the Murrain family to care for—"

"Don't. I don't want to hear."

"If you don't want to hear about that, then you must hear about the risk to you."

Jack stood with his back to the wall, arms folded, eyes downcast.

Pel had the beginnings of a headache. Perhaps shock had begun to get its teeth into her nerves at long last. *Hell . . . is that any surprise after the day I've had?*

Jacob talked. His grandson just shook his head, refusing to allow the words to have any meaning for him.

"Jack. Something's been happening in Crowdale. Over the last few days people have acted out of character. They've not been themselves—as the saying has been repeated so often recently. It wasn't Horace Neville who attacked his mother, or those police officers, or who visited me here; it was Justice Murrain."

"I believe it," Jack told him with a sigh. "I believe it."

"Good, because I need to explain—"

"Finally, I believe what the kids told me all those years ago; that I lived with a crazy man. Because I sure as hell don't believe you. And it rips my heart in two to say that."

The pain in Pel's forehead grew worse.

Jacob all but pleaded with his grandson. "Listen to me. It's true. The mosaic of our ancestor, the image they call the Ghost Monster, kept Justice Murrain locked out of this world. Him and his henchmen. Now that the sea is taking the cliff it's begun to destroy a sacred temple that has the mosaic at its heart. Every time a piece of the temple is lost it allows Justice Murrain and his Battle Men out. Horace Neville has been possessed by our ancestor. If you talk to him then you'll believe. No . . . Jack, don't go—please listen to me."

Pel shuddered. Something was happening to her that she didn't understand. The sensation changed from a headache to a sudden pressure above her eyebrows. In turn, that gave way to a certainty that a solid object, one icily cold, was being forced through her forehead. Pel tried to put her hands to her face. Only she couldn't move. The pressure increased; the pain became immense. Yet she couldn't cry out, couldn't breathe. *Dying,* she thought in panic. *I'm dying thousands of miles from home . . .*

Despite the agony, she sat absolutely still in the armchair. It seemed as if her mind had been displaced from where it usually sat, just behind her eyes. Now an icy presence occupied that seat of consciousness. Strangely, her panic passed. She found her sense of *self* thrust into the back of her skull. Pel could see Jack and his grandfather. They still argued. *Haven't they noticed what happened to me?* She tried to raise a hand to attract their attention. *Look, I'm ill. I've suffered a seizure . . . I can't talk . . .* However, the ability to raise even her arm had been lost to her. Try as she might, she could not cry out. Not a croak left her lips. As far as the shouting men were concerned she simply sat there quietly.

Just as she told herself that she'd suffered a stroke that left her paralyzed, her hand suddenly rose up in front of her. It turned to display her fingers . . . palm . . . wrist. As if suddenly the limb fascinated her. Yet this wasn't her doing. She didn't want to sit there staring at her hand like she'd never seen it before.

What struck Pel so forcibly was the impression that, as if she'd hitherto been in a room alone, now she knew that a person had entered through a secret door. It wasn't easy to put that feeling into words. Just that she felt so strongly there was an intruder in her presence . . . no, not in her presence . . . *but inside her.* This revelation filled her with horror. This was like suffering a physical attack but being unable to protest, never mind defend herself.

Wood smoke from the fire . . . to her it seemed impossibly pungent, as if her sense of smell had been absent for years. She saw Jacob imploring Jack. "Please, son, listen to me. I'm trying to protect you from the greatest danger you've ever encountered."

Jack Murrain grimly shook his head. He didn't want explanations.

The room tilted. Pel realized she'd stood up. And this frightened her because she'd not even tried. Her gaze swept round the room. The TV fixed to the wall wasn't even switched on but suddenly it became the most fascinating thing in the world. She tottered toward it. Her hand swam into vision, stroked the screen. Then darted toward the remote control. *Stop this*, she told herself, panicked. *What are you doing?* She pressed the power button. *Have I gone insane, is that what's wrong with me? Am I losing my mind?*

Three things happened in quick succession: One: Pop! The TV powered up. On-screen: Vivid images of children hurling beach balls at a clown. Two: A scream erupted from her lips. Exulting (not fear, oh no, nothing like fear); a scream of joy. Three: At last the two men realized the woman in their midst *was no longer herself.*

Jack took a step toward her. "Pel, what are you doing?" Then he noticed what must have been a crazed leer on her face. "What's happened to you?"

"Stay here!" Jacob Murrain caught his grandson by the arm. "They've got her."

"Who's got her? What the hell are you talking about?"

"Just as I've been trying to tell you, Jack. They've taken control of Pel."

"You're telling me that she has been possessed?"

"It'll be temporary. Another part of the temple must have collapsed into the sea. Every time it does, it allows them to escape for a while. Somehow, for now, it still manages to self-heal. When it fixes itself it draws the wandering spirit back to the mosaic." He watched Pel gleefully run her fingers over furniture in the room. "What we must do is make sure she doesn't harm anyone . . . or herself."

The moment Jacob released his grandson, Jack moved toward Pel.

"Easy, son. You're not dealing with Pel Minton anymore. That will be one of Justice Murrain's thugs."

"Thugs?" A lascivious voice oozed from Pel's lips. "My name is Anna. I'm Justice Murrain's night-wife. Hmmm . . . I kept his bed warm, his cock slick, and his hunger satisfied." She regarded the pair. "You two are his image. You know that? The Murrain gents always look the same, don't they. Big black hair. Big gray eyes. No doubt big appetites, too, for food and fucking. Care to taste my wares, sirs?" She fumbled with the zip of her fleece jacket.

"Pel, don't say those things."

"Jack. That isn't Pel Minton. Her mind has been overwhelmed. She's in there somewhere, but the spirit of a woman who calls herself Anna has taken control."

"So, if you don't want to plunge your pork swords into woman flesh, then what would you do with me? Beat me with your fists? Thrust my head into yonder blazing fire? Hmmm . . . I've not felt the tingle of love, nor a jab of hurt in centuries." She advanced toward the fire. "Even a burn on my finger would be something to savor after all these years."

"No." Jack surged forward to put his arms around her.

"Hmmm . . . such strength, sir. I'm sure this body I occupy yearns for you to enter." She stroked his face. "Oh, how I forgot how skin feels to the touch, sir. So smooth. But . . ." She broke free of his grip. "I'm not here for pleasure, my lords."

Jacob warned, "Jack, careful she doesn't harm herself. This Anna thing will soon be gone. It'll be Pel who has to deal with any injuries the monster leaves behind." Jacob examined Pel's face. "It's starting. The spirit's leaving her."

In the wall mirror, Pel Minton, still locked down inside her own skull, regarded the expression . . . *her expression.* The wanton leer faded . . . that air of confidence weakened. Pel had been in the grip of paralysis. Her possessor had taken control of her body. However, Pel focused her mind on bunching her right fist. To her relief she saw the fingers curl inward . . . it wasn't much, but it was a start. She was fighting back. Maybe, if she concentrated hard enough, she could push out this evil intelligence that had taken control of her.

Jacob cried, "Keep her away from the fire, and anything sharp. We'll soon have Pel back . . . the real Pel."

Yet, with a sudden burst of energy a possessed Pel Minton shoved Jack against the wall. "I'm not here for games. I bring a message from Justice Murrain. Soon he'll come for Jack, here. That's when the *real* games will start. Games of death." She laughed. "Then he'll take this she-creature." Pel rubbed her hands across her breast. "He'll take her for his wife. She'll give birth to his sons!"

At first, Pel thought the entire front of her head had been ripped off. When the spirit of Anna detached itself the agony nearly overwhelmed her. Instantly, Jack and his grandfather ran to support her as her knees folded.

The pain left her too breathless to speak. And at that moment she did need to reveal one important fact. *Horace Neville is back.* Jacob and Jack had their back to the window. And framed there, just inches beyond the glass, a giant of a man; all seven feet of him. Horace peered in, still clad in the blood-smeared forensic suit.

"The possessor is gone," Jacob said. "Pel's back with us again."

Pel couldn't speak, yet she still had to warn the pair that the killer stared in at them. The windows were covered by steel bars, but such a giant of a man could probably break down the front door with ease. She struggled.

"Take it easy," soothed Jacob. "You're safe now."

"*LOOK!*" The word exploded from her. "He's here!"

Both men spun to the window. Horace Neville didn't even flinch on being seen by the men. He merely smiled.

Jacob shouted, "There he is! That might be Horace Neville's body, but the person you are really seeing is your ancestor Justice Murrain."

Without hesitating Jack seized the gun case that contained the firearm. Swiftly, he slid the shotgun out, before starting to load shells into its breech.

Pel found she'd recovered her speech. "He's going . . . don't let him get away."

Jacob went to the window. "Sorry, Jack. You'll never catch him now."

All three watched Justice Murrain bound across the fields. Although ungainly, those legs were strong enough to carry him away into the distance.

Jack clenched the gun in his fist. "I'll get him next time—so help me."

CHAPTER NINE

Dusk fell. It brought more dark clouds from the sea. With that forbidding pall came yet more hailstones. Kerry Herne moved restlessly from one excavation trench to another. It frustrated her to the point of a hissing, foot-stomping fury that she'd been forced to shut down the dig early today. At lunchtime the civil engineers, tasked with building the sea defenses, had arrived with orders that the site on the cliff top must be vacated. Kerry had insisted that work up here wouldn't affect their surveys at the base of the cliff. She'd almost persuaded them when a section of cliff had collapsed onto the beach with the sound of a fist punching a torso (it had taken another rim section of Temple Central with it). After that, no amount of persuasion would change the engineers' minds. They suggested that archaeologists digging too near to the cliff's edge had compromised the "integrity of the subjacent soil." Therefore, excavation had to be suspended for the day. So, a heavyhearted Kerry ordered her team to pack up, climb into the convoy vehicles, then head back to the motel in Calder-Brigg.

Early that afternoon, she'd seen her own car (no doubt driven by Pel Minton) approach the site behind a pickup, which she didn't recognize. An assistant to the engineers guarded the access lane. From some 200 yards away Kerry had seen a man in a hard hat explaining that nobody was present at the site (*well, nobody but little old me*, fumed Kerry). Pel and the pickup driver must have accepted the guy's word, for they turned the vehicles round then headed away.

Kerry decided it would be simplest to call Pel. However, after searching the pockets of her formidable waterproofs, she realized she'd left her phone in the glove compartment of the very car that Pel was driving. Great, just great.

With nothing less than pit-bull tenacity, Kerry continued to work alone at the dig site. For one, she had no lift back to Calder-Brigg (she'd wrongly anticipated that Pel would be able to return with her car); secondly, Kerry, as chief archaeologist, could not bear the idea of wasting good daylight. Although the engineers had gotten her to agree to no more digging while they surveyed the beach, she single-handedly spent two hours sieving dirt heaps for finds. After bagging an eighteenth-century belt buckle and assorted Roman potsherds, she focused her energies on photographing tagged artifacts in the trenches (these awaited extraction in the morning). Then, as the light waned, she returned to an awning where she could cheat the approaching dusk by using a flashlight to work on the more humdrum stuff of time sheets and stock requisitions.

Despite her frustration at having to halt the team's work today, she felt relief—a delicious . . . no, call that GARGANTUAN relief, that the engineers were finally here. Once they'd completed their survey today, they'd call in the squad tomorrow to start building the barricade. Steel cages, filled with rocks, would prevent surf from munching away any more of those cliffs, which consisted of boulder clay. A substance so soft the entire coast might well have been made from chocolate chip cookies.

Kerry had every confidence that Jacob Murrain would turn up this evening to check on the mausoleum. He'd refill the lamp to make sure it burned through the night; its rose-colored light illuminating the portrait of his ancestor. Desperately, she needed to share with him the fact that the spirits of Justice Murrain and his cohorts were free to roam the area by day, something evidenced when she'd witnessed the possession of Nat yesterday.

"So, Mr. Murrain, where are you?" She slipped printed forms into a plastic wallet. By now, night had fallen. It turned the countryside into a mass of indistinct shapes that her imagination only too quickly turned into menacing, stalking figures. She had to look twice to reassure herself that figure of a hunched man was only a scrawny bush after all.

At one point she decided to check on the engineers. Surely, they couldn't remain on the beach for much longer. The tide would be coming in. Taking the flashlight, she picked her way through the gravestones. They, too, wanted to trick her imagination, so she'd think they were lurking goblin figures in the gloom. With an unsettling frequency, she thought she saw one of those grim tomb markers scuttle toward her. Then she'd have to shine the light directly onto it. Sure, it reassured her that the gravestone was still a gravestone, not a crouching assassin, but then she'd find herself reading the text chiseled there: IN MEMORY OF CATHERINE BROOKS. 1800–1824. CRUELLY DONE TO DEATH BY VAGABONDS. BLESSEDLY NOW FREE OF PAIN.

Kerry murmured to herself, "Did you have to be so specific in what you had engraved? RIP would have been enough."

As she threaded her way among the graves she found herself noticing yet more messages about the much lamented. Beneath the carving of a weeping angel: DROWNED BY SHIPWRECK, 1873. And another: A VICTIM OF TYPHOID. And: KILLED IN AN EXPLOSION AT MURRAIN QUARRY, 1 JUNE, 1933. Many a time, Kerry Herne wished that science would deliver the archaeologist a device that would allow them to see through the ground with perfect clarity. Alas, her imagination granted her just that gift when she walked through the cemetery. In her mind's eye, she could see down through the sod into the earth beneath, as if it were all as clear as white wine. Floating in that transparency would be the coffins. In those coffins she could picture yellowing bones. In the one belonging to the quarryman, whose life was snuffed out by dynamite, there'd be shattered ribs, femurs, thighs, spine, and, no doubt, pieces of the tin detonator case would be embedded in the bones of the face. *What a grisly way to go.*

Gritting her teeth, she hurried on along the cliff-top path. Here lay the buried remains of Temple Central. Beneath the gentle undulations would be ditches, linear mounds, buried "baby tooth" stones and the spirit roads—all of which formed the sacred site. One whose earliest beginnings dated back 8,000 years.

Kerry reached a point where the cliff curved enough to allow her a view of the beach. In the darkness she could make out white surf. Way in the distance, there were bobbing lights. Those must be the engineers' vehicles as they drove back along the sands to Crowdale. Satisfied they were safely on their way back to town, Kerry retraced her footsteps back to the cemetery. The flashlight cast a generous dash of radiance, so she could find her way through the bushes, clumps of gorse, and tombstones.

In the cemetery, she noticed a shadow moving about the mausoleum. Thank goodness for that. Jacob Murrain was here to tend his lamp. She'd hitch a lift back with him. Kerry hurried up the slope to the building. Its steel gate was open. A figure of a man hunched over the mosaic. *It must be Jacob. He's cleaning the portrait.*

When she was ten paces from him she said, "Jacob. Thank God, you're here; I've something to tell you."

But when he turned his head she saw it wasn't Jacob. This man had a heavy build. His blotchy face appeared almost purple in the lamplight. Instead of cleaning the mosaic, he rammed a chisel into it.

"Stop that," she barked. "You're damaging a site of historical importance."

But no, it was worse than that. The man was breaking the face of the Ghost Monster. She recalled, with a shiver, her conversations with Jacob, and the purpose of the mosaic. This held evil spirits. To destroy it would be the same as breaking open the gates of a jail.

The man used a hammer to pound the chisel's point deeper into the mosaic.

"I said, stop that!" Kerry rushed through the entrance to grab hold of the man's raised arm. "Get away from here. I'll call the police."

When he pushed her back against the wall she clearly saw his face.

"Get away from here," he snarled. "'S'nothing to do with you."

"I know you. You're Ross Lowe. You drove a truck onto the site. I warned you then that—"

Kerry saw the flurry of movement. At first, she felt no pain. Then she noticed a wetness stream down her forehead. Another blow felled her. In the glow of the oil lamp she could see splotches of red dropping from her face as she tried to hold up her head from the mosaic. It didn't seem right to rest her bloody head on the face of Justice Murrain. The portrait's huge gray eyes gazed up into hers. He seemed amused by her plight. Crimson splotches dappled the cheek in the picture.

A third blow. Nothing but darkness.

CHAPTER TEN

At ten minutes to midnight the bulky figure of Ross Lowe entered his mother's house. His brother sat with Ma in the lounge. Both Scott and their mother watched expectantly as he carried the hefty wooden box with low sides. Covering it, a thick plastic sheet.

"Just you look at this." Proudly, Ross set it down on the floor at his mother's feet. "Jacob Murrain's going to be in for a surprise."

The big man yanked back the sheet. There in the box, lit by the table lamp, was a face. A pair of gray eyes gazed up from the depths of the container. Spots of dried blood covered the portrait.

"I got it," Ross crowed in triumph. "I got that damned mosaic!"

No Days Left

CHAPTER ONE

Crowdale's town-hall clock had pealed out the chimes of midnight when it happened. The Murrain portrait had already been wrenched from the mausoleum. Spattered with blood, it now resided in the Lowe family home in the suburbs.

Justice Murrain's army of psychopaths, his "Battle Men," were free. The occult mechanism that had bound them to the earth beneath the mausoleum had been disabled. Through the darkness they glided, drawn to the defenseless people of Crowdale. There the evil spirits took possession of unsuspecting men and women.

In a shed down by the harbor two cousins gutted fish. A hard, electric light made the white-tiled walls shine. The men wore green plastic aprons and heavy-duty rubber gloves. They worked opposite each other across a steel table. The cousins selected fish from a tub of iced water, inserted the tip of a wickedly sharp knife into a fish belly, *slice*, then reached into the creature, pulled out its guts. Entrails went into a sluice hole in the table. Cleaned fish went into a trayful of ice. The cousins had gutted thousands of fish like this, six nights a week, for twenty years.

One grunted. "I think I'm getting a headache."

"You're not leaving me with two hundred fish to clean by myself. Keep working."

"Uh." The man pressed his hand to his forehead. "I don't feel right."

"Keep working," repeated the elder cousin.

"Very well," the other announced brightly, then jabbed the point of the knife into the man's belly. "Cooee! Offal!" The possessor laughed at the sight of the man's intestine streaming out through the wound in his stomach. Laughing giddily, he thrust steaming guts down through the hole in the table; then he hauled the dying man toward the trays of fish. Seconds later, he shoved the twitching body onto the neat rows of prepared fish. "To market! To market!" howled the murderer. Then, laughing with the sheer joy of being truly alive again, he raced from the gutting shed—knife still in hand.

Oh, after all those years languishing in the earth, he'd make the most of tonight.

Three men, stumbling home from the bar, couldn't believe their luck when a house door opened to reveal a nerve-tingling surprise.

"Boys. Come in for a while. It's cold out there."

The woman they knew to be a widow stood in the doorway. Thirty-eight years old, she looked good. *Downright sexy*, thought one of the men. And as she stood there naked in the doorway they appreciated just how well she maintained her figure, cared for her hair, kept her breasts pert. Now the nipples turned black, either from sexual excitement or cold—they didn't know which. They didn't care which.

Too drunk to know better, or question if this was an orgy that might go seriously wrong, the three hurried inside.

"Go straight up to the bedroom. I'll be right with you."

Before the possessed woman joined them, she locked the downstairs doors, disabled the smoke alarm, and set fire to the house. For a moment, she enjoyed the heat of the flames bursting from the sofa. Then, once upstairs, she let all three take her again and again on the bed. The men were so inebriated they didn't smell the smoke.

The woman uttered strange words as they took it in turns

to pound their groins against her body. "My name is Anna. I am Justice Murrain's bed-wife. I'm free again. I'm going to taste every kind of pleasure. It's my avowed wish to experience sensation until I am overwhelmed." She moaned in ecstasy. "Bite, sirs. Scratch away this skin, sir. I tenant it but for a short while. Press onto my throat as much as you like, sir. What's that, gentlemen? You'd like me to do what? By all means, sirs. All of you at once . . . I have the capacity to accommodate."

When they'd fucked to exhaustion she opened the bedroom door. The stairwell sucked flames upward to this floor like a chimney. The three drunks, shagged-out, disorientated, confused by the unfamiliar room, stumbled against the bed and the furniture; they cried out when they stubbed bare toes. When they realized that tongues of flame, ten feet long, had burst through the doorway they screamed to each other to get out of the house. Fumes from burning synthetics made them choke; their eyes streamed. Heat seared the tender skin of their genitals.

"Does that not excite you, sirs?" The possessed woman struck at their backsides as they milled about the bedroom. This confined space had become as bright as the heart of a lantern. The sheer intensity of light blinded them. Incredible heat scorched their naked bodies. Panic turned them into a screaming melee of limbs.

The woman jumped up and down on the bed, her breasts bouncing to the rhythm. She laughed herself breathless. Plastic hairbrushes melted into a pink pool on the nightstand. Mirrors shattered. Broken glass sliced bare feet. Blood didn't have time to soak into rugs. Heat surging up through the floorboards bubbled it dry. Perfume bottles exploded on a shelf. One of the men was blinded by shards of a scent bottle. Screaming, he blundered through the doorway, where he was engulfed by the roaring incandescence. Hair spray aerosols exploded. The force ripped away the second man's face. His fingers explored his mangled visage until they found an eyeball hanging down against his cheek. In his panicked state, not knowing what it was, he ripped the eye away. The pain broke his mind. After that, he squatted in the corner to babble nursery rhymes.

By now, flames from downstairs had all but devoured the floorboards. The third man had been trying to force open the bedroom window. His fingers blistered as he struggled with a lock that now glowed red-hot. He shouted in triumph when he finally pushed open the window. At the same moment, however, the timbers gave way beneath his feet. He plunged through the hole in a gust of sparks to land in a pool of burning foam rubber that had poured, lavalike, from the sofa in the room below.

On the bed, the possessed woman's hair caught fire. As it crackled with the ferocity of a firework she still bounced on the mattress. The flames were a golden halo. But Anna, Justice Murrain's mistress, was no saint. When she worked as a midwife she had a passion for stealing just-born babies (after she'd pushed a long pin through the ear of the babe's mother until it pierced her brain). Oh! How she bounced with joy.

The final male survivor still sang nursery rhymes. "Round and round the mulberry bush."

Anna shrieked with pleasure. The afterglow of sex mated with the heat of the flames to overload her senses with such erotic power. Her masochistic appetites were at last being gratified.

"I'm alive! I'm alive!" she trilled. "I'm alive, I'm—"

At last, gas pipes in the kitchen blew. Instantly, the naked woman ascended into the night sky with more than a ton of masonry. A fountain of fire and gory body parts.

Elsewhere in the town that night, the evil spirits of Murrain's Battle Men forced their way into the heads of men and women. Two hundred mortal minds were roughly shouldered from the seat of consciousness as the invaders took over. Not all would-be possessors were successful. Some mortal minds were so firmly rooted in the brain that they couldn't be displaced. When the would-be possessors realized it would be futile to persist they sought more vulnerable hosts. Ones with minds that hadn't such a tenacious grip of *self*.

After being confined in a never-never world beneath the mausoleum for more than two centuries the now-freed minds sought "feeling." They yearned to indulge the five senses. In the mini-mart at the all-night garage a youth raced in through the door. He wrenched the cap from a bottle of port wine, then drank so eagerly that red liquor cascaded down the front of his white T-shirt. Then he gorged from tubs of candy.

"Here, stop that," demanded the counter clerk.

The youth gurgled some response that from the tone suggested *Go screw yourself*—although through a mouthful of pink marshmallow no words were discernible. After the marshmallow he ripped the wrapper from a stick of butter then forced it into his mouth. All the time his jaws worked in sheer ecstasy; his eyes were glazed slits of pure enjoyment.

Far from happy with this display of gluttony (unpaid-for gluttony at that), the clerk rapped on the counter to attract the feeder's attention. "Get out or I'll call the cops."

"Ugh," was hardly an eloquent reply . . . it was all the youth could manage as he stuffed raw bacon into his mouth. Chocolate smeared his face; red liquor stained his clothes. His lips had split from trying to cram so much into his mouth, yet he still wanted more. Needed more. Lusted for more. He pressed slices of cheese into the bacon mulch that occupied his cake shoot. After that he broke open bags of sugar, flour, chili powder, desiccated coconut, coffee beans—all went into the chomping maw; along with bananas, grapes, bright green soap (he didn't even spit), eggs (shell and all), more chocolate, peppermint gum, beer, cookie dough . . .

"Hey, crazy man." The clerk had enough. "Look at the mess you're making. Guess who has to clean that up? Me! Now get out before I kick you out." He advanced on the youth.

Meanwhile, the glutton had turned his attention to the bakery shelf. The instant he picked up a loaf of bread the clerk seized him by the arm.

"You pig! Didn't I warn you!"

The glutton sensed he was about to be parted from the love of his (new) life: food, glorious food. He grabbed a hefty jar of barbecue sauce, then smashed it down onto the clerk's head. The force of the blow stove in the top of his skull. The guy fell down into a sitting position, his back to the dairy products refrigerator. Surrounding him, shattered remains of the glass jar, together with splotches of rich, dark sauce.

The youth started work on the loaf of bread. He tore off huge mouthfuls. Soon he started to cough as a dry crust stuck in his throat. He paused, his eyes searching for something to moisten his meal. When the possessor saw hot blood bubbling out of the broken crown of the clerk's head to mingle with zesty barbecue sauce he nodded as an idea took hold. Squatting beside the clerk, he happily dipped his bread into the massive head trauma.

Elsewhere, men and women spilled out into the streets. The town-hall clock struck one. On the cold air the single chime shimmered. At that time of night the place was largely deserted apart from the possessed townsfolk. Skanky Mal, the notorious Crowdale alcoholic, stuck his head out of the cardboard carton he called home. From there, Skanky Mal witnessed dozens of people walking by in their nightclothes; some pausing to peel off naked, then fuck each other in the road. A bunch of women turned over a car . . . just for the hell of it, he surmised. These folk had the appearance of long-lost friends who were meeting each other after years apart. Many of them danced. They sang songs he'd never heard before. Skanky Mal crawled out of his residence, then scrambled as quickly as he could to his feet (which for such a hard-drinking man wasn't especially speedy). Ten men linked arms as they walked abreast. They sang at the tops of their voices—something about a pirate's encounter with a ship full of feisty nuns. Skanky Mal gamely tried to join in the with the chorus. At the same time, he dragged a vodka bottle from his pocket. An inch or so sloshed in the bottom. He'd been saving that precious liquor for morning, but this spectacle called for a toast. Especially when these carousing revelers kicked over garden walls then threw the bricks through windows.

"Here's to you, at last!" hollered Skanky Mal. "How long have I been telling ya' boring buggers to loosen up? Now, you give this bloody town a damn good shaking! Cheers!"

Two hundred possessed adults approached the town hall. There on its steps stood a giant of a man; one clad in a white suit. They gathered in front of him to form a respectful audience.

The man pointed at individuals. "Do you know me?"

"Yes," cried a woman with joy. "You are our master!"

He pointed to a youth who carried a half-eaten watermelon in both hands. The giant demanded, "Who am I?"

"You be Justice Murrain, sir!"

"And you?" He pointed to a naked woman of thirty. Teeth marks speckled her shoulders from where she'd been willingly ravished—joyfully, passionately ravished.

"Justice Murrain. That's who you are. Our beloved Justice Murrain!"

His finger roved over the crowd. "Who am I?" As the digit's tip pointed at an individual they responded, "Justice . . . you are the Justice, sir."

"The Justice!"

"Justice Murrain."

"Our master! Our savior!"

The crowd raved with adulation—the tumult became a raw power in its own right.

"The Justice." A voluptuous woman, slinkily clad in a red nightdress, stepped forward. She boasted a cleavage to die for. "You are our master. We sacrificed ourselves for you and will do so again. *And again!*"

Another woman padded from the back of the crowd. She smiled with an erotic hunger. This femme fatale was clad in the dark uniform of a female police officer. "I am Anna, sir. Tonight I occupied two females, sir. The first I had the pleasure of burning. I baked with three men; we were like rabbits a-cookin' in a pie. Then I found this muscular young thing." She stroked her hands down the hips of the figure-revealing uniform. "Remember your Anna, sir? Your own sweet Anna? Back at Murrain Hall you kindly took me as your bed-wife." She pursed her full red lips. "I'm ready for whenever you need me, sir."

Others started to clamor, too; they were eager to serve.

Justice Murrain raised a white-clad arm to silence them. Then he launched into a thundering speech: "Tonight, after more than two centuries of confinement, we are free. Fully free. Not like those sips of freedom we experienced over the last dozen days. When we were only permitted a fleeting tenancy of men and women. Now, let me explain, if you have not yet grasped the truth of what is happening here. The mosaic created by my vile son trapped our souls. It must have been destroyed because we are no longer subject to its power. You, my followers, my courageous Battle Men should choose the men and women you wish to possess most carefully. Select the strong and the healthy, because together we will become warriors once more. We will exact our revenge on this feeble town. We will become its rulers, just like the days when we roved out from Murrain Hall, to take what we wanted, and whom we wanted."

The youth who gorged on watermelon blurted, "But they'll send the army like they did before. I remember the soldierman who fired his musket into my eye. They'll come with guns again, and bayonets fixed. How can we fight them?"

Justice Murrain smiled. "Oh, doubtless many of us will fall to their weaponry. This is a new age: they can fire rockets from sky machines. They have cannon that ride on horseless carriages."

The woman with the cleavage, which dived to who knows where beneath the nightdress, sobbed. "I have only just taken possession of this body. I don't want it to be torn apart."

A clamor of distress rose from the Battle Men.

Their leader raised up his hands, his smile triumphant. "Listen to me, carefully. Yes, the soldiers will come. They will fire their bullets into your hearts. But hear my words: *You cannot die.* Yes, the flesh that houses you might be destroyed. If that happens, leave the body and find a fresh, healthy one. If it helps you understand, imagine that the body you have possessed is a horse that you are riding. That horse might be killed in battle. What you would do is find a new horse to ride. Now, do you follow my meaning?"

Their mood of anxiety changed to one of joy.

"The Justice speaks the truth." Anna in her policewoman's uniform stepped forward. "Tonight I stole the body of a widow. I enjoyed the pleasures of three handsome bucks. Then the body I occupied burned to death. In the blink of an eye, I found this sturdy wench. It took no time at all to slide into her head, push her thoughts aside, and to take my seat in the saddle of her mind."

"Anna, my beautiful Anna, is correct," Justice Murrain boomed. "If the body that clothes you is destroyed, find another. And this is the most perfect truth of all." He held up his finger as he made the important point. "When the soldiers come, as they surely must, they will slaughter you. As soon as you leave the host body fly to the soldier-man that killed you. Enter his brain. Vanquish his mind. Then you will possess his body." The smile became a grin of utter wickedness. "Because then you will also possess his fine weaponry. See, my friends. We cannot lose."

An excited babble rose from the Battle Men; they were eager to wreak their revenge on Crowdale.

Justice Murrain beamed. "I know you are impatient to settle old scores. However, before you begin your bloody work, here are my rules—few though they are. One, do not touch any of the Murrain family. Jacob Murrain will die by my hand, and mine alone. Two: Soon I will shed this tiresome lump of flesh. To do that I need Jack Murrain's body. He is mine to possess. Three: There is a woman from the Americas. Her name is Pel Minton. Once I have housed my spirit in Jack Murrain she will become my bride. Thereafter, I shall lie with no other woman."

Anna clutched her heart as the awful truth finally penetrated her understanding. "Master! I gave you my life. For centuries I have waited patiently beside you beneath the mausoleum. Tell me you won't take a stranger as your one and only love. Promise that I can continue to be your mistress."

Justice Murrain took no notice of her distraught cries. With a benevolent smile he made fond shooing gestures. "Go, my friends. Tonight, enjoy yourselves. Because tomorrow our real work begins."

Laughing, hooting, yelling, singing, the Battle Men rushed along the streets. That look in their eye? Pure madness. Utter insanity. Yet there was lust, too. A burning lust for flesh, for blood, for violence—for every sensation this new world could yield: willingly or not.

CHAPTER TWO

Stars burned with a fierce, cold light. Frost made the cemetery grass crunch beneath their feet.

Jacob Murrain stopped dead. Anger, frustration, and anxiety clouded his face.

"Pel? Jack? Isn't there anything I can say to persuade you to drive to Calder-Brigg? It's dangerous here."

"If it's dangerous, Grandfather, I'm not going without you."

"But you don't understand what Justice Murrain is."

Pel said, "He's evil, I know that much."

"It's more than that." Jacob's voice rose. "Many a man has done wicked things to others. Only rarely are they wicked to their own children. Justice Murrain took a knife and cut off his baby son's thumbs. His henchmen were recruited from asylums for the criminally insane."

"We'll fight this together," Jack insisted.

"Justice Murrain told me today he planned to take possession of your body. Then he's going to find Pel here, and . . ." Pointedly, he didn't finish the sentence.

Pel grimaced. "One of those monsters got inside my head earlier. But I know what to expect now. I can fight it."

Hopeful, Jack said, "You believe you can stop it happening again?"

"You bet."

"I hope to God you're right, my dear." Jacob shivered. "Because the next few hours are going to be the most hazardous of our lives."

Pel walked between Jack and his grandfather. Jack carried the shotgun that he'd brought back from Calder-Brigg. All three used flashlights to scan this field of bones at the ocean's edge. She glimpsed the excavation trenches, which were so grimly reminiscent of open graves. Stone angels glittered with ice, as if dusted with diamonds. In the distance, the roar of surf. Once more it would be launching its assault on the cliff. Dear God, the sea was attempting to possess the land, just as the ghosts of Justice Murrain and his henchmen tried to possess the human beings on this godforsaken stretch of coast. Pel had made herself appear brave in the face of what happened today. Yet her insides fluttered. Her hands hadn't stopped trembling. Even though her mind had been suppressed by the spirit of someone called Anna, who had died physically more than two centuries ago, she had still known what had happened in the Murrain home. She could see, she could feel, she could hear. Her hijacker could have done anything using her body. Sex. Robbery. Assault. Murder. And she, Pel Minton, would have been powerless to stop it from happening.

Jacob limped toward the squat building. At this time, little more than an hour after midnight, it resembled a black box against a montage of grays that were the grass and stunted bushes.

"It'll just take a moment to check the mausoleum," Jacob told them. "Then we'll drive home. If need be, Jack, we'll turn it into a fortress to keep that ancestor of ours out." He shook his head. "What worries me, can we keep those phantoms out of our heads?"

"We'll watch out for each other," Pel reassured him. "We know the warning signs."

"The problem is that we . . ." Jacob's voice tailed away. "Something's wrong . . . the gate's open." Despite his years, and that painful limp, he ran toward the mausoleum.

Their flashlights revealed that the steel gate yawned open.

A broken padlock lay on the ground. Jacob froze in absolute shock. *He's suffering a heart attack.* That was Pel's reaction when she saw his pained expression. However, he pointed a trembling finger at the floor.

"My God . . . it's gone . . . the mosaic is gone!"

Jack hurried into the confines of the building. Sure enough, when he played his light on the three-by-three slab, in which the mosaic was embedded, it revealed a void of darkness.

Crouching, Jack examined the hole. "It's been hacked out." He picked up splinters of stone. "Probably by something sharp. A hand ax, or a chisel."

Pel shone the light, too, into the building in the hope that the mosaic had simply been abandoned there. What she saw disturbed her. "Aren't those bloodstains? There, Jacob. Near your foot." Quickly, she swept the light into the corners. For a second, she thought she saw a discarded coat, then: "Jack, there's a body."

Pel hurried to the crumpled figure.

"Careful," Jacob warned, "they might be dangerous."

"It's Kerry!" shouted Pel in horror. "Kerry Herne, my boss! Oh no . . . her face . . . look what they've done!"

Jack crouched beside the still form. He gently eased back her blood-soaked hair. "Head wounds. She must have disturbed whoever was stealing the mosaic. Damn it, when I get my hands on them."

It sickened Pel to see the once-beautiful, lively face now so cold and full of death. She held her hand just inches from Kerry's lips. "Jack! She's still breathing. I can feel it."

Jacob took the woman's wrist. "A pulse. Thank heaven. Jack, get her to hospital as quickly as you can."

After handing Jacob the gun, Jack gently, yet swiftly, gathered the unconscious woman into his arms. "Pel, lead the way with the light."

"I'm not coming," Jacob told them. "You take Ms. Herne to the hospital."

"For crying out loud, you can't stay here." Jack was aghast.

"That's exactly what I'm doing. I'll search for the mosaic. It may have been dumped nearby."

"For once, forget that blasted picture."

"Son, it's important. I've got to find it."

"I'm not going without you."

"Okay." Jacob nodded at Pel. "Tell him why the mosaic's so important."

As Jack stood there, with Kerry in his arms, her head still dripping blood, Pel said with considerable force, "This entire area is holy ground, an ancient sacred site. One that your ancestors have guarded and worshiped at for at least five thousand years. At its center is the holy of holies. Your grandfather has told you that the mosaic holds the ghosts of Justice Murrain and his thugs in the earth. Now that it's gone, they are free."

Jacob nodded. "Pel is correct. I must find it."

"But they've been free for days. They got a hold of me. Then we saw one take possession of Pel today. And Justice Murrain is using the body of Horace Neville."

"Justice Murrain was too clever for his own good. Horace is brain-damaged. Murrain is trapped in a malfunctioning mind. The others were only freed temporarily when part of the temple complex was destroyed by the sea. After a while, this occult mechanism can heal itself. It drew the wandering spirits back to the mausoleum and locked them down out of harm's way. But with the mosaic gone . . ."

Pel supported Kerry's head. "Jack, please. She's so cold. If we don't go now we'll lose her."

Jack struggled to make the right decision.

"Go, son." Jacob handed Pel the shotgun. "Take this. I'll be fine here until you get back."

Clearly, Jack's loyalties were divided. "If anything happens to you I'll never forgive myself."

"Jack, my boy." The man gave a grim smile. "We are Murrain. With the blood of Justice Murrain running in our veins it is *we* who do the frightening. Now, please save this brave lady's life."

Jack gave a single nod. "Look after yourself. We'll be back in an hour."

How wrong he was. This night of terrors had only just begun.

CHAPTER THREE

Ross and Scott Lowe watched their mother. Even though the clock revealed it was one thirty in the morning she refused to go to bed. She paced the room. Every few moments she'd go regard the mosaic in the crate. Then her eyes would burn with an unsettling intensity. After that, she'd pace the room again. At times she'd pause to study her reflection in the mirror. At the ruin inflicted by fire all those years ago.

Once more, she returned to lock eyes with those of the Murrain ancestor in the mosaic portrait, which Ross had removed intact. How closely the long-dead Justice Murrain resembled Jacob Murrain. To see the gray eyes staring up into hers made her heart beat faster.

At one forty that morning she took a deep breath before announcing, "You've done good work, Ross. But it's not enough. I want Jacob Murrain here in the house. I want him down on his knees, begging me for forgiveness."

The two middle-aged brothers exchanged puzzled glances.

"Remember what I told you, boys," she murmured. "Don't lay a finger on Jacob Murrain. You must hurt the ones he loves."

CHAPTER FOUR

Justice Murrain strode through the center of town. Crowdale was his. Two centuries ago, his pet lunatics had served him well. They'd terrorized the townsfolk so completely that they'd given him money, food, and drink. They'd also supplied him with young men and women as playthings. Fresh flowers of youth to be enjoyed until they were all broken up and useless. Soon, he would ensure that fine old custom was restored.

Tonight, he was content for his Battle Men to enjoy their recreation. They'd been confined so long in the cemetery dirt beneath the mausoleum that they needed to taste life again. It was essential they reacquaint themselves with sensation, pleasure, and gratification. Numbering some 200, comprising both male and female, his Battle Men experimented with their new bodies. The gluttonous youth had finished the watermelon. Now he discovered the joys of discarded pizza in a Dumpster behind an Italian restaurant. A naked woman dabbled in a motor car. She drove it at lightning speed up and down the street. Its original owner had caught his foot in the seat belt as she'd hurled him from the vehicle. His mangled corpse painted crimson lines on the blacktop as it was dragged at ninety miles an hour.

Justice Murrain knew that the phantoms, which had taken possession of those modern men and women, would be learning from the minds they had conquered. Their speech would adopt a modern idiom. They'd soon understand modern technology—all those computers, phones, cameras, vehicles, televisions, and so on, which adorned the lives of modern humans. When the woman smashed the car into a house, the force of the impact catapulted her body through the windshield, through the living room window, and no doubt deposited mangled meat and bone on the carpet.

No matter. Though the ghost would be evicted from dead flesh, his Battle Man would find a new host in moments. Good, they'd soon learn that they could discard a broken body for new. His henchmen would become consummate Bone Jackers. He smiled. He enjoyed using the phrase. That's what they were now. *Bone Jackers*.

Pleased, he whistled a merry tune; then he sang himself a little ditty. "Hey, hey-ho, my boys, a bone-jacking we will go."

One of his Battle Men, wearing striped pajamas, raced past him. He pushed a terrified woman in a wheelchair. Its silver wheels spun. She clung onto the arms of the chair for dear life. Whether her abductor intended pleasure or pain Justice Murrain could not say. Not that it mattered. He watched fondly as the man sprinted along the road, pushing the wheelchair, and the screaming woman, in front of him.

A window smashed. From a house, a pair of femme fatales were laughing as they dangled a youth from an upper window by his ankles. He was starkly bare. Blood ran from the area of his groin. He still managed a din of a noise, though. His yells were enough to set dogs barking in the neighborhood. The two women soon tired of this merrymaking. On the count of three they released the yowling teen. Smartly, he dropped headfirst onto a concrete path. The blow silenced his voice, while simultaneously it released his brains onto the ground. In this cold air they steamed, billowing clouds of white.

Enjoying what he saw—and approving mightily of his Battle Men's bloody games—he walked on.

CHAPTER FIVE

Scarlet numerals, blazing from the bus station clock, pulsed 2:03. Pel Minton sat in the back of the pickup, cradling Kerry's blood-soaked head on her lap. The injured woman's breathing was frighteningly shallow; her eyelids hadn't so much as flickered during the drive here. Time and again, Pel had gently tried to wake her boss but she remained deeply unconscious. "Don't die on me," Pel urged. "Please hang on; we're nearly at the hospital." Then to Jack, who drove the pickup. "How long now?"

"Less than two minutes." He crushed the gas pedal to the floor. The motor screamed as he raced along the deserted road. Only it wasn't deserted for long. When he turned at a crossroads, he braked hard.

"Jack," Pel begged, "don't slow down. Kerry's pulse is so weak I can hardly feel it."

"We've got to go back." He slammed into reverse.

"Listen, I don't think she's going to last much longer."

"Take a look for yourself. We won't be using this road."

Pel lifted her head so she could see through the windshield. She was astonished to see a dozen cars had been smashed into an unholy tangle of scrap metal outside a KFC. One car blazed with such brilliance she had to screw her eyes almost shut. The pyramid of fire reached as high as the surrounding buildings.

"Dear God. There must have been a riot."

"In sleepy old Crowdale?" Jack sounded grim. "I doubt it.

In fact, I'd be a happy man if it was just a homespun civil disturbance." He reversed the truck hard to the crossroads, then took another road.

"You mean this is Justice Murrain's doing?"

"You bet." He accelerated along another shopping street. "Don't worry, this'll get us to the hospital just as quickly."

By now, the stench of burning plastics stung Pel's nostrils. Intruder alarms blared out into the night. The reason was clear to see. Even from here, Pel could count six stores that had their plate glass smashed. On a bed, in the window display of a furniture store, a pair of naked bodies mated with brutal enthusiasm. The woman thrust her thumbs into the eyes of the man as orgasms shuddered her flesh. Just along the street, a man danced with a wheelchair, spinning it round in an extravagant waltz. A middle-aged woman, clinging desperately to the chair, to prevent herself being flung out, must have been screaming fit to burst—her mouth was a huge O shape. However, alarms belted out their intruder warning so loudly Pel couldn't hear the cries. Jack reached across for the shotgun.

"Whatever you do, Jack, don't stop. We can only save one person at a time. Right now, Kerry needs our help." Pel knew that Jack wanted to rescue the wheelchair rider from her lunatic dancer. "Please, Jack, drive on."

Jack eased by the wheelchair-waltzing maniac, not wanting to collide with the woman, confined in more senses than one to the chair (Pel noticed a piece of blue string looped around her neck, then tied to the wheelchair frame). Her legs flip-flapped loosely at the wild gyrations.

No sooner had he maneuvered the car safely past the pair, then a wail of police sirens cut through even the din of intruder alarms.

"Hang on tight," Jack warned her. "Trouble's coming our way."

They didn't have to wait long for him to be proved right. A purple ice-cream truck tore past them, "come-up-and-buy-one" chimes sang from the speaker set in a giant cone on the truck's roof. Chasing it, a pair of police cars. Blue lights pumped out warnings for other road-users to get the hell out of the way. The possessed driver of the ice-cream truck lost control. The machine slammed through the window of a boutique. Arms and legs from fashion mannequins flew. A plastic head, complete with scarlet lips and frizzy blonde hair, bounced out onto the pavement. Chimes still tinkled discordantly from the vehicle.

Its driver staggered out from the wreck. The police cars pulled up just paces from him. A cop from each car sprang from their vehicles. Only they didn't rush to arrest the crazed driver. One cop pounced on the other. Straightaway, he commenced pounding his colleague with his fists. Soon the pair were wrestling on the blacktop.

The speedster from the ice-cream truck lumbered toward the pair. A broken jaw left him with an expression of slack-jawed amazement at the brawling constables. Despite his injuries, he aimed kicks at the cop who'd gotten the upper hand and straddled his adversary.

Jack smoothly accelerated away. Behind him chaos reigned. The guy pushing the wheelchair joined the fight in the street. He used the chair as a battering ram against the melee.

Thankfully, Jack turned a corner: Pel was spared witnessing the fate of the woman who'd been pushed into the knot of struggling men.

"It's Justice Murrain's Battle Men." Pel's heart clamored. "They're possessing the townspeople, aren't they?"

Jack drove hard, tires screeched. "And they're causing mayhem. Two hundred years ago they used to terrorize the place. They ran a protection racket; abused families in their homes. They murdered people for the fun of it. Now the Battle Men are hell-bent on starting a new reign of terror."

A naked woman darted from a side street. She ricocheted off the side of the car. Despite the red flash of a graze down her nude hip, she didn't stop running. She didn't stop laughing, either. It struck Pel that the benighted creature was so hungry for sensation anything would do—sex, gluttony, speed, exertion, pain; an overwhelming lust for being human with feelings again had intoxicated her.

Jack called back, "See what I mean?" The pickup's taillights bathed the running nude in a ruddy glow. "The possessors are insane. They don't care whether they live or die."

"But that's not the worst of it. Those two cops back there were fighting each other. Which man was possessed? Which was normal? We can't tell friend from foe."

Jack gave a sour laugh. "If you don't feel yourself, you will shout me a warning, won't you?"

"That goes for you, too." She wasn't joking, she meant it.

Ahead, lights blazed from a large building. A sign by the gate announced CROWDALE DISTRICT HOSPITAL.

Jack sang out, "Made it!"

To Pel, the building no longer promised to be the haven of safety and healing that she'd hoped for. As Jack pulled up she found herself chilled by a sense of foreboding. "After what we've seen back there, you've got to wonder what we're going to find in there." She shivered. "I can't stop myself from imagining what a bunch of crazed people would do with a bunch of very sharp surgical instruments."

CHAPTER SIX

The drunk tried to paw Anna's backside as she passed a gateway marked CROWDALE DISTRICT HOSPITAL. "I haven't seen a policewoman as hot as you before. I love your sexy shirt. Your stab-vest is hot. What a long black baton you got. That's hot . . . that's really hot. And you've got this really, really . . ." He struggled to find the appropriate word. "Hot! Hot eyes. Sexy, hot mouth."

Anna had been planning to find some enjoyment with the drunk. Aged about fifty he had piercingly bright blue eyes. He wore a white shirt with a red necktie that was covered with a design of tiny gold farm tractors (maybe he sold such vehicles for a living). Now she debated what she should do with liquor breath. Kiss him? Squeeze his balls? Or peel the skin off his face with the butcher's knife she'd looted from a supermarket? She'd tucked the blade inside a zip pouch in the stab-vest. Justice Murrain's promise to make a stranger, by the name of Pel Minton, his bride enraged her. Why should that woman take her place? Couldn't both women serve their master? Anna felt cheated out of her rightful role as the Justice's favorite. He'd ridden Anna many a night. He'd sighed with pleasure when she'd mouthed his flesh. She'd never, ever denied him the use of her body, even when his frequent bouts of rage had left her thighs bloody after lovemaking. Then she'd been accustomed to such treatment in the Pennine Asylum before Justice Murrain had selected her to join him at Murrain Hall. Many a night, warders and fellow inmates had dragged Anna by her long hair round and round the dinner hall, while folk had whipped her with belts, or used strong fingers and thumbs to snatch away strands of her pubic hair to garnish their dishes. Alas, such was the uncouth behavior in an old-time bedlam.

However, the Battle Men had a new world to savor. *The past is dead.* Anna liked the body she possessed. It had such firm breasts. The limbs were strong. This body had belonged to a lioness of a woman. And it was Anna's now. She found she could dip into her host's mind. From it, she could tease information about how life is lived today. Anna knew her host was employed by the police force. Though British police do not carry guns, as a rule, her host had firearms training. In a strong room at the building that housed the constables there were pistols, rifles, grenades, and something called *machine guns* (that name seemed unusual to Anna; even so, she could draw an image from her host's brain; that image revealed a short stump of a gun that fired dozens of bullets with a *dat-dat-dat-dat* sound).

The hand of the drunk patted her rear again. "Ms. Cop . . . hot Ms. Cop. I know you want me. You've been giving me that 'come on' look, haven't you? *Haven't you?*"

Because she'd ignored him, he rammed both hands into her back. The push sent her to clatter face-first into a chainlink fence that surrounded the hospital grounds. Straightaway, she saw a familiar figure open the door of a vehicle. Her heart surged with such excitement she didn't even notice the drunk's sudden anger. For a moment, she was convinced that Justice Murrain was not fifty paces from her. And it was the Justice Murrain she remembered from their time together more than two centuries ago.

But that can't be, she realized with a surge of disappointment. *Her* Justice Murrain had housed himself in the body of the giant clad in white. This young buck must be Jack Murrain. Anna had seen him at the house earlier when she'd possessed the Americas woman, Pel Minton.

The drunk growled, "You wanted me a few minutes ago. Now you're ignoring me. Not good enough, am I? Got your eyes on some cocksure detective, no doubt." He shoved her against the fence again. "I'll show you what you need. I'll have you begging for mercy . . ." He talked like a man possessed, but this was a regular guy, not one of the Battle Men. Though it would be fair to say he'd been possessed by the spirit of the whiskey distiller's art. He gripped her hair as he uttered profanities jumbled with threats of pain and erotic pleasure. Roughly, he shoved her face against the fence. But a greater force than pain worked on her now. Anna couldn't take her eyes off the handsome face of Jack Murrain. She longed to rub her cheek against the mane of black hair. As she watched through the wire mesh, he gently eased an unconscious figure from the backseat of the car. Straightaway, another figure stepped out from the vehicle.

Then Jack hurried toward the entrance with that bundle of humanity in his arms. He paused to call back to the figure who followed. "Pel!" he called. "Pel!" He nodded at the vehicle. "Bring the gun. We might need it!"

Pel! This is the Pel Minton woman? The very woman that my master will make his bride! In her mind's eye, Anna saw Justice Murrain tenderly kiss that interloper, while murmuring fondly, "I love you, Pel. There is no other to match you. You will be my wife, forever and ever." Still Anna didn't even notice the drunk's rough groping of her breasts. Only the distressing image of *her* man loving that Pel woman to the exclusion of all others filled her head right now.

Just fifty paces away Jack Murrain, a devilishly handsome man who made her heart flutter, carried a sick or wounded woman through the hospital doors. Meanwhile, Anna's despised love rival hurried back to the pickup. The woman hadn't noticed that she was being spied upon. Intruder alarms wailing across the neighborhood ensured she didn't hear the couple at the fence, either.

"Get your clothes off," grunted the soused oaf. "It'll do

here, right up against the fence. Gonna make you squeal. Ha!" He got a fistful of her boob . . . squeezed . . . squeezed until he moaned with pleasure.

Enough. Anna reached into her host's mind where it had been driven into a few strands of cerebral matter. There, Anna searched until she found the information she required. The entire process took mere seconds. As soon as she realized the purpose of the canister that dangled from a hoop on her belt she snatched it, then aimed it back over her shoulder as she closed her own eyes.

"Gonna make ya beg, ya bitch. I'm—" Whatever he intended to threaten didn't leave his lips. Instead, a jet of pepper spray entered his mouth. After that, the torrent of chemical irritant hit his eyes. Choking, blinded, not knowing what had assaulted him, he stumbled backward from Anna. Saliva hung in strings from his mouth. The pepper spray robbed him of his much-professed *hots* for the comely policewoman. Anna didn't intend wasting time on the drunk. She had a quest of burning urgency. So, after delivering a sharp kick to the man's testicles, which felled him as effectively as a head shot, she raced to the hospital gate.

By this time, she saw her rival for Justice Murrain fully lit by the hospital's floodlights. To Anna, she appeared young and strong. The full breasts and broad hips were evidence of excellent nourishment. This well-fed stranger radiated fecundity. She would possess the healthy womb that would bear many a strong Murrain child. *Ye gods. That must not happen. Once you are dead the Justice will realize that I shall be his wife. This strong body I have stolen for myself will give him sons aplenty. Just one glistening drop from his shaft will impregnate me. I know that to be the truth!*

Silently, Anna raced toward the woman who hurried toward the hospital doors. In Pel's hands, a formidable gun with two barrels fixed side by side. Nevertheless, Anna smirked with confidence. *I'll strike her before she realizes I'm even there.* There was nobody else around. Jack had vanished into the building with his burden.

Thirty paces away. Anna unzipped the pouch on the front of the stab-vest.

Twenty paces away. Still not seen by the interloper. Pel walked along a line of parked ambulances.

Fifteen paces away. Anna took the knife by the handle.

Ten paces. Good, the woman was too preoccupied to notice the figure approaching from behind. Anna circled one of the parked ambulances. She could pounce on the Pel bitch from behind the vehicle. Take her completely unawares. Knife in hand, Anna got ready to pounce.

Just one second from springing out at her victim, another figure lumbered from the shadows of the parking lot. A huge, shambling figure clad in white.

It seized the fist that held the knife, then a second hand, the size of a dinner plate, clamped tight over Anna's mouth. Before she could even struggle, Justice Murrain had picked her up, as if she had no more substance than a straw dolly. Quickly, he lumbered away with her back into the shadows.

Once they were hidden from sight he threw her to the ground. She was a piece of garbage now. A filthy, worthless object that he didn't even wish to soil his hands with.

Winded, she struggled to her knees. "I love you. She's not right for you."

He raised his fist. "I've told you, Anna. I will make the woman from the Americas my wife. You will not interfere again."

"You can't kill me, sir. Once my spirit has left this body it will find another . . . then another, if needs be." She added with absolute defiance, "I'll come looking for you. I'll never leave you."

"Go."

"You loved me once, Justice Murrain. I shared your bed. We were happy together."

"You don't understand. Modern people have learned something of the human condition. There is a germ called a 'genetic.' I've reached into the mind of the man I've possessed and learned about it. You have bad blood, Anna."

"But you've taken the body of an idiot. It'll serve you wrong. No good can come of it."

"Be quiet." He yanked Anna to her feet. "That woman I have chosen has muscle on her bones. She has a strong mind. Intelligence, aye, she has much intelligence. When I have taken my rightful ownership of that young buck, Jack Murrain, I will be wed to her. Because the gene she carries is perfect—unlike yours—her children will be strong warriors. A time will come when Jack's body wears out; then I will transfer to his son. I will be a young man again. This I can do for all eternity."

"She'll be the destruction of you, master. I can see it. Even a fool can make such a prophecy. Pel Minton will ruin everything."

"That's what you think, jealous little whore." He grinned. "But what words will come out of those lips when you witness our wedding rites. Hmm?" With a laugh he flung her aside, then loped away into the darkness.

Though Anna was certifiably mad, she embraced one clear, indestructible line of thought: *I love Justice Murrain. I will fight to win him back.*

CHAPTER SEVEN

In the hospital: pandemonium.

Pel Minton had never needed to use the word before. But that's what she saw now. Total pandemonium. Medical staff in green scrubs (many splattered with shining scarlet gore) worked like crazy. Without exception they all wore expressions of deep anxiety. Victims of violence either lay groaning on gurneys, or sat on chairs in the waiting area. Most had been bandaged in a hurry. All were in shock.

Pel still carried the shotgun. Her grip tightened on it when she noticed that there were perpetrators of violence, too. A guy of around seventy, with a white beard that would have impressed Santa Claus, snarled like a mad dog. His wrists were handcuffed to a radiator.

"Come fight me! I'll take you all!" He bellowed a string of curses.

The man's dazed wife repeated to everyone in earshot, "He's never like this. I do apologize. My husband isn't himself. He's Reverend Pearson from St. Jude's. I do beg your pardon. I don't know what's got into him."

"I do," Jack whispered to Pel. "One of the Murrain Battle Men." Jack found an empty gurney so he could gently set Kerry down. Once he'd done that, he took the shotgun from Pel.

Pel grabbed tissues from a dispenser then carefully tried to clear the blood from her boss's face. "My God. I don't know if she's alive or dead. Try and find a doctor."

"I'll do my best." He scanned the room for one of the green-clad medics; however, now there were none to be seen. They'd taken the casualties to the treatment rooms. "The place has gone to hell. What we're witnessing here is one of the Battle Men's jaunts into town." He added grimly, "Just like the good old days, eh? When my ancestor used to send his thugs into Crowdale to teach the locals a lesson. Payback time." With the words, "Sit tight, I'll see if I can find a doctor," he headed down a corridor.

From packs of surgical dressings on a trolley, Pel did her best to bandage the cuts on Kerry Herne's head. Blood matted the woman's long dark hair, which was her pride and joy. The bestial roars of some patients (who'd been restrained) suggested that at least eight people were possessed by Justice Murrain's damned banshees.

More wounded were brought in by distraught relatives. Soon after that, a mother and father wheeled in the kind of cage you use might use to transport a large dog. Behind its shiny steel bars a youth of around sixteen had been crammed in tight. He roared, "Give me a cutlass! I'll take off all your pretty heads!"

"Stop it, Beckham," the mother pleaded to her caged son. "You're making such a show of yourself. You don't want people staring at you, do you?"

The boy raged. "My name is Valdemar! With these bare hands I strangled five men in a single night."

Dad slammed his hand down onto the cage. "Shut your stinking mouth!"

Nerves aren't frayed, Pel decided. *They're well and truly shredded.*

Just then, Jack returned. He led a frazzled-looking guy in a green uniform; the man carried a hefty rucksack over his shoulder that was emblazoned with a big red first-aid cross.

"What we got here?" The man had a strong Eastern European accent.

"This is Kerry Herne," Pel told him. "She was attacked earlier tonight."

"Welcome to the party. That makes about three hundred other people."

"Doctor, can you tell me if she's still alive?"

"I'm no doctor. I'm a paramedic. Doctors are operating on the most badly injured." He began to examine her with swift professionalism. "Ah . . . she's so cold. How she get so cold?" His accent became more pronounced as he focused on Kerry's injuries.

Jack said, "We found her at the archaeological site on the cliff top."

"Then we can add exposure to head trauma. But her vital signs are not so terrible." He raised her eyelid, then shone a penlight to gauge pupil reaction, and for the first time in the maelstrom of activity he noticed Jack carried a gun.

"You won't add to my workload with the bang-bang, huh?"

Jack almost seemed embarrassed. "I don't always carry this. But Crowdale's a battlefield tonight."

"Tell me about it, sir." The paramedic lightly touched the cuts on Kerry's scalp. "Not twenty minutes ago, a dear old white-haired grandma drove her car through the back doors of the hospital. She knocked down two security guards before they could put restraints on her. She's a demon. A woman possessed."

Jack and Pel exchanged glances.

Pel murmured, "You're closer to the truth than you think."

"Pardon me?"

"Nothing."

"There are accounts in the Bible of demonic possession." The man checked Kerry's pulse in her neck. "But then who am I to know these things? I'm just a paramedic. My work is with the mortal body, not the eternal soul, huh?" He checked the unconscious woman's limbs. "No broken bones. And good news about those cuts. They are superficial. The problem is that she is suffering from concussion *and* hypothermia. How long has she been in a warm place?"

Jack checked his watch. "She's been in a car with the heater on full for twenty minutes."

"And in here for almost fifteen," Pel added, feeling a surge of relief for Kerry.

"Good. Her body temperature will be rising. Now, let's see if we wake Sleeping Beauty." The paramedic dug his thumb into her breastbone then, pushing down hard, made a screwing motion. "Not pretty to do this. Pain, however, is a powerful stimulant."

At the third attempt, grinding his thumb into Kerry's chest, she said distinctly, "Do that again, and I'll black your eye."

Pel hugged Kerry as she lay there on the gurney. "You're alive. Thank God!"

Kerry blinked. "This isn't the motel. Where's Nat?" She groaned. "I didn't get drunk and misbehave, did I?" Her dazed eyes found the paramedic. "Sir, if I kissed you I do apologize."

"Kerry," Pel said quickly. "You haven't been drinking. We found you at the mausoleum."

Kerry jerked bolt upright. "Oh hell, the mosaic, I remember. This man had a chisel. He was hacking at it." Suddenly panicky, she asked, "The mosaic? Is it still there?"

"It's gone," Jack said simply. "We need to find it."

Pel squeezed Kerry's hands in hers. "Did you see who took it? Was it a man dressed in a white coverall?"

"A white what?" Confusion clouded Kerry's face. "Oh, my God. If the mosaic's gone, it's like opening a prison door. Justice Murrain and his phantom thugs will have escaped."

The paramedic angled his head. "The lady has suffered hard blows to the cranium. There may be confusion. Hallucinations."

Kerry regained her composure. "Whatever was trapped under the mosaic is able to invade our heads. They take possession of people—then they cause absolute mischief." All at once she seemed to realize where she was. She glanced round at the wounded townsfolk. Those, and the raging men and women—and the boy in the cage who now regaled everyone with a lusty story about a pair of insatiable milkmaids in a hayrick. Her attention swung back to the shotgun in Jack's hands. "It's happened." Understanding crossed Kerry's face. "The shit's hit the fan, hasn't it?"

Jack nodded, grimly, then: "This is important, Kerry. Can you describe the person who stole the mosaic?"

The paramedic flinched in surprise. *"There really is a mosaic?"*

Nobody answered his question. Instead, Pel asked Kerry, "Can you tell us what the thief was like?"

"I'll do better than that. Jack, here, saved you from him when he smashed that truck into the graveyard. He goes by the name of Ross Lowe."

"You're sure?"

"Absolutely. We were standing toe-to-toe when he whacked me."

The paramedic began, "The attack on you, lady, is a matter for the police. With war breaking out in the street, however, they seem to be in short supply."

Pel put her arm round Kerry's shoulders. "When can you get her onto a ward? And won't she need X-rays?"

"X-rays be damned. Just patch me up." Kerry sounded insulted. "I've got a head like a rock. I'm fine."

"Kerry, you've—"

"I'm coming back with you two. Just grab an arm each. I'll be able to walk to—"

Suddenly, yells battered Pel's eardrums. Those that weren't possessed were all staring in horror. It soon became obvious what had happened. The old guy with the Santa Claus beard had broken the handcuff links. With youthful vigor, he punched a security guard to the floor. Then he rifled through the trolley where Pel had found the surgical dressings. Leering, he picked up a slender paper envelope.

"Oh, sweet Mary, no," uttered the paramedic. Clearly, he'd recognized what the envelope contained.

Santa-beard ripped open the sterile package to expose a silvery object.

"Keep back from him," the paramedic warned. "He's got a scalpel."

The old man took savage delight in holding the ultrasharp blade to the light. "It might not be Excalibur . . . but it will carve your Adam's apple."

The possessed men and women applauded and hooted with vulgar pleasure at the arming of one of their kind. The teen in the cage slapped his palms against the cage. "I know you, old friend! You are Griffin! Tom Griffin!"

"And you are Valdemar. I'd know you in any guise, sir." Santa-beard laughed. "I'll have you out of there in a twinkling."

The elderly wife caught hold of the possessed man's arm. "You're not yourself, Clarence."

"Ah! By Jove, you speak the truth!" boomed the man. Then he slashed the blade across her throat. An ugly wound exposed veins that resembled cream-colored spaghetti. Then the deluge. Blood drenched her yellow cardigan. Crimson rain fell on the floor. With an expression of absolute horror distorting her features, the woman toppled forward. After that, the only movement was a rapid twitching of her fingers.

Santa-beard advanced toward where Pel stood alongside Kerry on the gurney. The light flashed against the blood-streaked steel blade. Those shocked occupants of the waiting area had fallen silent as they gaped at the menacing figure. Then the silence ended with a huge bang. The old boy with the scalpel jerked backward. Blood jetted from wounds in his chest. His eyes rolled. Staggering backward, he reached the wall where he slid down into a sitting position. The eyes no longer rolled but stared fixedly in the direction of his outstretched legs.

Pel turned to Jack. He remained there with the butt of the shotgun hugged to his shoulder. Smoke oozed from its muzzle.

"You killed him," gasped the paramedic. "You gunned down an old, old man."

Pel spun toward him. "It was either him or us."

"But you—" The paramedic flinched. His hand went to his forehead. "Ah, that bang gave me a headache. I . . . I . . ." Paralysis gripped the man. His eyes went frantic as if he experienced a terrible panic. Quickly it passed and a stark, cold certainty returned to that gaze.

Kerry gasped. "What's wrong? Sir, talk to us."

The paramedic smiled. "You don't get rid of old Tom Griffin so easily." With utter confidence the *thing* that possessed the paramedic sang out, "Don't fret Valdemar. I'll have you sprung from that cage in a trice!" Quickly, he reached into the first-aid bag. He plucked out a familiar envelope. Before anyone could react he'd ripped it open to reveal a new scalpel. "Ah, another Excalibur for Tom Griffin. A dwarf Excalibur but it will still carve your Adam's apple."

The possessed went nuts. They applauded with a ferocious passion. The teen crammed in the cage banged his face against the bars with sheer joy.

Jack aimed the shotgun at the creature that had, just a moment ago, been a paramedic. Pel shoved the weapon upward.

"Jack, no!"

"He's one of those things now."

"Jack, think it through. Kill him and he might take you. If you're possessed, you'll turn the gun on us."

"She's right!" Kerry sprang from the gurney. "What we've gotta do is run." She shouted to everyone there. *"That goes for you all! Get away from here! Run for your lives!"*

Most fled. Some, however, stayed with their loved ones. But by now the sight of violence in the hospital waiting area had inflamed the possessed with a roaring bloodlust. Two of the monsters snapped their restraints. They wasted no time attacking anyone near them.

Pel pushed Jack ahead of her. "Don't kill them. You saw

what happened. As soon as the host is dead they simply find another."

"Okay! Okay! I won't kill them." But before following Kerry, he fired at the feet of the possessed paramedic. Birdshot ripped away the end of one foot. Pain didn't bother the crazy man, but running with half a foot became a problem. Spilled blood made it worse. Before he could slash at Pel he slipped on the slippery gore. In another part of the room the teen broke the bolt on his cage. With the speed of a jack-in-the-box he sprang out onto his bemused parents.

"Beckam! Beck—"

Pel didn't wait to hear, or see, what happened in that new battle zone. Moments later, they were outside, where the cold night air felt so good. The sheer heat generated by the mayhem in the building had been suffocating.

Jack helped Kerry to the pickup. In his free hand he still carried the shotgun (which had for obvious reasons become as dangerous to its shooter as to its victim). *Those deranged spirits jump ship fast.*

Pel felt better when they locked themselves into the truck. Jack started its motor.

"Where now?" Pel shouted.

"We've got to find the mosaic," Kerry told them. "If we can return it to the mausoleum, we might have a chance to put a stop to all this."

Jack accelerated toward the gates. "Ross Lowe. We'll go to his place. If he doesn't give up the mosaic I'll break every bone in his body."

A wild-eyed man raced along the road, pushing a wheelchair. In the chair, a woman laughed as gleefully as he did. Both possessed, both crazed.

Pel saw that Jack would have dearly liked to barrel over them. But he heeded her earlier warning about possessors finding new bodies pronto. Instead of running them down, he swerved round the cavorting pair.

Fire tore through the whole neighborhood. The possessed

still made merry with the regular townsfolk. Fear and panic pulsated on the night air. Sirens wailed. Cars burned. Dogs howled in fear.

Pel knew that Jack hated leaving innocent people to the not-so-tender mercies of the Battle Men—and to Justice Murrain, wherever he lurked in those streets.

Gently, she rested her palm on the hard muscle of his forearm. "It's fine, Jack. This is the right thing to do." She gave him a reassuring smile. "Find the mosaic. We can make everything okay again."

CHAPTER EIGHT

"Battle Men . . . My Bone Jackers!" Justice Murrain marched along the street. "Come on my boys. You've had your pleasures! It's time to work. The work we were born to do!" The figure in the white forensic coverall beckoned the possessed as he marched. "Join me, boys. Join me, fair maids." The possessed had been ripping up the town. They'd enjoyed the fruits of Crowdale's populace, as well as its stocks of food and wine. Though many of the possessed wore pajamas, nightgowns, or were in a state of complete undress, they all wore expressions of elation (not to mention smears of their victims' blood mixed with chocolate stains, liquor spills—you name it; they'd indulged themselves royally). As soon as they heard their master's summons they quit whatever barbarous acts they were committing and ran happily to join him.

Soon, Justice Murrain marched along Main Street, 200 possessed men and women following him. He led them to a suburb where dozens of cars were parked neatly in driveways. There, in one smart avenue, he turned to his ruthless band of warriors.

"You are accustomed to your hosts' bodies by now. You will also be learning how to plunder their minds for knowledge. Bit by bit you will be gaining an understanding of this new world." The Battle Men nodded vigorously. "I'm sure you appreciate this is a world built not by the sweat of hard toil in the blacksmith's workshop, the tanner's yard, or the cornfield, but this is the world of electrical slaves and motorized vehicles."

"Yet a woman's lips taste the same today as they did two hundred years ago," cried a man in a chauffeur's uniform.

"Indeed they do." Justice Murrain laughed. "Now, listen. This body of the idiot giant is tiresome to me. Its limbs are cumbersome. Sometimes the idiot's thoughts intrude on mine. Therefore, I intend to take possession of my descendant Jack Murrain. I will do it tonight. But everything must be prepared. This has to work the first time. Therefore, it's essential that I have these two hands on Jack Murrain when I make the transfer." He held up two huge paws, fingers splayed. "We will take these cars, then drive to my descendant's house. I wish to rehouse my spirit as soon as possible."

"Don't we need ignition keys, master?"

"Oh, you'll find them in the houses there. If the occupants give you any trouble simply dispose of them. All I ask is for you to make haste, make haste!"

Gleefully, the Battle Men rushed to break down doors. Soon intruder alarms were yowling. Lights came on in upper windows, heads appeared; there were shouts that residents were calling the police.

"Call away." Justice Murrain laughed with such rich pleasure. "Call away, fools. The constables are far too busy tonight to bother with you."

Anna, in the apparel of a female police officer, hung back in the darkness beyond the streetlights. She would ride with them in the convoy to the Murrain home. But she would accompany Justice Murrain on her own terms. A plan had begun to form in her mind—a mind warped and degraded centuries ago. In her hands, she held a submachine gun that she'd managed to steal away from police headquarters. The place had been in chaos as constables struggled to contend with arson and murder on a glorious scale. Clad as she was in the uniform none of the other officers even challenged her.

One of the Battle Men reversed a BMW through a pair of

gates (neglecting to open them first). Nearby, Justice Murrain had taken a seat in a 4x4. Hugging the machine gun to her chest, Anna slipped into the passenger seat behind the driver of another vehicle. Seconds later, the convoy rumbled out of the avenue. Anna and her master were now on course to meet their rightful destiny.

CHAPTER NINE

"Kerry. Try to keep your head still."

"Then ask Jack to drive in a straight line."

"I would," he called back from the front, "but it would mean driving through fields to avoid going round corners."

Pel said, "Stick to the road, Jack, bendy though it is. I'm nearly done with my grumpy patient."

As Jack drove out of town at three that morning, Pel had scrambled into the backseat with a first-aid kit. During the swaying, tire-screeching ride she'd managed to get Kerry's head bandaged. Blows and exposure to the cold night air had only briefly robbed the woman of her forthright nature. Kerry was back on form.

Pel tutted, "Just let me get this sticky tape on—it should hold the bandages in place."

"My God." Kerry appraised her reflection in the rearview mirror, the top of her head swathed in white bandage. "It's Halloween in a couple of weeks. Remind me not to turn up at a party dressed as an Egyptian mummy."

"When this is over," Pel told her, "you'll be good as new."

Jack killed the lights, then swung the nose of the car through an entrance marked LOWE BROS. HAULAGE. A yard, filled with a motley bunch of vehicles, stopped someway from the house. Jack braked the pickup next to a footpath that ran through bushes to the front door.

"This is where the man who attacked you lives." Jack checked that the shotgun had a full complement of ammo. "And where he's probably brought the mosaic."

"Probably?" Pel asked.

"If you have any religious inclinations, it's time to say your prayers. We won't be the only ones after the mosaic. Justice Murrain will want it, too, even if it's only to smash it into a million pieces." He opened the door. "Stay here."

"No way." Pel opened her door. "We're with you all the way."

"I want the pair of you here. Because I know for a fact that Ross and Scott have guns. When I get back to the truck with the mosaic I'll need to leave this yard like a bat out of hell."

"It'll be heavy," Kerry told him. "If it's still in one piece."

"I'm sure it will. They'll want it intact so they can effectively hold it to ransom. Those two are hell-bent on tormenting my grandfather." He gently eased his door shut. "I want to take them by surprise. Now, sit tight."

Pel watched Jack move through near darkness toward the house.

Kerry whispered, "Once he has the mosaic it needs to be set back into the mausoleum floor. If our theory about the occult mechanism at the site is correct then, once it has repaired itself, it will work its magic again. It'll yank Justice Murrain's henchmen back where they belong. Back into their graves."

A shiver trickled down Pel's spine. "You said *once it has repaired itself*. The effect won't be instant, then?"

"Magicians, priests, shamans, and warlocks of the past believed that their magic wasn't a transient thing. When they created sacred sites it was accomplished with great precision, using all kinds of devices, such as arrangements of standing stones, ditches, mounds, magic pathways, and walls—all laid out with geometric precision; there would be buried animals, or even humans, that had been ritualistically sacrificed. Each component had its own special value, or built-in power. Just like the components of a computer have specific tasks, such as conducting electricity, or governing the flow of information, or processing data, so the components of Temple Central each have specific duties. Some act as glue to stick the souls of the dead in a particular area of earth within the complex. Some of the components are designed to repair the temple if it is damaged. You see, the ancients believed that their religious structures were organic. They could be made to act more like living flesh rather than inanimate bricks or sterile mortar. Don't we do exactly the same today? When we enter a house for the first time, don't we pause for a moment to sense how it *feels* to us? Whether it is a happy or unfriendly place to be? Oh my God, I'm lecturing again." Kerry managed a tired smile. "When I should be groaning that my head hurts I grandly hold forth on the mythology of ancient temples. I'm sorry. And sorry for being a grouch, too, when you were trying to fix my bashed noggin."

"There's nothing to be sorry about." Pel smiled. "You're the main reason I stayed working on the dig."

Kerry feigned surprise. "Gosh, you mean to say that you weren't there for the glamour of sieving mountains of dirt, or our lavish wages?" She nodded, smiling. "I take that as a compliment."

The night air chilled Pel to the bone. "Jack's taking too long. Where is he?"

She leaned toward the side window to try to catch a glimpse of Jack at the house. A pair of eyes glared in at her. Before she could even cry out the front doors of the pickup opened.

A gruff voice uttered, "What the hell kept you? I thought you'd be here before now."

Two middle-aged men, thickset, reeking of liquor, slid into the front seats of the vehicle. The balding one chuckled. "Look here, Brother. The fool even left the keys in the ignition."

"Get out of here." Pel aimed a blow at the head of the man behind the wheel.

"Keep your mouth shut," said the other. "Don't worry, we'll take care of you two beauties."

"You're Ross Lowe," Pel shouted. "You almost killed this woman tonight. You'll do jail time for what you did to her."

Kerry added, "And where the hell is the mosaic?"

"I told you to shut up." Scott Lowe, in the passenger seat, raised a shotgun.

Pel didn't back down. "We must have the mosaic. Because you've moved it there's wholesale carnage in the town."

Scott pointed the gun at her face. "I told you to shut that trap of yours." Then to his brother: "Okay, better get this shifted before Murrain finds there's no one home."

The moment that Ross started the pickup Jack reappeared from behind the house. He must have been searching for a weak point so he could break in. Even though he raced toward them, Ross managed to get away with ease. The vehicle fishtailed as he accelerated across the dirt yard. In no time at all, he was through the gates, then out onto the road.

Over the roar of the motor Pel hollered, "Where are you taking us?"

Scott grinned at her along the gleaming gun barrel. "To a place where there's a lovely view of the ocean."

CHAPTER TEN

3:20. The convoy of Battle Men rumbled through darkness toward Jacob Murrain's house: fifty vehicles forming a line lit by each other's headlights. In a Ford Anna nursed the machine gun on her lap. Gripped by desperation, she knew she must prevent Justice Murrain from taking Pel Minton as his bride. As her fellow Battle Man drove she glanced at him. *Chauffeur*, she thought. Or rather he occupied the body of a chauffeur. As the man drove he eased scalpels from surgical wrappers.

"These are my Excaliburs," he explained as he stuck them point first into the cushioned surface of the dashboard. Soon, he had made himself a little forest of shiny surgical instruments. "Tonight, I occupied the body of a priest, then a paramedic. When the paramedic was disabled by gunfire I transferred to the body of a chauffeur who'd taken his master to the hospital. Simple, isn't it?" He added another scalpel to his steel forest. "I'll carve many an Adam's apple with these. Ha!" He glanced back at the machine gun on her lap. "So you have your own Excalibur, eh? A mechanical Excalibur that fires myriad musket balls at once . . . no, not musket balls. These modern weapons discharge bullets through a rifled barrel." The dashboard lights revealed his smiling face. "It's delightful to rummage through my host's mind and find such information. Easy. Like 'tis easy to drive this motor machine." They rumbled along for a while before he said, "You have taken possession of a female constable. You're Anna, aren't you?"

"And your demeanor makes me think you are Tom Griffin, right?"

"Correct. I remember you from the old days, when we all lived at Murrain Hall we were happy. Now we will be happy again."

"Will we?"

"Of course. I have a strong, young body. You are once more a beautiful woman. Isn't that better than being bones in a grave?"

"Then I'm happy for you, Tom."

"Ahhh . . ." He understood. "You once shared the master's bed, didn't you?"

"I was his wife . . . or as good as."

"Now, he's set his heart on the lady from the Americas. I see the problem."

"Do you?"

"Of course. You want your man back. But the Justice has plans that don't include you."

"Does he?" Her voice grew cold.

"Don't interfere, Anna, my sweet. If you make him angry he will destroy you. Have no doubt of that."

Anna didn't reply—she was thinking hard.

CHAPTER ELEVEN

Pel Minton stretched her aching limbs. "Dawn's breaking." Her voice echoed back from the classroom walls. "If those two aren't coming back, isn't it time we found a way out?"

"See for yourself." Kerry sat with her back to the wall. Patches of crimson had seeped through the bandages around her head. "There's steel mesh over the windows on the landward side. The only door that hasn't been nailed shut is the one that pair of thugs brought us through. And it's made of solid timber, with locks that would keep a barbarian horde out."

"We can't just sit here. Ross and Scott might be planning to execute us."

"Thanks for the optimistic prediction."

"Kerry, sarcasm isn't going to break down the door, is it? The Lowe family have got a vendetta against the Murrains. The first time I encountered them they were trying to ram trucks into the mausoleum. The second time they were slashing tires on Jack's pickup."

"Sorry, Pel. My head's sore. The wounds are still . . . seeping, to put it mildly. And . . ."

"And?"

"I know where we are."

Pel stopped pacing. "I know we're in an old school, that much is for sure." She gestured at upended desks that lay along one wall. On that wall were children's drawings of boats, houses, and stickmen. "I understood that the moment the oafs shoved us through the doorway."

"I mean, I know the place." Kerry grimaced. She had the emperor of all headaches. "This is Thorpe-Upton. I saw the sign as we arrived. It's a little village north of our graveyard dig. We—"

"*Help! Can anyone hear us!*" Pel didn't spare her vocal cords. "*Help!*" The power of the yell loosened dust from the roof beams overhead. In the morning light the falling particles formed a golden snow. "*Get us out of here. Help . . . HELP!*"

Kerry scrunched up her face as the yell made her headache a whole lot worse. "Thorpe-Upton is one of the cliff-top villages . . . to be more accurate, Pel, one of the *abandoned* cliff-top villages."

"The Lowes are smarter than they look. They knew nobody would hear us."

"Absolutely."

"Then we can't assume we'll be found. We have to save ourselves."

"Pel? Forgotten something? Locked door. Screens over windows."

Pel dragged a desk upright. "Now that it's getting light we should be able to see out." She slapped dust from her hands. "I guess the school's builders set the windows so high to stop the kids from gazing out and daydreaming."

Wearily, Kerry said, "We did a survey of Thorpe-Upton. Little of archaeological interest. A nineteenth-century school, which we're sitting in, field patterns of possibly Saxon origin. A Norman motte-and-bailey castle, circa 1070 AD— that is to say, a mound of dirt surrounded by a ditch. It formed a low-budget defense system."

"You're lecturing again, Kerry."

"You know something? I don't care anymore. Because I learned the motte and bailey fell into the sea last week."

"I'm sorry to hear that."

"And so you should. The site of it lies just outside the boundaries of this very school."

Pel had climbed onto the rickety desk. It wobbled. It wobbled very badly. On hearing those words she froze, forgetting to stay focused on her balance. "Pardon?"

"The earthworks fell into the sea. So where that puts the school in relation to the cliff is anyone's guess."

Pel nearly toppled from the rickety desk. At the last moment she caught hold of the windowsill. Heart clamoring with a panicky rhythm, she peered out through the glass. Now her heart really did miss a beat. "Oh, my God." She took a deep breath. "Kerry. We've got to get out of here. Did you hear me? *NOW!*"

CHAPTER TWELVE

The fifty vehicles in Justice Murrain's convoy halted on the road near Jacob Murrain's house. It didn't take long to establish that neither Jacob nor Jack were home.

Justice Murrain kicked down the door. The giant of a man made short work of the timbers. Even so, he suspected he'd broken at least three toes on the assault on the door. No worries. He'd make the switch soon to Jack Murrain, a young healthy body, through which Murrain blood coursed. Justice Murrain took time to explore the home of his descendants. When one of the Battle Men helped himself to whiskey from a bottle in the kitchen Justice Murrain punched him down to the floor.

"This will be my home," he bellowed. "Touch nothing!"

Then he lingered over photographs of the Murrain lineage that covered much of the dining room walls.

Anna crept in to stand silently behind him. Yet he knew she was there. They still shared a bond.

"Look at all these . . ." He indicated the photographs. "The Murrain men. Don't we look so very much alike?"

"You are all very handsome," she told him.

"Ha. That we are. I'm sure a Murrain man watched the Roman soldiers march into this godforsaken strip of coast two thousand years ago. And that very Murrain man, in his blue face paint, and wolf-skin cape, would have worn these features." He frowned. "Of course, I don't wear a Murrain face at present. But I will soon." He examined his features in a wall mirror. "Not pretty is it, this face? It was a mistake to possess the idiot boy. However, I judged a body of such size and strength would be useful to me. It is, Anna. Only it is so clumsy." Uneasy, he ran his fingers through his hair. "Sometimes the idiot's thoughts wrestle with my own. When they do . . . I . . . It becomes difficult to think clearly. There are times I . . ." An uncharacteristic air of perplexity surrounded Justice Murrain. Usually, his mind possessed absolute clarity. His judgments were invariably sound. "Only in the last few hours . . ."

"Anything wrong, master?"

"Wrong? No, nothing's wrong. Nothing at all."

He walked toward the broken front door.

"Where now, master?"

"The mausoleum. We'll probably find my kin there. I know that for Jacob Murrain the mosaic is an obsession."

They emerged from the house to find dawn's first light touching the treetops. Justice Murrain gave a booming order for everyone to climb back into the vehicles.

The driver in the lead car called, "In which direction are we headed, master?"

Irritated by what seemed such a foolish question, Justice Murrain snapped, "We're going to . . ." The force went from his voice. "Why . . . it's over there near the . . ." Once more his voice failed.

It seemed that all his followers in the vehicles stared at him through the windows. The giant in the white forensic suit cast glances about the garden. Then over the fields, where shadows yielded to the approaching day.

Concerned, Anna touched his arm. "Master?"

"It's really time I quit this ungainly flesh." He rubbed his face. "Anna?"

"Sir?"

"Tell me. Do you see a little figure over there on the lawn?"

"A figure, master?"

"Of course," he snapped. "A—a tiny goblin of a man. He's grinning . . . blasted, vile grin. *Bobby!* Uh . . . I don't know why I said that . . ." He rubbed his face again. This time he noticed his hands were shaking.

The driver who headed the convoy called out, "What's the matter?"

Anna replied loudly, "Nothing's the matter. Give the master a moment to consider his plans!"

She took Justice Murrain's arm. "I'll look after you. Step this way. Once you're in the car, you can rest a while." Pleased, she guided the man she loved to the lead vehicle. To its driver she snapped, "Drive to the graveyard. The rest will follow."

CHAPTER THIRTEEN

Pel Minton stared out of the school window in horror. No land presented itself. Instead, only ocean. Mile upon mile of gray briny water. In the dawn light she could see the dredgers already gouging at the ocean bed. They looked about as pretty as dreadnoughts, too. Those boats, hauling huge iron scoops, were responsible for the plight of the old school building. They'd destabilized the seabed for miles around. Coastal erosion greedily devoured the land. Day by day, ground had fallen into the surf by the ton. Now, the little village school stood (as precarious as Pel on the rickety desk) on the very edge of the cliff. When Pel pressed her nose to the cold glass she could make out the waves pounding the base of the cliff. Ocean scents spiked her nose.

In a dull, lifeless voice Kerry stated, "We're just about to fall into the sea, aren't we?"

"This building might. But we aren't going down with it." She scrambled from the desk, then opened a connecting door to the next classroom. The L-shaped building only consisted of a pair of classrooms. And those had high windows that were intended to cheat easily distracted pupils of the views. Pel rushed about to gain some overall picture of the school that the Lowe brothers had turned into a prison. As she did so, she shouted, "Kerry. Pull yourself together. We must find a way out of here."

"My head's sore. I'm weak as a mouse." She didn't budge from where she sat with her back to the wall beneath one of the high windows.

Pel's swift survey of the village school revealed that, apart from two classrooms, there was a miniscule closet that contained the remains of a heating system. An equally miniscule kitchen area with a disproportionately large Belfast sink. This room must be where the staff made their coffees, swapped stories about the children's antics, or whispered eagerly about colleagues' love affairs. Between the boiler room and the kitchen she discovered a narrow door that opened onto a set of stairs. These ascended to an attic space that served as the school's office. No furniture remained but a filing cabinet, its empty drawers yawning open. A calendar revealed that the school had been abandoned a couple of years ago. A rather alarming inscription above a wall hook read SPARE THE ROD, SPOIL THE CHILD. Pel didn't doubt for a moment that in the time of yore a formidable cane, which would have been used to beat mischievous children, once hung from the hook.

Most importantly for Pel, the office had two sets of windows set in the sloping ceilings. One had terrifying views of the sea. The second overlooked a road that ran to the edge of the cliff (the missing section of road must lie on the beach now). The surviving section passed between boarded-up homes, then uphill through woodland. These windows weren't covered with screens. *Can I persuade Kerry to climb out onto the roof? There might be a way of shinning down to the ground.* But then Kerry displayed signs of clinical shock. She had no energy, nor inclination, to do anything other than sit against the wall and utter pessimistic predictions about their approaching doom.

Pel scuttled down the stairwell, her feet clattered on the wooden risers. In the classroom, Kerry sat in a daze. Rather than alarm at being incarcerated by vengeful thugs she appeared on the verge of drifting into unconsciousness.

"Kerry. Don't go to sleep. We've got to get away from here." Pel clapped her hands. "Stay awake, please."

Clapping or her pleas didn't stir the woman.

Pel tried again. "Listen to me, don't go to sleep. Come on, there might be a way out of here."

Kerry muttered drowsily, "Leave me here. I'll be fine."

On the word *fine* a series of sharp clicks filled the room. The clicks became a cracking sound. A cracking that rose in volume. A staccato, nightmare cacophony. Pel froze in horror. In front of her the smooth white wall began to transform. First a spider pattern of delicate black lines appeared. Those black lines soon became ragged cracks. Plaster dropped from the walls. Windows shattered. Then the entire wall sagged outward.

"Kerry!"

At last, Kerry snapped to her senses. She scrambled away on all fours. At the same time, the classroom wall that faced the sea fell outward. A ton or so of brickwork plunged onto the beach below. Cold air gusted through the new opening. Even as the roar of falling masonry receded the wooden floor began to slope downward. Kerry still crawled on her hands and knees. However, the incline became so steep that she'd begun to slip backward. Aghast, Kerry tried to hook her fingernails into the smooth floor. No doing. Relentlessly, she slid back toward a clear blue sky where the wall had once stood.

Pel raced forward. She grabbed her boss by the wrists then dragged her back to the comparative safety of the wall at the far side of the classroom—the landward side.

"Thank you . . . thank you . . ." Kerry panted as Pel put her arms round the woman to comfort her.

By now, they caught a far-from-pleasant glimpse of rocks at the base of the cliff. That disconcerting view told them that they were a good hundred feet above the beach. A height that would ensure that they broke pretty much every bone in their body if they fell. *Add to that the school falling on top of us if we do*, Pel thought grimly. *This situation is about as lethal as you can get.*

From behind her, Pel heard a loud guffaw. Ross and Scott

Lowe stood there in the doorway to the room. They grinned hugely.

Pel shouted, "You've got to let us out."

The grins, if anything, got even more huge.

"Please," she begged, "at any minute the cliff will give way under us. The entire school's going to fall into the sea."

Ross enjoyed the women's terror. "Do you want to say anything else about your predicament?"

Kerry yelled, "What the hell are you talking about? You can see for yourselves. Get us out. Or we'll be killed!"

"That's it. Movie gold."

Then Pel understood. Ross held a cell phone in his hand. He'd filmed what happened when the walls collapsed; now he recorded their reaction to the danger.

Scott asked, "Did you catch it all on camera, Ross?"

"That I did, Scott. That I did." The burly man nodded with satisfaction. "Ma's going to love seeing this." He laughed. "Then I'll send it to Jack Murrain."

Scott remarked, "I wish I could see Murrain's face when he watches his girlfriend and the other bitch screaming their heads off. The picture of fear they are. The very picture!"

"Bastards!"

Pel would have attacked the men if Kerry hadn't held on to her.

Still filming the pair, together with a vast aperture in the wall revealing views of the ocean, Ross retreated through the doorway into the second classroom. His brother performed a kind of burlesque dance with the shotgun, so whoever viewed the film would realize that gravity wasn't the only danger the women faced. A pair of armed thugs featured, too. Pel Minton knew full well that this, the incarceration, and filming their terror, was another act in the brothers' vendetta against the Murrains.

Whether Pel and Kerry survived to hear how Jack did react to the footage remained to be seen.

With calls of "Hang on tight," "Lovely view, isn't it?" and

"Don't leave the place in a mess," the brothers exited through the only functioning door to the outside world. By the time Pel had raced to it she found it securely locked once more.

For now, they were staying put in the school, as it stood precariously on the edge of the cliff. More bricks fell from the wall. A crack appeared in the ceiling.

Kerry murmured, "One way or another, our stay here will only be a short one."

CHAPTER FOURTEEN

Jacob Murrain warmed his bones by the fire he'd made. An early morning sun poured a fierce light upon the gravestones. They cast long ultrablack shadows, which pointed like scores of accusing fingers at the mausoleum. A mausoleum that he'd failed to protect. Many a time that night he'd threaded his way between tombs and the archaeologists' trenches. With dread making every step echo a condemned man's walk to the gallows, he'd revisit the mausoleum. Sight of the raw, dark hole in its floor made him wince. Ever since the son of Justice Murrain had installed the mosaic in the 1700s, a Murrain had ensured that no harm befell the image: for his ancestors believed that the mosaic had the power to contain the monstrous spirit of Justice Murrain. Now he, Jacob Murrain, had botched his family's duty. On his watch he'd allowed the mosaic to be stolen. Justice Murrain and his henchmen were free again to take possession of innocent men and women. Jacob knew that they'd wreak carnage.

Jacob's eyes filled with tears. "I'm sorry. I've failed you." The man directed the words at his ancestors, who'd successfully discharged their duty. "I've let you down." Did the ghost of his father, and grandfather, and all the other Murrains, hear his apology? He prayed that they did, yet it did not ease his shame. Suddenly, he had a clear mental image of his Stone Age ancestor who was the shaman of this place in prehistoric times, long before the Christian graveyard existed. Jacob pictured a tall, straight figure clad in animals' skins.

That trademark mane of black hair would adorn his head. Those gray eyes that graced the Murrain men were gazing at Jacob. The man stood in the midst of the pagan temple, surrounded by a complex arrangement of ring mounds and ditches. Spirit roads, surfaced with crushed limestone to make them a shining white, would radiate outward into the surrounding forests. These were the magic highways along which the ghosts of yet even more ancient ancestors would travel to the heart of this sacred place. At that instant, he was both his ancestor from an age long past of flint blades and forest gods, and he was Jacob Murrain, a modern man of this age of steel blades and computer technology.

When he murmured these words they issued from his lips, and from the lips of the figure dressed in wolf pelts: *"Blood . . . Murrain blood will heal all."*

Jacob blinked. He stood before the open gate of the mausoleum. Gales that had been born in the Arctic tugged his hair. It seemed as if he'd woken from a trance. For a while, he wasn't sure if he'd been standing by the fire he'd made earlier to stop the cold killing from him, or if he'd been wandering in a daze through the cemetery, calling out to his ancient bloodline to help him.

An engine thundered on the cold air. Shielding his eyes against the sun's glare, he saw a huge, flat-backed truck barreling along the lane to the cemetery. There, it screeched to a stop by the gates. From it leaped a familiar figure.

"Jack? Jack, my boy! You're safe!" His heart could have burst with joy at that moment. However, the expression on Jack's face soon killed the relief he felt. "What's wrong?" he asked as Jack reached him.

"It's Pel and Kerry . . . the Lowe brothers have got them!"

"Those thugs are as insane as their mother. Do you know where the women are?"

Jack shook his head. "Kerry recovered consciousness at the hospital. She told us that it was Ross who'd attacked her last night. She'd caught him hacking at the mosaic. Then about three hours ago I drove to the brothers' place to confront them. Damn it, the pair had it all planned out. They knew I'd come looking for the mosaic. So they lay in wait to kidnap Pel and Kerry. The bastards drove off with them in my pickup." Anger as much as exertion made him breathless. "It took me almost two hours to break into their office so I could get the keys to one of their trucks."

"We must find them. They'll torture the women." Jacob spoke with such stark clarity that Jack grimaced. "To the brothers' warped minds it will be vengeance. Their mother believes I was responsible for the accident that destroyed her face."

"Where do we even begin looking?"

"Scott and Ross could have taken them almost anywhere by now. In the meantime, Justice Murrain and his Battle Men will be doing whatever the hell they want."

"So far, that's amounting to arson, looting, physical abuse, murder." Jack recapped the events of last night. How they'd struggled to find a route through the mayhem to reach the hospital. Jacob sighed with relief on hearing that Kerry's wounds weren't serious. Yet he appeared physically nauseated on hearing accounts of wholesale bloodshed in Crowdale.

"So," he began when Jack had finished, "we're fighting a battle on two fronts. There's Scott and Ross Lowe to tackle. Then we must deal with Justice Murrain." Deep in thought, he gazed at the ocean. "The trouble is, it will be fruitless killing the possessed. The spirits of the Battle Men will readily leave a dead husk behind to find a new body to occupy. That will become worse when police reinforcements arrive from other towns. Soon they'll be possessed, too. We won't know who is friend and who is foe." He blew into his cold hands. "How we can combat them I don't know. But there's got to be a way. There has to be. Or we'll—" He stopped talking the moment that Jack's phone trilled. "Quickly, Jack, that might be Pel or Kerry." The man was almost pathetically grateful for the merest sign of hope.

On checking the phone's screen Jack grimaced. "It's Ross Lowe."

"He's got your number?"

"That's no mystery. It's painted on the side of my pickup they stole." He thumbed a key, then frowned, puzzled. "I don't like the look of this. They're sending me video footage."

"Brace yourself for a shock, son. It probably makes for grim viewing."

Stone-faced, Jack held the phone so both men could see the screen. First: shots of a building. Clearly, a former village school; its windows were covered with mesh to prevent any lowlife breaking in. A stout timber door hove into view. A hand appeared in the shot to unlock the door. The rest of the unhappy film unfolded in one long shot that picked up sound with fearsome clarity.

Jacob's blood ran cold as he watched events unfold. The little screen showed him the interior of a disused classroom. Windows set high in a wall. Tumbled desks. Discarded picture books. Kerry sat on the floor, her back to the wall. Pel stood in the center of the shot. She appeared to be imploring Kerry. At that instant the entire wall collapsed outward to reveal blue sky and ocean. On all fours, a panicked Kerry rushed away from the demolition. Pel grabbed hold of her, dragged her to safety, where the women sat on the floor, their arms round each other.

One of the Lowe brothers must have been operating the camera phone. Both their voices, however, rumbled from the speaker as they approached their victims. Pel noticed her captors; she called out to them.

Then one of the men asked, *"Do you want to say anything else about your predicament?"*

Kerry replied, and this time the phone caught her voice. *"What the hell are you talking about? You can see for yourselves. Get us out. Or we'll be killed!"*

Ross: *"That's it. Movie gold."*

Scott: *"Did you catch it all on camera, Ross?"*

"That I did, Scott. That I did. Ma's going to love seeing this. Then I'll send it to Jack Murrain."

Even on such a tiny screen Pel Minton's face expressed utter fury. Her eyes blazed. She'd have beat the men with her fists if she could. Off camera, one of the brothers commented that he wished he could have seen Jack's reaction when he watched their vile little kidnap movie.

Jacob began to move as fast as his legs could carry him in the direction of the parked truck. "Jack! Fire her up!"

"Where are we going?"

"I know where that school is. It's Thorpe-Upton—just ten minutes north of here!"

Jack easily kept pace with the man; even so, Jacob managed an impressive jog, despite his limp.

"If they gave away the place where they're keeping them so easily," Jack said, "then might it be a trap?"

"Of course it's a trap. The women are bait. They want to lure me there."

"Then we're going to walk right into it."

"Got a better idea, son?"

Once they were in the cab Jack started the motor. Flooring it, he swung the heavy truck round across the meadowland, crushing a fence; then he pushed the vehicle hard.

"Turn right at the crossroads," Jacob told him. "You can't miss Thorpe-Upton. It's the end of the road. Literally."

CHAPTER FIFTEEN

In the lead car of the Battle Men convoy Anna sat beside a brooding Justice Murrain. The man appeared troubled. More than once he muttered to himself, "Time's running out . . . I need to make the transfer to Jack Murrain soon . . ."

One of the Battle Men had found a pair of binoculars. He stood on the passenger seat with his upper half through the sunroof. The man eagerly scanned the way ahead. Every so often he'd call out such comments as, "I see the cemetery." A moment later: "By God's breath! The ocean is closer now than in our day. Murrain Hall is entirely gone!" Then more crucially, "Master, a large vehicle is leaving the cemetery." He checked out the machine with his binoculars. "Sire, I can see two men through the glass." His voice pealed out with excitement. "Both are Murrain! One is old, the other quite young!"

"We're closing in on Jack Murrain." Justice Murrain nodded with satisfaction. "Good. Follow them." He smiled. "They'll soon be in our hands."

CHAPTER SIXTEEN

Over at the school the women's situation became increasingly perilous. They'd retreated into the second classroom, which was the farthest from the edge of the cliff. This wouldn't grant them much more time. Erosion steadily nibbled the cliff away. Sometimes it took formidable bites. Already half of the floor in the next classroom had slipped away down to the beach a hundred feet below. Even in the classroom they occupied huge cracks appeared in the walls. If Pel had been crazy enough to risk losing a finger or two she could easily have slipped a digit inside the masonry.

She told Kerry, "We can't just sit here waiting for the school to topple off the edge of the cliff."

The woman in her bloodstained bandages shrugged helplessly. "What do you suggest? The only way is through the main door. That timber's hard as iron."

"If we can inch our way toward the side of the classroom that's fallen away, maybe there'll be enough of the cliff top remaining. We might be able to escape along that."

"You're out of your mind."

"Worth a try, wouldn't you say?"

They passed through a short linking corridor. Enormous stresses from warping walls had split the white Belfast sink in two in the kitchen. The stairs up to the office had buckled, too. Plaster dust fell as steadily as snow. Every so often, glass would shatter as frames twisted under the stress.

As they moved slowly into the classroom, or rather what

remained of it, the building began to groan. It groaned from the depths of its failing foundations to the top of its cockeyed roof timbers. The edifice could have been some sick old beast that was close to death. With every deep, weary groan the floor shivered. More cracks burst the wall plaster. Children's pictures stuck there split in two. From the vast opening created by the fallen wall the sea winds gusted in.

"Move with your back to this wall." Pel motioned Kerry. "The floor's sagging in the center."

So they slid toward the raw, open wound of this mortally wounded building. Gravity and coastal erosion conspired to be its assassins. Another groan. The incline of the floor increased. A desk tumbled over the edge. Soon after that they heard a thud as it struck the rocks below.

Pel inched her way to where the wall ended. Beyond that, nothing but ice-cold air. The sea sparkled in hard sunlight. Ships plied their lazy routes through the ocean a dozen miles away from this precarious life-and-death battle. Another groan. Tremors shivered through the building. This time, roof slates skidded off the timbers to fall in a black rain just inches from Pel's head.

"Can you see if there's any way out?" shouted Kerry.

"Take my hand . . . hold on tight. I'm going to lean out past the end of the wall."

"I've got you."

Pel stretched out as far as she dare. Moments ago, there had been a hundred-year-old wall here. Now she could see it on the rocks far below. All of it reduced to individual bricks by the shattering force of its fall. Mixed among those, a hell of a lot of debris from the school. Gales blew her hair. The cold had such intensity it made her teeth ache. When she leaned out a little farther she could tell that the cliff had eroded back *under* the building. This side of the structure overhung the rock face with nothing to support it but a salty breeze. That meant this section of floor had nothing beneath it, either, other than a long drop. To her left, just behind the wall she leaned against, there was no cliff. From this angle she couldn't even see it. To her right, the remains of the pupils' toilet block. One elevation had fallen away. The line of white ceramic toilet bowls that had been revealed reminded her, bizarrely, of white teeth set in a human gum. The building convulsed again. Pel watched the toilet block come adrift. It tumbled down the sheer cliff in a mess of brickwork, dust, and shining ceramic bowls.

"No way out this way, Kerry! Pull me back!"

Quickly, the pair shuffled back the way they'd come, spines pressed hard to the wall. Soon they were back in the only intact classroom. Albeit one showing signs of distress. Dust hung thick in the air to tickle their throats. Kerry fired off a volley of sneezes.

"I'll give the building thirty minutes—at most." Pel shivered as structural timbers groaned. "Then, whether we want to or not today, we'll be visiting the beach."

CHAPTER SEVENTEEN

Jacob hung on to the grab handle on his side of the truck cabin. His grandson drove the huge vehicle as if it were a sports car. Just ahead lay the abandoned houses of Thorpe-Upton. The school on the cliff's brink possessed a strangely ragged appearance now that part of it had collapsed. Roof beams poked upward, the displaced bones of that sad edifice.

Jacob had two warnings: "Easy, Jack, the road ends at the cliff's edge." And, second: "See your pickup? The Lowe brothers are here, too."

Jack had a warning of his own. "We've picked up some followers." He jerked his thumb back over his shoulder. "About fifty vehicles, half a mile behind us."

"Justice Murrain and his Battle Men, no doubt."

Jack gave a grim smile. "Events are about to become ever so interesting."

When the school was some hundred yards away he slowed the bucking vehicle. Straightaway, three figures stepped from the pickup.

Jacob clicked his tongue. "Ross and Scott Lowe, plus deranged mother."

After stopping the truck, Jack pulled the shotgun out from behind his seat. Then both decamped from the cab; two eerily similar men, despite the age difference of sixty years.

Jack approached the three. He grimaced when he saw the ruinous state of the old woman's face. One half had been burned until it resembled a Halloween mask. The two men aimed their shotguns at Jack.

"This madness has gone far enough," Jacob told them.

His grandson added with some force, "Hand the women over, Scott. I know you're no killer." He shot Ross a filthy look, his meaning clear. *Ross, however, is beyond redemption.*

"Where are they?" demanded Jacob.

Gleefully, Rebecca Lowe shrilled, "In yonder schoolhouse. They're going down with all that bricks and mortar—you'll watch the bitches fall with 'em."

"Rebecca. There's no need for this. We've been at odds for thirty years. But keep innocent people out of it."

"I couldn't hurt you, Jacob Murrain. You thrive on noble self-sacrifice. If I hurt the ones you care about, that's another thing entirely. See this?" She pushed her hair away from the medley of oranges, yellows, rifts, and puckered flesh. "That's your doing, Murrain. After that night in the cemetery not another man lusted over me again. Boys, tell him how I've endured a life of torment."

The pair appeared close to tears. Their mother's outpouring of emotion shook them to the core. Ross tightened his finger around the gun trigger. "Just give me the word, Ma. Just give me the word! I'll blow his head off!"

From the building came a rending sound. Another ton or so of masonry parted from the structure to crash to the beach.

Jack said, "Scott. Do the right thing."

"My mother isn't long for this world. Her heart's failing. We promised her." He pointed the gun at Jack.

Jack aimed at the old woman. "Pull that trigger and I'll fire before I die. I'm promising you."

Jacob spoke gravely. "Rebecca. It's time to tell your boys to stop this. We have to bury our differences."

"Oh? What puts you in a position where you can demand anything?"

"Because of them, Rebecca." He pointed at the approaching line of vehicles. "You've heard of my ancestor Justice Murrain and his Battle Men. You know about the terrible things they did in Crowdale."

"That was hundreds of years ago." She laughed. "Losing our mind are we, Jacob?"

The Lowe brothers watched the approaching convoy. They exchanged glances of alarm.

"I guarded the mosaic of my ancestor, Rebecca. My grandson was destined to follow me in my duty. You see, the portrait of Justice Murrain kept his restless soul locked in the earth. Now that your sons have removed it they have opened the prison door. Evil spirits are free, Rebecca. You know the legends of the Ghost Monster. They were told often enough by our parents and the townspeople."

Scott frowned. The vehicles were only seconds away from reaching them. Something about their occupants unsettled him. "Ma, is this true?"

"Pah! Jacob Murrain and his family are crazy. Obsessed they are. The damned picture in the mausoleum means everything to them. I remember Jacob's grandfather when I was a girl. He trudged through snowstorms to make sure the lamp still burned there. Jacob, here, inherited the madness. The night this happened"—she touched her disfigured features—"I followed Jacob up to the cemetery. I watched him and laughed at him as he oh so carefully swept the mausoleum floor. Then he got a little rag to oh so gently wipe the grubby face of his ancestor. And he fiddled with the lamp to make it all rosy and warm. Foolish man."

Jacob asked, "Do you want to know the truth, Scott? Do you, Ross? We were—"

"Shut up, Jacob," she shrieked.

"We were lovers. And sometimes even the best love affairs go wrong."

Jack warned, "Grandfather. They're nearly here."

"Shoot the pair of them," howled Rebecca. *"Kill them!"*

Ross would have obeyed, but Scott pushed the muzzle upward so it aimed harmlessly skyward. "Ma, is he telling the truth?"

"Tell them, Rebecca. We had three happy years together. Then I fell sick with influenza. You never liked to be kept waiting, did you?"

Ross had locked onto the notion of killing the Murrains. "That's not important. You did that to Ma's face. That's why I'm going to blow your heads off."

Jacob cast glances at the approaching vehicles. Already, he glimpsed Justice Murrain in the lead car. Yet he took the remaining moments to explain calmly: "Scott. We'd broken up, your mother and I. There were attempts at reconciliation after that, but . . . well, anyway, I'd gone to the mausoleum one night to check everything was all right. Your mother followed me up there. I know she was simply being playful, but she grabbed the lamp. I begged her not to. When she saw that she'd succeeded in teasing me she ran off with it. I followed her, because she'd gone into the ruin of Murrain Hall, which stood on the cliff. It was dangerous. Like the school, here, it was falling into the sea. As I tried to catch up with your mother she tripped. When she fell the lamp broke. The oil ignited and . . ." He sighed. "I'm so sorry what happened to you, Rebecca. However, it was an accident. Nobody was to blame."

"Scott, this is your mother telling you the truth. Murrain is responsible for this." She seized her son's hand, pressed it to that withered orange-peel flesh. "Kill the pair of them." Mad lights danced in the woman's remaining eye. "Tear them apart!"

Scott, however, couldn't help but stare at the approaching vehicles. They trundled in line along the narrow lane, flanked by stout brick walls. "That bloke there in the car," he said. "That's Horace Neville."

His mother snarled, "The idiot boy. So?"

"Horace Neville killed three cops. They say he murdered his own mother."

Jack called out, "Now will you believe us? Those men and women have been possessed by the spirits of Justice Murrain's thugs."

"Possessed by spirits?" Rebecca spat in disgust. "Jack Murrain, you're as deranged as your grandfather."

Scott wasn't so sure his mother spoke the truth. "Ma. Some of those people are in their nightclothes. This doesn't look right to me."

"There'll be a *sane* explanation. See? In the front car with Neville? That's a policewoman. They must have arrested the simpleton, then—"

At that point, the policewoman did something that none of the Lowes expected. As the car turned sideways on, just thirty paces from them, the pretty woman in the police uniform pushed the muzzle of a submachine gun from the open window, then fired a burst in the direction of the Lowe family. One of the rounds smashed into Scott's thigh.

"Damn!" he exclaimed before firing back. The pellets shattered a side window. Even from here Jacob saw blood spill from the driver's head.

Howling, Rebecca begged her sons to kill Jacob. Ross stood there gawping, too dim to know what to do next. Scott reached a decision.

"Jack!" Scott tossed the man a key. "Get the women out of the school, then run."

"What are you doing?" shrieked Rebecca. "This isn't what I wanted!"

"Maybe not, Ma. But if it's the last thing I do, I'm going to make up for all the trouble we've caused. You're with me, aren't you, Ross?"

Ross appeared torn between obedience toward his mother and allegiance to his younger brother. At last: "I'm with you, Scott. Sorry, Ma, but we think you need help."

"No . . . No!" She threw the queen of all tantrums. By the handful, she ripped out her hair, as she wept and yelled.

Jack ran to the school's main door. As he wrestled with

the key, in a no-doubt rusty and underused lock, another chunk of school collapsed over the edge of the cliff.

Jacob prayed that the two women had managed to find some relatively safe corner of the building.

Meanwhile, the bulk of the convoy emerged from the narrow section of lane to fan out into the area that once comprised the village green. From vehicles, there spilled a strange assortment of half-dressed, or even completely undressed citizens of Crowdale. Most wore leers. They anticipated violent entertainment. What's more, they didn't appear troubled that Scott, Ross, and Jack toted shotguns. Jacob saw that the possessed had armed themselves with hammers, screwdrivers, and knives. Most formidable of all, the policewoman with the machine gun. Behind him, a series of thuds told him that yet more of the school had tumbled into the ocean.

"Talk about being caught between the devil and the deep blue sea," he murmured. Then he called to his grandson. "Jack. Hurry!"

At last Jack managed to unlock the door. Only the door frame had warped from the building's decidedly seaward slant. After shouldering it three times it slammed inward. Instantly, Pel and Kerry burst free.

All four charged across to where the big flatbed truck stood nearby.

Jack suddenly paused. Then to the Lowe family, who'd bunched together to support a wounded Scott, he shouted, "Come with us. I can get you away from them."

Scott called back, "You know we'll get jail for what we've done. We've reached the end of the line: Ma, Ross, and me. This is what we want. To all go together."

Dozens of Battle Men advanced across the road toward both the Murrain group and family Lowe.

Jacob hissed, "The Lowe brothers are as crazy as their mother." Then he shouted to Scott. "Where's the mosaic?"

At that moment Ross let fly with the gun. A pair of possessed middle-aged men were felled by the single blast. Some of the Battle Men threw knives and screwdrivers. One pierced Rebecca Lowe's shoulder. She gave a piercing scream. Now both men fired their guns into the crowd.

Jacob searched for the giant form of Justice Murrain. When the shooting started he'd retreated quickly. Eventually, he saw him hanging back at the rear of his mob of thugs. The policewoman guarded him, machine gun at the ready. Clearly, Jacob's ancestor wasn't prepared to risk his own neck during the attack. Then Jacob had begun to suspect that Justice Murrain's choice of host, the brain-damaged Horace Neville, might have been deeply misguided.

When the Lowe brothers had finished discharging their weapons Jacob shouted, "For God's sake. The mosaic. Where is it? We can stop all this if you tell us where it is!"

This time it was Ross who spoke. "You'll find it at our house. Under the cellar stairs."

"Thank you, Ross. Thank you, Scott. In the end, you were good men." With that, Jacob pointed at the truck. "Get us out of here, Jack."

Soon they climbed into the cab: Jacob and Jack in the front. Pel and Kerry scrambled into the bunk area at the back. Jack fired up the big motor. Just yards away, the school collapsed like a house of cards. Brick dust billowed. In the bright sunlight it formed a crimson fog that momentarily obscured the confrontation in the road. By the time it cleared, Scott and Ross had reloaded. They fired again. Their mother stood between them, still howling and wringing her hands. Eight of the possessed lay flat on the blacktop, lifeblood oozing from gunshot wounds. The 200 or so other Battle Men took their time to savor the fact that they closed in on their prey.

Pel said, "When Jack shot one of the possessed in the hospital the spirit simply transferred to a new host. Why isn't that happening here?"

"My guess is," Jacob replied, "that the possessors are becoming deeply embedded in their host's brains. So when the body is killed it is taking longer for the spirit to disentangle from the flesh." He nodded at the figure in the white forensic suit. "As for Justice Murrain, I figure he's got another problem entirely."

Jack shot his grandfather a surprised glance. "And that is?"

"Just wait and see. And pray that I'm right."

From the back of the cab Kerry shouted, "Look at Ross. Something's happening!"

Jacob peered through the windshield as Jack turned the rig across open grass. Ross appeared as if he'd suddenly become distracted from their fight. His body stiffened. He rubbed his temple with the heel of his hand, afflicted by a headache. Then his usual expression of mulish bad temper was replaced with an expression of cunning. A smile spread across his face. Then without any further ado he raised the shotgun. *Bang.* His brother's head vanished in a puff of crimson. Then he jabbed the muzzle into his mother's stomach. Squeezed the trigger. The womb that had given him life was obliterated in a blast of lead.

That done, whatever had taken possession of Ross Lowe strolled over the road to join its comrades.

Jacob noticed an agitated Justice Murrain beckon his Battle Men back to the vehicles. "It looks as if we'll have that lot chasing us."

"Then let's make life difficult for them," shouted Jack. He drove the truck along the line of vehicles. When he reached the convoy's tail some cars still remained between the two walls where the lane was narrowest. Jack eased past them, braked, then slammed the truck into reverse. "Warn me if any of those devils try to jump on board." Then he backed the truck into the tail end of the convoy. Effortlessly, the big rig shoved cars as if they were toys. Soon, a jumble of wrecked vehicles effectively blocked the lane. Jack gave a grim smile. "That road's the only way out of the village.

They'll have to shift a hell of a lot of scrap metal before they even can think of following." That said, he slammed the truck into gear. In no time at all, it lumbered forward, carrying them away from the carnage of wrecked vehicles and bloody cadavers.

CHAPTER EIGHTEEN

At the cemetery dig site Nat experienced conflicting emotions. When he'd arrived there that morning with a pair of dirt monkeys, he'd looked over the edge of the cliff, then let out a huge whoop of joy. It gladdened his archaeologist heart that Temple Central, and all its precious earthworks, would be saved for future generations. For there, on the beach below, a row of wagons armed with mechanical claws lowered steel cages full of rock onto the sands at the base of the cliff. These would run for a mile along the shore. Although they wouldn't stop the cliff getting wet at high tide, they'd rob the surf of its destructive force.

Then Nat visited the mausoleum. This time a cry of despair erupted from his lips. The mosaic had vanished. Some vandal had hacked it out during the night. He recalled his impromptu lecture on Temple Central being a supernatural mechanism. At its heart, the mosaic that formed the image of Justice Murrain. *Just imagine,* he thought, *if what Jacob Murrain had said was true then all hell would be let loose.*

One of the dirt monkeys, an attractive blonde, walked unsteadily toward him. "I'm going to sit in the car. Start of a head cold I think. I'm not feeling myself." She swayed.

"Chelsea, are you all right?"

"I'm not Chelsea!" The blonde seized a shovel from a soil mound. Then she raced toward Nat. From the expression on her face he had no doubt she lusted after blood. His blood.

CHAPTER NINETEEN

Jack Murrain hammered the truck along the lane. Jacob sat alongside him. On the bunk in the back of the cab, two dazed women. Kerry rubbed her head where the bandage started to itch. Her eyes were empty.

Pel Minton had seen hell. Touched hell. Felt hell embrace her. Felt its fiery lips on hers. For the first time since she left Providence one humid day, with the promise of thunder advancing across the heights of Swan Point Cemetery, she wondered if she'd not only left the United States, but if she'd also left the world behind. England, she'd discovered, could be a strange place. *They drive on the wrong side of the road. Elevators are called lifts. Englishmen devour piecrust filled with pig kidneys. They relish sausages made of blood. Now this . . . is this madness so unexpected? Here I am on a coast being munched away by the ocean. Ghosts have broken out of their occult prison to take possession of English men and women. Have those people resisted the mind invasion? Or did they secretly welcome it? Does the Englishman secretly crave domination? If they are conquered by alien strength, does that absolve them from responsibility? Do they long to shed their buttoned-up lifestyle? Are they aching for one of excess, debauchery, sexual freedom? Will random violence purge them of their ancestors' crimes?*

Pel found herself drifting into a state of altered consciousness. The ride became strangely soothing. It seemed she traveled in some phantom machine that rose and fell in a smoothly rhythmic way. After the tension of being imprisoned in a school that had been falling piecemeal into the ocean, and witnessing a bloody shootout on the village green, this influx of relaxation was a healing balm. Exchanging terror for security, albeit fleeting, eased her aching limbs as absolutely as morphine.

Even though her body swayed in harmony with the swerves of this drive along a narrow country lane, she was at peace. She thought: *Perhaps this is how it feels when you're preparing to die. Warmth. Comfort. A sense of letting go* . . . In front of her, the two near-identical black manes of hair of the Murrains. Beyond the Murrains, the windshield. Beyond that, a river of black tar on which their iron ship of the highway glided.

Grandfather and grandson conversed: "*Did you see Ross Lowe?*"

"*The spirit of a dead Battle Man left the corpse; then it entered him.*"

"*It happened so fast. Ross killed Scott and his mother in cold blood.*"

"*As they will do to me, Jack. The moment they get the opportunity.*"

"*Nobody's safe from being slaughtered.*"

"*All except you, Jack. The truth is, son, Justice Murrain plans to steal your body from you. Then, in the words he used yesterday, he intends to make Pel Minton his 'bride.'*" In a quiet voice, which Jacob clearly thought she couldn't hear, he added, "*Keep a couple of shotgun cartridges in reserve. Just in case. Whatever happens, don't let Pel be captured by the madman.*"

As Jack accelerated onto the main highway, troubling images flowed through Pel's mind. She'd been drawn to Jack by his otherworldly beauty. His quiet English manner had enticed her, too. She'd wanted to test his boundaries. Wouldn't it be downright sexy to provoke him into a fiery outburst of passion? Now, in that trancelike state, she saw him as a darkly occult figure. One as deeply embedded in this ancient land-

scape as the venerable oak tree in the meadow. If Justice
Murrain took possession of his descendant, she would be
powerless. A sudden flash-forward, and a vision of her wedding night seared her brain. Jack's body would crush her naked flesh against the bed. His dark hair would brush her skin
as he kissed her. But it would be Justice Murrain, the psychopath, the Satanist, the murderer, the mutilator of his own son
who would have possession of Jack's brain. Then, remorse-
lessly, coldly, callously, the possessed man would exert a formidable pressure. He'd crave to penetrate her body. Crying
would be futile. His eyes would blaze; he'd glory in his con-
quest of her. She felt the sting of that pressure now. A bittersweet sting that once would have inflamed her desires . . . now
a violation.

"*Here!*"

Jack's shout startled Pel so much that she almost screamed.
It felt akin to waking from a deep sleep. Dazed, she wondered
why she rode in a truck that careered through the gates of a
haulage company. She watched parked vans blur by. Jack appeared to be in no hurry to stop. Then, as she gathered her
wits, memories streamed through her head—the trip to the
hospital with Kerry. Crowdale in flames. The possessed. How
they ran amok. How they reveled in carnage. Being incarcerated in the cliff-top building that threatened to carry them to
their deaths.

Pel saw a sign on a wall: LOWE BROS. HAULAGE.

Jacob warned, "The house will be locked, Jack. It'll take
time to break in."

Pel's mind snapped into focus. "We can't be delayed in getting the mosaic back to the cemetery."

"No problem," Jack sang out. "I'm onto it."

He didn't slow before the fence that separated parking lot
from garden. The truck slammed through wooden rails. Jack
kept his foot on the gas. Thundering like the god of war, the
huge motor propelled the vehicle—across the lawn, through
bushes, over flower beds, then—*crash!*—it plunged into the

front of the house. Jack reversed the rig back from the debris. Brickwork covered the hood. More masonry tumbled on the lawn. Dust billowed in the morning sunlight.

"I'll be right back."

"You'll find it under the stairs in the cellar," Jacob told him. "For the pity of mankind be quick! The Battle Men will be here soon!"

Jack raced through that yawning hole in the house created by the collision. Moments passed. Jacob glanced back at the road. Pel willed Jack to move lightning fast. Kerry kept repeating, "If we can only get the mosaic back in its setting, we might have a chance. It may draw those devils back."

At last! Jack loped over the debris. In his hands, a wooden crate. He shoved it into the cab's foot-well beneath his grandfather's feet.

Both Pel and Kerry leaned over the front seats to get a better view. For there, in the crate, a familiar face peered out. Justice Murrain. Huge gray eyes. Mane of black hair. A Satan rendered in fragments: shards of pot, chips of stone, glass splinters—all carefully gathered from the ruins of Murrain Hall.

Over 200 years ago the son of Justice Murrain, *sans thumbs*, had patiently assembled crud from the ancestral home into a likeness of his father. A portrait that had sealed the monster's troublesome spirit into the ground for centuries.

God willing, Pel told herself, *he will soon be back in the earth where he belongs.*

"Hold on tight." Jack reversed the truck toward the road. "Next stop, Temple Central!"

Pel added, darkly: *"Next stop is our destiny."*

CHAPTER TWENTY

Nat Stross rubbed the painful bump above his left eyebrow. "Dianne? What came over her?" he asked his young female colleague. "That isn't what Chelsea does. She's usually shy as a mouse." He gazed down at the leering, foul-mouthed creature that lay in the cemetery grass. Her limbs were bound with the fluorescent orange tape they normally used to mark out excavation grids.

Dianne shrugged. "Did you make one of your improper suggestions?"

"Absolutely not! At least, not for a couple of days." Nat rooted for a possible reason for Chelsea's attack. "Time of month?"

"Don't even go there."

"All right."

Dianne couldn't take her eyes from Chelsea's wild leer. "But what can we do with her? They say there's been a riot in Crowdale. The army have cordoned off the entire town."

Nat rubbed his jaw. After his insensitive "time of month" suggestion he had a sudden reluctance to venture any plan other than, "We could let her rest here for a while. She might come to her senses."

The creature yelled, *"Take me! You know you want to!"*

"I'll fetch the thermos," Nat said quickly. "We could do with a coffee."

To the woman Chelsea hissed. "Rip off my clothes. Get handfuls of that graveyard dirt; big moist handfuls. Smear it over my body. I want to feel it—all those bits of bone and body and death! Rub it into my breasts good and hard. Ha, turning you on, aren't I? Admit it, your heart's beating faster. You want to lick your lips. Your starting to picture yourself fondling me. Come on . . . pull away my bra. Cup me with your hands . . ." Chelsea convulsed, trying to snap the plastic strips that bound her. "Come and take me, lover girl!"

Nat hurried in the direction of the car. "I'll try calling Kerry again."

He'd not gone far when the sound of a motor swelled on the cold breeze. In the distance a flatbed truck appeared. It roared toward them along the cemetery lane. At that moment, it seemed it would stop for nothing. Nat foresaw it reach the cliff's edge without even slowing. Then it would sail out . . . out . . . through the blue sky before plunging into the sea.

CHAPTER TWENTY-ONE

Pel Minton shared Nat's thought. *Jack's not going to stop. He's going over the edge of the cliff. He doesn't want us to be possessed. This is his solution. To drive us to our deaths.* She imagined the truck lumbering off the cliff, then the dizzying fall.

"*Hang on, tight!*" Jack hauled the wheel. The action almost caused the rig to jackknife. Yet he held its course true. A moment later it smacked through the fence then followed the route the Lowe brothers had carved from the cemetery, when they'd driven their trucks through it, nearly crushing Pel Minton in the process.

Fat tires bumped over already-felled tombstones. The iron behemoth's vibrations would make the bones of the dead tremble in their tombs. This was a matter of life and death. Jack didn't intend wasting time by neatly parking in the lane, then hauling the decidedly weighty mosaic block up to the mausoleum by hand.

Kerry shouted, "It's happening here. Nat's been having problems, too."

By the mausoleum Nat had rejoined Dianne. Both stood beside a figure that lay on the grass, bound in orange tape.

"That's Chelsea." Pel clung on as the cabin bucked wildly. "She must have been taken."

"Be on your guard," Jacob warned.

Seconds later, Jack braked hard. The truck skidded to a stop in the cemetery, not twenty paces from the mausoleum.

A bewildered Nat met them as they climbed out of the cabin. "It's crazy . . . everything's crazy. Contractors have started work on the beach. The barrier's going up. But someone stole the mosaic. And Chelsea's gone nuts . . . absolutely raving nuts."

"Oooh," cooed Chelsea on the grass. "All of you take pleasure from my body. Come on, everyone. Don't wait in line. Take me! Rip yourself a handful of flesh; I don't mind. Nice . . . tasty . . . sexy . . ."

Nat appeared close to tears. "What can we do to help her?"

"Never mind that now." Kerry spoke briskly. "We'll take care of Chelsea later. First things first. We've found the mosaic."

Jacob helped his grandson lift it down from the cab. "But we've got to get it back into the mausoleum."

Pel collected the shotgun from the truck, then called out, "Make it fast. The bad guys are on their way."

"What bad guys?" asked a bewildered Nat.

"Very bad guys," Pel said with feeling.

Jack hefted the crate containing the image of his ancestor. "Pel, hold the gate open for me, will you?"

Pel ran to grab the ironwork that sealed the mausoleum. She hauled it open. Chelsea rolled over on the ground toward her. The possessed woman strained her head forward to try and bite Pel's leg.

Kerry shouted, "Dianne. Sit on her."

Soon Kerry, Jack, Pel, and Jacob had squeezed into the small building. Pel leaned the gun against a wall. Meanwhile, Jacob, with Kerry's help, eased the mosaic out of its box. Justice Murrain's eyes glared up at them. The expression of hate made Pel shudder.

Jacob told them, "We need to make sure it goes back in the same position. The orientation will be important."

Rough handling of the ancient artifact disturbed Nat. "Easy with it. You're losing some of the blue glass edging."

"Nudge it an inch your way," Jack told Kerry.

Car engine sounds grew louder, an ominously throaty note on the chill air.

Anguished, Nat cried out. "Kerry, this isn't accepted archaeological practice! First we should discuss our options, while comparing photos of the mosaic when it was in place."

Outside, Chelsea moaned with pleasure. "Justice Murrain is coming. He's here with his Battle Men. They'll strip you naked and dance you over the cliff. Ha!"

"The slab doesn't fit." Jacob had managed to lay the cement block flat over the hole. "Why won't it go back in?"

Kerry pressed it down with both hands. "It's got to. Otherwise those monsters stay free."

Pel warned, "The convoy's going to be here any minute."

Nat counseled a more cautious approach. "We should discuss a strategy to replace this precious artwork. I've got plans at the motel that show how—"

Kerry screamed in exasperation. "Just ram the bloody picture back into the hole!"

Everyone who could get close enough in that confined space placed their palms flat on the mosaic. Pel felt as if she pressed cold corpse flesh when she touched the image of Justice Murrain. Nevertheless, she gulped down her fear.

Jacob panted, "On the count of three! One, two, three!"

All five pairs of hands depressed the slab. They pushed down as hard as they could. It resisted their force. It was as if malign spirits heaved upward from the grave soil to thwart their efforts. Then: CLICK! The mosaic slid down into the opening from where it came. To Pel, seeing it slip back into place offered the same kind of satisfaction as the last piece of a jigsaw being clicked into the puzzle.

Panting, they stood up.

"How long until it starts to work?" Kerry asked.

Jacob gave a pained shrug. "Who can say? There's damage to both the mosaic and this sacred site."

"We know it has the capacity to self-heal."

"But the damage might be more severe than we can tell. Besides, it will take time to for the power to reassert itself."

Nat groaned. "Am I crazy? Or are we all listening to the old man's crazy, crazy talk like we believe it?"

"He's not crazy," Kerry assured. "Jacob is intelligent. We should have listened to him from the start. If we had, lives might have been saved."

Kerry touched Nat's arm. "Don't struggle to suspend disbelief, Nat. See these people coming across the cemetery? They're going to convince you that Jacob was right all along."

Through the cemetery trooped 200 people. They were an odd assortment of characters: men and women from early twenties upward. Some clothed. Some nude. All carried makeshift weapons—knives, screwdrivers, hammers, wrenches. Leading them, a huge figure in a white coverall.

"Nat. In a moment," Jacob murmured, "you're going to meet Justice Murrain."

"You mean the guy in the . . ." Dumbfounded, Nat's eyes rolled down to the mosaic.

Jack took the shotgun from where Pel had leaned it against the inner wall.

Nat blinked. "You're going to shoot those guys?"

"There's no point in killing them. What's inside those people cannot die. If the worse comes to the worst, this gun is for us."

"Absolutely," Kerry agreed. "Death rather than possession."

Justice Murrain, accompanied by the woman in a police uniform who toted a machine gun, approached to within fifty paces of the mausoleum.

"Jacob Murrain." The giant beckoned. "It's time to end this now. Step out here. Your death will be painless. Jack Murrain will not be harmed, rest assured."

"But you intend to possess him with that sick soul of yours."

"He will live, Jacob."

"No deal," Jack called. "You will use me to hurt others."

Kerry shouted, "The mosaic is back in place. It's you and your thugs that have reached the end."

Justice Murrain pointed at his Battle Men. "See? My warriors are still with me. The magic doesn't work anymore. We still possess these pieces of flesh. You are defeated. Come now. We'll end it here. Don't suffer anymore. You'll be at peace."

"Except for me," Pel snarled. "You want me for your bride."

"And so you will be." He beamed his monster's smile—all wickedness and lust. "When I have taken Jack's body I will take you as a wife. Why worry? You will wake beside that handsome young buck every morning."

Jacob exited through the mausoleum gate to stand beside Chelsea. She lay on the grass, a delighted grin on her face. Still sitting on her was Dianne, who watched the proceedings with utter bemusement.

The gun-toting cop took a threatening step forward. "I can kill him now, master." She aimed the weapon at Jacob's heart.

"Not yet, Anna. I don't want a stray bullet harming either Jack or Lady Pel."

Pel Minton immediately noticed Anna's scowl. Clearly, the woman would be delighted if a stray bullet found Jack or her. *Especially her.* Jacob, she noticed, suddenly perked up.

"Anna?" Jacob asked. "Is that Anna De Suisse?"

"What if it is?" Anna mixed defiance with a hint that Jacob should elaborate.

"Anna De Suisse. Family legend has it, my dear, that you were Justice Murrain's second wife."

Justice Murrain sniffed in contempt. "Anna took her pleasures in my bed. Nothing more. No ceremony took place. No marriage rites."

"Yet, the pair of you lived as husband and wife. Isn't that so, Anna?" Jacob fixed her with his sharp eye. "So you consent to your master being wedded to Pel Minton here?"

His words produced a flash of anger in Anna. "I'll do as my

master asks. If he wishes to make the lady his bride. Then my mind is easy."

"Okay. As you wish. Then he found you, Anna, in a lunatic asylum. Perhaps you don't understand what is happening regarding yourself and Pel Minton? That her charms are superior to yours. "

A dangerous game you're playing, Jacob. Yet Pel knew he made such an apparent offhand sleight about Anna's mental competence for a reason.

Jacob continued. "But what of your master here?" These words he directed at the Battle Men. The man grew in confidence. Even his stature appeared to increase as he stood straighter, stronger. "Here before you is my ancestor; the robber, the slayer of innocent men and women; the devil incarnate. He isn't the potent force that he once was, you know? In truth, my friends, he's losing his most important battle. The one he fights in there." Jacob pointed at the man's skull. "That battleground inside his head."

"Anna." Justice Murrain spat the words. "Kill the old man."

Anna appeared too wrapped up in her own worries to act.

Justice Murrain, however, didn't appear fazed by the strange look in the woman's eye. "Battle Men. It's time to destroy my bothersome descendant. It was he who kept us prisoner."

"Or you could listen to what I have to say?" Jacob took another step toward the giant in the white forensic suit. "Your master made a bad choice when he invaded the body of Horace Neville. You see, Horace's brain was damaged at birth. But it isn't a weak mind. It is strong. And it has been fighting the spirit of Justice Murrain. Do I need to tell you which one is winning?" When Jacob was ten paces from his adversary he paused. "Tell them that you find it difficult to think clearly, Justice Murrain. Explain to your men that strange ideas intrude."

"Don't listen to him. He's trying to save his own neck."

Moments ago, the Battle Men had shown every inclination to hack Jacob apart. Now they appeared uneasy. An air of doubt hung over them.

"Kill him!" Justice Murrain thundered.

"Wait." Jacob pointed at a patch of grass to the right of the white-clad man. "Justice Murrain. Anna stands on your left. Who stands on your right?"

"Destroy the fool, or I'll do it myself."

Jacob shouted, "There! Beside you! Who is it?"

The little fellow! The words spurting, unbidden, from Justice Murrain's own lips pained him more than blows. "Bobby! My friend! He . . . he's been crying. Frightened. Very frightened! Bobby wants—" The giant clapped his palm to his mouth to prevent any more words escaping.

The Battle Men muttered among themselves. They'd witnessed how their master's voice had changed from that of a full-blooded tyrant to one that tremored with childlike fear.

Justice Murrain recovered his composure. "Do as I order. End that man's life!"

However, the Battle Men called to him:

"What's wrong, master?"

"Have they done witchcraft on you?"

"Is it really you, master. Are we being deceived?"

Through this exchange of words Pel and Jack had emerged from the mausoleum. The mood of the Battle Men had changed from naked aggression to confusion.

"Tell them what you see," Jacob boomed with such authority that the Battle Men were silenced. It made the rabble uneasy. Here was a man who was clearly a blood Murrain; he possessed an undeniably forceful charisma, while the giant, who claimed he was Justice Murrain, had begun to appear weak; his eyes had become shifty. Jacob continued: "Justice Murrain. Or am I speaking to Horace Neville? Tell everyone what you can see there on the ocean."

"Pirate ships. Jolly Roger. Big sails all flip-flapping in the breeze . . ." The voice changed as if the possessor vied for control. "*I am . . . am Justice Murrain. Bring Jack to me. I will transfer now.*" His gaze wandered in confusion. Then the Neville voice returned: "I've seen foxes in the supermarket. Nobody else knows they shop there. I've seen 'em . . . seen 'em plenty. Clever foxes. Buying their chickens and chocolate, and—*no, I am Murrain! I lived at Murrain Hall. I will build an empire!*"

Pel noticed a battle of sorts in Anna's expression. Jacob had revealed that Anna had been brought to Murrain Hall from an asylum. Now, it appeared the old psychosis had returned. Madness flared in the woman's eyes. And when she glared at Pel they blazed with pure jealousy . . . a soul-devouring jealousy . . . one that craved the destruction of her love rival.

Pel recognized a ploy that might push the psychosis into all-out insanity. "Listen to me! I, Pel Minton, accept Justice Murrain's offer. I will become his bride."

Jack stared at her. "Are you crazy?"

"No," she murmured, so only he would hear, "but I know a very angry girl who is just about to be." Then to Justice Murrain she held out her arms. "Prove to everyone here that you are serious in your intentions. Kiss me!"

Tears flashed in Anna's eyes. Her fists trembled as she gripped the machine gun.

"At last!" Justice Murrain recaptured control of his host's body. "Bear witness to my power. Watch me take my bride by the hand!"

The Battle Men appeared convinced. They cheered. Then cheered even more loudly for their master. Victory was theirs.

Convulsions of sheer misery jolted Anna's body. "No! Stop that! Don't applaud her—I'm telling you not to!"

The Battle Men were ecstatic. They cheered, applauded, waved their knives and hammers in the air. An explosively psychotic Anna De Suisse bit down on her own lip so forcefully that blood spurted. When she screamed that blood atomized into a spray of crimson. Then she snapped.

Pel realized that the scorned woman's anger might be directed at her. However, the approbation of the Battle Men enraged her the most at that instant. She raised the machine gun then discharged the weapon into those yelling faces. Every single one of the ammo clip's thirty high-velocity rounds flew at the mob. At least a dozen of the possessed were felled. Some fell silently. Many collapsed, shrieking, as they spurted blood.

"Anna!" roared Justice Murrain. "I order you to stop."

Anna's mind had exploded into lethal psychotic shrapnel. Hurling aside the machine gun, she raced toward Pel Minton. As she ran, she drew a long-bladed knife from her belt. With bloodlust uppermost in her broken mind, she raised the weapon. Jack stepped in front of Pel.

Anna, in her confusion, couldn't differentiate between the man she'd loved two centuries ago, or the bloodline descendant. Both looked so much alike. Her eyes locked onto his large gray eyes. She absorbed his demeanor; his mane of black hair. Then she saw he shielded the woman who would steal Justice Murrain from her. Anna flung herself forward, aiming a desperate blow at Pel as she did so.

Jack blocked the attack. However, the knife sliced into his chest. The sight of Murrain blood pouring from the wound finally crushed Anna's own heart. Sobbing, she dropped to her knees.

Pressing his hand to his ribs, Jack stepped backward. That bright, luscious red—the stuff of life—ran free through his fingers.

Justice Murrain raged. "He wasn't supposed to be hurt. His body is mine!"

The surviving Battle Men showed no desire to attack. What they saw before them was a Murrain with his life hemorrhaging from him. They, too, had been gathered up from asylums across the county. Their logic, faulty at best, failed them when they saw someone, who so closely resembled their master, staggering toward the mausoleum, an open wound in his breast.

Jacob Murrain shouted, "I know why the mosaic hasn't healed itself." His next words were as chilling as they were inexplicable: "*Blood . . . Murrain blood will heal all.*" Then he went to his grandson. "Jack? Will you do something for me?"

Although weakening, Jack nodded.

"Jack. Go into the mausoleum. Allow your blood to fall onto the mosaic. It's important . . . vitally important."

"Grandfather." He grimaced. "I said harsh things. About how the mosaic had ruined my life. But I wouldn't have it any other way. You, and my entire family, even the old devil himself"—he nodded toward Justice Murrain—"you all made me what I am."

Pel tore away her fleece jacket. "Here. I can stop the blood with this. Let me hold it to you."

Jack shook his head. "There's a need for this stuff." He managed to smile. "Can't waste this vintage Murrain." He dropped to his knees on the mosaic. Now the blood fell—a scarlet offering on the portrait of his ancestor. Not a sacrificial gift to Justice Murrain, but to more ancient spirits: ones that an even more ancient ritual had woven into the layers of soil beneath the cemetery.

Pel felt her own life drain away as she watched that selfless act of giving. His blood cascaded in luscious red drops onto the portrait's eyes, mouth, nose, and jaw. The blood trickled into the gaps between the image and where the mosaic had been brutally hacked from the ground. Soon, the red fluid had filled the fissures. Then it darkened. As it did so, that congealing blood became fresh mortar that cemented the mosaic into the floor. In turn, that living adhesive joined the mosaic with the earth once more.

"It's working," Pel whispered.

"We're not there yet." Jacob nodded in the direction of Kerry and Nat.

The pair pressed their fingers to their temples as if their heads hurt. Already their expressions had become unfamiliar. The spirits that had been evicted from the bullet-riddled corpses of the possessed had found new hosts.

"Anna De Suisse," Kerry grunted. "I'll have her hide for firing on us."

Pel willed the magic to work once more. For the self-healing to be complete. Because at that moment the Battle Men began to close in on the mausoleum. Justice Murrain led them, his face set to kill.

"You're going to die, Jacob Murrain," snarled a possessed Kerry Herne. "We'll make your people pay for this."

Jack gave a groan. He toppled sideways, so weakened by blood loss he couldn't stay in that crouching position any longer. Pel doused her hand in his blood, then swept her palm over the mosaic until a scarlet emulsion covered every inch.

The sky went dark all of a sudden. A profound blackness. A void between worlds. And the air was still. Kerry and Nat sighed. Their expressions of fury morphed into one of utter vacancy. Outside, the view of their surroundings changed. The archaeologists' trenches vanished. The once-eroded gravestones became more regular. Newer. On the cliff a mansion stood tall.

Pel heard Jacob say, "Murrain Hall. It's back. But like the olden days, when it was new."

She turned her attention back to the mosaic. It had vanished. As simply as that. Instead, she peered down a deep well . . . at least that's what it resembled. A well going down and down and down and . . . vertigo tugged hard. For a moment, she feared it would pull her in headfirst.

Suddenly, out on the cliff top, the hall had vanished. Now there were no gravestones. Instead, a ring mound enclosed the ancient holy site. A figure clad in animal skins and vines stood motionless at a point where a host of radiating white paths all came together. Temple Central as it was 4,000 years ago. The figure made priestly gestures with his hands—slow, dignified, with such precision. His dark hair fell on his shoulders. Briefly, his gray eyes fixed on hers. Then the Battle Men yelled as one.

From their direction flew small dark shapes. Their speed, and the fact they were only glimpsed fleetingly, reminded Pel of bats flying at dusk. They streamed through the darkness toward the mausoleum. One by one, they sped toward the pool of night once occupied by the mosaic. Then each flitting shape plunged down into it. Flying down and down, as if to the center of the earth.

Kerry and Nat groaned even louder. They clutched their heads. Something fast, dark, and almost too fleeting to see, shot from them; then those two shadows vanished into the pit, too. Pel knew those dark knots of shadow were the souls of the Battle Men. Now, at last, they returned to their prison in some dark heart-soil of the earth.

Slowly, the day began to brighten again. Pel pressed the fleece to the wound in Jack's chest. He seemed stronger. What's more, he insisted on standing.

Silent, they stepped out into the growing light. On the ground, still bound in orange tape, Chelsea complained, "Dianne? Why are you sitting on me?"

Kerry and Nat were Kerry and Nat again. They hugged each other. The air smelled of ocean; a zing of ionized breeze that brought their senses back to life with renewed freshness.

The men and women were no longer possessed. They either sat on the ground, or wandered away in confusion, or asked one another what they were doing here in their nightclothes, or without clothes at all.

Pel supported Jack as they approached Justice Murrain and Anna.

Anna said, "It's better like this. I'd rather lie with Justice Murrain in the ground forever than be in this flesh and lose him." Her features appeared to flicker as the spirit lost its grip on the stolen body. "I love him. Now we'll be together."

Jacob shook his head. "I'm sorry, my dear. Justice Murrain has a new prison. He can't escape the brain he occupied."

"No! He's got to come back with me." She clutched his arm. "Please, master. Say you will!"

"At last," Justice Murrain whispered, "I understand. Isn't it always the way? That you never appreciate what treasure you possess until it is lost? I am sorry, Anna. Truthfully, you were special to me." He kissed her tenderly.

"*Woah!*" The woman pushed him back. "You do not kiss a police officer. That is actionable as an assault. Touch me again and I will arrest you!" She blinked, suddenly aware of her surroundings.

"Anna." Justice Murrain's voice wavered. "My Anna . . ."

"Don't you Anna me." The policewoman frowned. "How did I get here? I . . . I thought I was just finishing work when . . ." Puzzled, she regarded the prone bodies, and all those puzzled men and women, who wandered through the cemetery asking one another questions that none knew the answers to.

"My Anna's gone." Grief clouded Justice Murrain's eyes.

"And back where she should be," Pel told him. "Back under the mosaic."

"As for you," Jack told him, "you'll live out your days in a secure unit."

Jacob added, "I, for one, find that satisfying. Very satisfying. You recruited your thugs from asylums for the criminally insane. Now you're going to find yourself living in one until the day you die."

"I'm trapped in this thing?" With an expression of absolute horror Justice Murrain touched the head that imprisoned him. "There's no escape?"

Jacob shook his head.

Shocked to the core, Justice Murrain walked away from the group. They watched him peer at tombstones, then into the trenches, then at the sun shining brightly in the sky. Beneath one of the archaeologists' awnings, he found a pair of plastic chairs, the kind that grace summer patios. Slowly, he picked them up, one in each hand; then he found a level area that had a fine view of the ocean. There he set the chairs side by side. He sat down in one; the other he put his arm round.

In a childlike voice he said, "I'm Horace Neville. This is my friend." He patted the vacant chair beside him. "Bobby's been poorly. But he's all right now."

AFTER

Police cars took survivors of the mass possession home. Fleets of ambulances carried the injured away. Black vans collected the dead.

Jack patiently waited his turn for a ride to the hospital. When he noticed that Pel's expression of concern hadn't diminished, he reassured her. "It was only a glancing blow. Soon I'll be good as new."

She managed a tired smile. "Glad to hear it. And you'll have a hero scar to show your buddies, when it's too hot to wear a shirt."

"My thoughts exactly." He glanced at his grandfather, who in turn kept a watchful eye over Horace Neville, as he placidly sat beside a best friend nobody ever saw; but who was perhaps, in the end, his most powerful ally.

Pel shivered. "Will they ever come back?"

"They might," Jack allowed. "If the mosaic is taken again. Or if this sacred site is compromised."

"Then someone will have to take care of it forever."

"Ah, that's where we Murrains come in. When my grandfather retires I'll be the one to guard it."

"A lifetime commitment?"

"Of course." There was a pause, and then he added, "Things got hectic round here over the last few days."

She smiled. "That I did notice, Jack."

"I did plan to ask if you'd stick around for a while."

"In Crowdale?"

He nodded.

She gave a noncommittal shrug. "Give me time to think about it, won't you?"

"Naturally."

Pel considered for a moment. "Do you like kidney pie? I could never spend time with a man who ate kidney pie."

"Will that help you reach a decision?"

"Hmm. Absolutely."

"Kidney pie? Me? No, I never touch the stuff."

"Yup, that helps."

They stood together in the October sunlight. Pel was thinking hard. If she didn't quit this ancient corner of England, would something of its spirit ultimately take possession of her, one way or another? And if there ever came a time she needed to leave the country, and Jack Murrain, could she? Would she?

Or one day, years and years from now, might her bones rest beside those of Jack in this very cemetery?

So? Leave or stay? Eventually, she'd come to the right decision. For now, however, she took pleasure in the calm and the peace that had been restored to her world . . . She closed her eyes, and listened to the steady beat of her heart. And if she listened intently enough, and faithfully enough, would she find the answer to her question?

□ YES!

Sign me up for the Leisure Horror Book Club and send my FREE BOOKS! If I choose to stay in the club, I will pay only $8.50* each month, a savings of $7.48!

NAME: _____

ADDRESS: _____

TELEPHONE: _____

EMAIL: _____

□ I want to pay by credit card.

□ VISA   □ MasterCard.   □ DISCOVER

ACCOUNT #: _____

EXPIRATION DATE: _____

SIGNATURE: _____

Mail this page along with $2.00 shipping and handling to:
Leisure Horror Book Club
PO Box 6640
Wayne, PA 19087
Or fax (must include credit card information) to:
610-995-9274
You can also sign up online at **www.dorchesterpub.com**.
*Plus $2.00 for shipping. Offer open to residents of the U.S. and Canada only.
Canadian residents please call 1-800-481-9191 for pricing information.
If under 18, a parent or guardian must sign. Terms, prices and conditions subject to change. Subscription subject to acceptance. Dorchester Publishing reserves the right to reject any order or cancel any subscription.

GET FREE BOOKS!

You can have the best fiction delivered to your door for less than what you'd pay in a bookstore or online. Sign up for one of our book clubs today, and we'll send you *FREE* BOOKS* just for trying it out... **with no obligation to buy, ever!**

As a member of the Leisure Horror Book Club, you'll receive books by authors such as **RICHARD LAYMON, JACK KETCHUM, JOHN SKIPP, BRIAN KEENE** and many more.

As a book club member you also receive the following special benefits:
- **30% off all orders!**
- **Exclusive access to special discounts!**
- **Convenient home delivery and 10 days to return any books you don't want to keep.**

Visit www.dorchesterpub.com
or call 1-800-481-9191

There is no minimum number of books to buy, and you may cancel membership at any time.
*Please include $2.00 for shipping and handling.